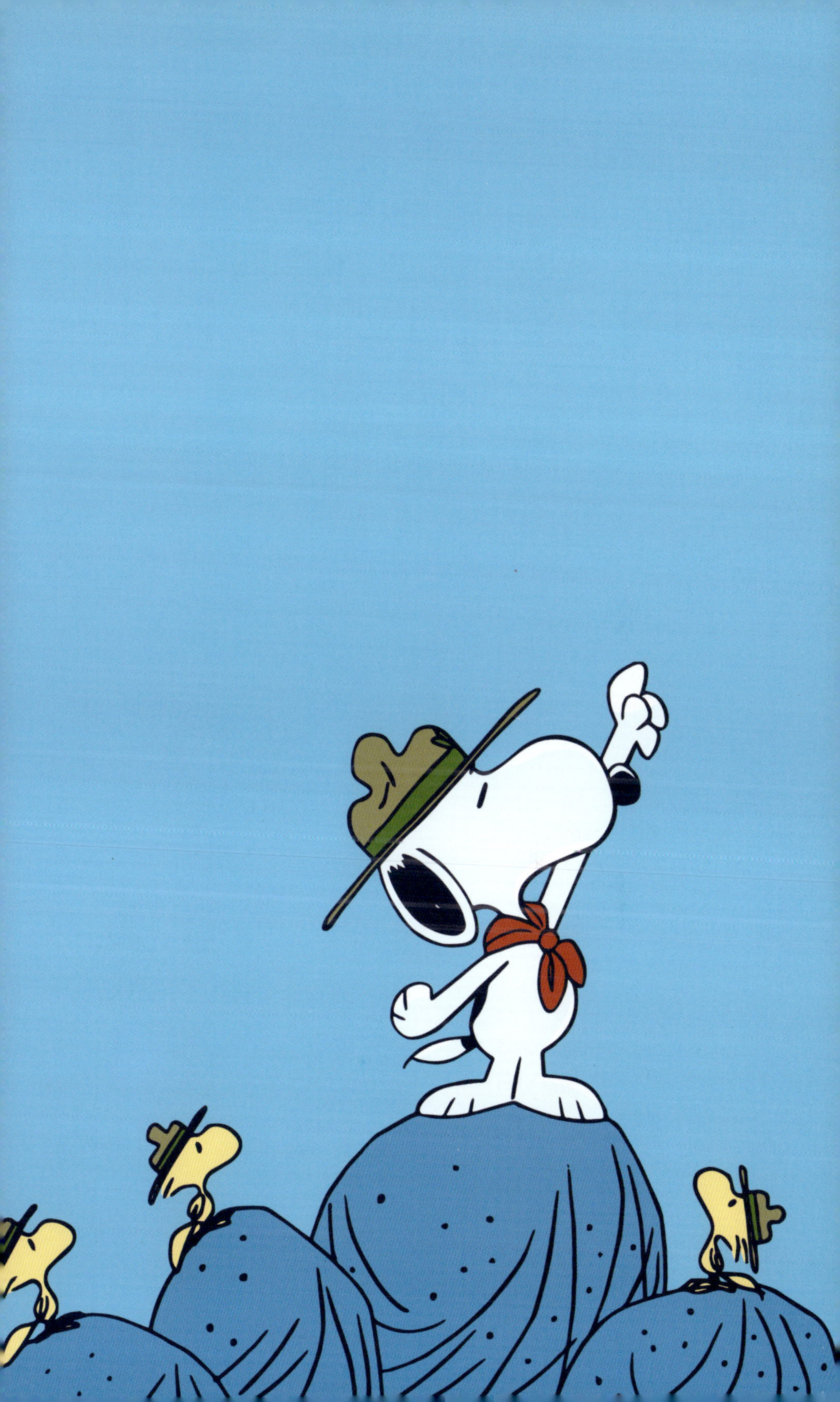

PEANUTS® GRAPHIC NOVELS

Snoopy's Beagle Scout Tales

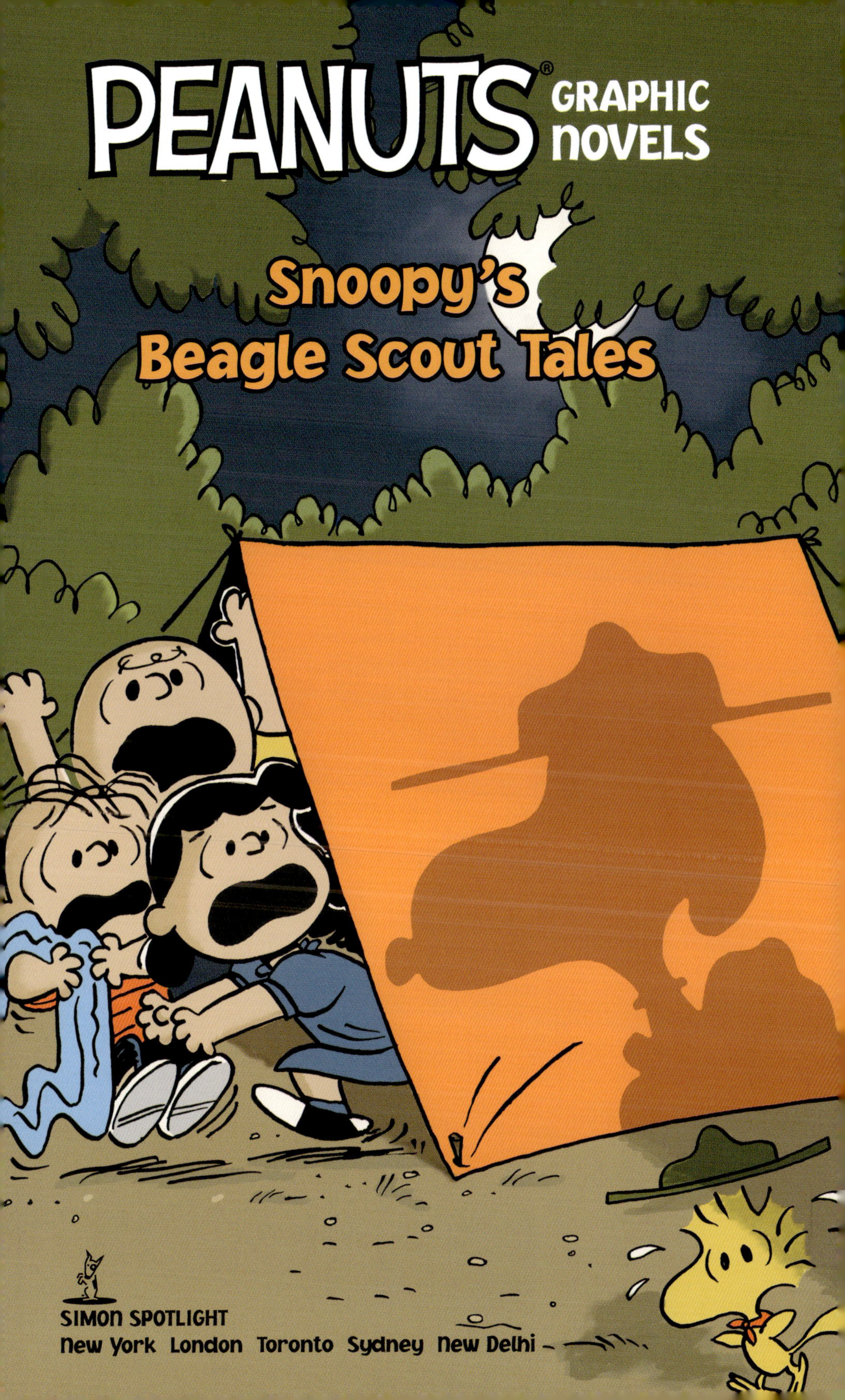

SIMON SPOTLIGHT
New York London Toronto Sydney New Delhi

PEANUTS
by Schulz

SIMON SPOTLIGHT
An imprint of Simon & Schuster Children's Publishing Division
1230 Avenue of the Americas, New York, New York 10020
This Simon Spotlight edition May 2024
Peanuts and all related titles, logos, and characters are trademarks of Peanuts Worldwide LL
© 2024 Peanuts Worldwide LLC. • *Race for Your Life, Charlie Brown* © 2018 Peanuts Worldwide LL
• *It's Summer Camp, Charlie Brown* © 2015 Peanuts Worldwide LLC. • *Movie Time* © 2013 Peanu
Worldwide LLC. • *Toodle-oo, Caribou* © 2014 Peanuts Worldwide LLC. • *Harriet Takes a Hike* © 20:
Peanuts Worldwide LLC. Most stories in this volume were originally published in the PEANUTS com
series by Boom Studios. All rights reserved, including the right of reproduction in whole or
part in any form. SIMON SPOTLIGHT and colophon are registered trademarks of Simon & Schuste
LLC. • Simon & Schuster: Celebrating 100 Years of Publishing in 2024 • For information about speci
discounts for bulk purchases, please contact Simon & Schuster Special Sales at 1-866-506-19
or business@simonandschuster.com. Manufactured in China 0124 SCP • 10 9 8 7 6 5 4 3 2 1
ISBN 978-1-6659-5241-5 (hc) • ISBN 978-1-6659-5240-8 (pbk) • ISBN 978-1-6659-5242-2 (ebook)

Contents

Cover art by Robert Pope

Race for Your Life, Charlie Brown 7
Story by Jason Cooper
Art by Robert Pope
Colors by Kat Fraser & Jewel Jackson
Letters by Donna Almendrala & Hannah White

Classic Peanuts by Charles M. Schulz 93

It's Summer Camp, Charlie Brown 95
Story by Charles M. Schulz
Pencils by Vicki Scott
Inks by Paige Braddock
Colors by Bill Bedard
Letters by Donna Almendrala

Classic Peanuts by Charles M. Schulz 125

Movie Time 127
Story by Nat Gertler
Art by Andy Hirsch
Colors by Lisa Moore
Letters by Steve Wands

Classic Peanuts by Charles M. Schulz 135

Toodle-oo, Caribou 137
Story, Art, and Letters by Donna Alemendrala
Colors by Bill Bedard

Classic Peanuts by Charles M. Schulz 145

Harriet Takes a Hike 147
Story by Jason Cooper
Art by Robert Pope
Colors by Jewel Jackson
Color Assists by Caitlin Leonard
Letters by Bryan Stone

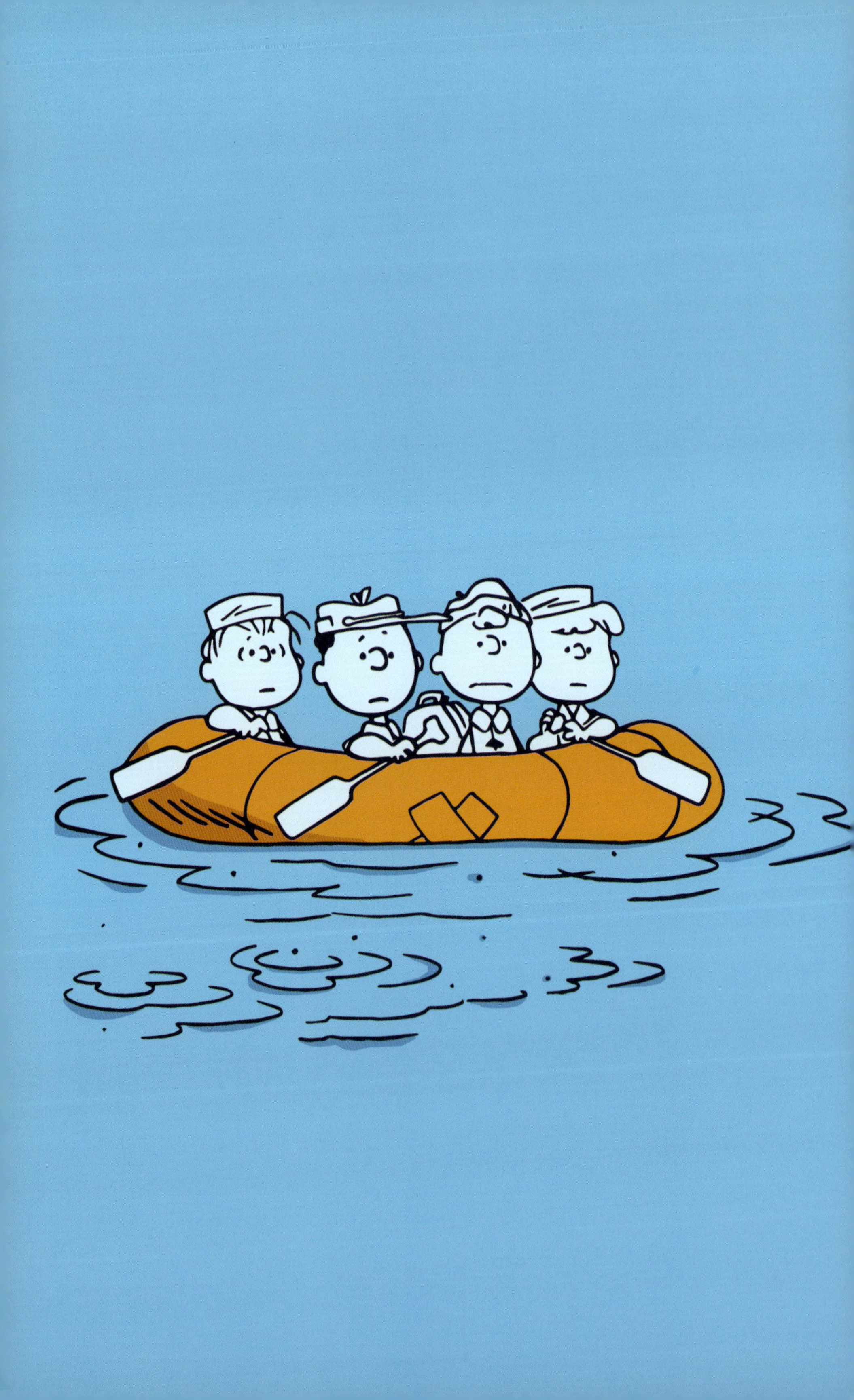

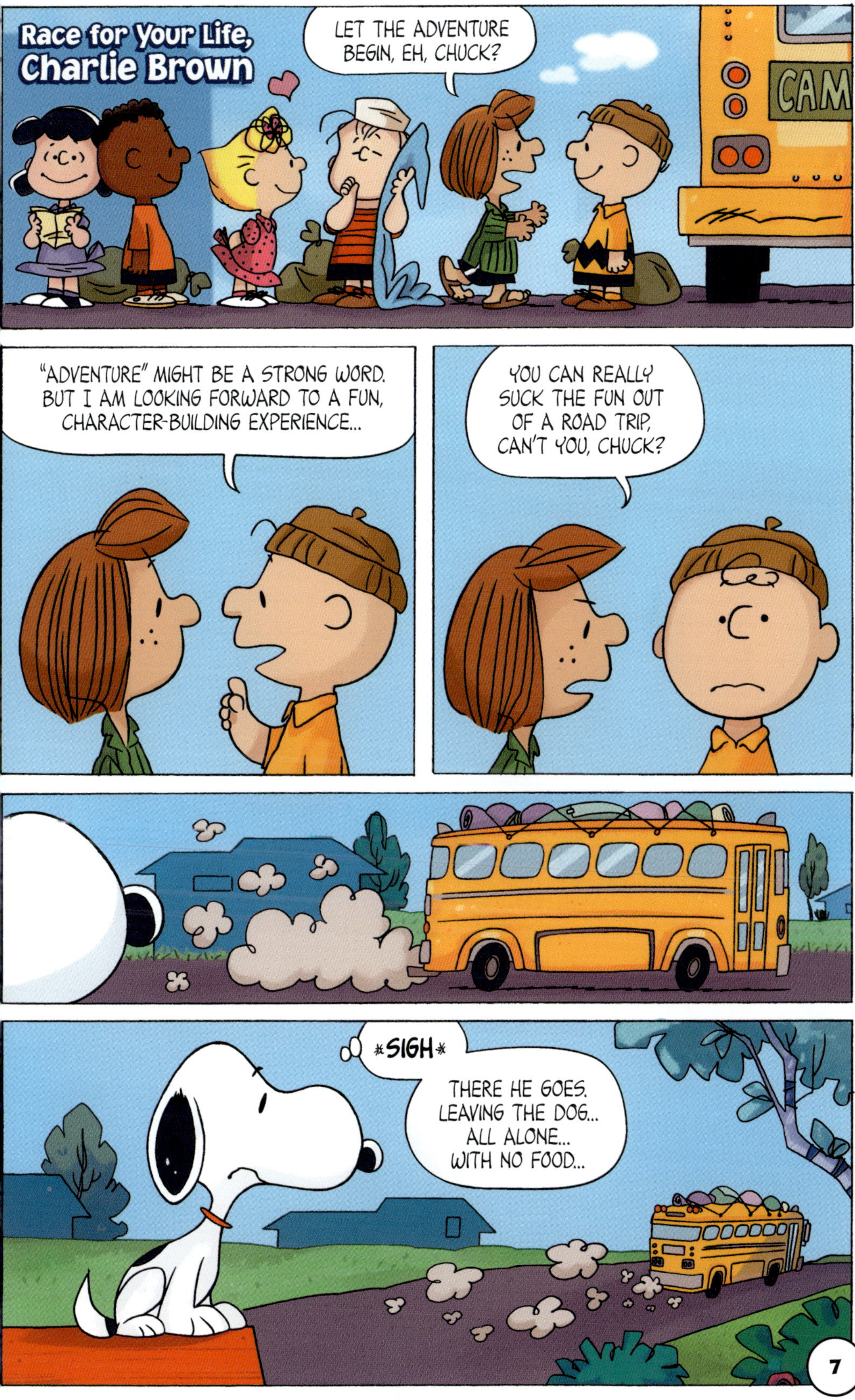
Race for Your Life, Charlie Brown
LET THE ADVENTURE BEGIN, EH, CHUCK?
CAM
"ADVENTURE" MIGHT BE A STRONG WORD. BUT I AM LOOKING FORWARD TO A FUN, CHARACTER-BUILDING EXPERIENCE...
YOU CAN REALLY SUCK THE FUN OUT OF A ROAD TRIP, CAN'T YOU, CHUCK?
SIGH
THERE HE GOES. LEAVING THE DOG... ALL ALONE... WITH NO FOOD...

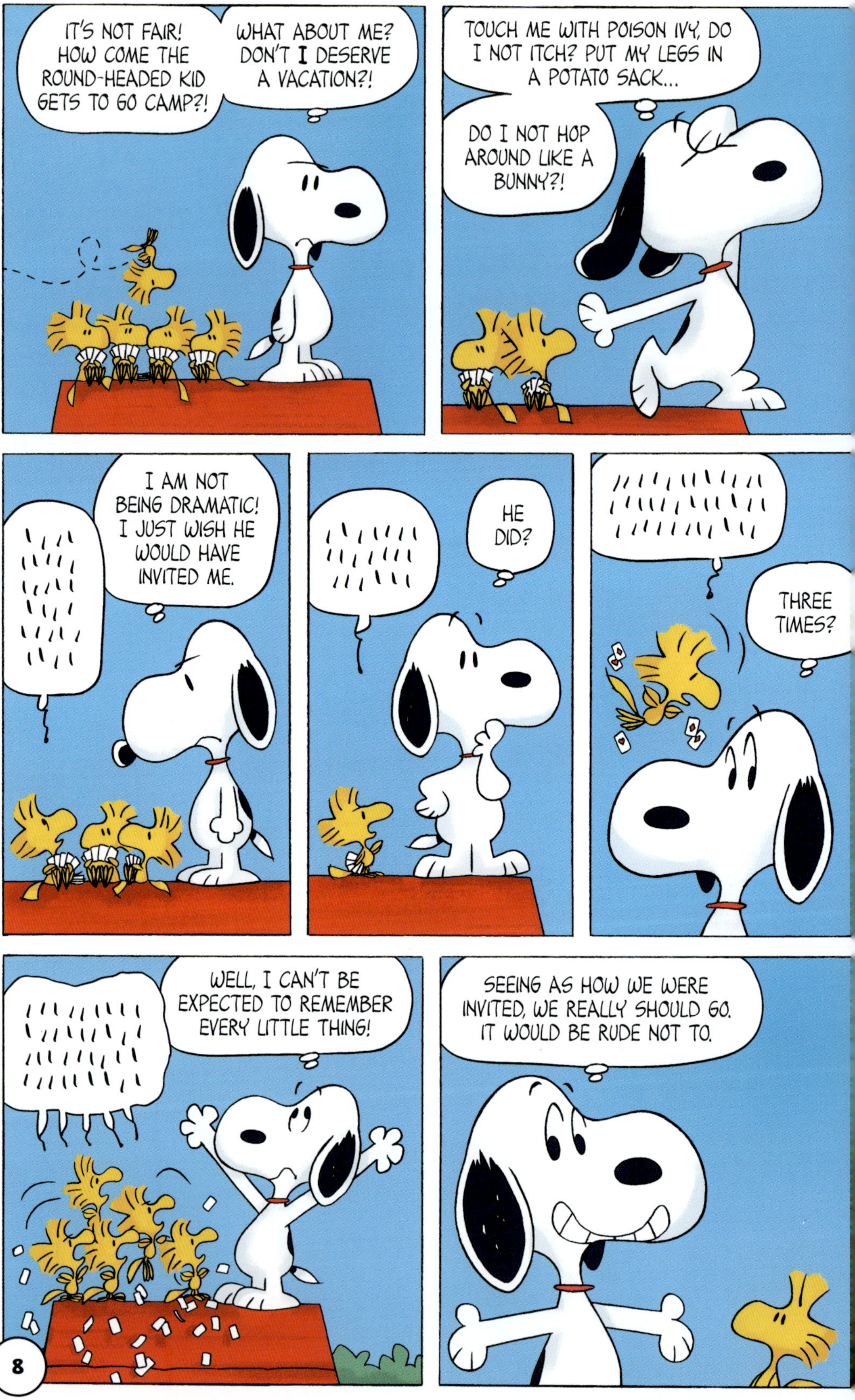
IT'S NOT FAIR! HOW COME THE ROUND-HEADED KID GETS TO GO CAMP?!
WHAT ABOUT ME? DON'T I DESERVE A VACATION?!
TOUCH ME WITH POISON IVY, DO I NOT ITCH? PUT MY LEGS IN A POTATO SACK...
DO I NOT HOP AROUND LIKE A BUNNY?!
I AM NOT BEING DRAMATIC! I JUST WISH HE WOULD HAVE INVITED ME.
HE DID?
THREE TIMES?
WELL, I CAN'T BE EXPECTED TO REMEMBER EVERY LITTLE THING!
SEEING AS HOW WE WERE INVITED, WE REALLY SHOULD GO. IT WOULD BE RUDE NOT TO.

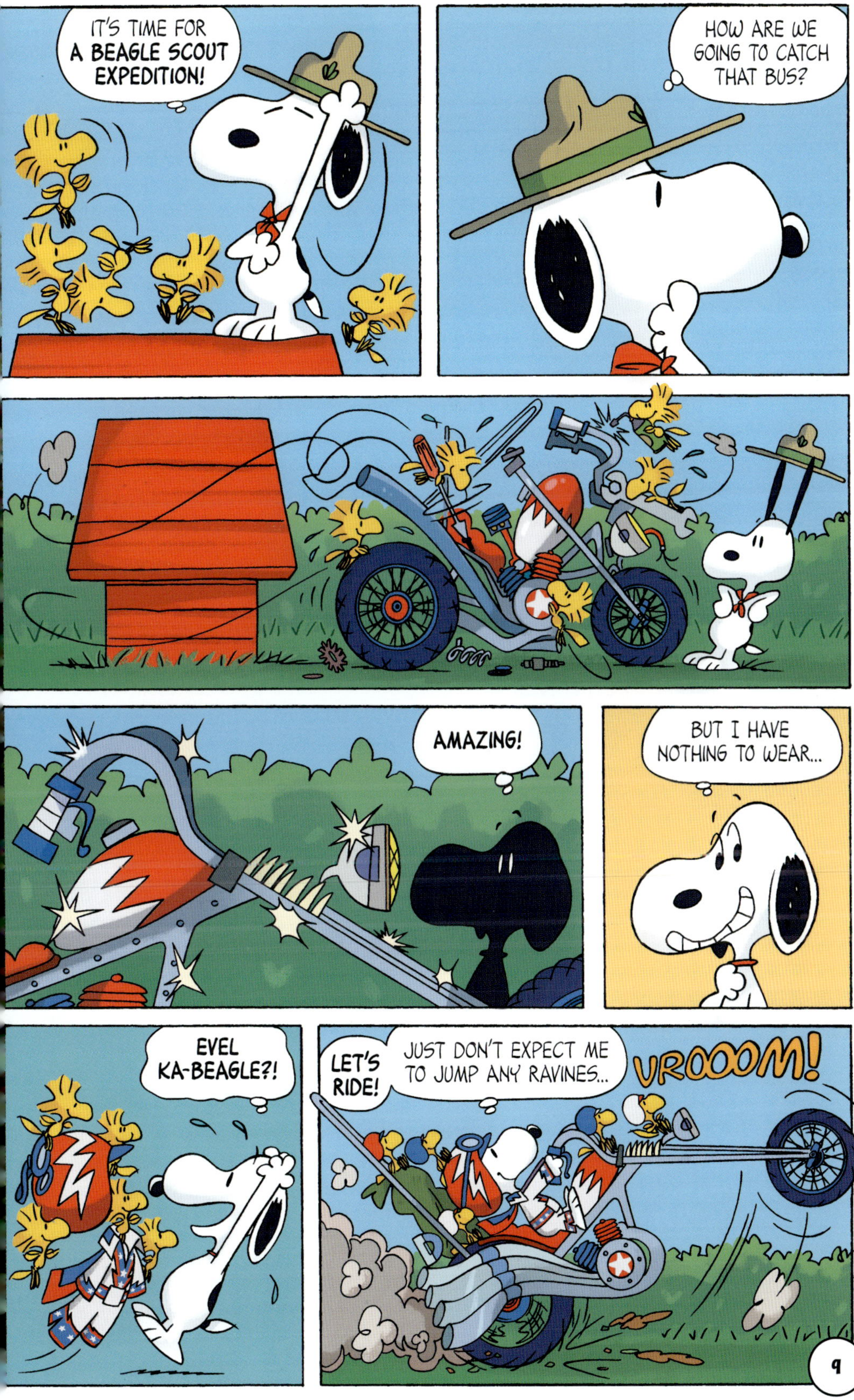
IT'S TIME FOR A BEAGLE SCOUT EXPEDITION!
HOW ARE WE GOING TO CATCH THAT BUS?
AMAZING!
BUT I HAVE NOTHING TO WEAR...
EVEL KA-BEAGLE?!
LET'S RIDE!
JUST DON'T EXPECT ME TO JUMP ANY RAVINES...
VROOOM!

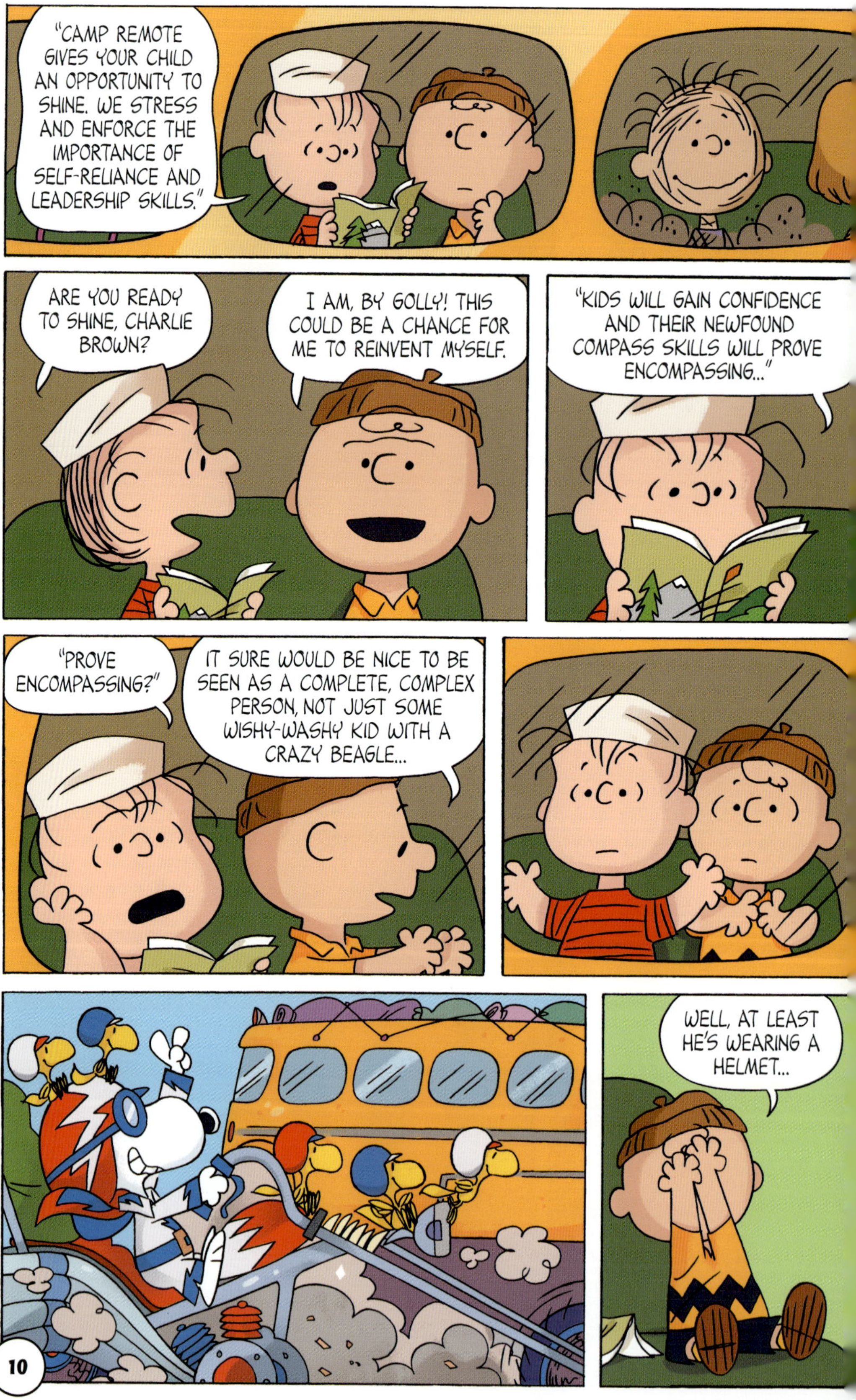
"CAMP REMOTE GIVES YOUR CHILD AN OPPORTUNITY TO SHINE. WE STRESS AND ENFORCE THE IMPORTANCE OF SELF-RELIANCE AND LEADERSHIP SKILLS."
ARE YOU READY TO SHINE, CHARLIE BROWN?
I AM, BY GOLLY! THIS COULD BE A CHANCE FOR ME TO REINVENT MYSELF.
"KIDS WILL GAIN CONFIDENCE AND THEIR NEWFOUND COMPASS SKILLS WILL PROVE ENCOMPASSING..."
"PROVE ENCOMPASSING?"
IT SURE WOULD BE NICE TO BE SEEN AS A COMPLETE, COMPLEX PERSON, NOT JUST SOME WISHY-WASHY KID WITH A CRAZY BEAGLE...
WELL, AT LEAST HE'S WEARING A HELMET...

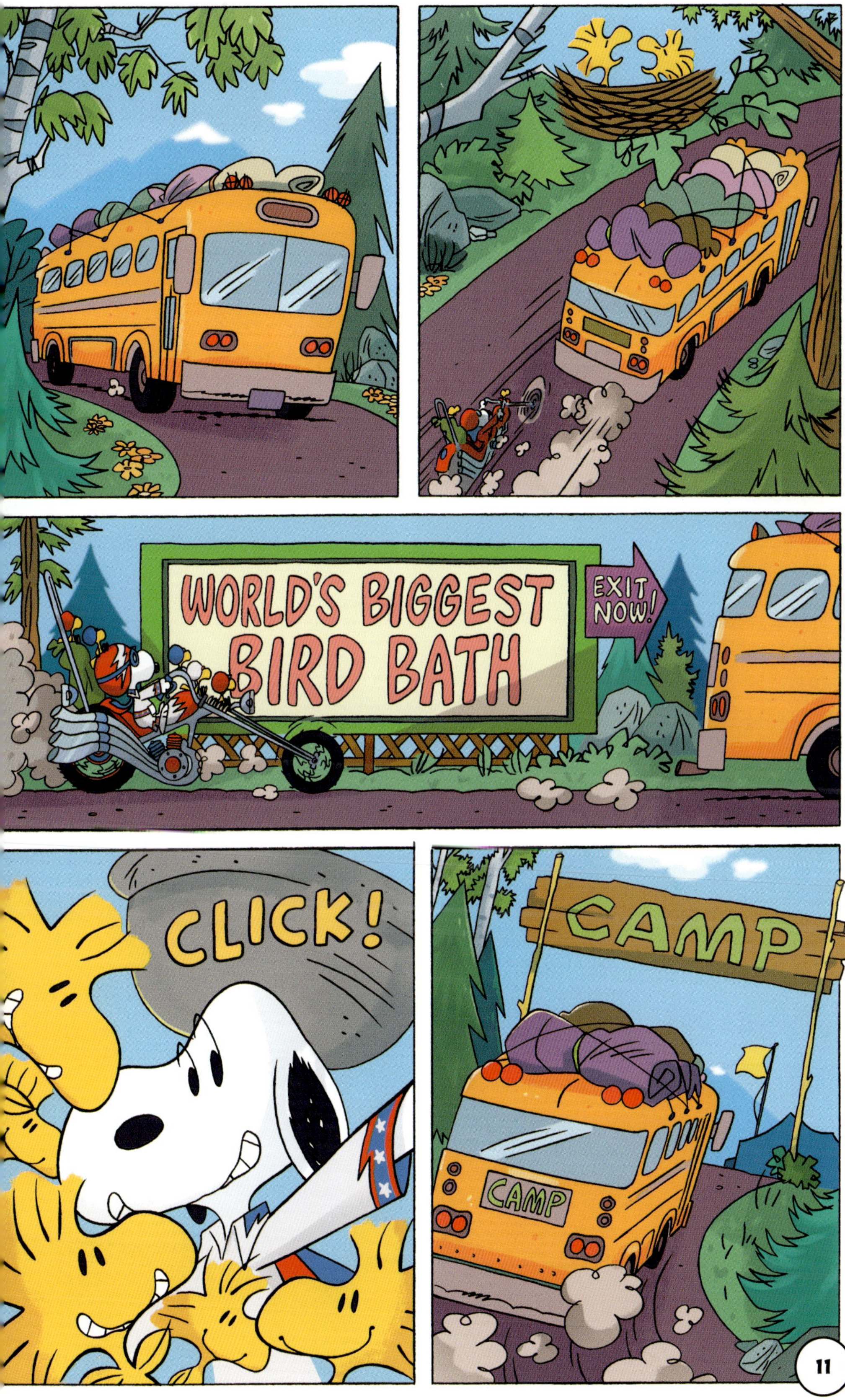
WORLD'S BIGGEST BIRD BATH
EXIT NOW!
CLICK!
CAMP
CAMP

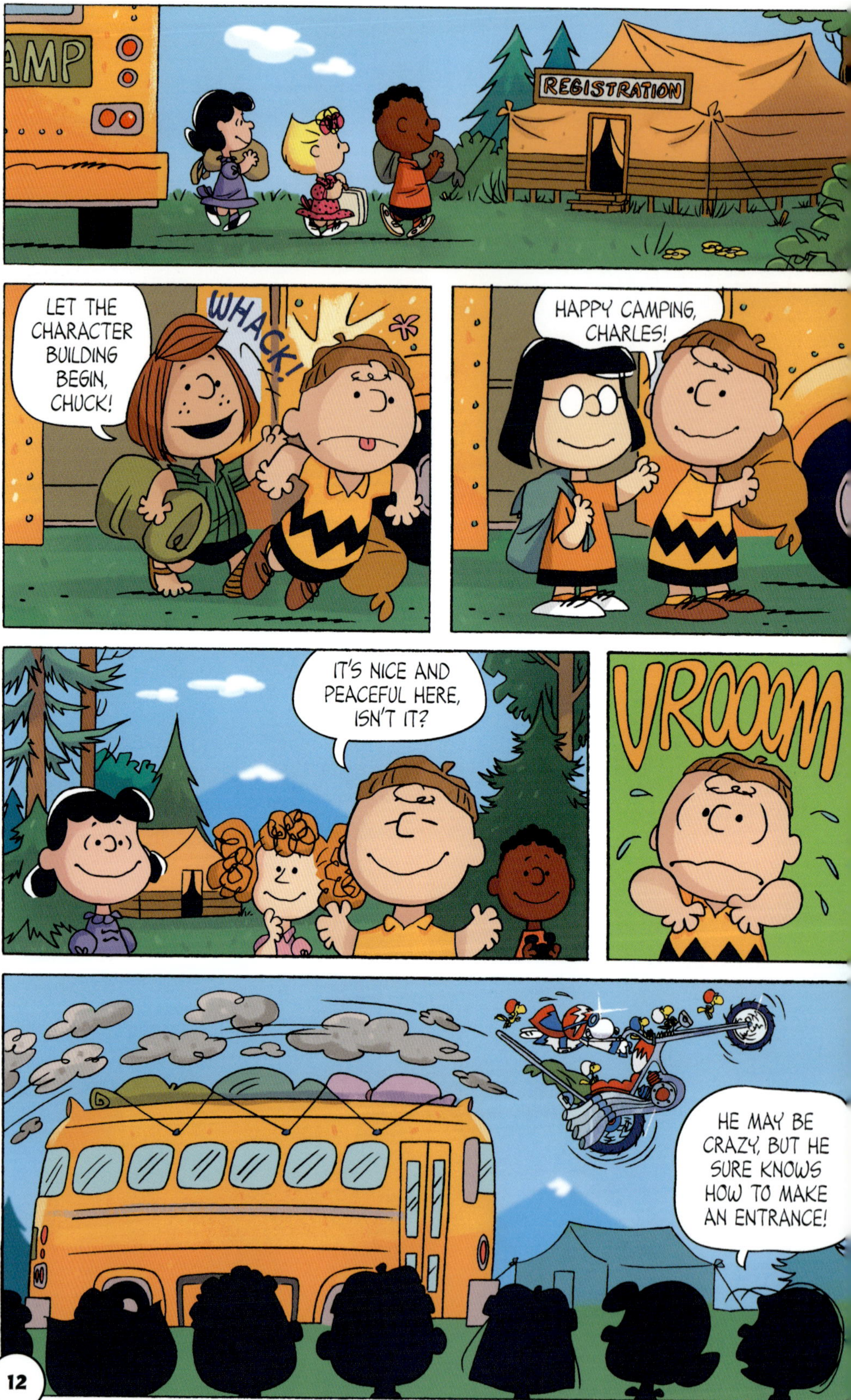
AMP
REGISTRATION
LET THE CHARACTER BUILDING BEGIN, CHUCK!
WHACK!
HAPPY CAMPING, CHARLES!
IT'S NICE AND PEACEFUL HERE, ISN'T IT?
VROOOM
HE MAY BE CRAZY, BUT HE SURE KNOWS HOW TO MAKE AN ENTRANCE!

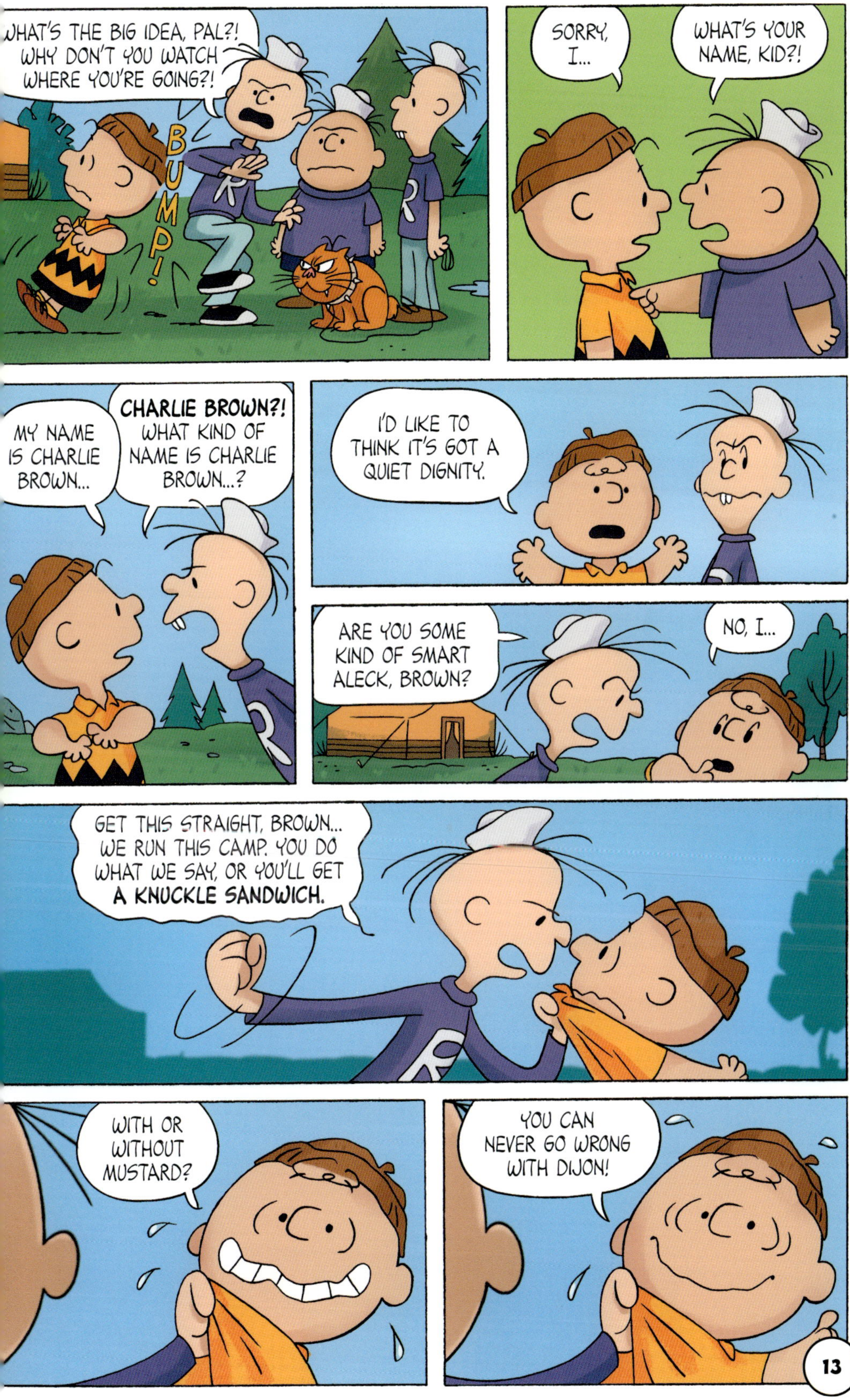
WHAT'S THE BIG IDEA, PAL?! WHY DON'T YOU WATCH WHERE YOU'RE GOING?!
BUMP!
SORRY, I...
WHAT'S YOUR NAME, KID?!
MY NAME IS CHARLIE BROWN...
CHARLIE BROWN?! WHAT KIND OF NAME IS CHARLIE BROWN...?
I'D LIKE TO THINK IT'S GOT A QUIET DIGNITY.
ARE YOU SOME KIND OF SMART ALECK, BROWN?
NO, I...
GET THIS STRAIGHT, BROWN... WE RUN THIS CAMP. YOU DO WHAT WE SAY, OR YOU'LL GET A KNUCKLE SANDWICH.
WITH OR WITHOUT MUSTARD?
YOU CAN NEVER GO WRONG WITH DIJON!

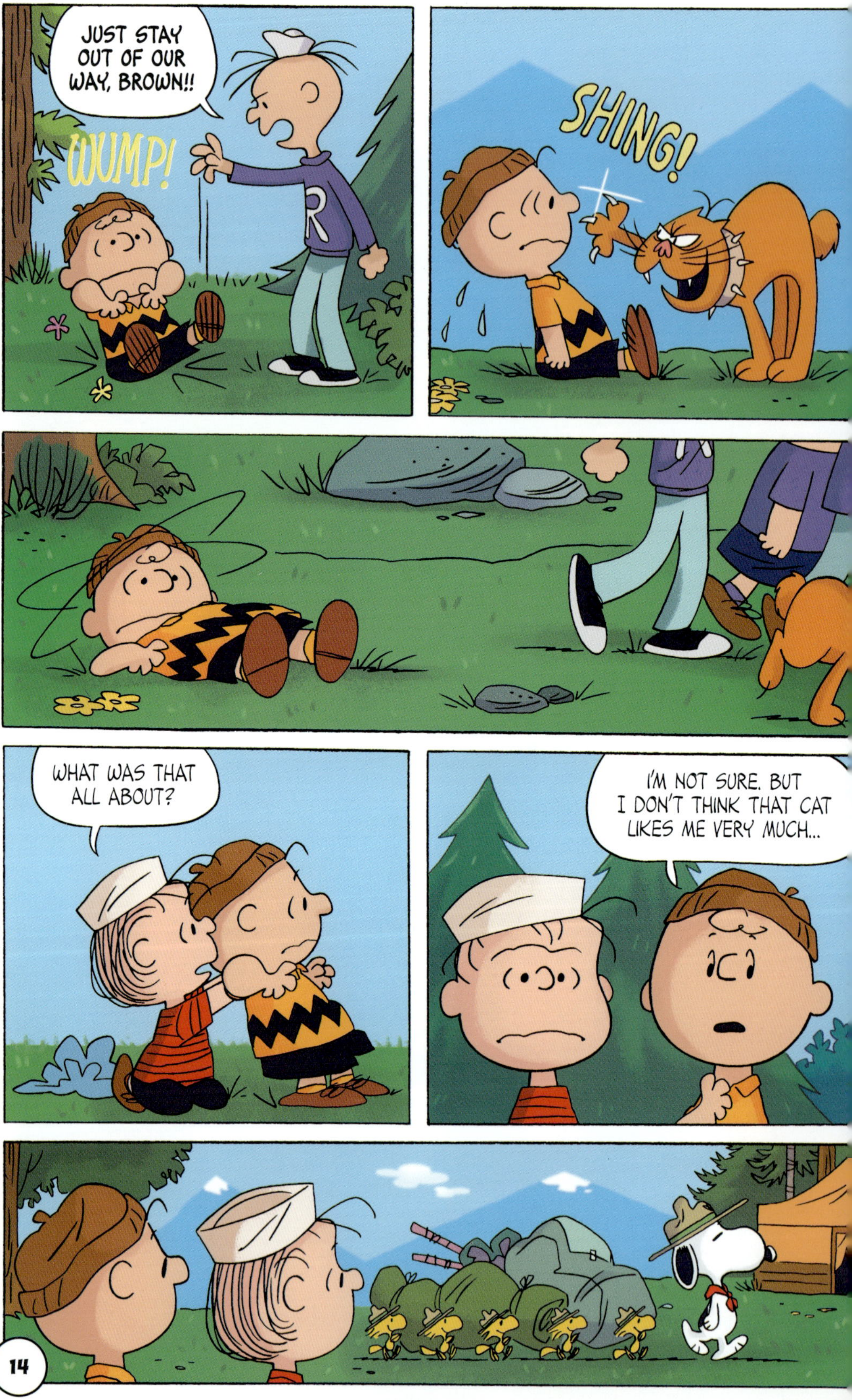
JUST STAY OUT OF OUR WAY, BROWN!!
WUMP!
SHING!
WHAT WAS THAT ALL ABOUT?
I'M NOT SURE. BUT I DON'T THINK THAT CAT LIKES ME VERY MUCH...

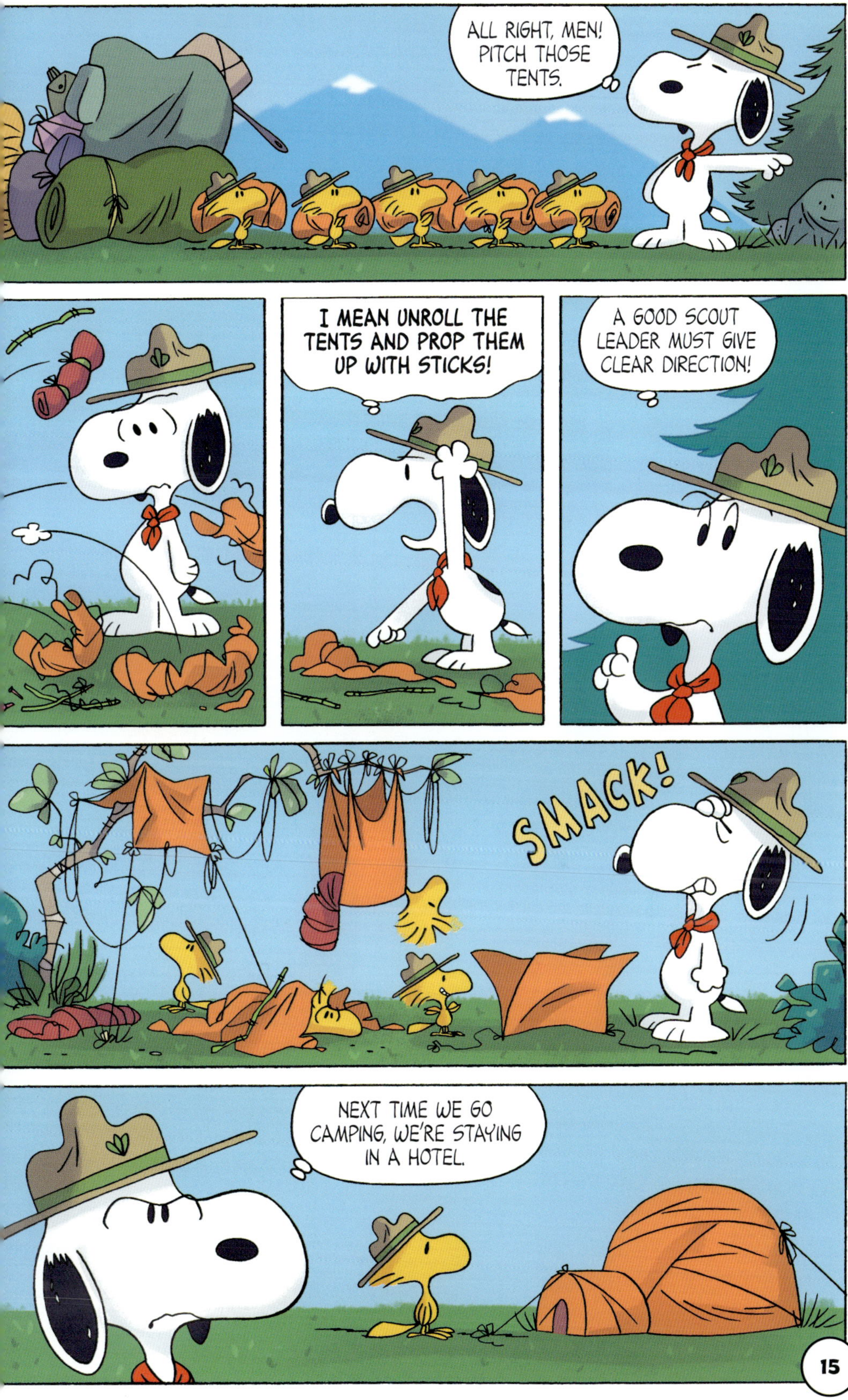

ALL RIGHT, MEN! PITCH THOSE TENTS.
I MEAN UNROLL THE TENTS AND PROP THEM UP WITH STICKS!
A GOOD SCOUT LEADER MUST GIVE CLEAR DIRECTION!
SMACK!
NEXT TIME WE GO CAMPING, WE'RE STAYING IN A HOTEL.

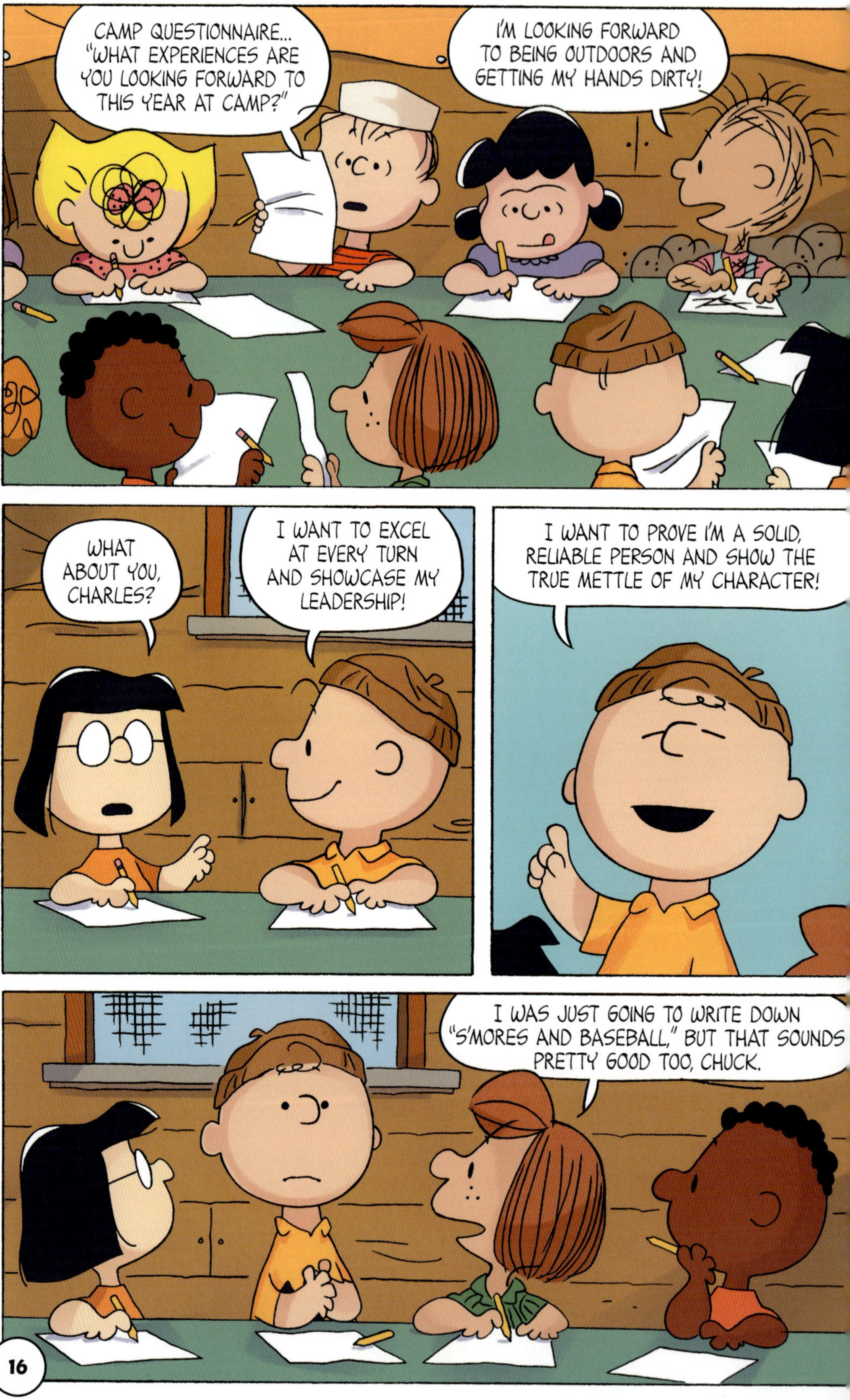
CAMP QUESTIONNAIRE... "WHAT EXPERIENCES ARE YOU LOOKING FORWARD TO THIS YEAR AT CAMP?"
I'M LOOKING FORWARD TO BEING OUTDOORS AND GETTING MY HANDS DIRTY!
WHAT ABOUT YOU, CHARLES?
I WANT TO EXCEL AT EVERY TURN AND SHOWCASE MY LEADERSHIP!
I WANT TO PROVE I'M A SOLID, RELIABLE PERSON AND SHOW THE TRUE METTLE OF MY CHARACTER!
I WAS JUST GOING TO WRITE DOWN "S'MORES AND BASEBALL," BUT THAT SOUNDS PRETTY GOOD TOO, CHUCK.

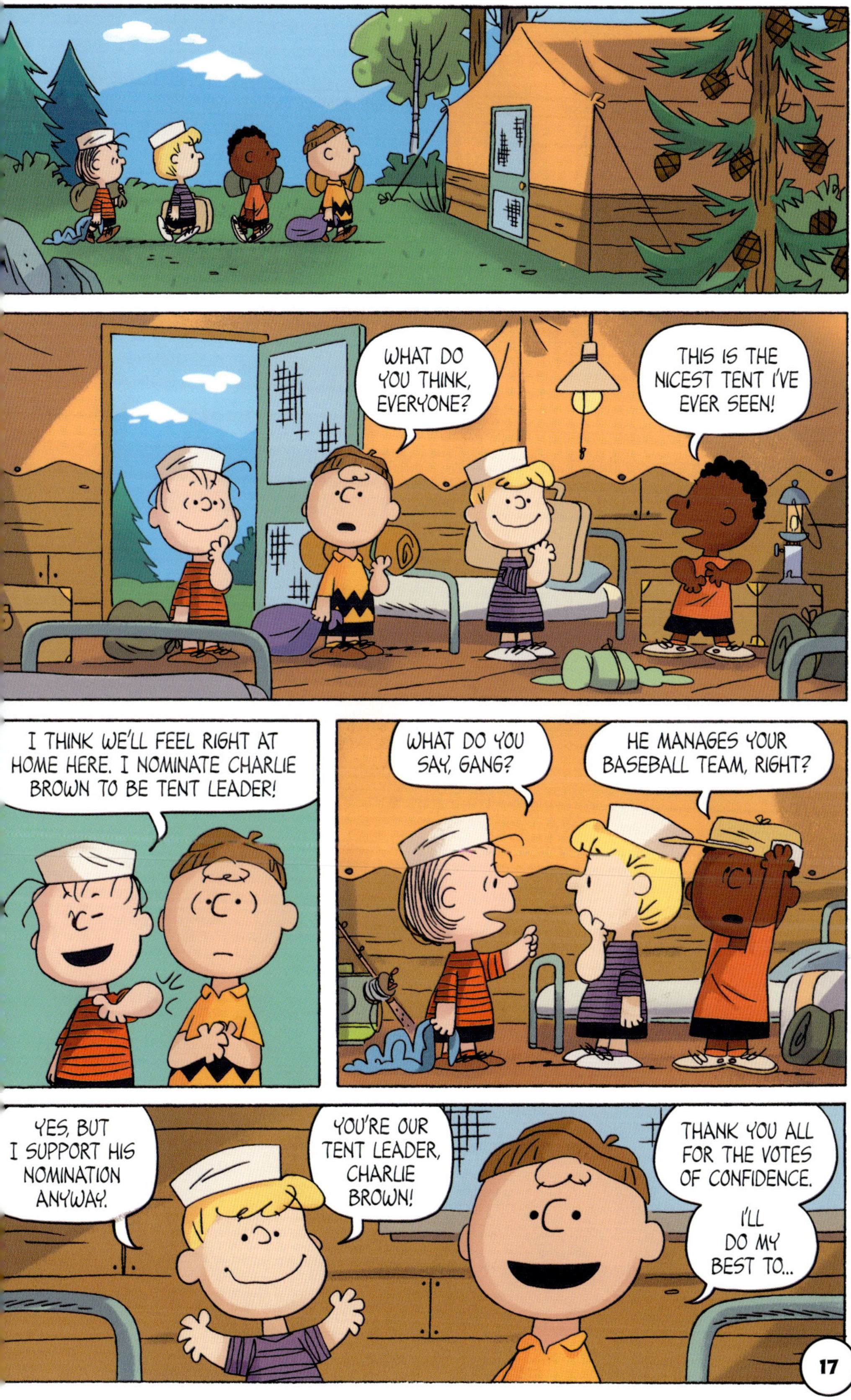
WHAT DO YOU THINK, EVERYONE?
THIS IS THE NICEST TENT I'VE EVER SEEN!
I THINK WE'LL FEEL RIGHT AT HOME HERE. I NOMINATE CHARLIE BROWN TO BE TENT LEADER!
WHAT DO YOU SAY, GANG?
HE MANAGES YOUR BASEBALL TEAM, RIGHT?
YES, BUT I SUPPORT HIS NOMINATION ANYWAY.
YOU'RE OUR TENT LEADER, CHARLIE BROWN!
THANK YOU ALL FOR THE VOTES OF CONFIDENCE.
I'LL DO MY BEST TO...

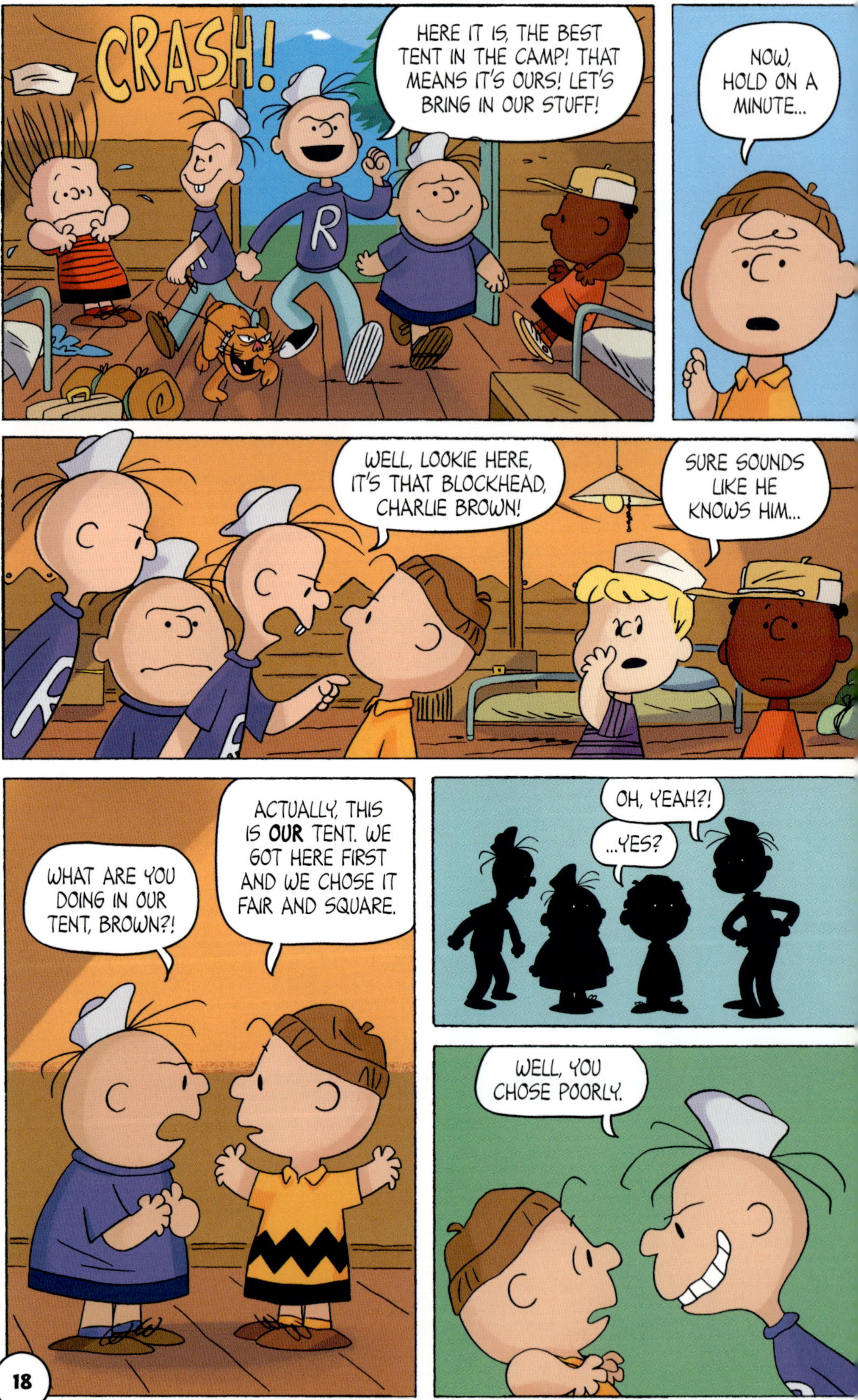
CRASH!
HERE IT IS, THE BEST TENT IN THE CAMP! THAT MEANS IT'S OURS! LET'S BRING IN OUR STUFF!
NOW, HOLD ON A MINUTE...
WELL, LOOKIE HERE, IT'S THAT BLOCKHEAD, CHARLIE BROWN!
SURE SOUNDS LIKE HE KNOWS HIM...
WHAT ARE YOU DOING IN OUR TENT, BROWN?!
ACTUALLY, THIS IS **OUR** TENT. WE GOT HERE FIRST AND WE CHOSE IT FAIR AND SQUARE.
OH, YEAH?!
...YES?
WELL, YOU CHOSE POORLY.

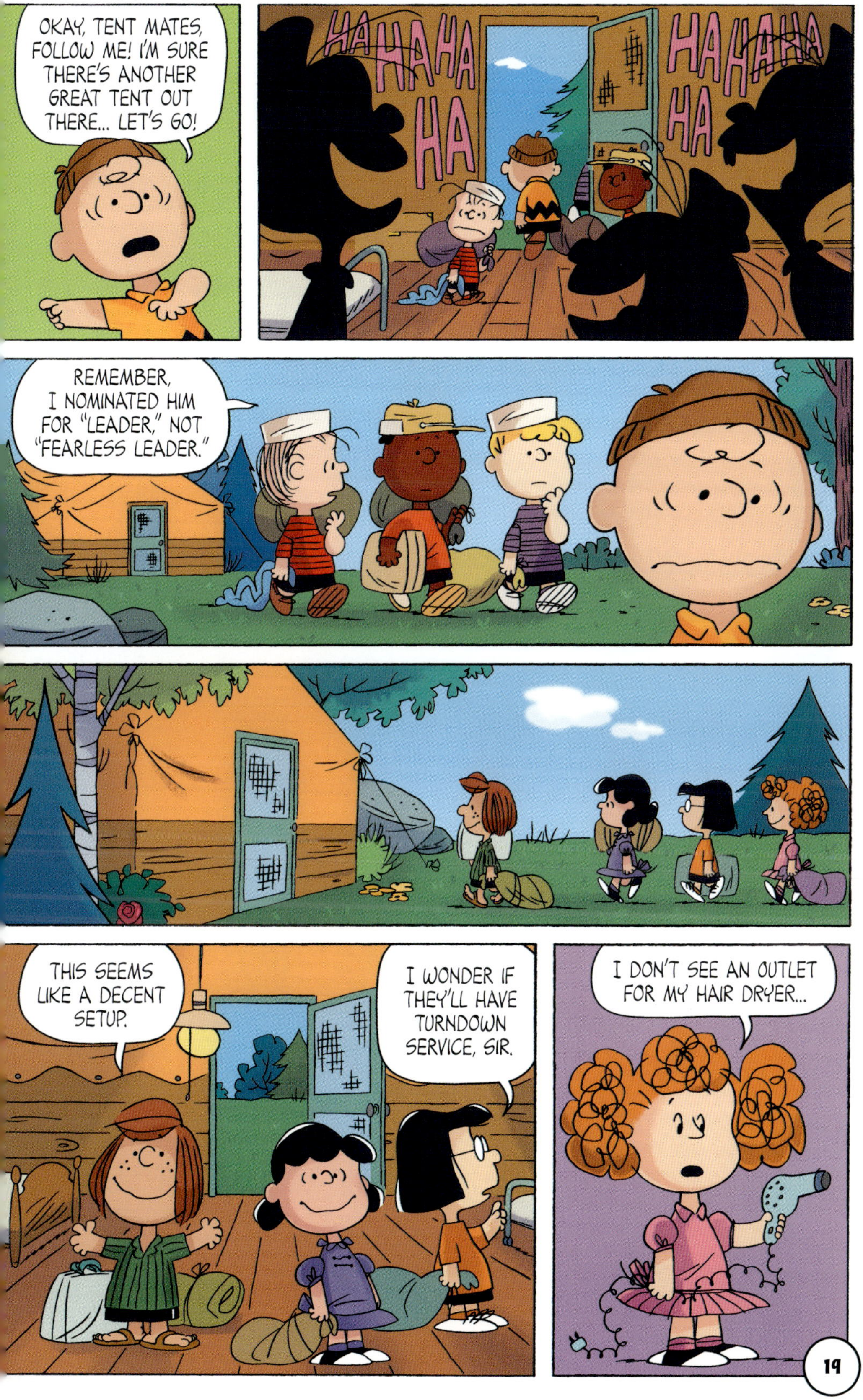

OKAY, TENT MATES, FOLLOW ME! I'M SURE THERE'S ANOTHER GREAT TENT OUT THERE... LET'S GO!
HAHAHAHA HA
HAHAHAHA HA
REMEMBER, I NOMINATED HIM FOR "LEADER," NOT "FEARLESS LEADER."
THIS SEEMS LIKE A DECENT SETUP.
I WONDER IF THEY'LL HAVE TURNDOWN SERVICE, SIR.
I DON'T SEE AN OUTLET FOR MY HAIR DRYER...

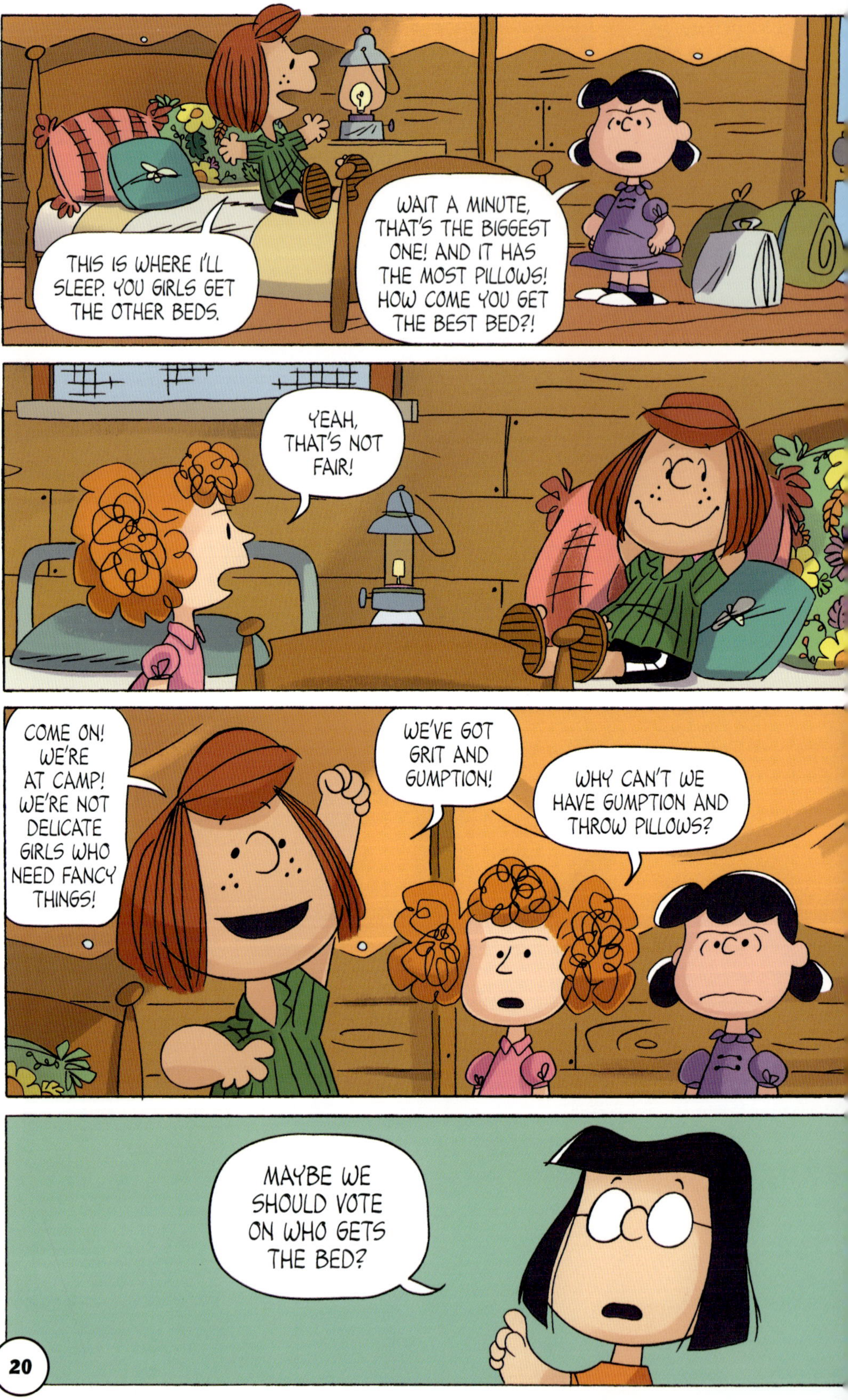
THIS IS WHERE I'LL SLEEP. YOU GIRLS GET THE OTHER BEDS.
WAIT A MINUTE, THAT'S THE BIGGEST ONE! AND IT HAS THE MOST PILLOWS! HOW COME YOU GET THE BEST BED?!
YEAH, THAT'S NOT FAIR!
COME ON! WE'RE AT CAMP! WE'RE NOT DELICATE GIRLS WHO NEED FANCY THINGS!
WE'VE GOT GRIT AND GUMPTION!
WHY CAN'T WE HAVE GUMPTION AND THROW PILLOWS?
MAYBE WE SHOULD VOTE ON WHO GETS THE BED?

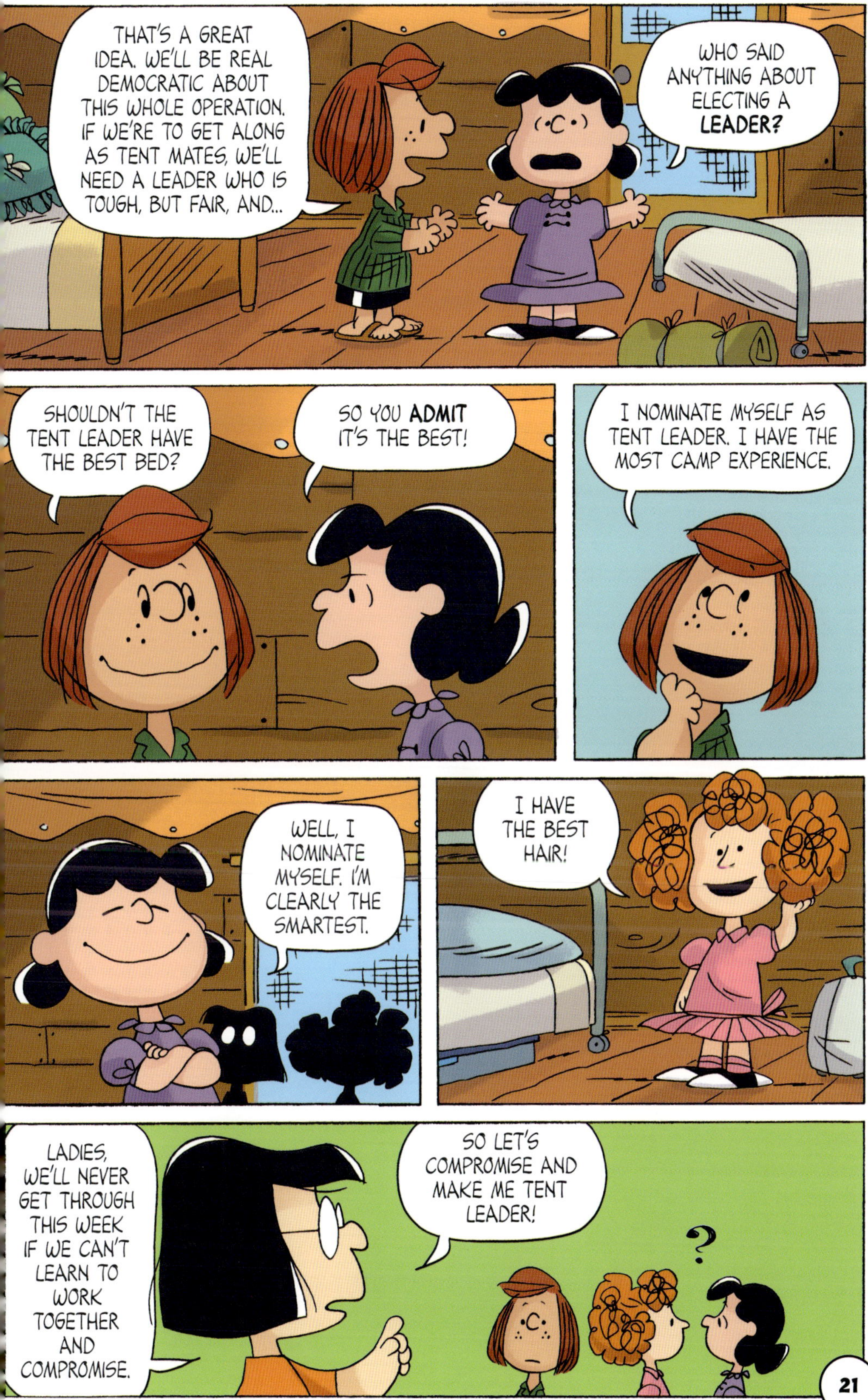

THAT'S A GREAT IDEA. WE'LL BE REAL DEMOCRATIC ABOUT THIS WHOLE OPERATION. IF WE'RE TO GET ALONG AS TENT MATES, WE'LL NEED A LEADER WHO IS TOUGH, BUT FAIR, AND...
WHO SAID ANYTHING ABOUT ELECTING A **LEADER?**
SHOULDN'T THE TENT LEADER HAVE THE BEST BED?
SO YOU **ADMIT** IT'S THE BEST!
I NOMINATE MYSELF AS TENT LEADER. I HAVE THE MOST CAMP EXPERIENCE.
WELL, I NOMINATE MYSELF. I'M CLEARLY THE SMARTEST.
I HAVE THE BEST HAIR!
LADIES, WE'LL NEVER GET THROUGH THIS WEEK IF WE CAN'T LEARN TO WORK TOGETHER AND COMPROMISE.
SO LET'S COMPROMISE AND MAKE ME TENT LEADER!
?

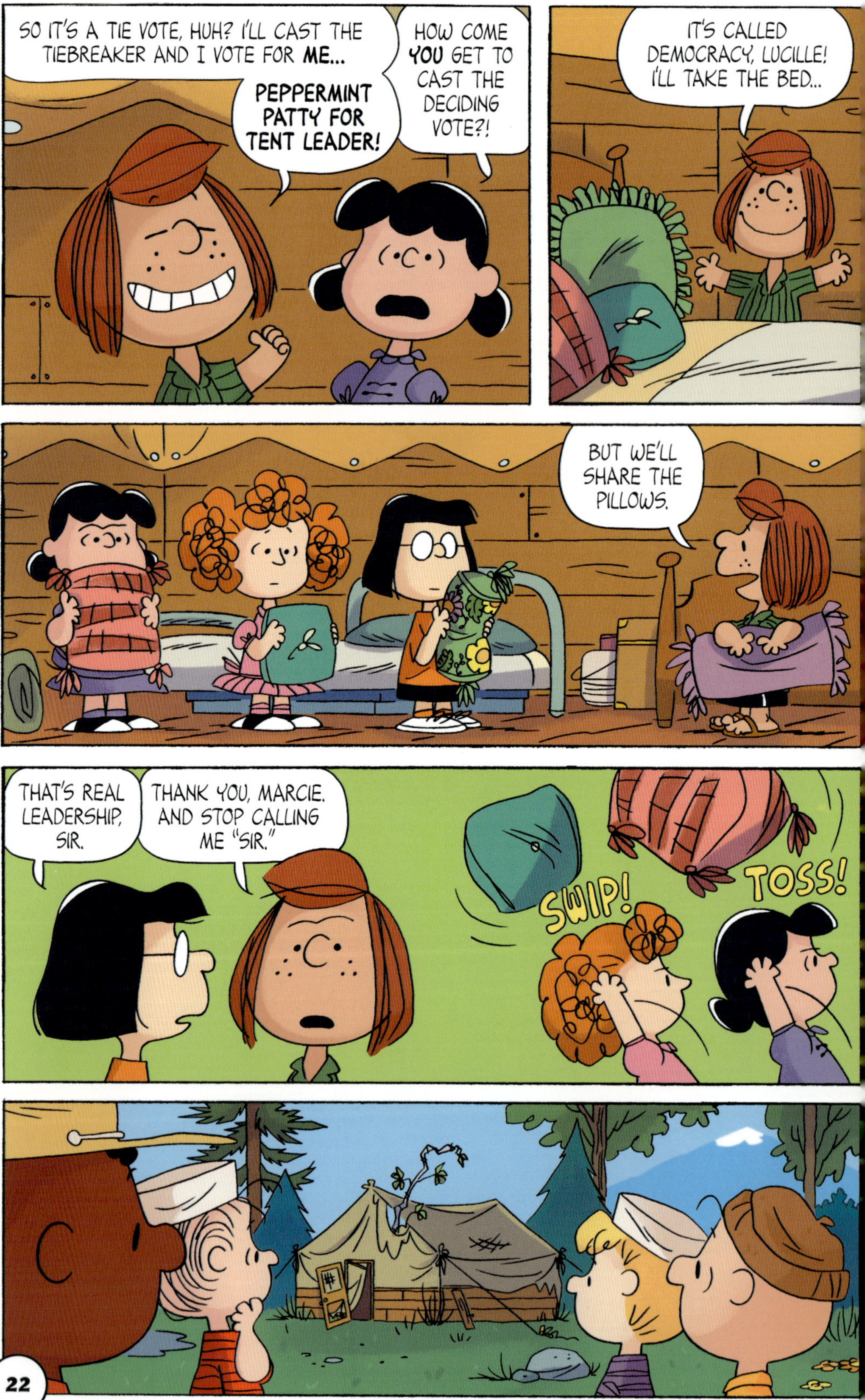

SO IT'S A TIE VOTE, HUH? I'LL CAST THE TIEBREAKER AND I VOTE FOR **ME...**
PEPPERMINT PATTY FOR TENT LEADER!
HOW COME **YOU** GET TO CAST THE DECIDING VOTE?!
IT'S CALLED DEMOCRACY, LUCILLE! I'LL TAKE THE BED...
BUT WE'LL SHARE THE PILLOWS.
THAT'S REAL LEADERSHIP, SIR.
THANK YOU, MARCIE. AND STOP CALLING ME "SIR."
SWIP!
TOSS!

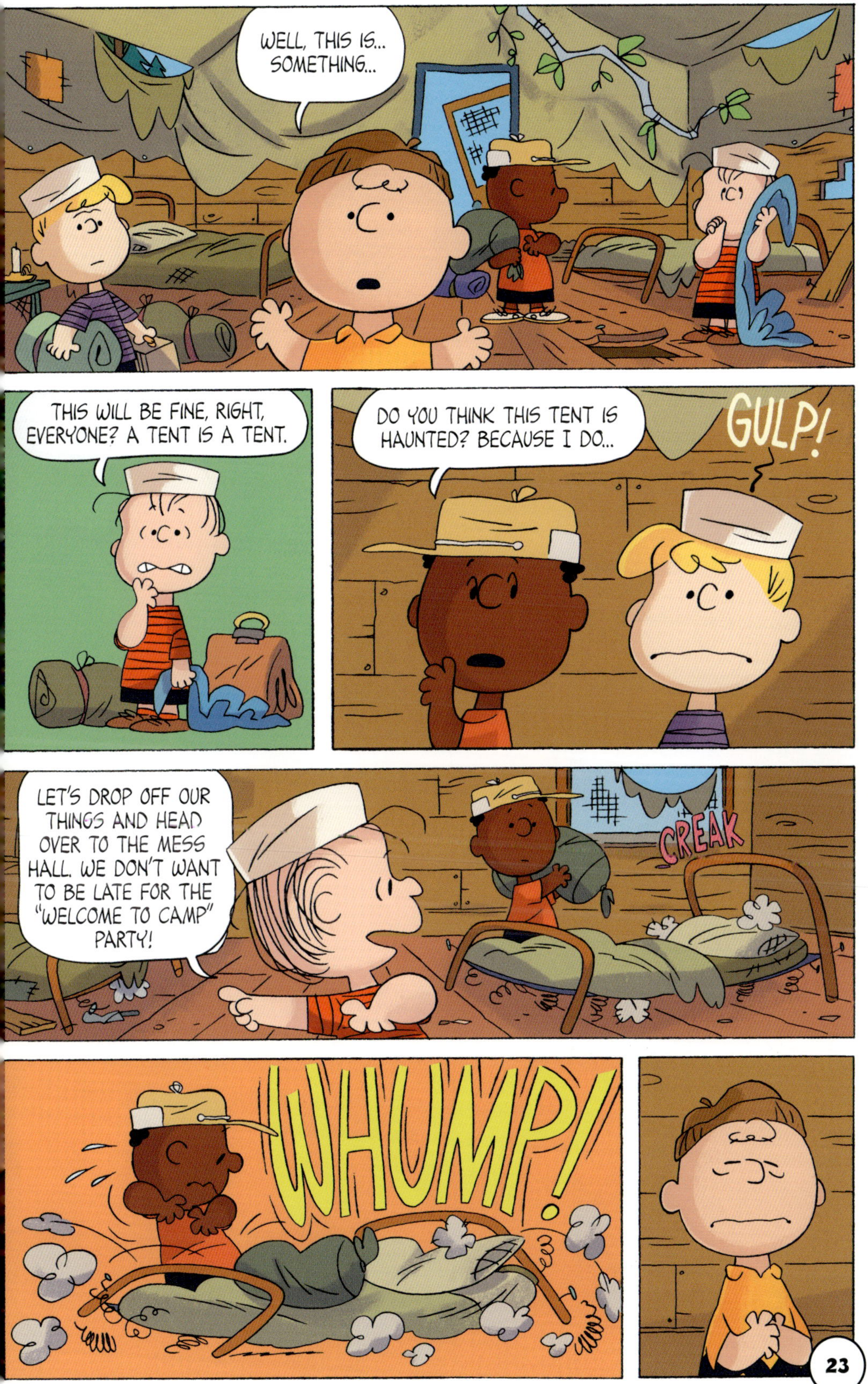
WELL, THIS IS... SOMETHING...
THIS WILL BE FINE, RIGHT, EVERYONE? A TENT IS A TENT.
DO YOU THINK THIS TENT IS HAUNTED? BECAUSE I DO...
GULP!
LET'S DROP OFF OUR THINGS AND HEAD OVER TO THE MESS HALL. WE DON'T WANT TO BE LATE FOR THE "WELCOME TO CAMP" PARTY!
CREAK
WHUMP!

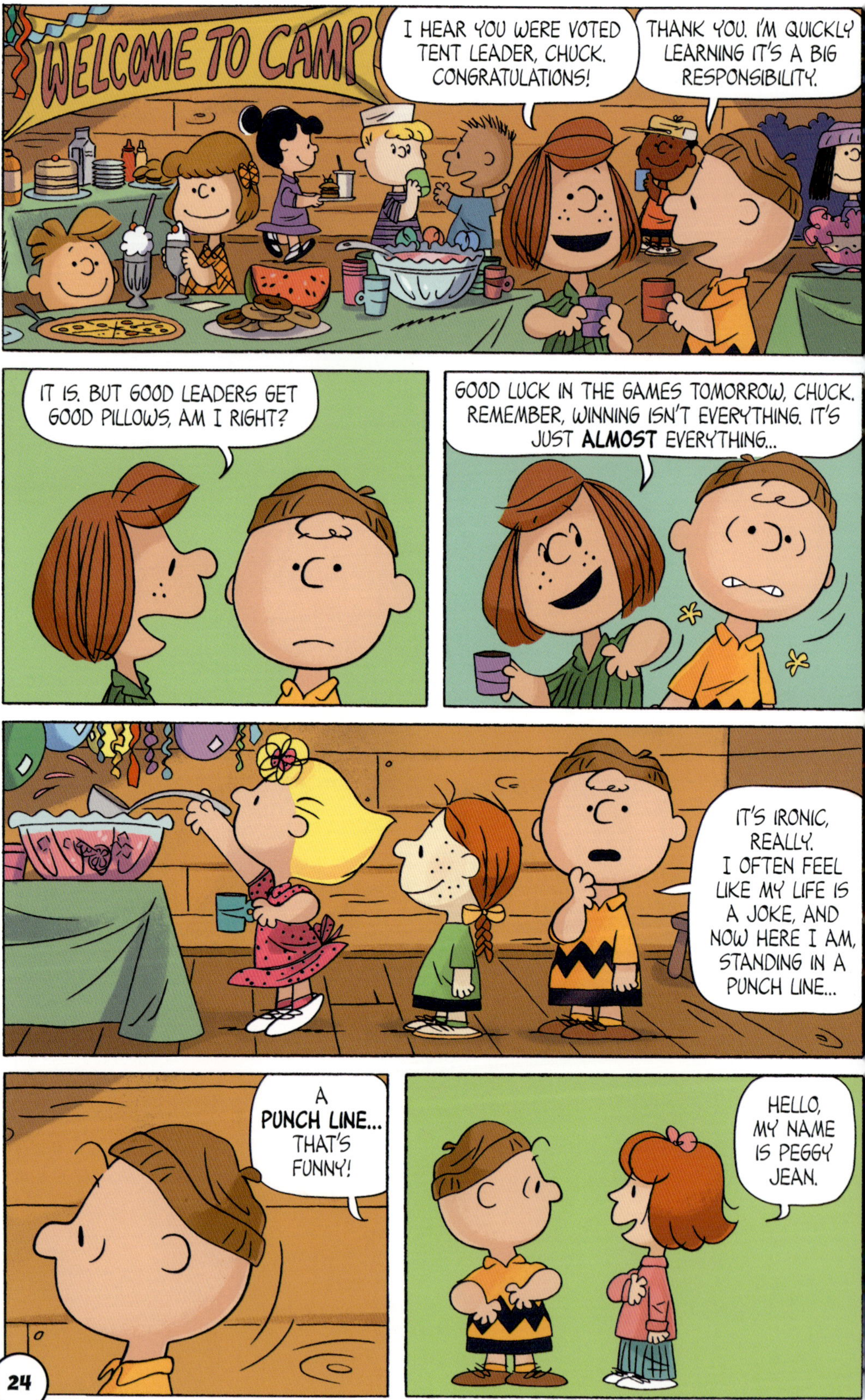
WELCOME TO CAMP
I HEAR YOU WERE VOTED TENT LEADER, CHUCK. CONGRATULATIONS!
THANK YOU. I'M QUICKLY LEARNING IT'S A BIG RESPONSIBILITY.
IT IS. BUT GOOD LEADERS GET GOOD PILLOWS, AM I RIGHT?
GOOD LUCK IN THE GAMES TOMORROW, CHUCK. REMEMBER, WINNING ISN'T EVERYTHING. IT'S JUST **ALMOST** EVERYTHING...
IT'S IRONIC, REALLY. I OFTEN FEEL LIKE MY LIFE IS A JOKE, AND NOW HERE I AM, STANDING IN A PUNCH LINE...
A **PUNCH LINE...** THAT'S FUNNY!
HELLO, MY NAME IS PEGGY JEAN.

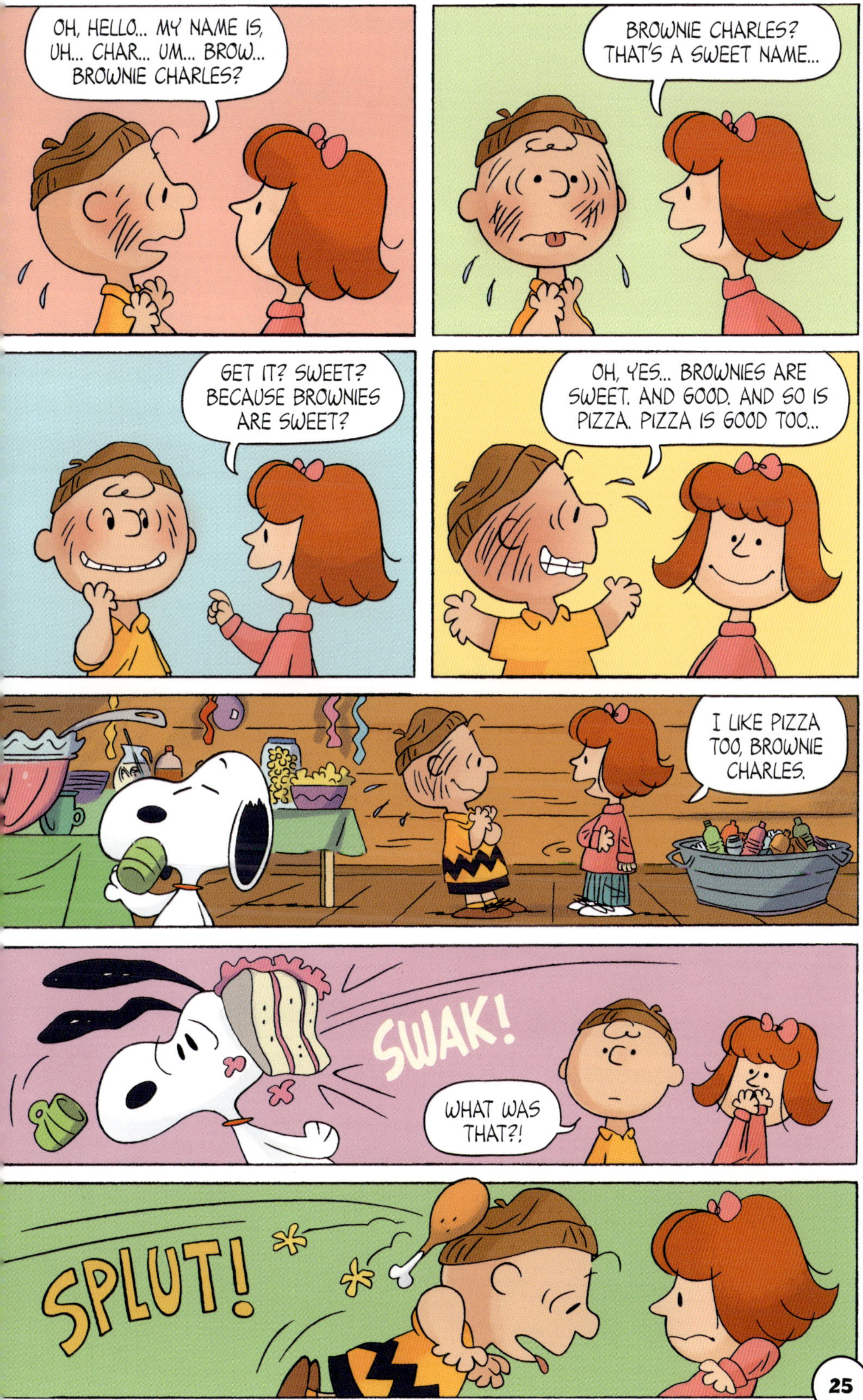
OH, HELLO... MY NAME IS, UH... CHAR... UM... BROW... BROWNIE CHARLES?
BROWNIE CHARLES? THAT'S A SWEET NAME...
GET IT? SWEET? BECAUSE BROWNIES ARE SWEET?
OH, YES... BROWNIES ARE SWEET. AND GOOD. AND SO IS PIZZA. PIZZA IS GOOD TOO...
I LIKE PIZZA TOO, BROWNIE CHARLES.
SWAK!
WHAT WAS THAT?!
SPLUT!

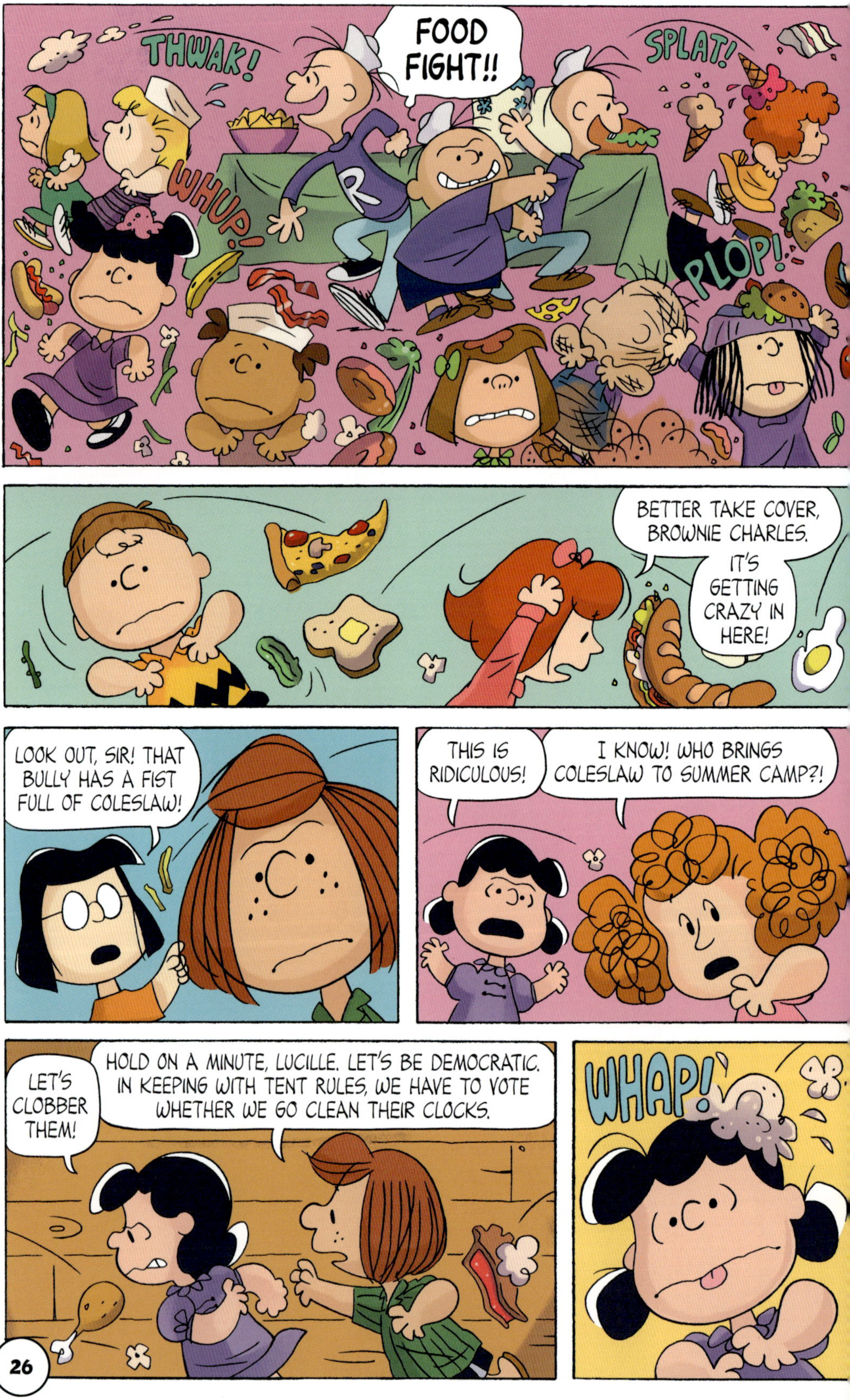
THWAK!
FOOD FIGHT!!
SPLAT!
WHUP!
PLOP!
BETTER TAKE COVER, BROWNIE CHARLES.
IT'S GETTING CRAZY IN HERE!
LOOK OUT, SIR! THAT BULLY HAS A FIST FULL OF COLESLAW!
THIS IS RIDICULOUS!
I KNOW! WHO BRINGS COLESLAW TO SUMMER CAMP?!
LET'S CLOBBER THEM!
HOLD ON A MINUTE, LUCILLE. LET'S BE DEMOCRATIC. IN KEEPING WITH TENT RULES, WE HAVE TO VOTE WHETHER WE GO CLEAN THEIR CLOCKS.
WHAP!

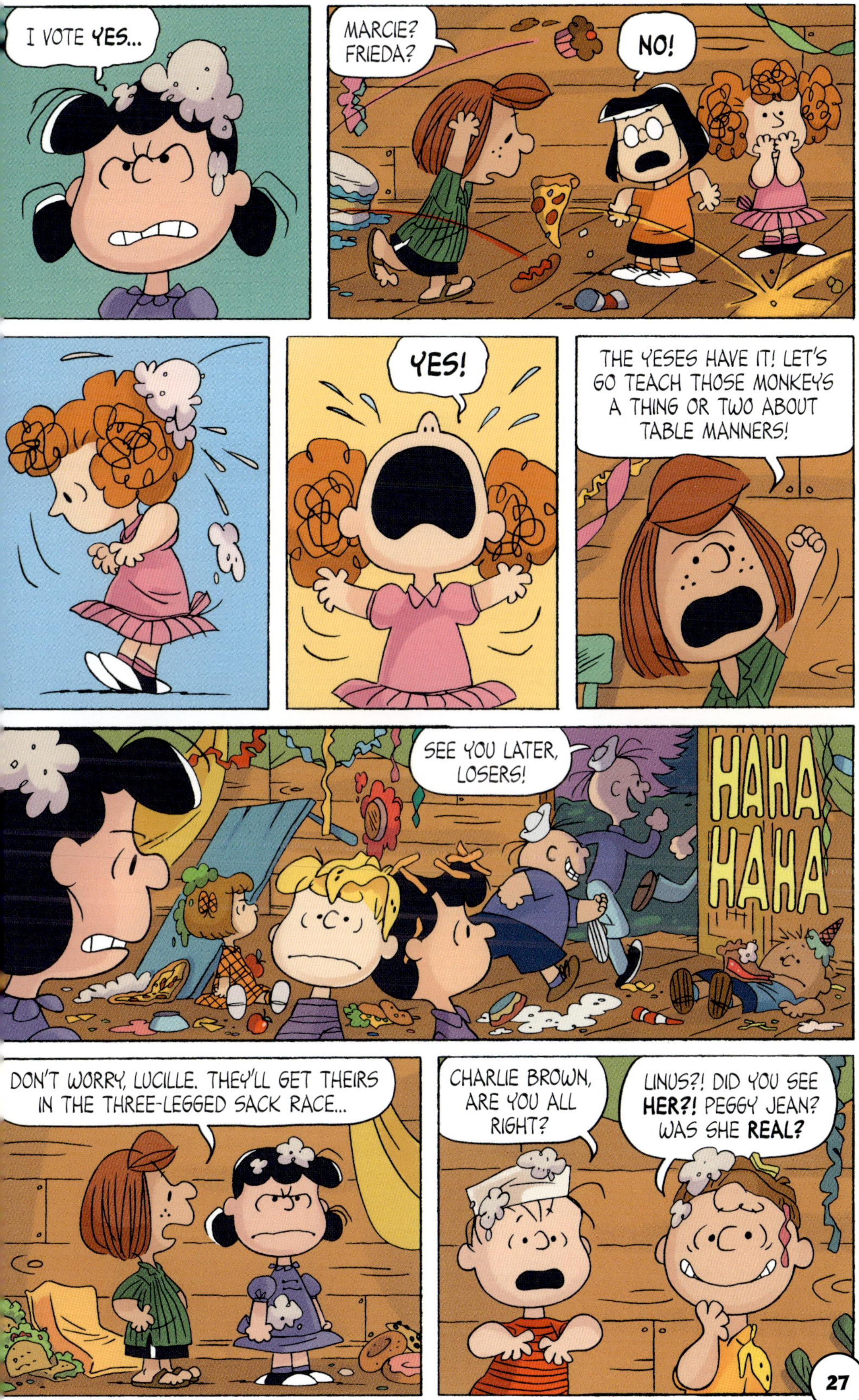
I VOTE YES...
MARCIE? FRIEDA?
NO!
YES!
THE YESES HAVE IT! LET'S GO TEACH THOSE MONKEYS A THING OR TWO ABOUT TABLE MANNERS!
SEE YOU LATER, LOSERS!
HAHA HAHA
DON'T WORRY, LUCILLE. THEY'LL GET THEIRS IN THE THREE-LEGGED SACK RACE...
CHARLIE BROWN, ARE YOU ALL RIGHT?
LINUS?! DID YOU SEE HER?! PEGGY JEAN? WAS SHE REAL?

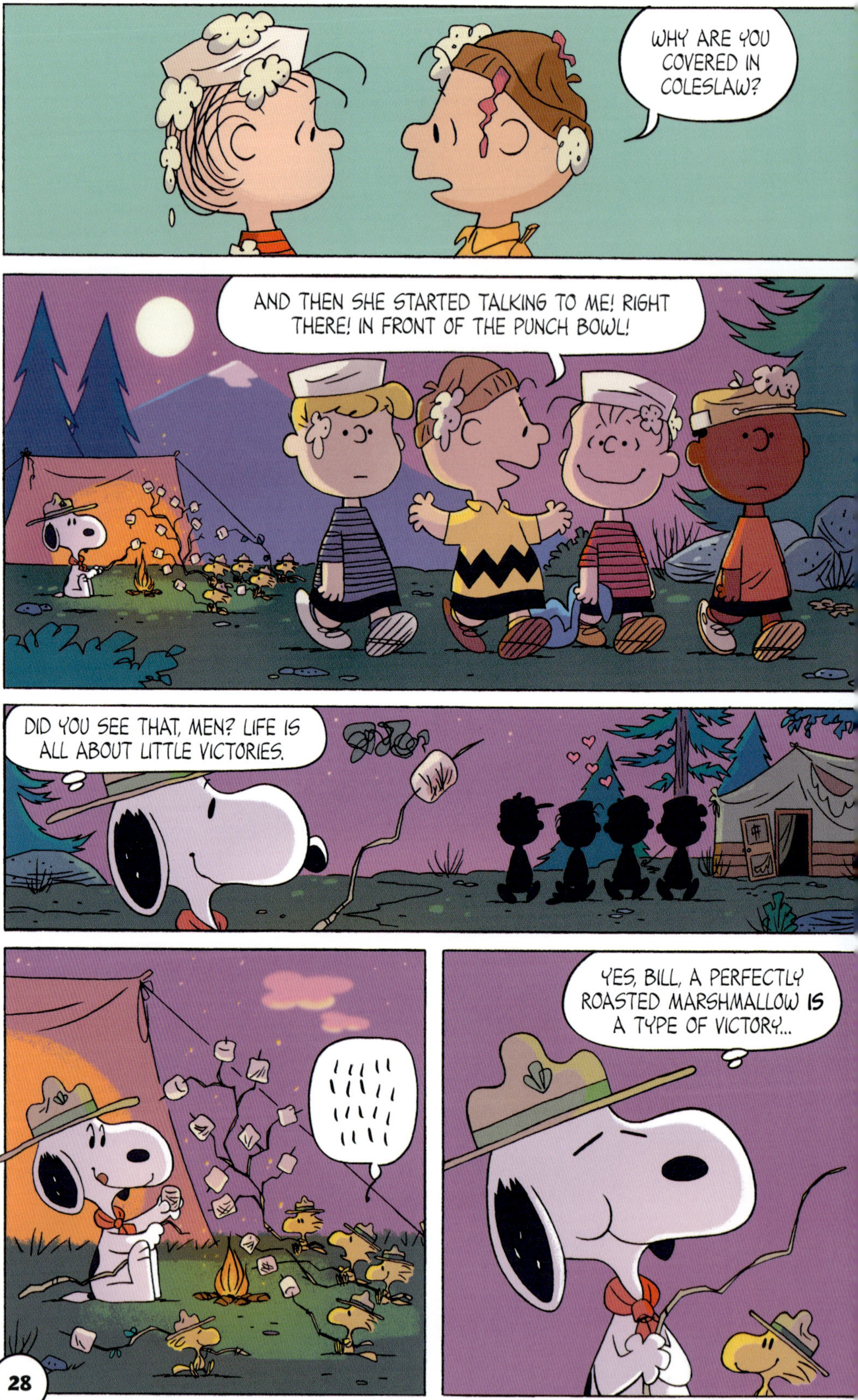
WHY ARE YOU COVERED IN COLESLAW?
AND THEN SHE STARTED TALKING TO ME! RIGHT THERE! IN FRONT OF THE PUNCH BOWL!
DID YOU SEE THAT, MEN? LIFE IS ALL ABOUT LITTLE VICTORIES.
YES, BILL, A PERFECTLY ROASTED MARSHMALLOW **IS** A TYPE OF VICTORY...

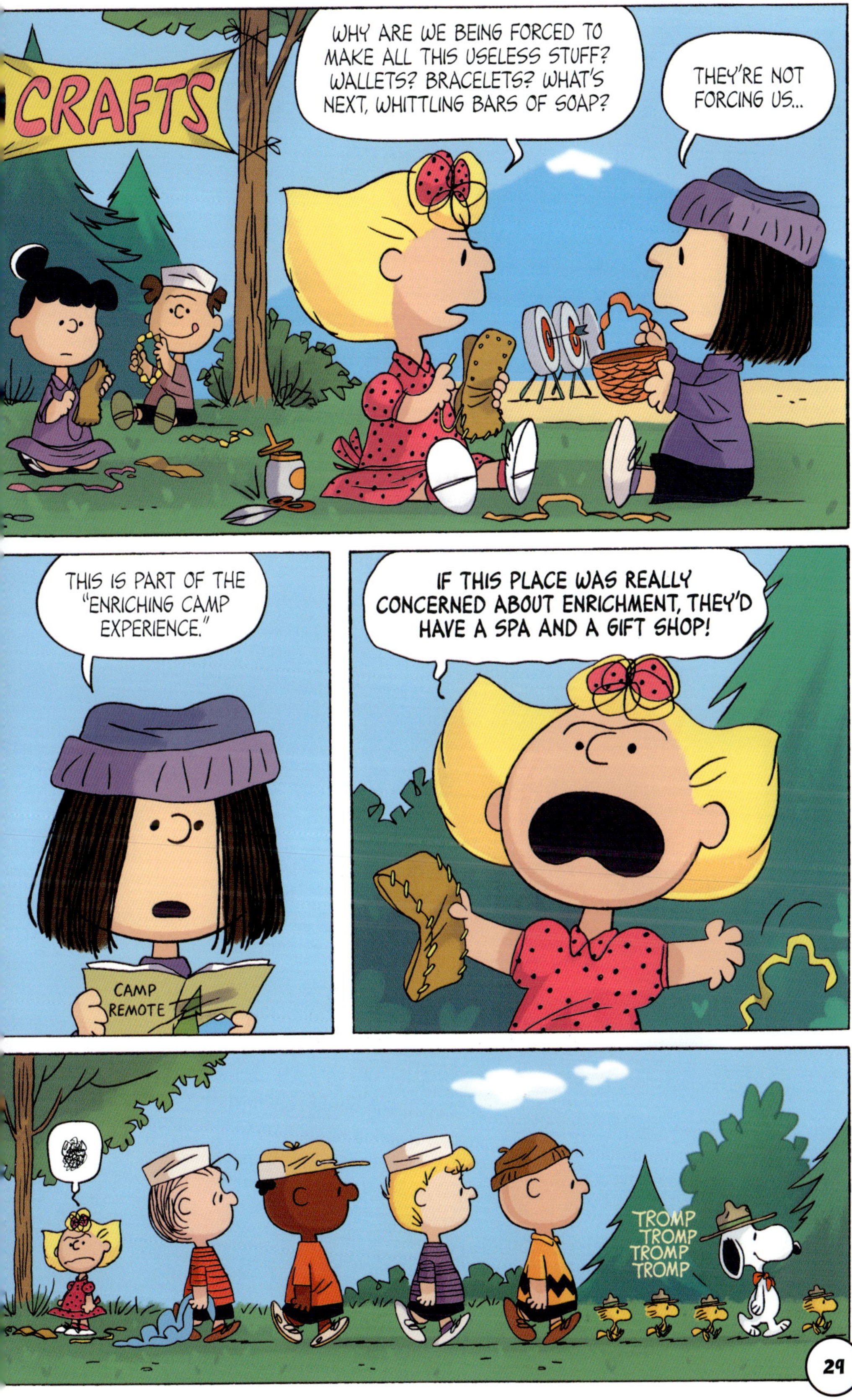
CRAFTS
WHY ARE WE BEING FORCED TO MAKE ALL THIS USELESS STUFF? WALLETS? BRACELETS? WHAT'S NEXT, WHITTLING BARS OF SOAP?
THEY'RE NOT FORCING US...
THIS IS PART OF THE "ENRICHING CAMP EXPERIENCE."
CAMP REMOTE
IF THIS PLACE WAS REALLY CONCERNED ABOUT ENRICHMENT, THEY'D HAVE A SPA AND A GIFT SHOP!
TROMP
TROMP
TROMP
TROMP

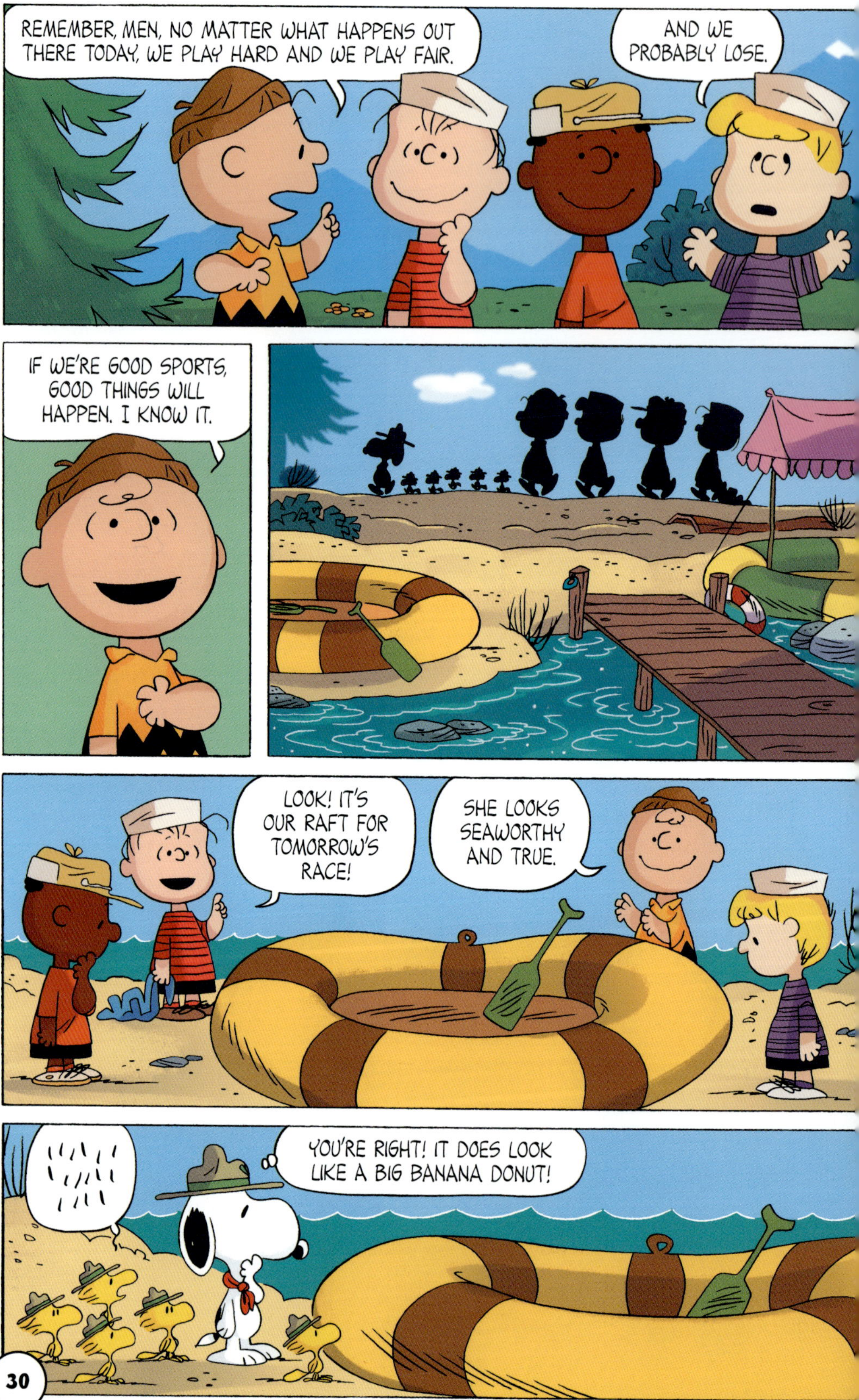
REMEMBER, MEN, NO MATTER WHAT HAPPENS OUT THERE TODAY, WE PLAY HARD AND WE PLAY FAIR.
AND WE PROBABLY LOSE.
IF WE'RE GOOD SPORTS, GOOD THINGS WILL HAPPEN. I KNOW IT.
LOOK! IT'S OUR RAFT FOR TOMORROW'S RACE!
SHE LOOKS SEAWORTHY AND TRUE.
YOU'RE RIGHT! IT DOES LOOK LIKE A BIG BANANA DONUT!

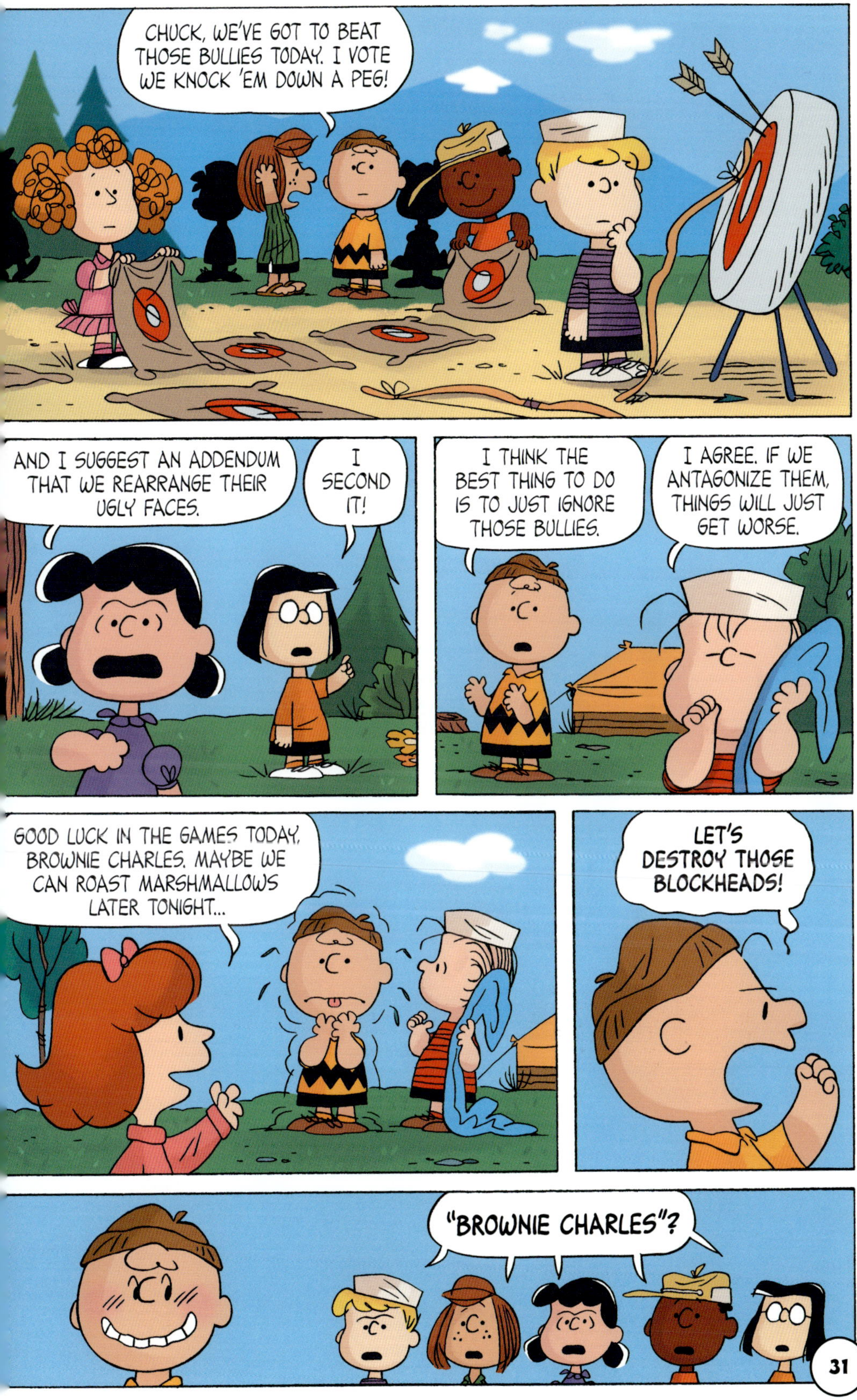
CHUCK, WE'VE GOT TO BEAT THOSE BULLIES TODAY. I VOTE WE KNOCK 'EM DOWN A PEG!
AND I SUGGEST AN ADDENDUM THAT WE REARRANGE THEIR UGLY FACES.
I SECOND IT!
I THINK THE BEST THING TO DO IS TO JUST IGNORE THOSE BULLIES.
I AGREE. IF WE ANTAGONIZE THEM, THINGS WILL JUST GET WORSE.
GOOD LUCK IN THE GAMES TODAY, BROWNIE CHARLES. MAYBE WE CAN ROAST MARSHMALLOWS LATER TONIGHT...
LET'S DESTROY THOSE BLOCKHEADS!
"BROWNIE CHARLES"?

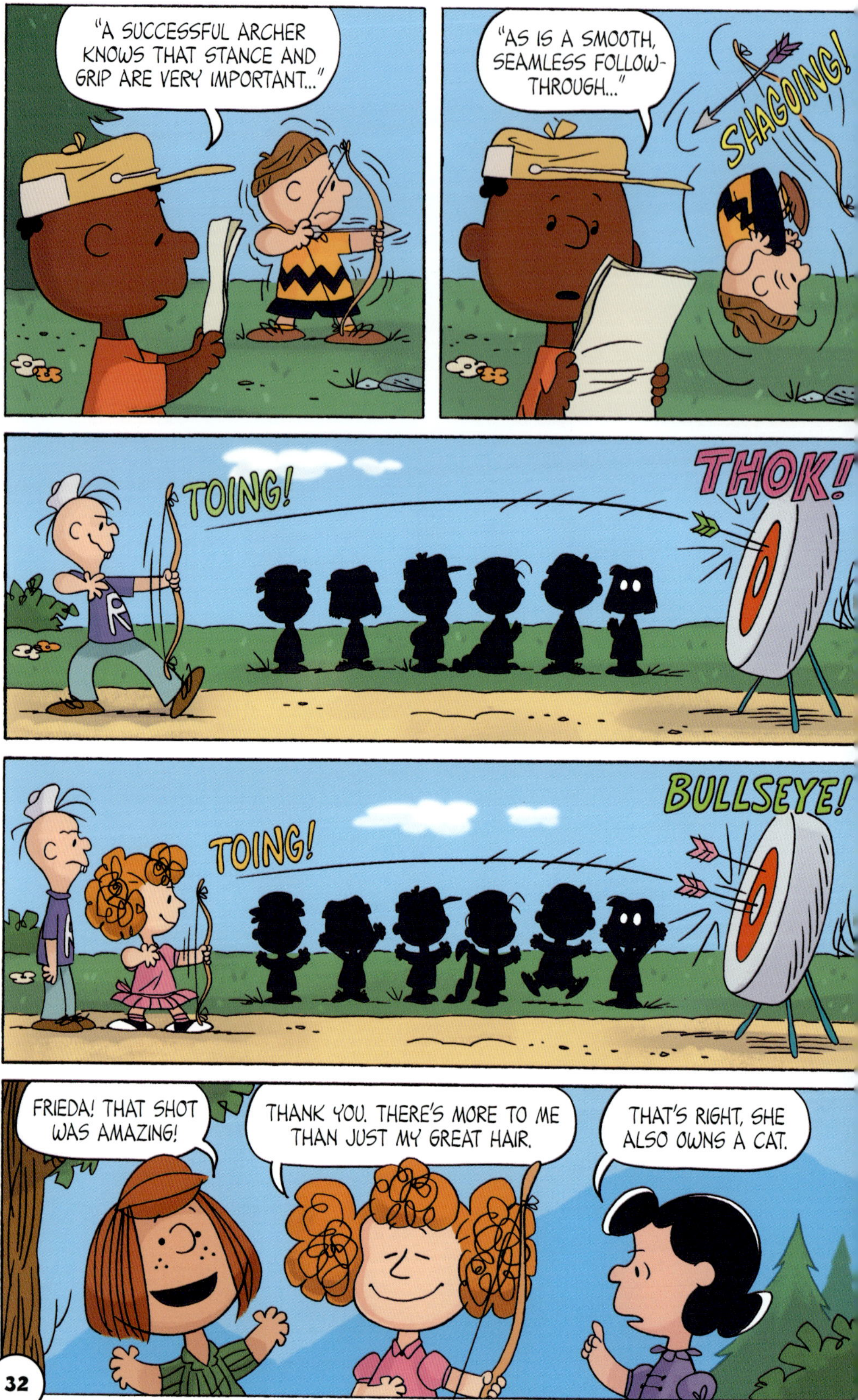
"A SUCCESSFUL ARCHER KNOWS THAT STANCE AND GRIP ARE VERY IMPORTANT..."
"AS IS A SMOOTH, SEAMLESS FOLLOW-THROUGH..."
SHAGOING!
TOING!
THOK!
TOING!
BULLSEYE!
FRIEDA! THAT SHOT WAS AMAZING!
THANK YOU. THERE'S MORE TO ME THAN JUST MY GREAT HAIR.
THAT'S RIGHT, SHE ALSO OWNS A CAT.

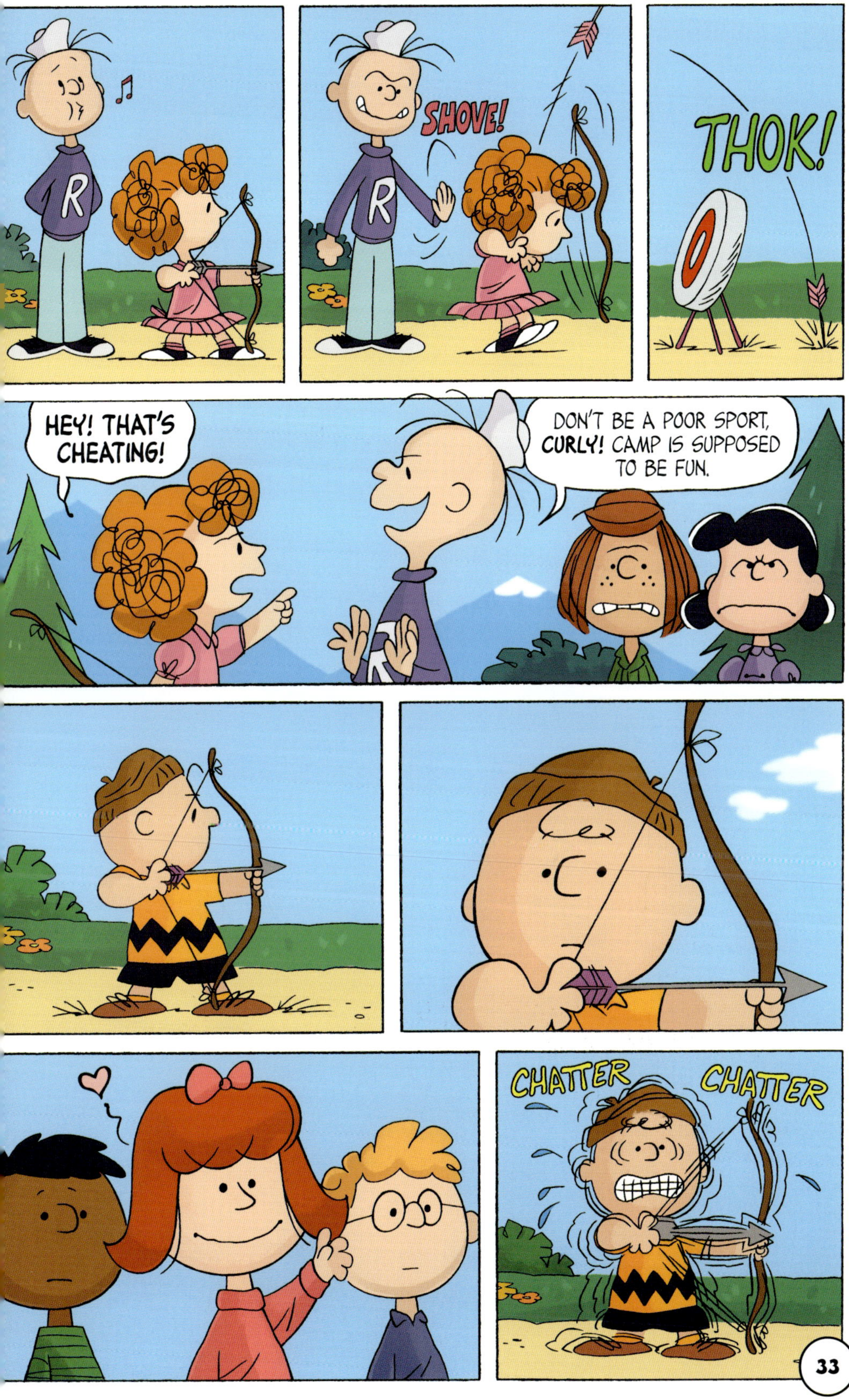

SHOVE!
THOK!
HEY! THAT'S CHEATING!
DON'T BE A POOR SPORT, **CURLY!** CAMP IS SUPPOSED TO BE FUN.
CHATTER
CHATTER

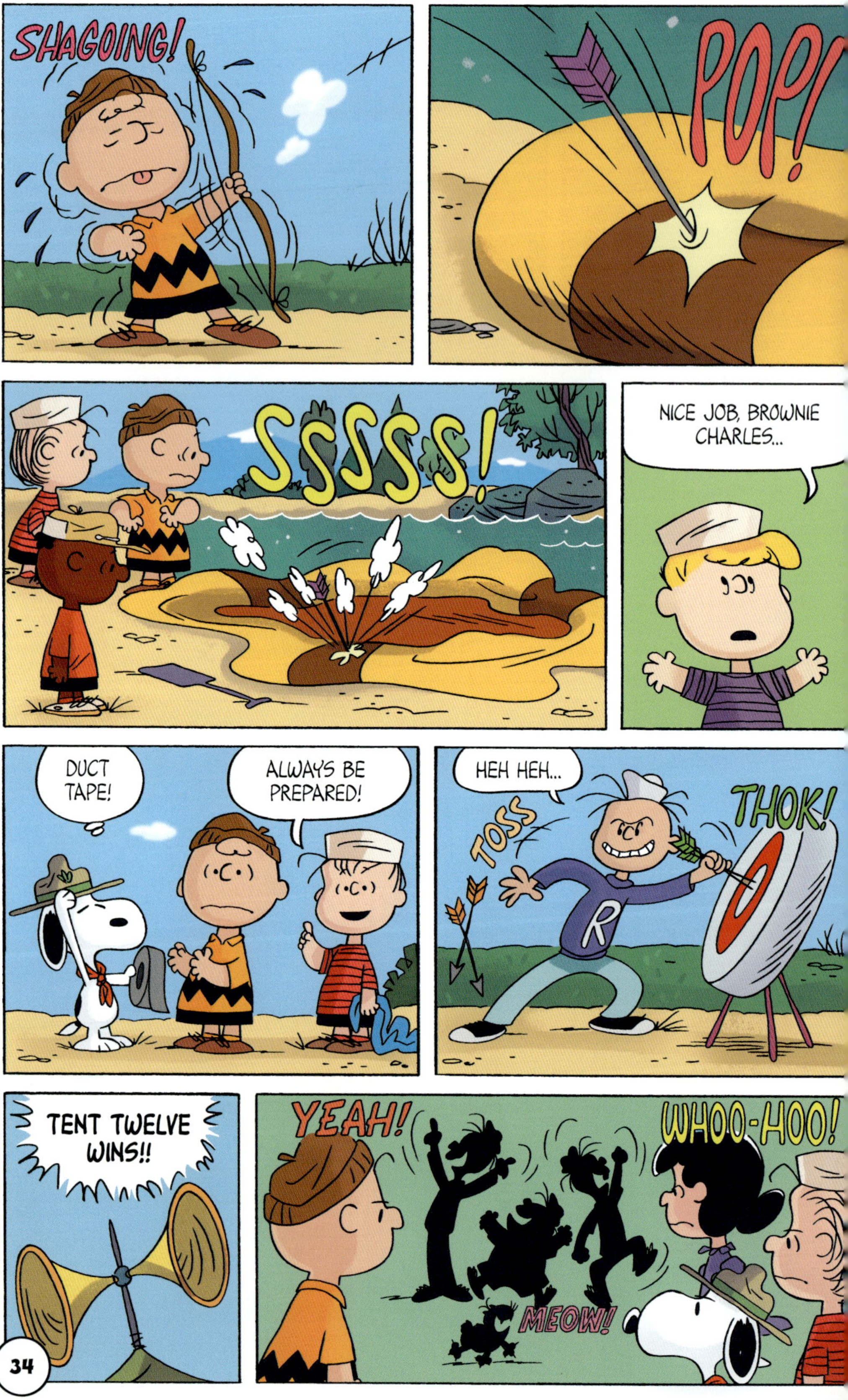
SHAGOING!
POP!
SSSSS!
NICE JOB, BROWNIE CHARLES...
DUCT TAPE!
ALWAYS BE PREPARED!
HEH HEH...
TOSS
THOK!
TENT TWELVE WINS!!
YEAH!
WHOO-HOO!
MEOW!

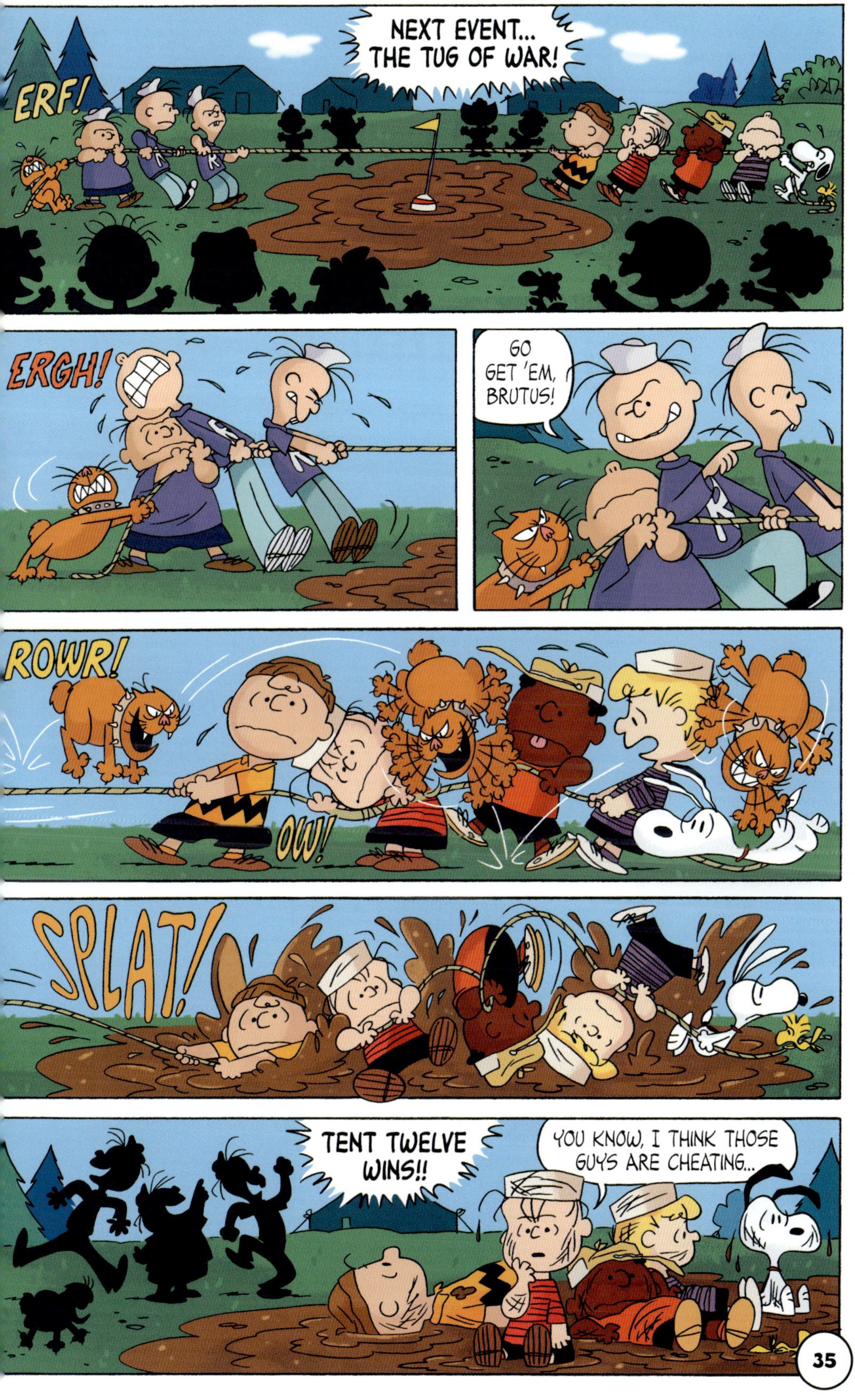
NEXT EVENT... THE TUG OF WAR!
ERF!
ERGH!
GO GET 'EM, BRUTUS!
ROWR!
OW!
SPLAT!
TENT TWELVE WINS!!
YOU KNOW, I THINK THOSE GUYS ARE CHEATING...

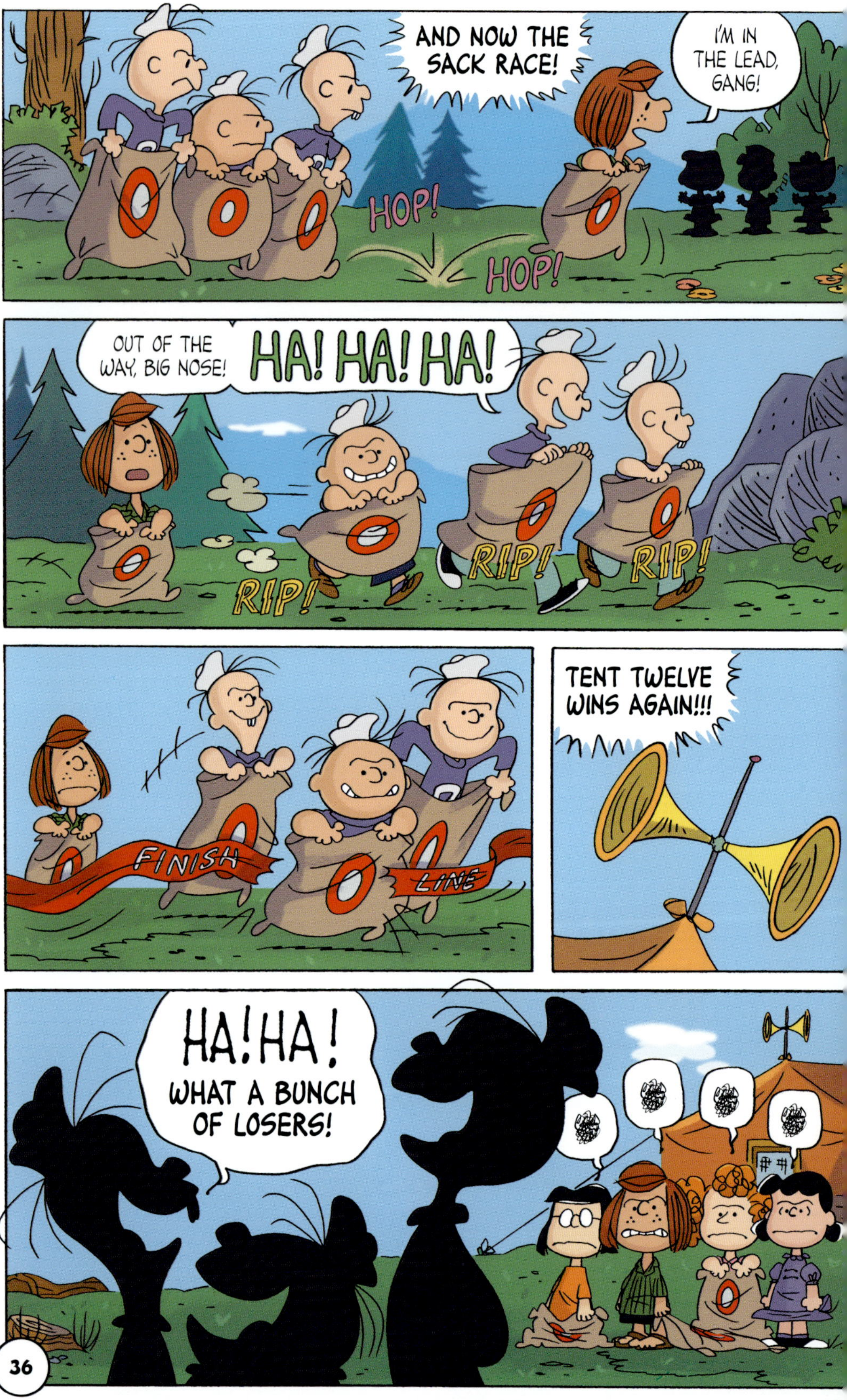
AND NOW THE SACK RACE!
I'M IN THE LEAD, GANG!
HOP!
HOP!
OUT OF THE WAY, BIG NOSE!
HA! HA! HA!
RIP!
RIP!
RIP!
FINISH
LINE
TENT TWELVE WINS AGAIN!!!
HA! HA! WHAT A BUNCH OF LOSERS!

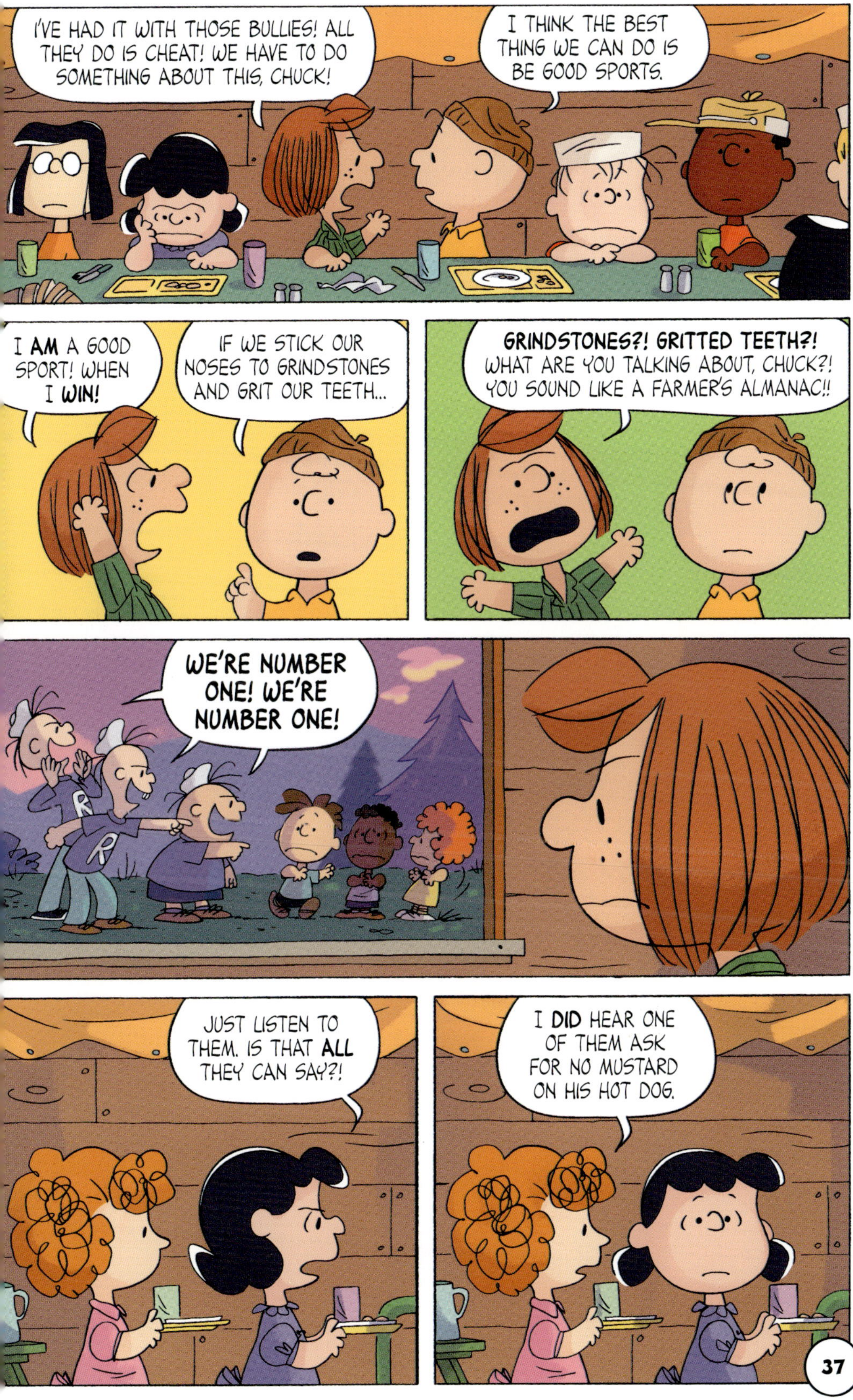

I'VE HAD IT WITH THOSE BULLIES! ALL THEY DO IS CHEAT! WE HAVE TO DO SOMETHING ABOUT THIS, CHUCK!
I THINK THE BEST THING WE CAN DO IS BE GOOD SPORTS.
I AM A GOOD SPORT! WHEN I WIN!
IF WE STICK OUR NOSES TO GRINDSTONES AND GRIT OUR TEETH...
GRINDSTONES?! GRITTED TEETH?! WHAT ARE YOU TALKING ABOUT, CHUCK?! YOU SOUND LIKE A FARMER'S ALMANAC!!
WE'RE NUMBER ONE! WE'RE NUMBER ONE!
JUST LISTEN TO THEM. IS THAT ALL THEY CAN SAY?!
I DID HEAR ONE OF THEM ASK FOR NO MUSTARD ON HIS HOT DOG.

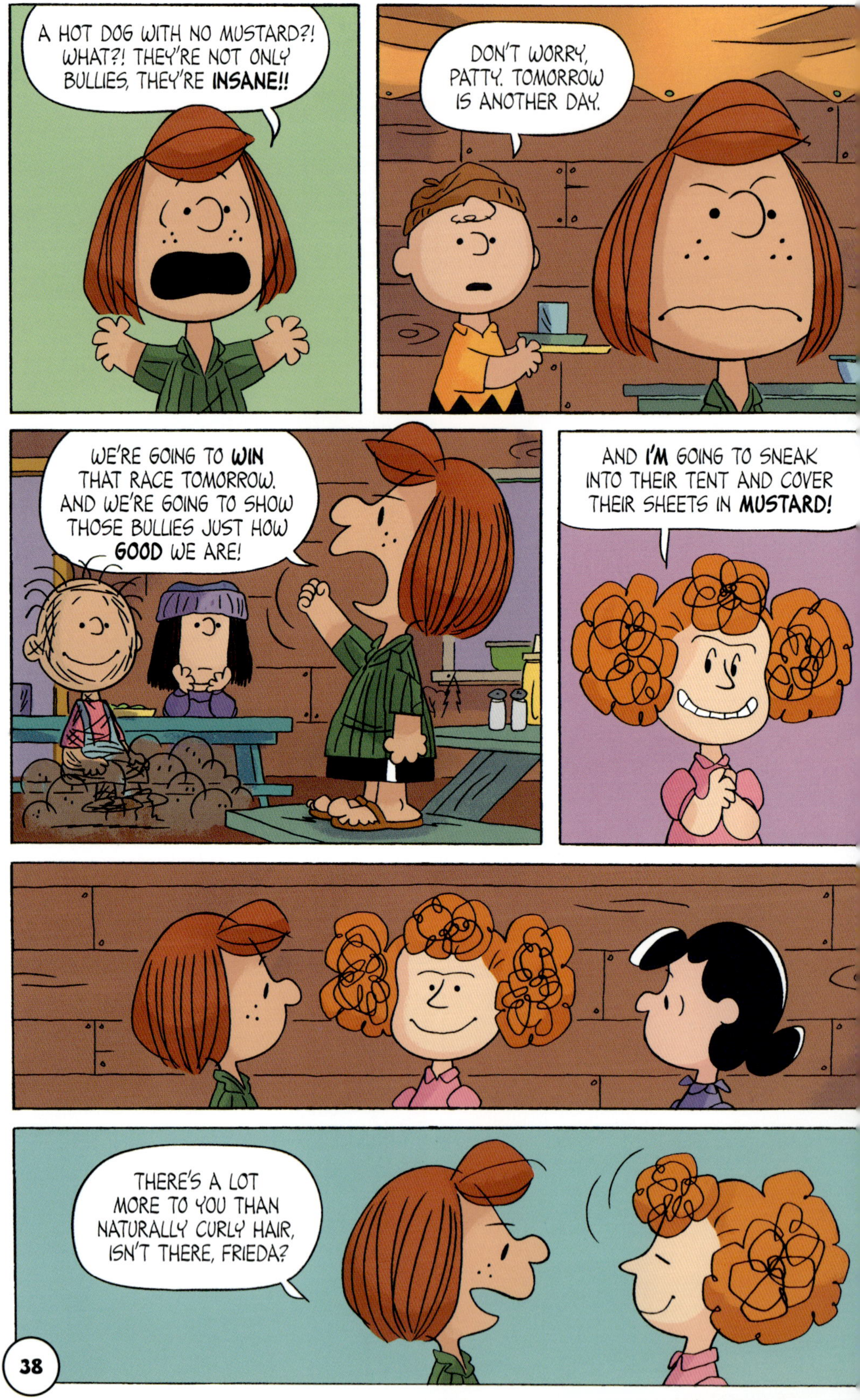
A HOT DOG WITH NO MUSTARD?! WHAT?! THEY'RE NOT ONLY BULLIES, THEY'RE **INSANE!!**
DON'T WORRY, PATTY. TOMORROW IS ANOTHER DAY.
WE'RE GOING TO **WIN** THAT RACE TOMORROW. AND WE'RE GOING TO SHOW THOSE BULLIES JUST HOW **GOOD** WE ARE!
AND **I'M** GOING TO SNEAK INTO THEIR TENT AND COVER THEIR SHEETS IN **MUSTARD!**
THERE'S A LOT MORE TO YOU THAN NATURALLY CURLY HAIR, ISN'T THERE, FRIEDA?

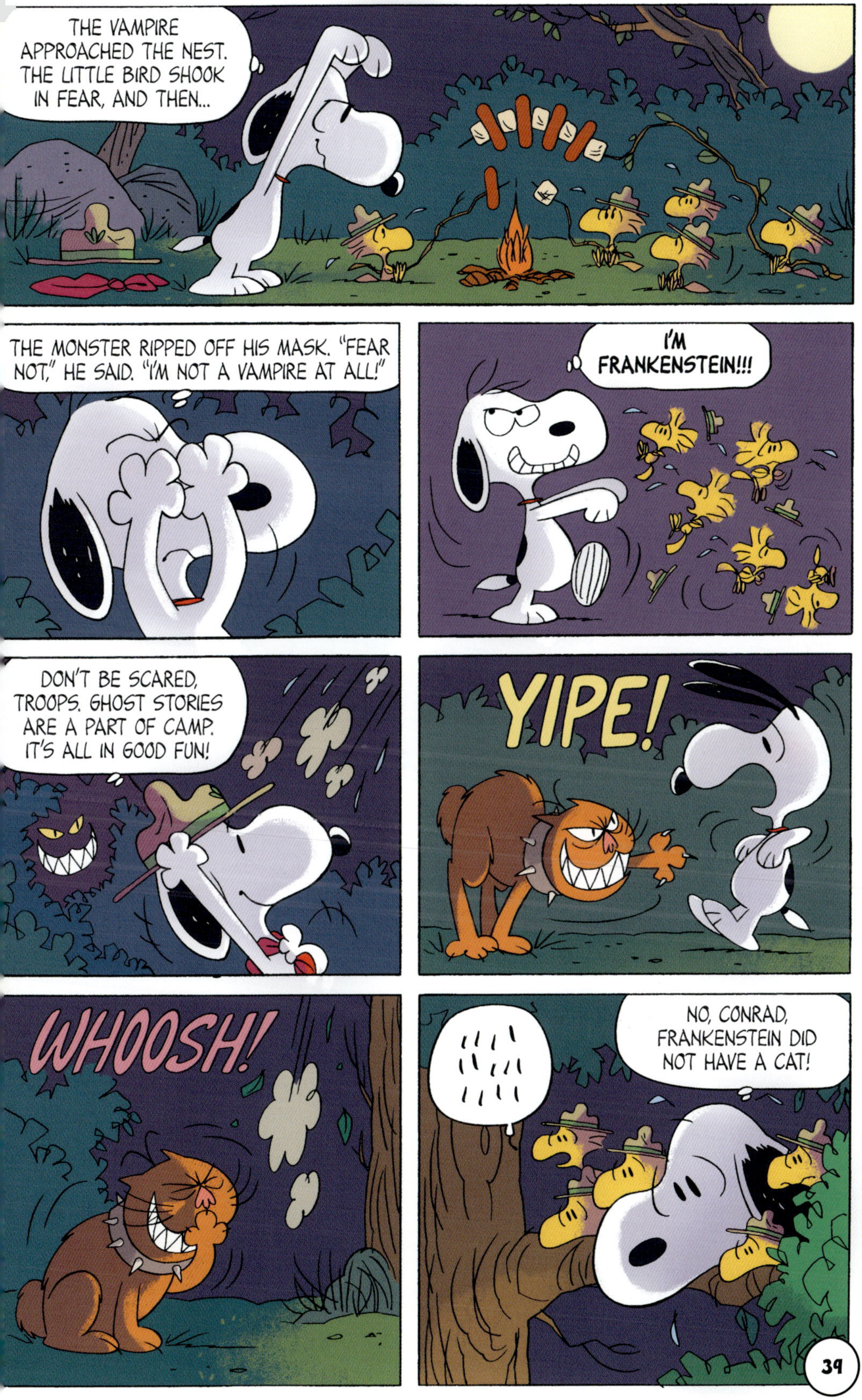
THE VAMPIRE APPROACHED THE NEST. THE LITTLE BIRD SHOOK IN FEAR, AND THEN...
THE MONSTER RIPPED OFF HIS MASK. "FEAR NOT," HE SAID. "I'M NOT A VAMPIRE AT ALL!"
I'M FRANKENSTEIN!!!
DON'T BE SCARED, TROOPS. GHOST STORIES ARE A PART OF CAMP. IT'S ALL IN GOOD FUN!
YIPE!
WHOOSH!
NO, CONRAD, FRANKENSTEIN DID NOT HAVE A CAT!

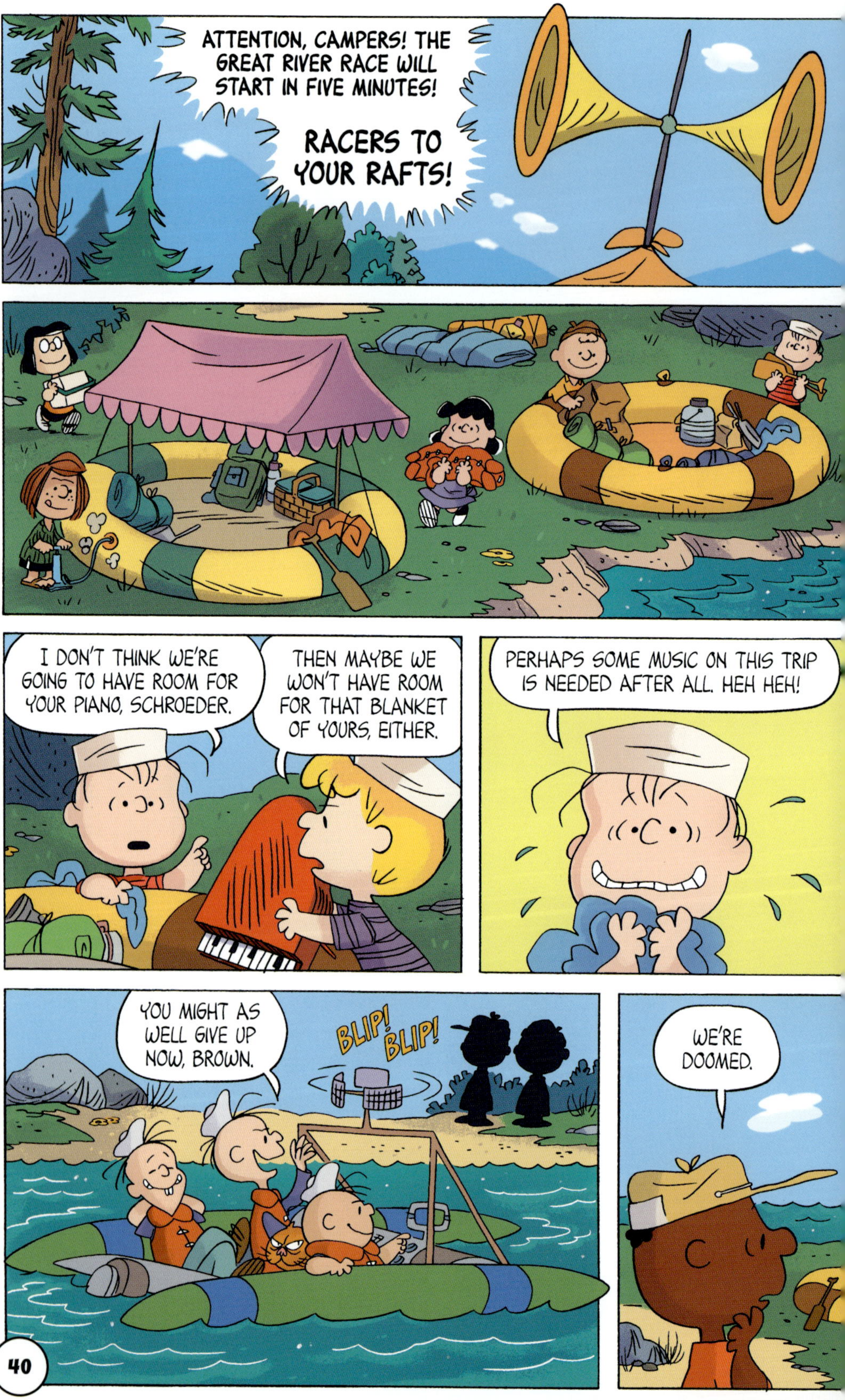
ATTENTION, CAMPERS! THE GREAT RIVER RACE WILL START IN FIVE MINUTES!
RACERS TO YOUR RAFTS!
I DON'T THINK WE'RE GOING TO HAVE ROOM FOR YOUR PIANO, SCHROEDER.
THEN MAYBE WE WON'T HAVE ROOM FOR THAT BLANKET OF YOURS, EITHER.
PERHAPS SOME MUSIC ON THIS TRIP IS NEEDED AFTER ALL. HEH HEH!
YOU MIGHT AS WELL GIVE UP NOW, BROWN.
BLIP! BLIP!
WE'RE DOOMED.

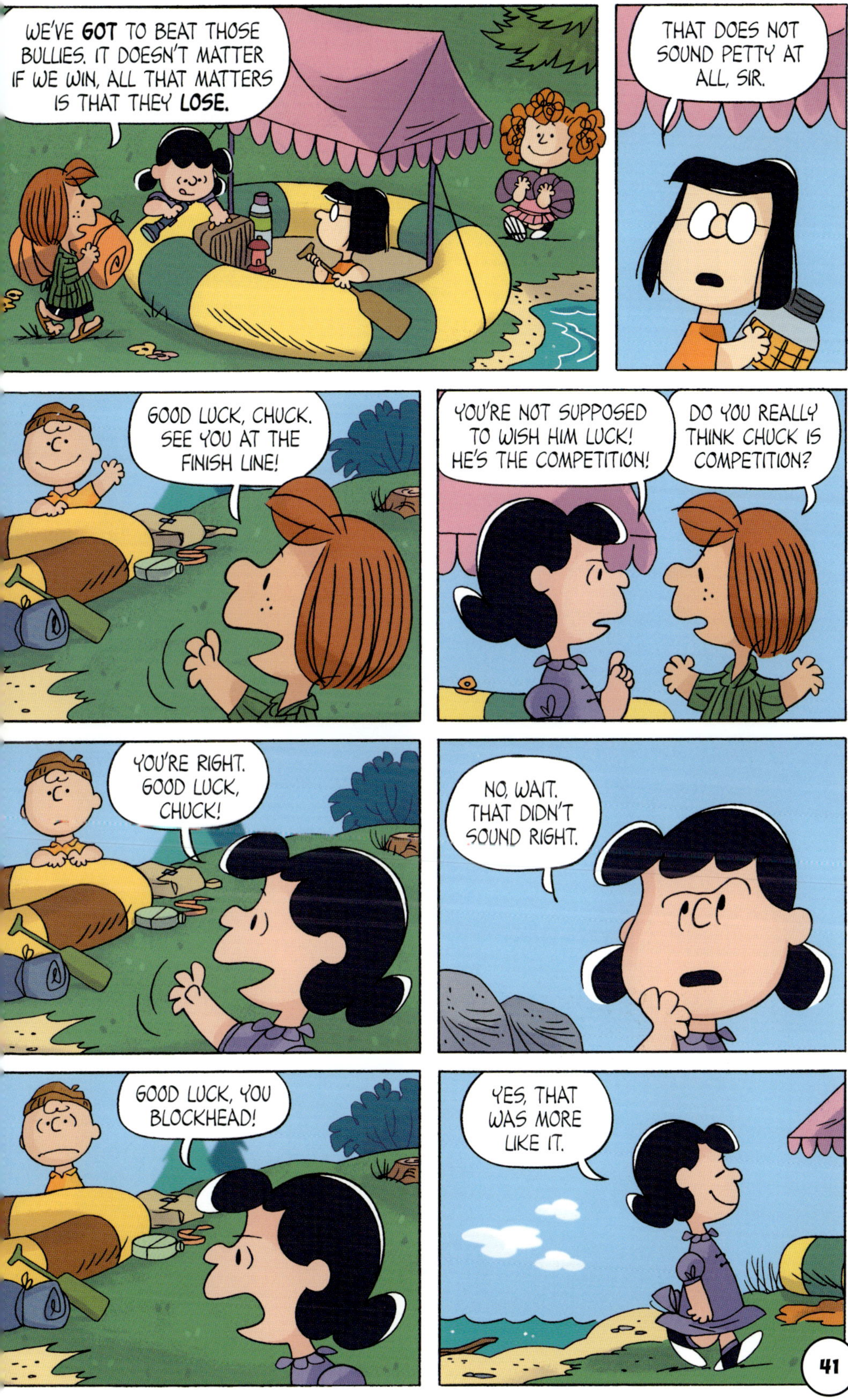
WE'VE **GOT** TO BEAT THOSE BULLIES. IT DOESN'T MATTER IF WE WIN, ALL THAT MATTERS IS THAT THEY **LOSE.**
THAT DOES NOT SOUND PETTY AT ALL, SIR.
GOOD LUCK, CHUCK. SEE YOU AT THE FINISH LINE!
YOU'RE NOT SUPPOSED TO WISH HIM LUCK! HE'S THE COMPETITION!
DO YOU REALLY THINK CHUCK IS COMPETITION?
YOU'RE RIGHT. GOOD LUCK, CHUCK!
NO, WAIT. THAT DIDN'T SOUND RIGHT.
GOOD LUCK, YOU BLOCKHEAD!
YES, THAT WAS MORE LIKE IT.

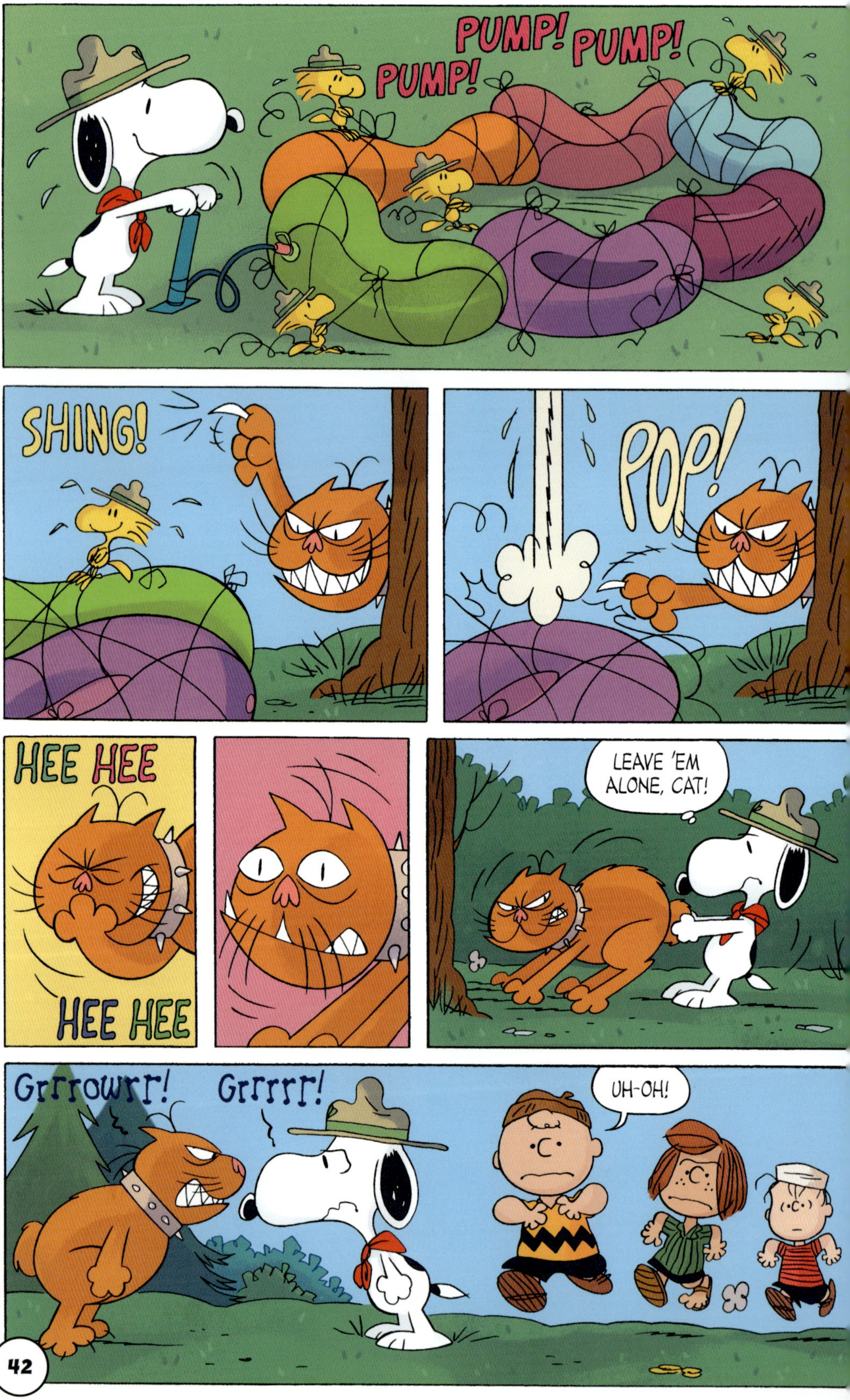
PUMP!
PUMP!
PUMP!
SHING!
POP!
HEE HEE
HEE HEE
LEAVE 'EM ALONE, CAT!
Grrrowrrr!
Grrrrr!
UH-OH!

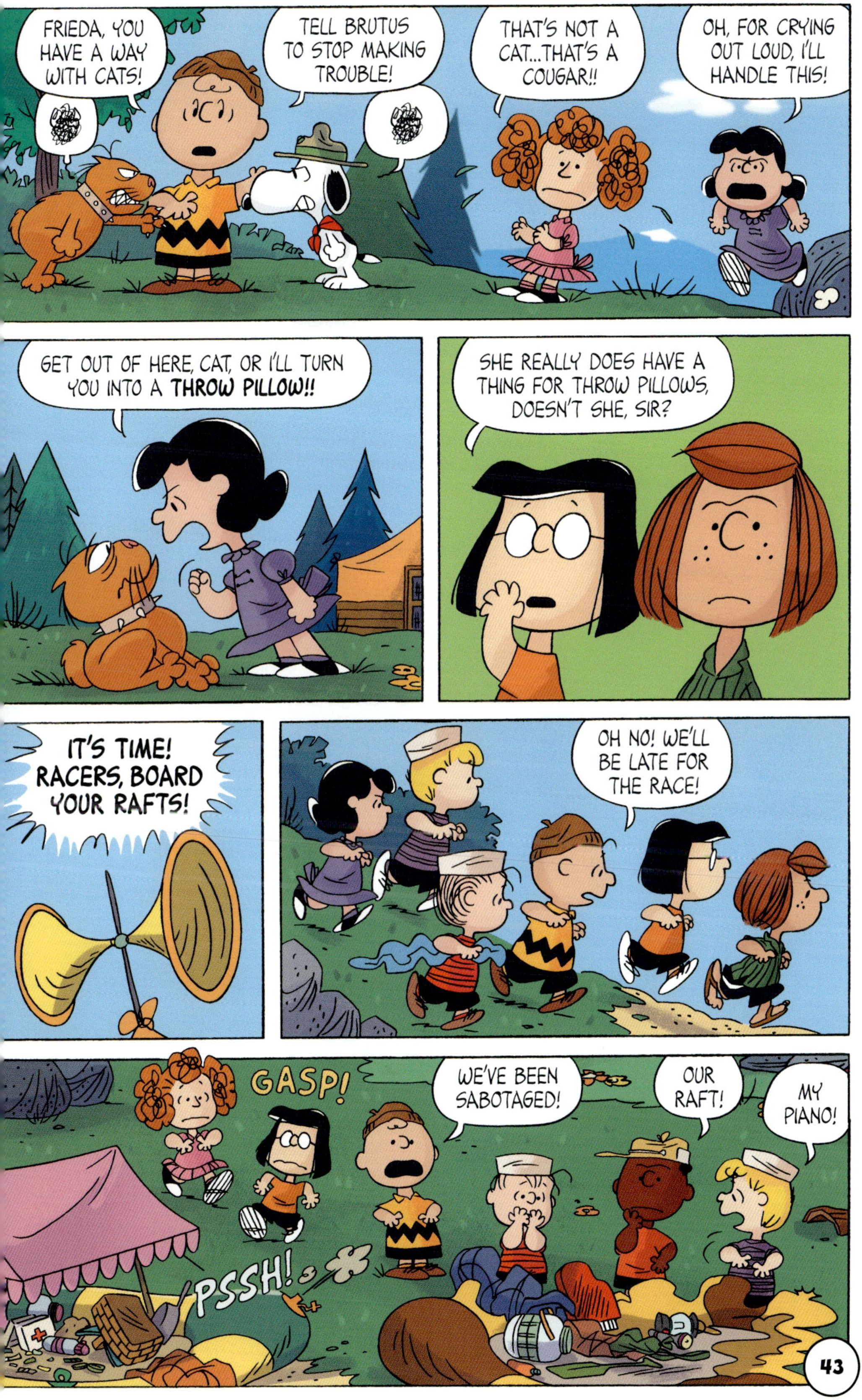
FRIEDA, YOU HAVE A WAY WITH CATS!
TELL BRUTUS TO STOP MAKING TROUBLE!
THAT'S NOT A CAT...THAT'S A COUGAR!!
OH, FOR CRYING OUT LOUD, I'LL HANDLE THIS!
GET OUT OF HERE, CAT, OR I'LL TURN YOU INTO A THROW PILLOW!!
SHE REALLY DOES HAVE A THING FOR THROW PILLOWS, DOESN'T SHE, SIR?
IT'S TIME! RACERS, BOARD YOUR RAFTS!
OH NO! WE'LL BE LATE FOR THE RACE!
GASP!
WE'VE BEEN SABOTAGED!
OUR RAFT!
MY PIANO!
PSSH!

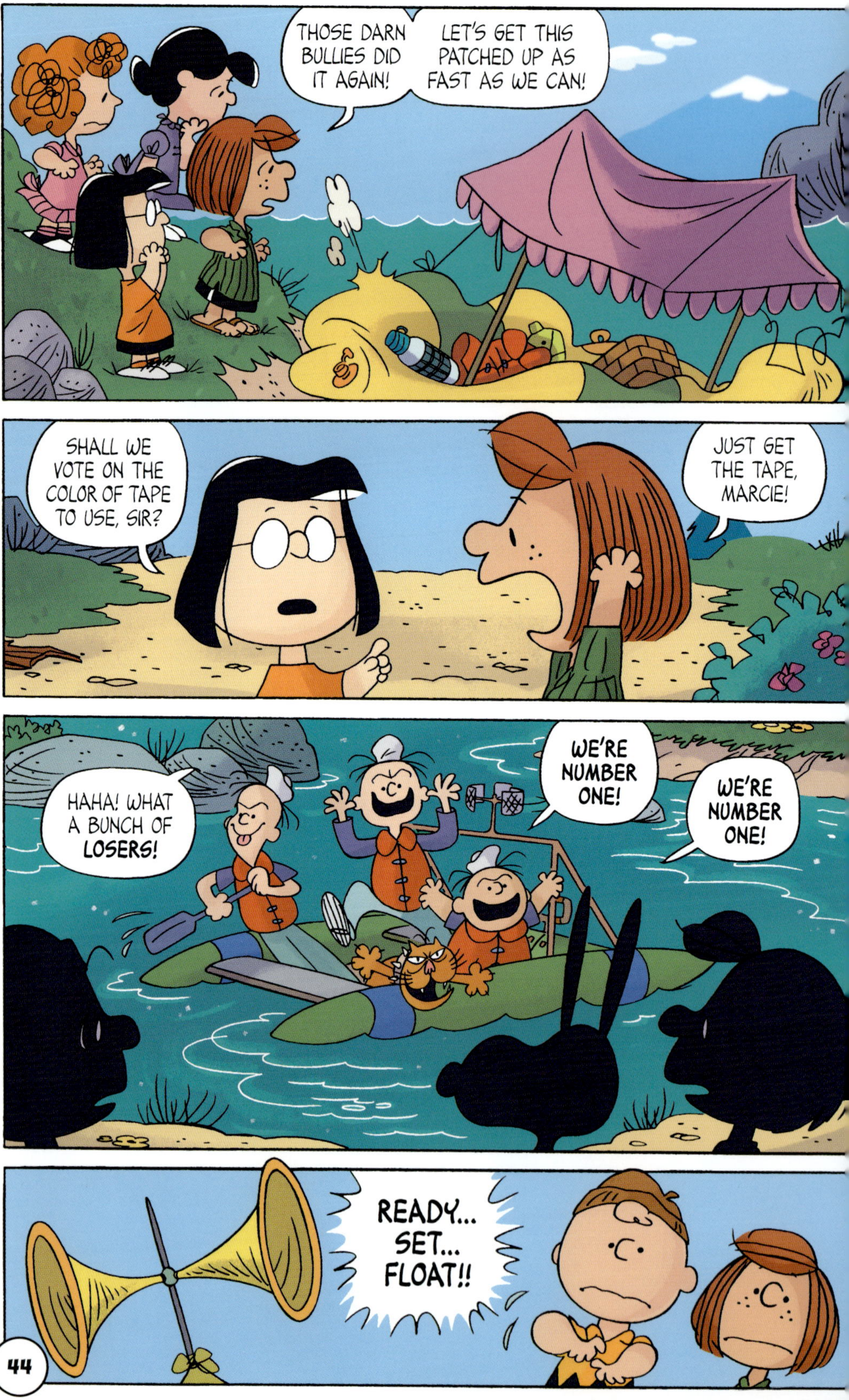
THOSE DARN BULLIES DID IT AGAIN!
LET'S GET THIS PATCHED UP AS FAST AS WE CAN!
SHALL WE VOTE ON THE COLOR OF TAPE TO USE, SIR?
JUST GET THE TAPE, MARCIE!
HAHA! WHAT A BUNCH OF LOSERS!
WE'RE NUMBER ONE!
WE'RE NUMBER ONE!
READY... SET... FLOAT!!

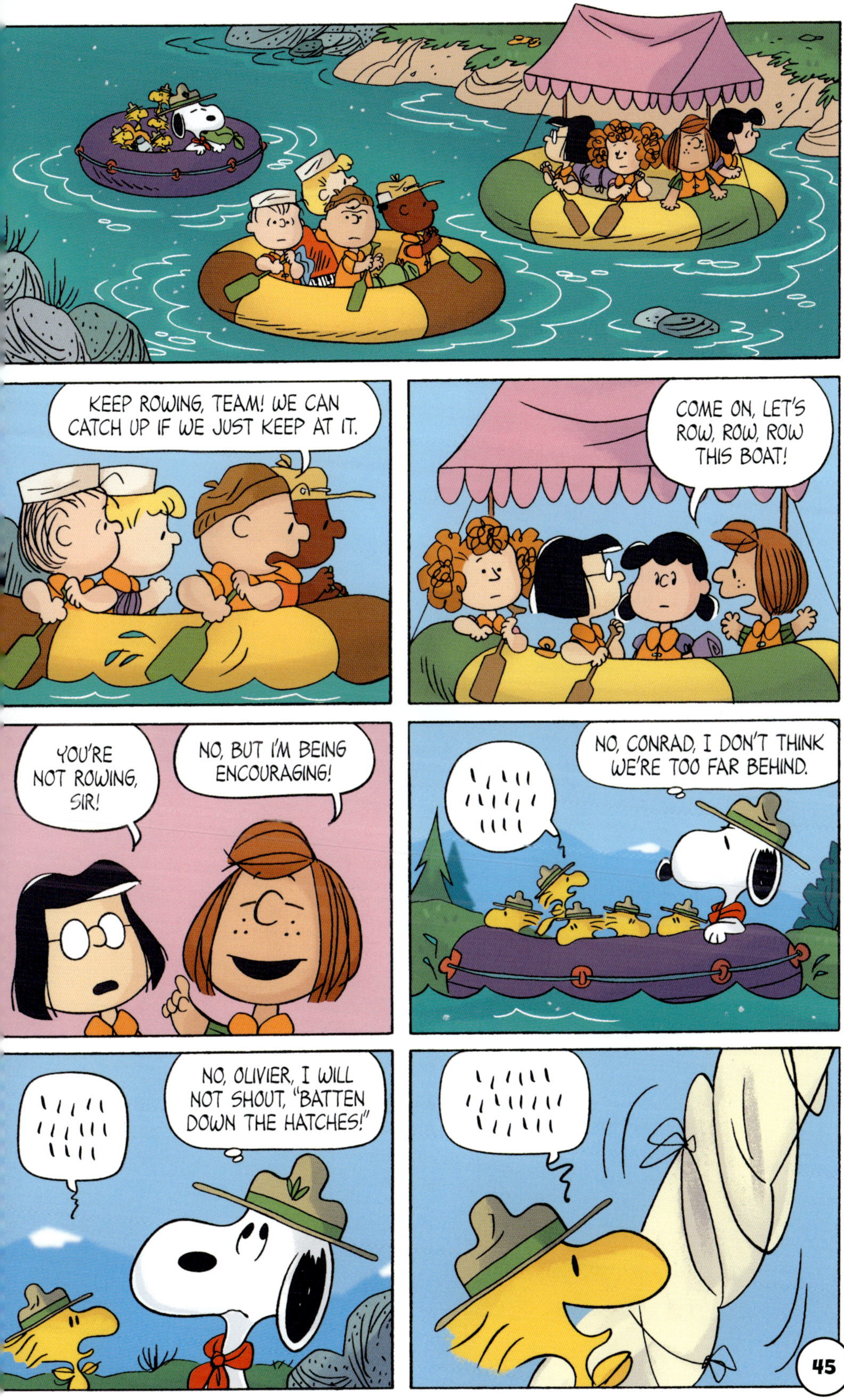
KEEP ROWING, TEAM! WE CAN CATCH UP IF WE JUST KEEP AT IT.
COME ON, LET'S ROW, ROW, ROW THIS BOAT!
YOU'RE NOT ROWING, SIR!
NO, BUT I'M BEING ENCOURAGING!
NO, CONRAD, I DON'T THINK WE'RE TOO FAR BEHIND.
NO, OLIVIER, I WILL NOT SHOUT, "BATTEN DOWN THE HATCHES!"

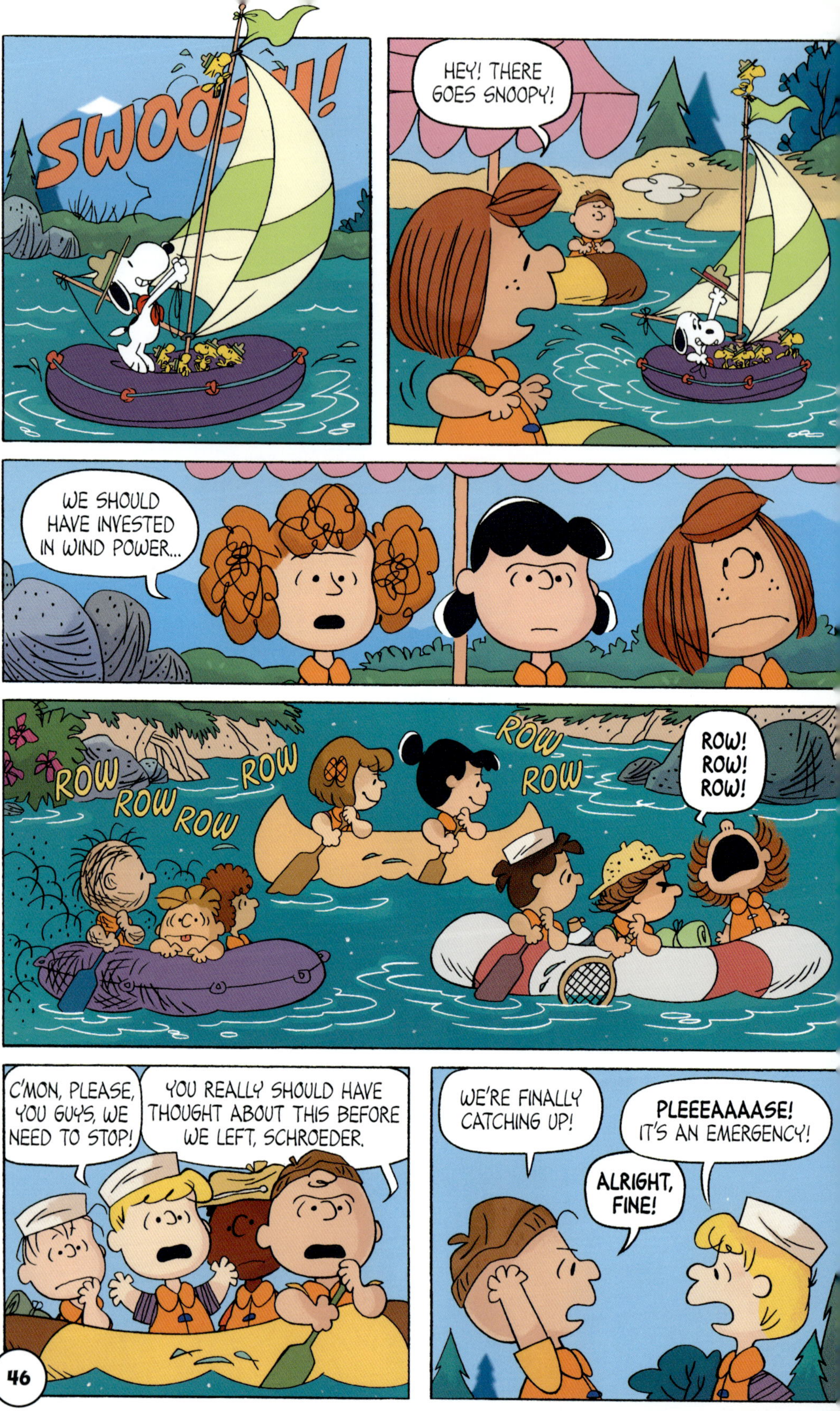
SWOOSH!
HEY! THERE GOES SNOOPY!
WE SHOULD HAVE INVESTED IN WIND POWER...
ROW
ROW
ROW
ROW
ROW
ROW
ROW! ROW! ROW!
C'MON, PLEASE, YOU GUYS, WE NEED TO STOP!
YOU REALLY SHOULD HAVE THOUGHT ABOUT THIS BEFORE WE LEFT, SCHROEDER.
WE'RE FINALLY CATCHING UP!
PLEEEAAAASE! IT'S AN EMERGENCY!
ALRIGHT, FINE!

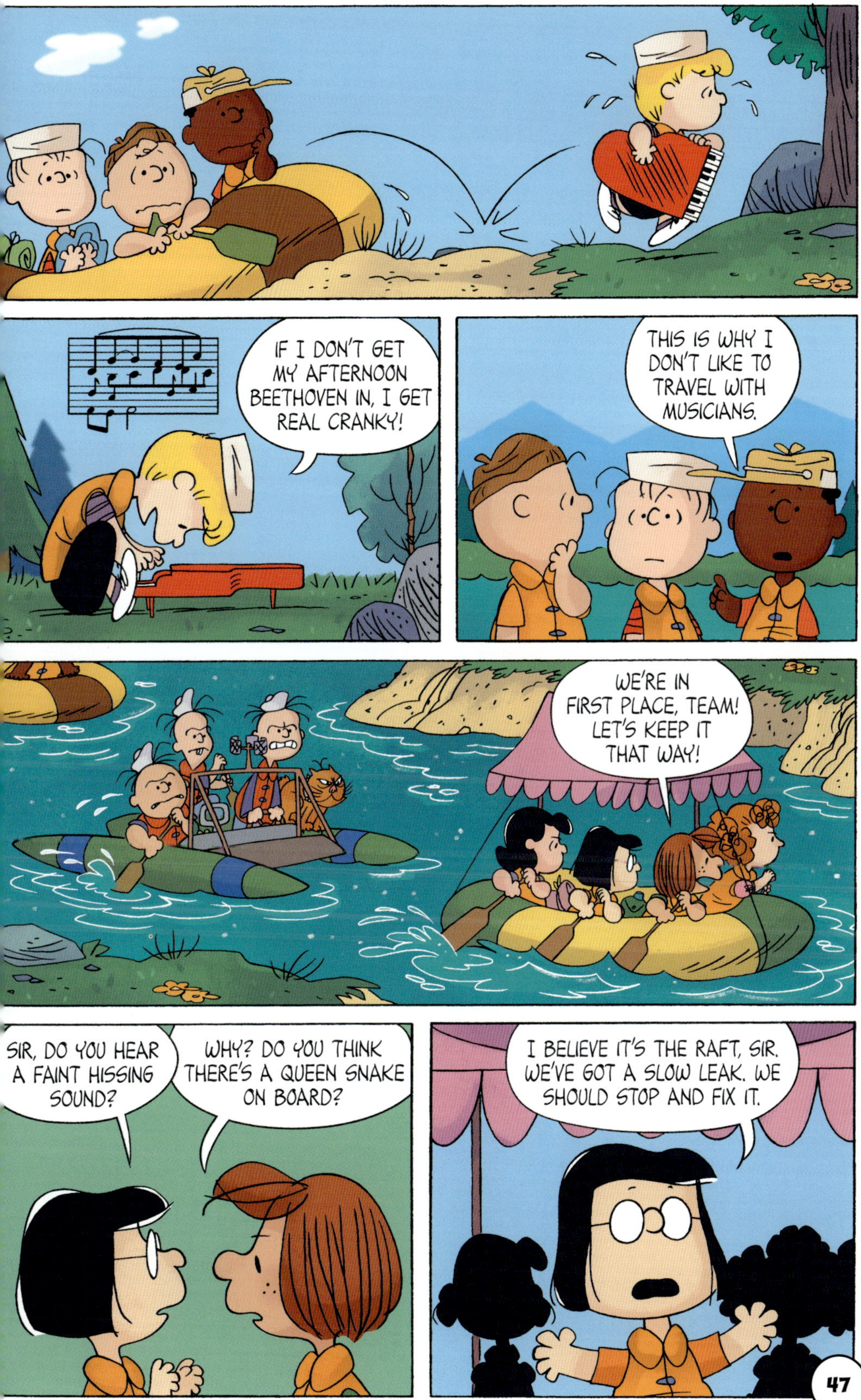

IF I DON'T GET MY AFTERNOON BEETHOVEN IN, I GET REAL CRANKY!
THIS IS WHY I DON'T LIKE TO TRAVEL WITH MUSICIANS.
WE'RE IN FIRST PLACE, TEAM! LET'S KEEP IT THAT WAY!
SIR, DO YOU HEAR A FAINT HISSING SOUND?
WHY? DO YOU THINK THERE'S A QUEEN SNAKE ON BOARD?
I BELIEVE IT'S THE RAFT, SIR. WE'VE GOT A SLOW LEAK. WE SHOULD STOP AND FIX IT.

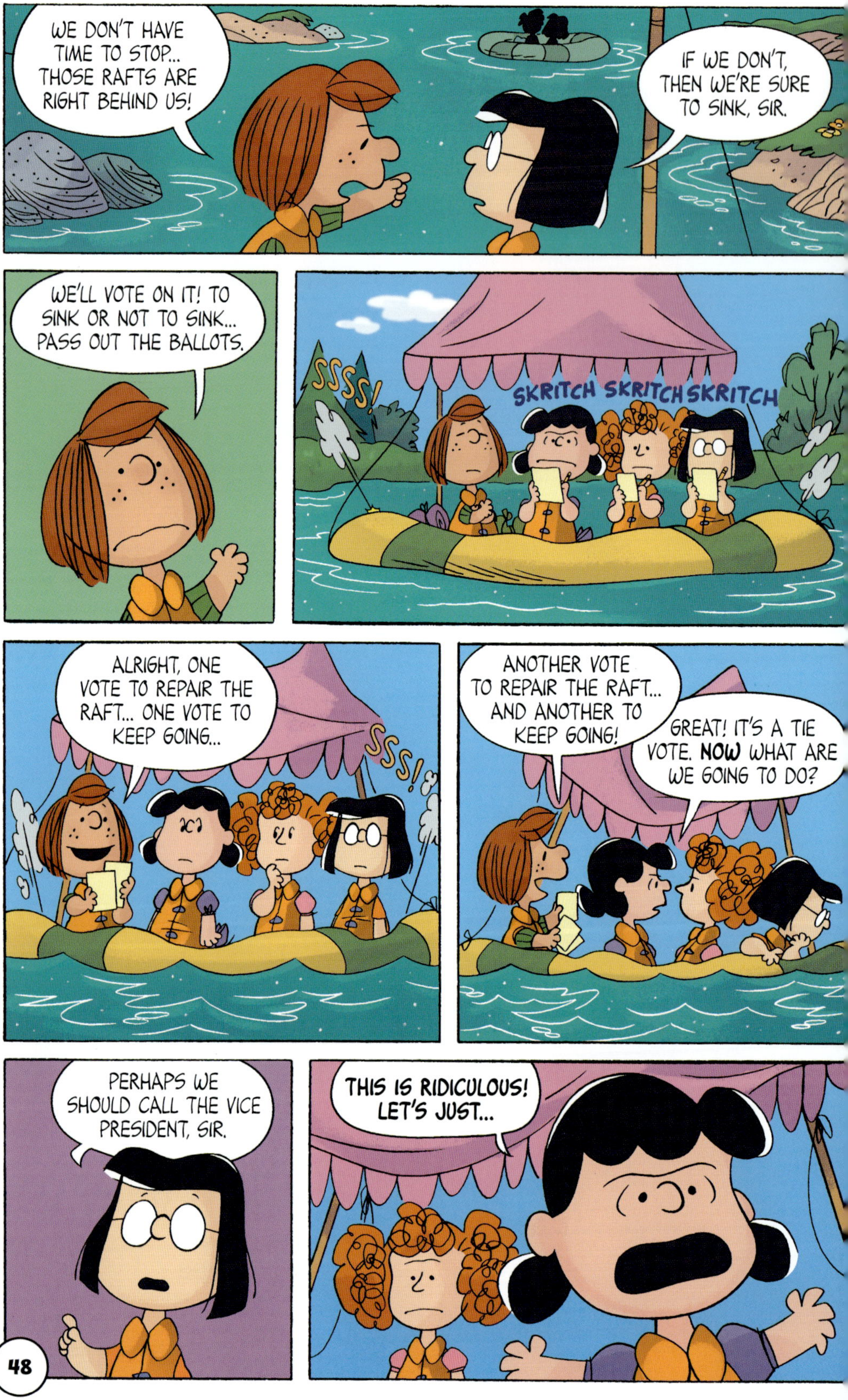
WE DON'T HAVE TIME TO STOP... THOSE RAFTS ARE RIGHT BEHIND US!
IF WE DON'T, THEN WE'RE SURE TO SINK, SIR.
WE'LL VOTE ON IT! TO SINK OR NOT TO SINK... PASS OUT THE BALLOTS.
SSSS!
SKRITCH SKRITCH SKRITCH
ALRIGHT, ONE VOTE TO REPAIR THE RAFT... ONE VOTE TO KEEP GOING...
SSS!
ANOTHER VOTE TO REPAIR THE RAFT... AND ANOTHER TO KEEP GOING!
GREAT! IT'S A TIE VOTE. **NOW** WHAT ARE WE GOING TO DO?
PERHAPS WE SHOULD CALL THE VICE PRESIDENT, SIR.
THIS IS RIDICULOUS! LET'S JUST...

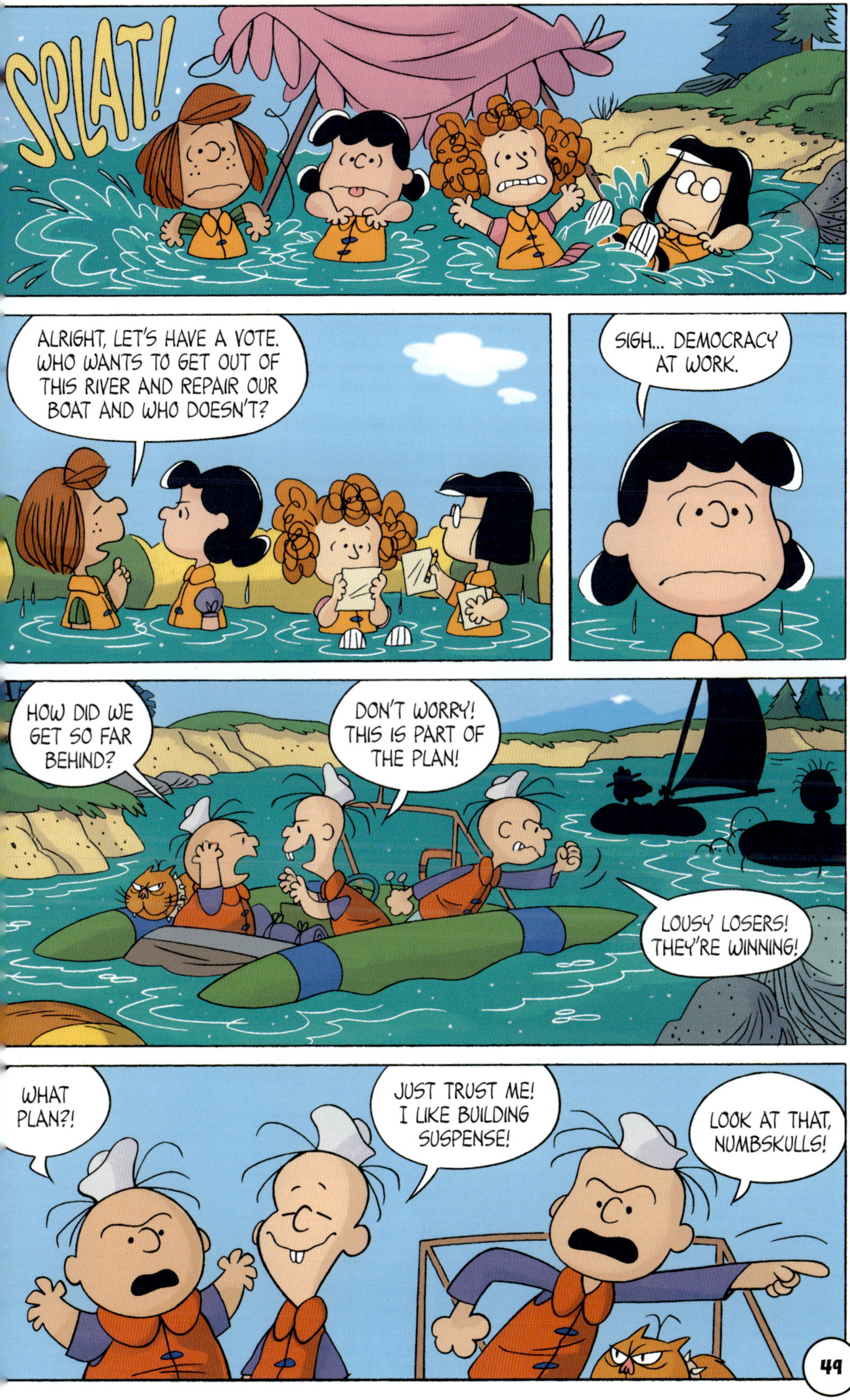
SPLAT!
ALRIGHT, LET'S HAVE A VOTE. WHO WANTS TO GET OUT OF THIS RIVER AND REPAIR OUR BOAT AND WHO DOESN'T?
SIGH... DEMOCRACY AT WORK.
HOW DID WE GET SO FAR BEHIND?
DON'T WORRY! THIS IS PART OF THE PLAN!
LOUSY LOSERS! THEY'RE WINNING!
WHAT PLAN?!
JUST TRUST ME! I LIKE BUILDING SUSPENSE!
LOOK AT THAT, NUMBSKULLS!

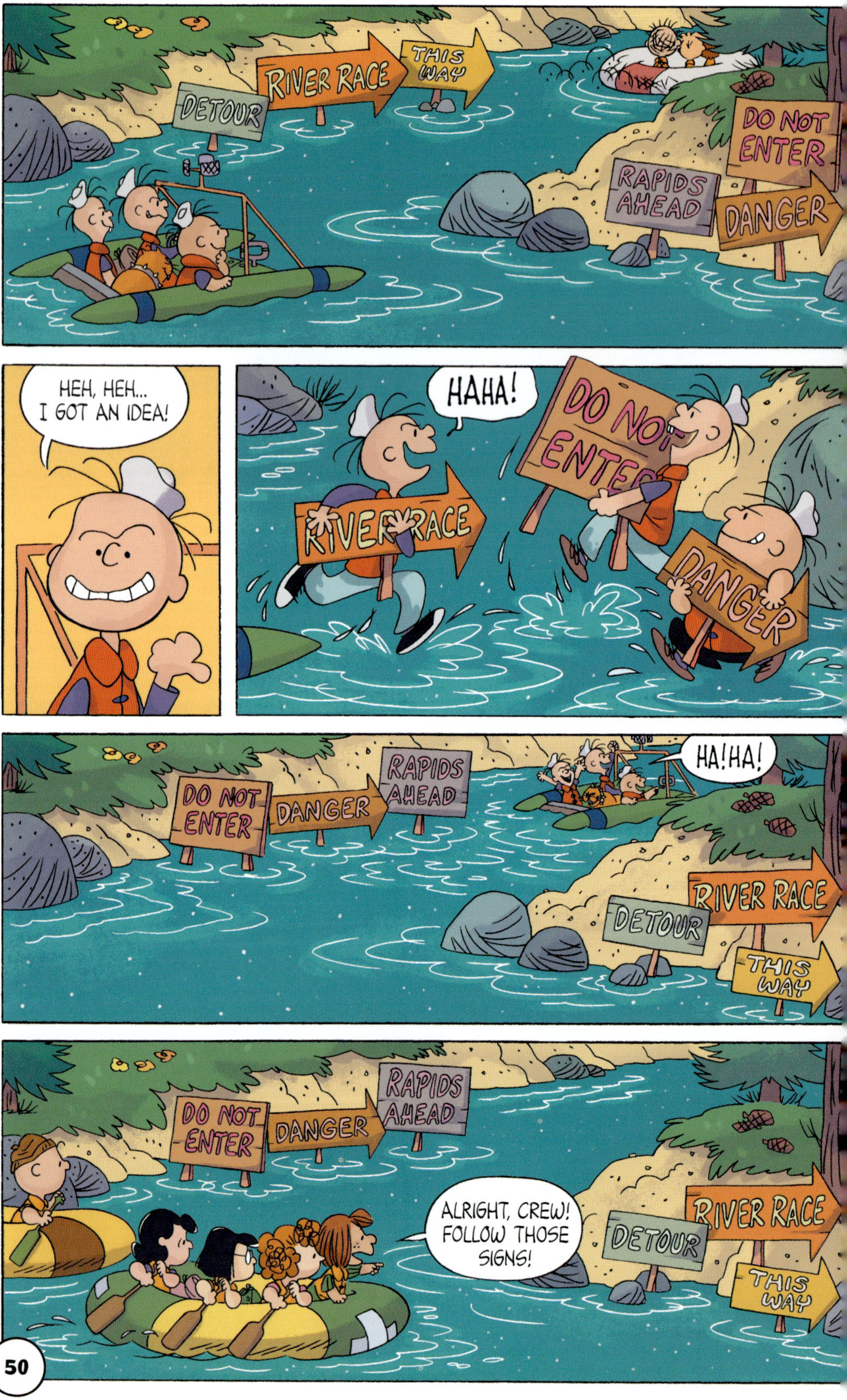

DETOUR
RIVER RACE
THIS WAY
DO NOT ENTER
RAPIDS AHEAD
DANGER
HEH, HEH... I GOT AN IDEA!
HAHA!
RIVER RACE
DO NOT ENTER
DANGER
DO NOT ENTER
DANGER
RAPIDS AHEAD
HA! HA!
RIVER RACE
DETOUR
THIS WAY
DO NOT ENTER
DANGER
RAPIDS AHEAD
ALRIGHT, CREW! FOLLOW THOSE SIGNS!
RIVER RACE
DETOUR
THIS WAY

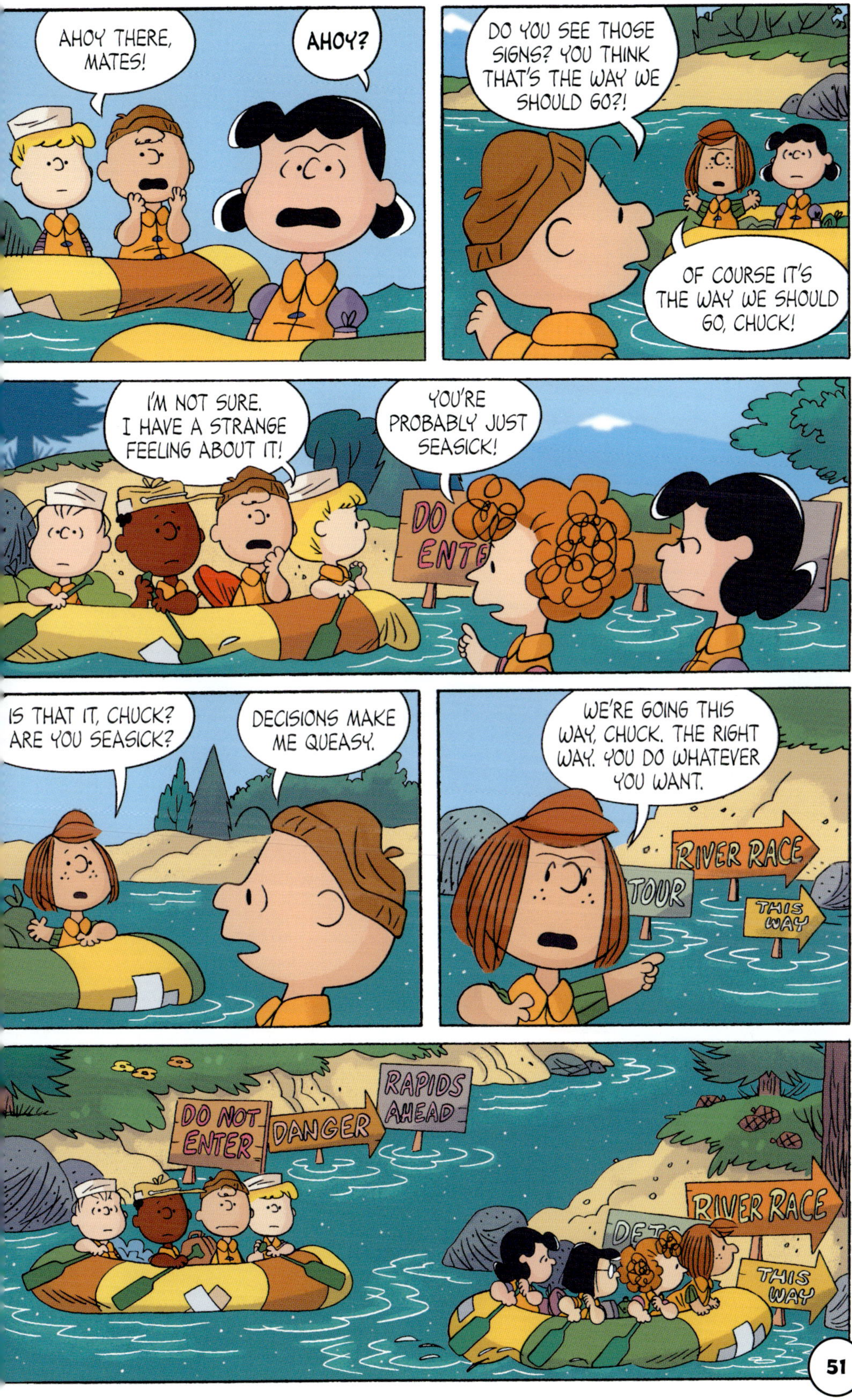
AHOY THERE, MATES!
AHOY?
DO YOU SEE THOSE SIGNS? YOU THINK THAT'S THE WAY WE SHOULD GO?!
OF COURSE IT'S THE WAY WE SHOULD GO, CHUCK!
I'M NOT SURE. I HAVE A STRANGE FEELING ABOUT IT!
YOU'RE PROBABLY JUST SEASICK!
IS THAT IT, CHUCK? ARE YOU SEASICK?
DECISIONS MAKE ME QUEASY.
WE'RE GOING THIS WAY, CHUCK. THE RIGHT WAY. YOU DO WHATEVER YOU WANT.
RIVER RACE
TOUR
THIS WAY
DO NOT ENTER
DANGER
RAPIDS AHEAD
RIVER RACE
THIS WAY

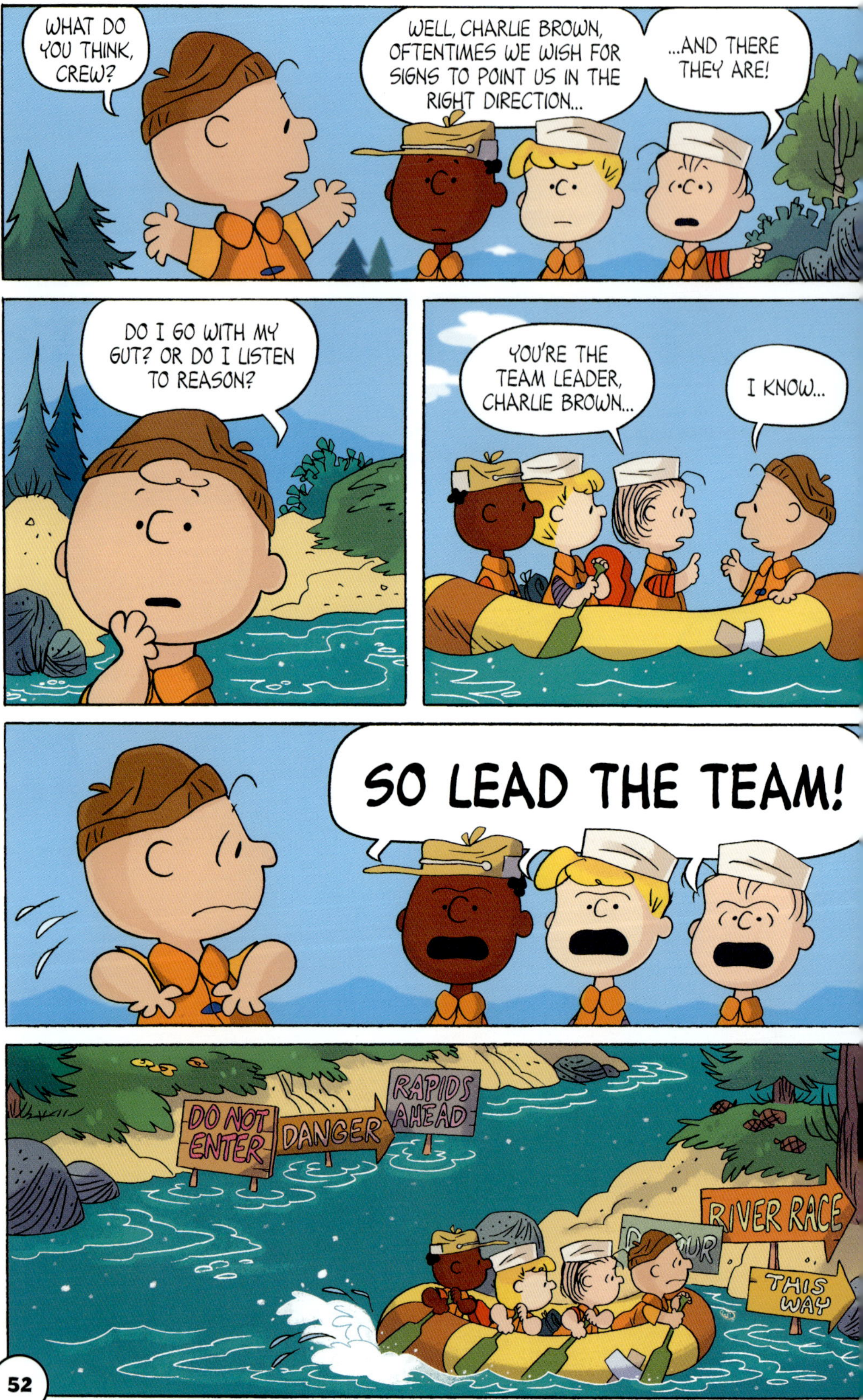
WHAT DO YOU THINK, CREW?
WELL, CHARLIE BROWN, OFTENTIMES WE WISH FOR SIGNS TO POINT US IN THE RIGHT DIRECTION...
...AND THERE THEY ARE!
DO I GO WITH MY GUT? OR DO I LISTEN TO REASON?
YOU'RE THE TEAM LEADER, CHARLIE BROWN...
I KNOW...
SO LEAD THE TEAM!
DO NOT ENTER
DANGER
RAPIDS AHEAD
RIVER RACE
THIS WAY

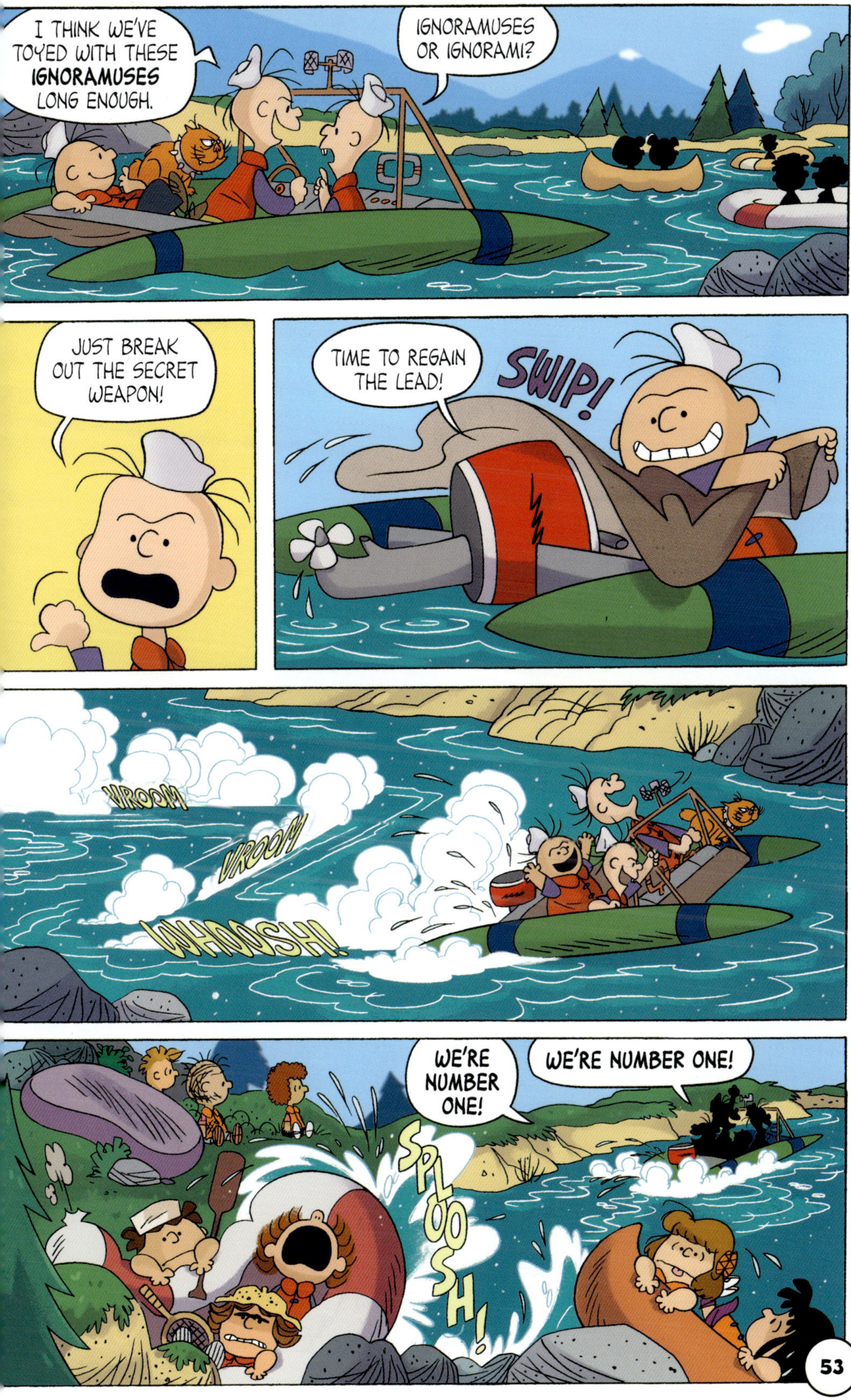
I THINK WE'VE TOYED WITH THESE **IGNORAMUSES** LONG ENOUGH.
IGNORAMUSES OR IGNORAMI?
JUST BREAK OUT THE SECRET WEAPON!
TIME TO REGAIN THE LEAD!
SWIP!
VROOM
VROOM
WHOOSH!
WE'RE NUMBER ONE!
WE'RE NUMBER ONE!
SPLOOSH!

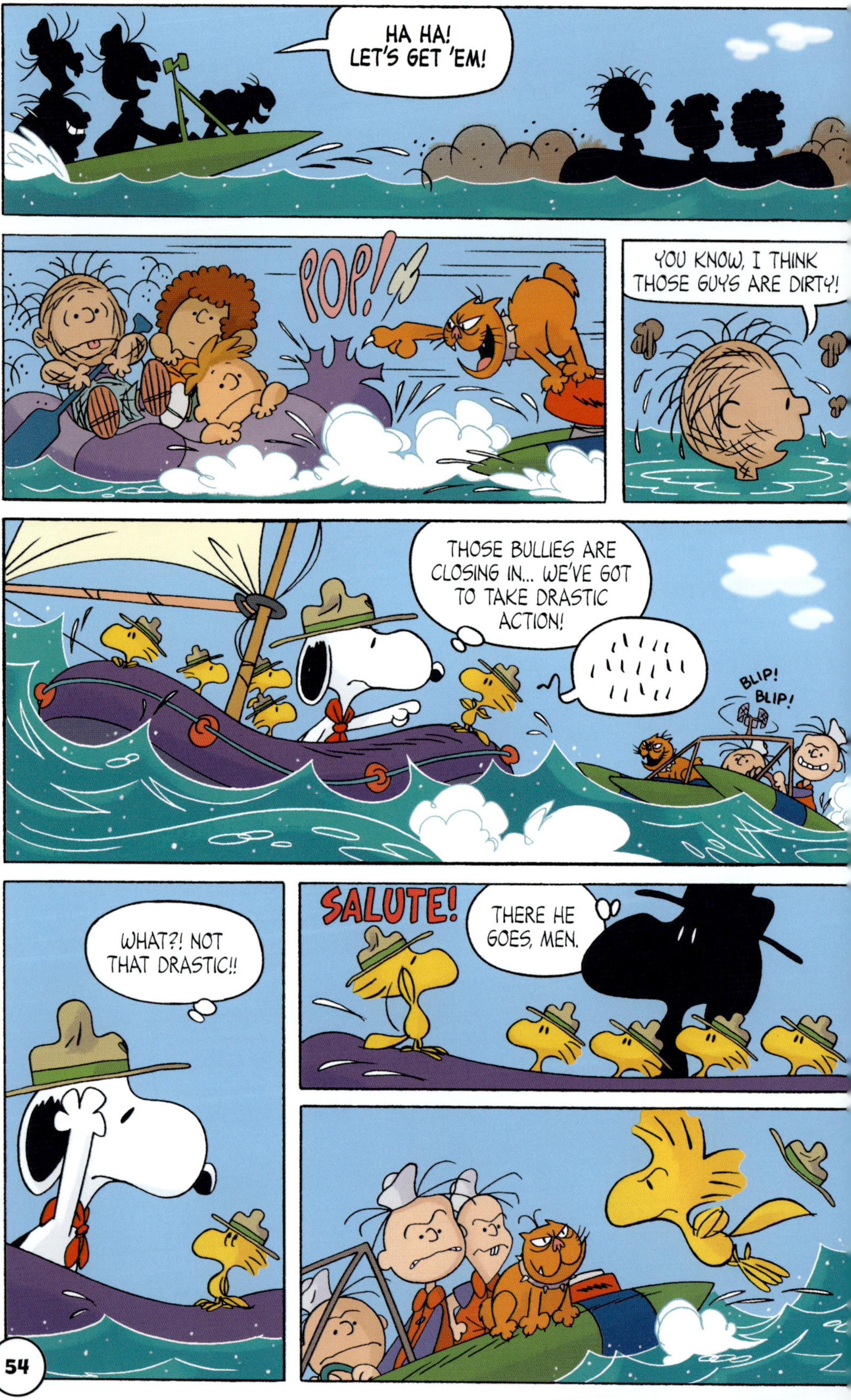
HA HA!
LET'S GET 'EM!
POP!
YOU KNOW, I THINK THOSE GUYS ARE DIRTY!
THOSE BULLIES ARE CLOSING IN... WE'VE GOT TO TAKE DRASTIC ACTION!
BLIP!
BLIP!
WHAT?! NOT THAT DRASTIC!!
SALUTE!
THERE HE GOES, MEN.

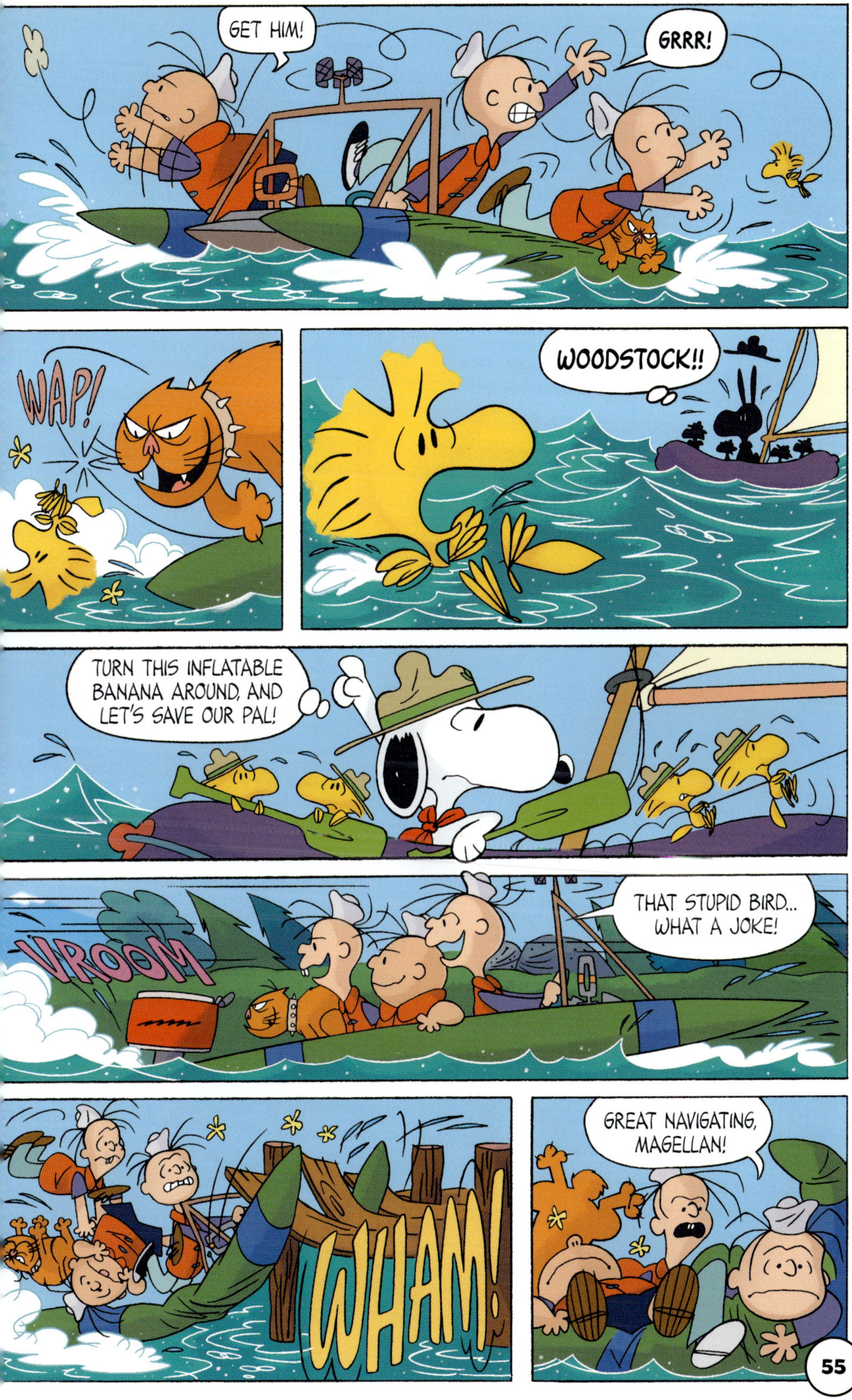
GET HIM!
GRRR!
WAP!
WOODSTOCK!!
TURN THIS INFLATABLE BANANA AROUND, AND LET'S SAVE OUR PAL!
VROOM
THAT STUPID BIRD... WHAT A JOKE!
WHAM!
GREAT NAVIGATING, MAGELLAN!

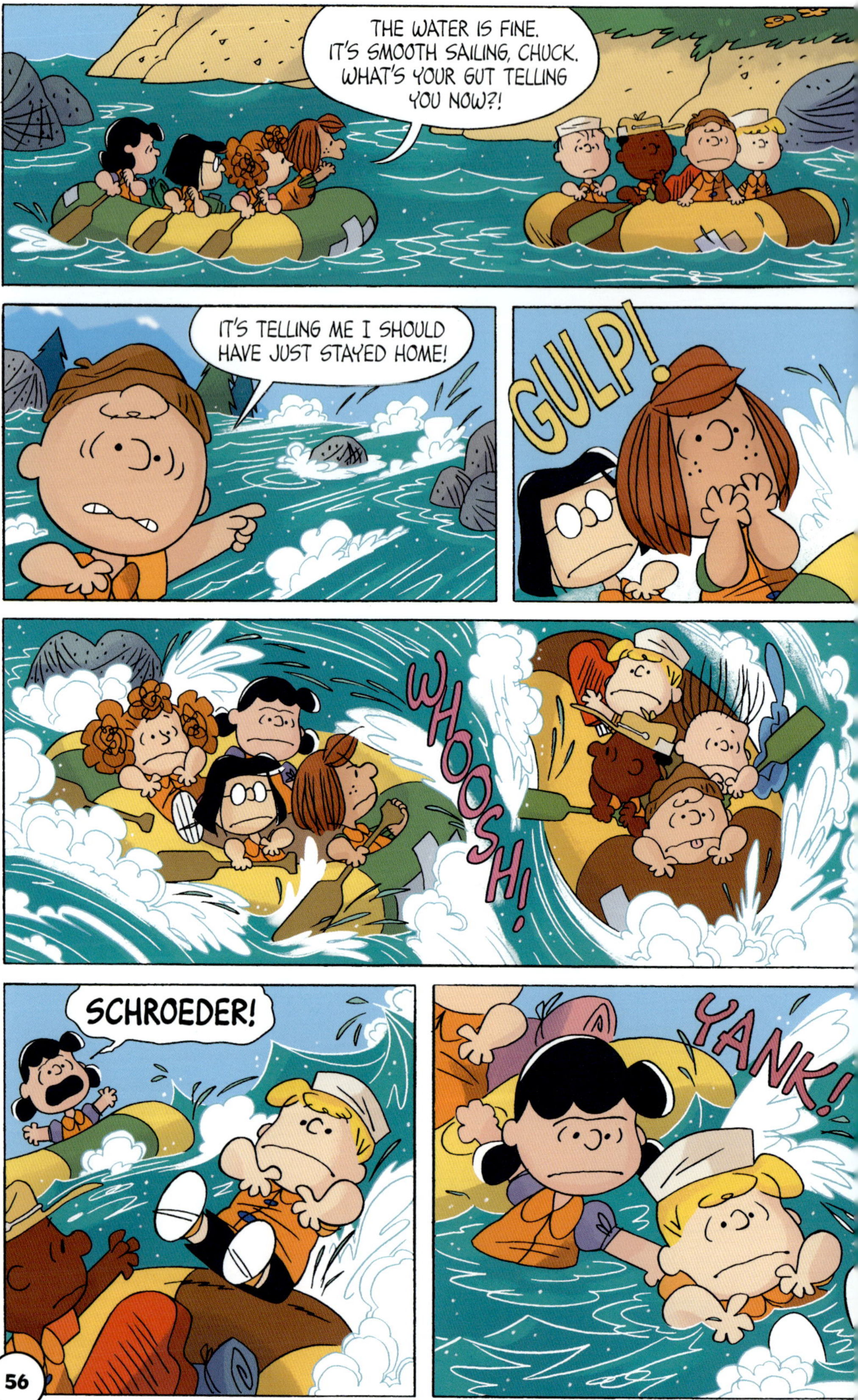
THE WATER IS FINE. IT'S SMOOTH SAILING, CHUCK. WHAT'S YOUR GUT TELLING YOU NOW?!
IT'S TELLING ME I SHOULD HAVE JUST STAYED HOME!
GULP!
WHOOSH!
SCHROEDER!
YANK!

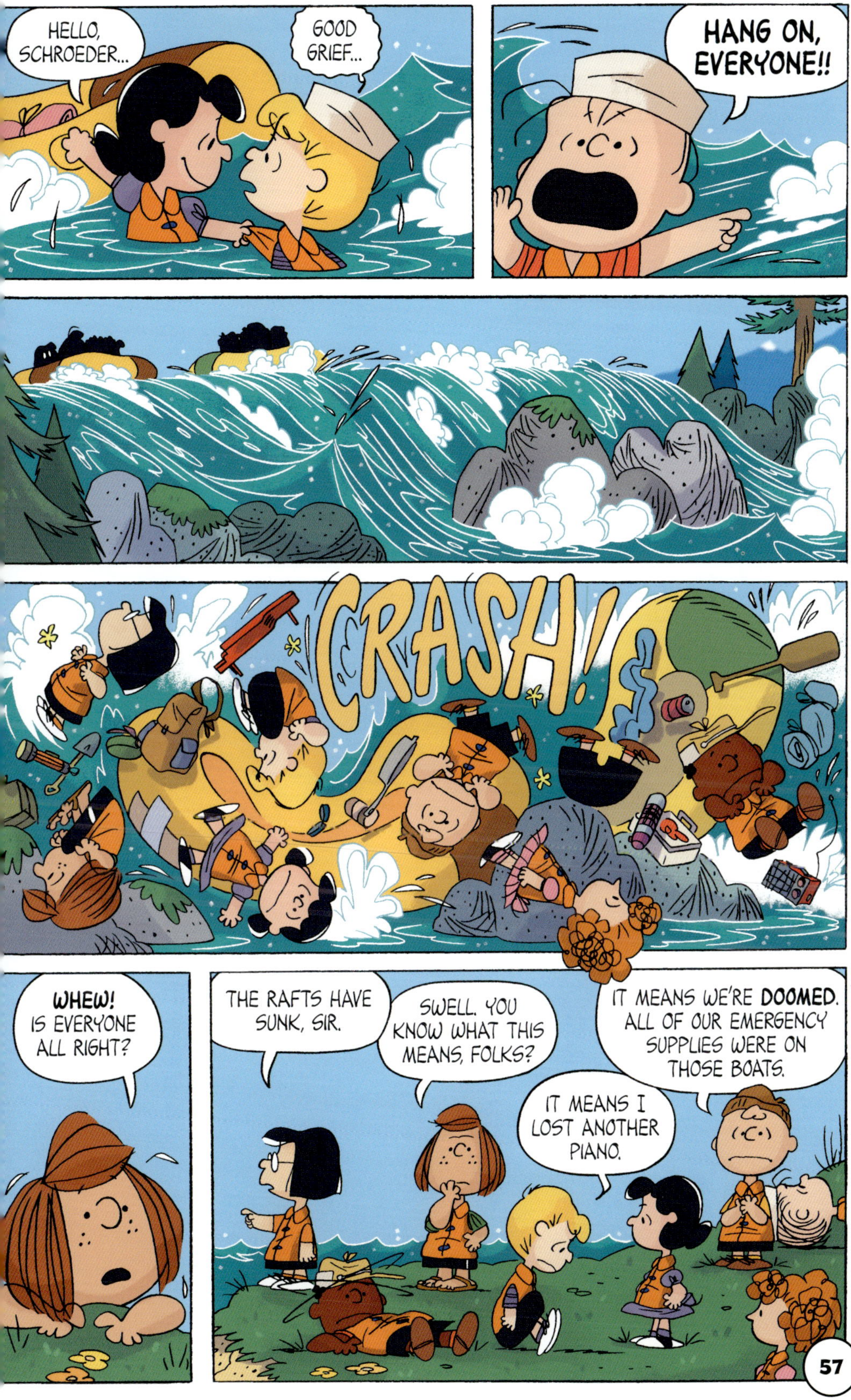
HELLO, SCHROEDER...
GOOD GRIEF...
HANG ON, EVERYONE!!
CRASH!
WHEW! IS EVERYONE ALL RIGHT?
THE RAFTS HAVE SUNK, SIR.
SWELL. YOU KNOW WHAT THIS MEANS, FOLKS?
IT MEANS WE'RE DOOMED. ALL OF OUR EMERGENCY SUPPLIES WERE ON THOSE BOATS.
IT MEANS I LOST ANOTHER PIANO.

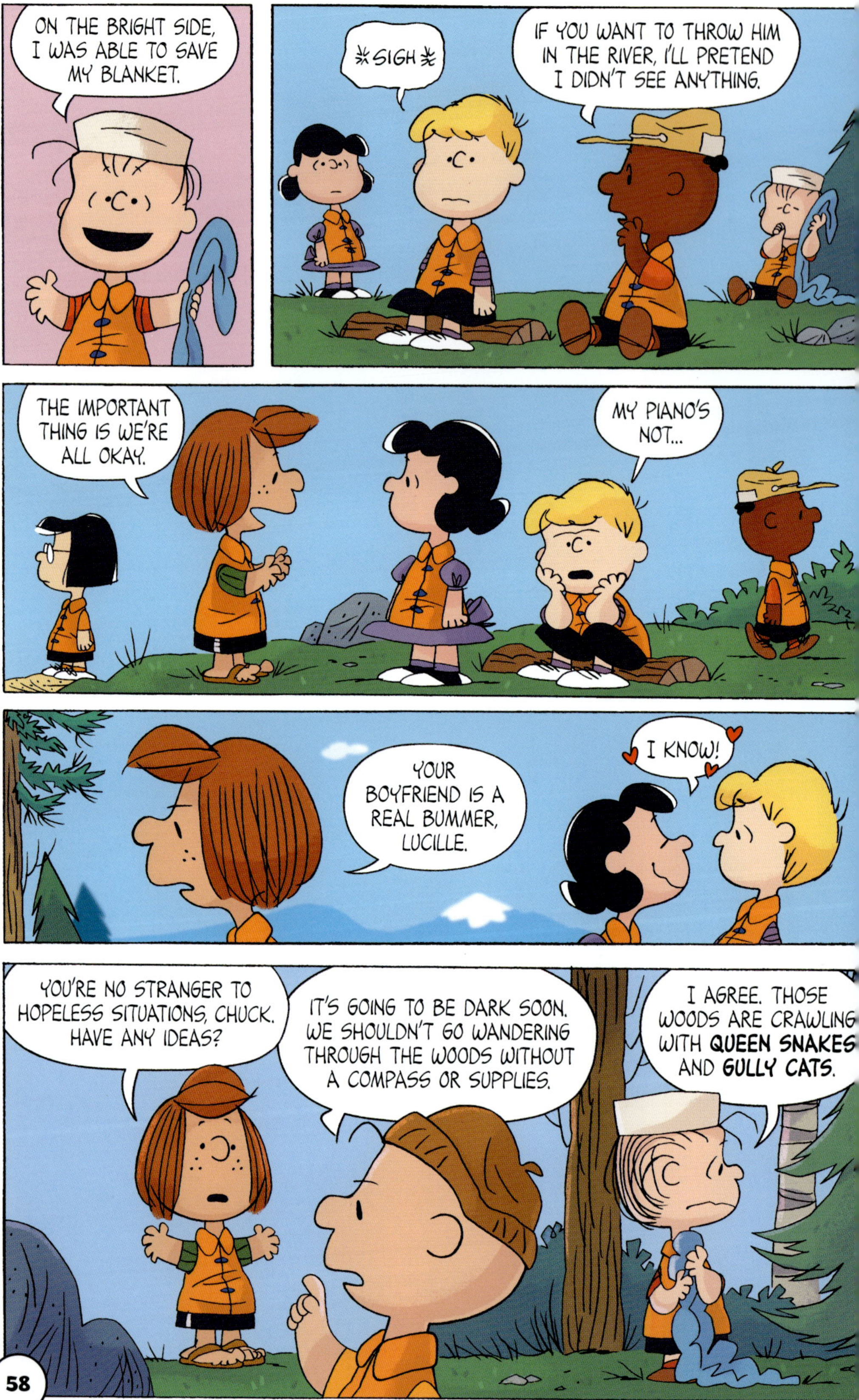

ON THE BRIGHT SIDE, I WAS ABLE TO SAVE MY BLANKET.
SIGH
IF YOU WANT TO THROW HIM IN THE RIVER, I'LL PRETEND I DIDN'T SEE ANYTHING.
THE IMPORTANT THING IS WE'RE ALL OKAY.
MY PIANO'S NOT...
YOUR BOYFRIEND IS A REAL BUMMER, LUCILLE.
I KNOW!
YOU'RE NO STRANGER TO HOPELESS SITUATIONS, CHUCK. HAVE ANY IDEAS?
IT'S GOING TO BE DARK SOON. WE SHOULDN'T GO WANDERING THROUGH THE WOODS WITHOUT A COMPASS OR SUPPLIES.
I AGREE. THOSE WOODS ARE CRAWLING WITH **QUEEN SNAKES** AND **GULLY CATS**.

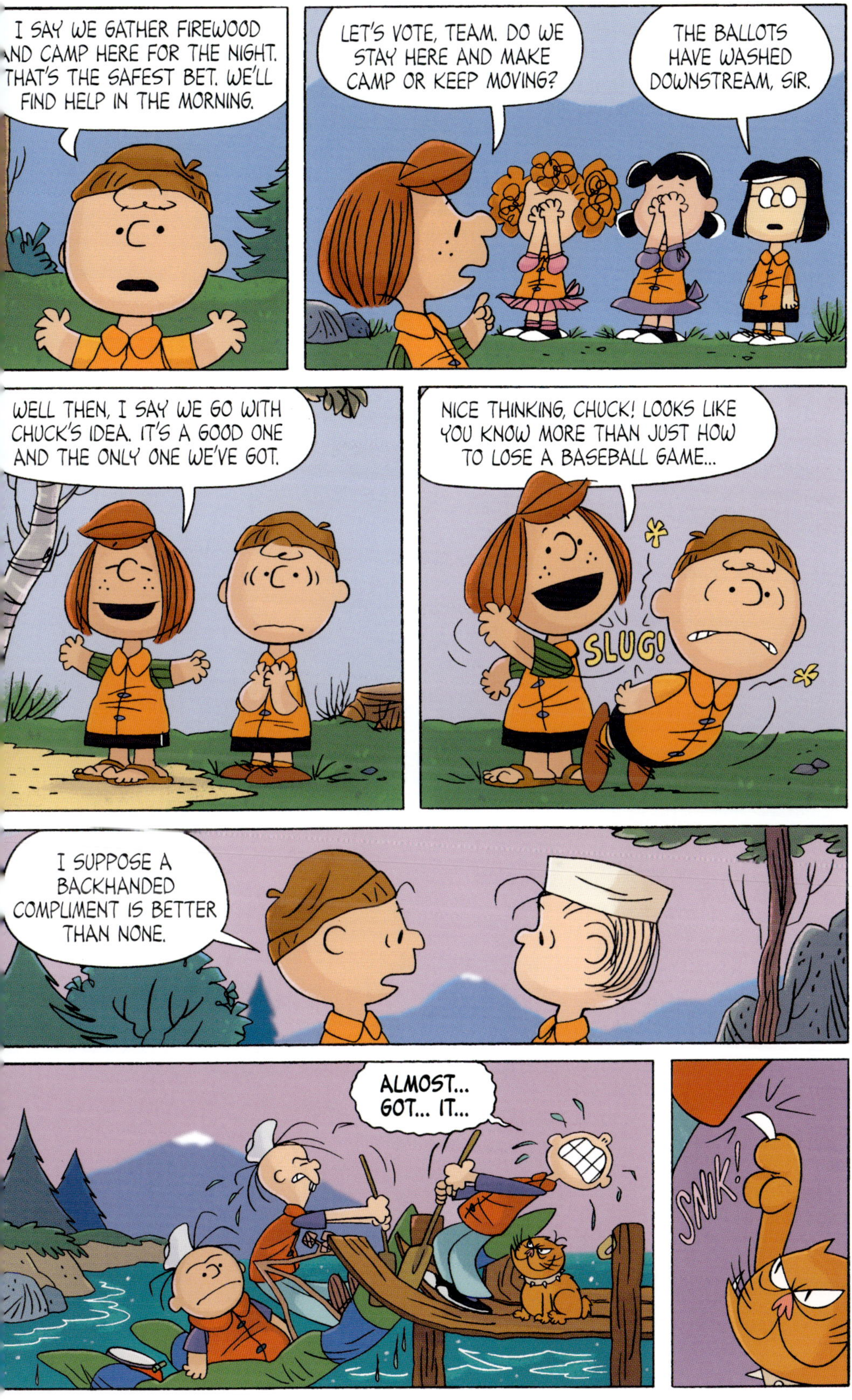
I SAY WE GATHER FIREWOOD AND CAMP HERE FOR THE NIGHT. THAT'S THE SAFEST BET. WE'LL FIND HELP IN THE MORNING.
LET'S VOTE, TEAM. DO WE STAY HERE AND MAKE CAMP OR KEEP MOVING?
THE BALLOTS HAVE WASHED DOWNSTREAM, SIR.
WELL THEN, I SAY WE GO WITH CHUCK'S IDEA. IT'S A GOOD ONE AND THE ONLY ONE WE'VE GOT.
NICE THINKING, CHUCK! LOOKS LIKE YOU KNOW MORE THAN JUST HOW TO LOSE A BASEBALL GAME...
SLUG!
I SUPPOSE A BACKHANDED COMPLIMENT IS BETTER THAN NONE.
ALMOST... GOT... IT...
SNIK!

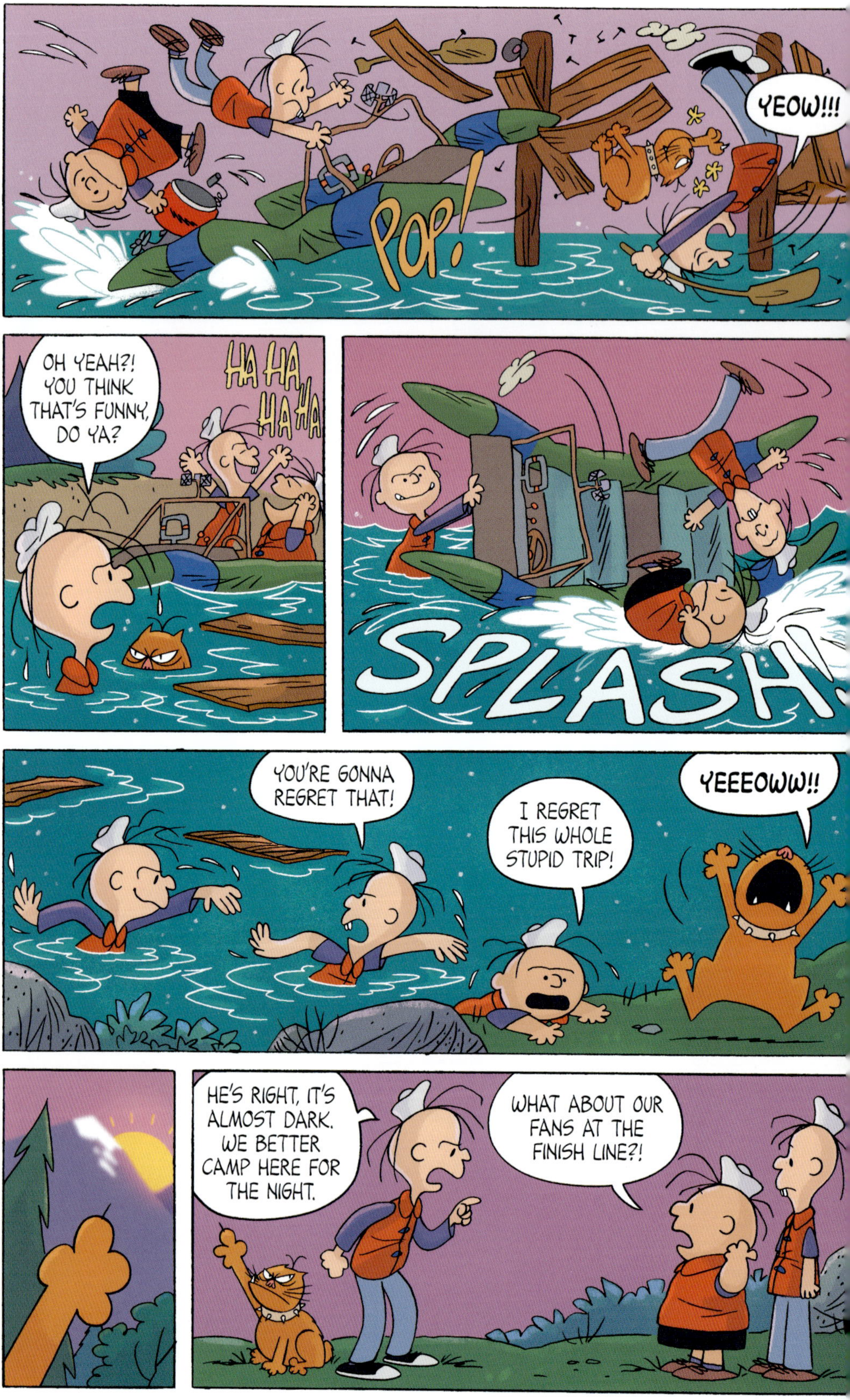
POP!
YEOW!!!
OH YEAH?! YOU THINK THAT'S FUNNY, DO YA?
HA HA HA HA
SPLASH!
YOU'RE GONNA REGRET THAT!
I REGRET THIS WHOLE STUPID TRIP!
YEEEOWW!!
HE'S RIGHT, IT'S ALMOST DARK. WE BETTER CAMP HERE FOR THE NIGHT.
WHAT ABOUT OUR FANS AT THE FINISH LINE?!

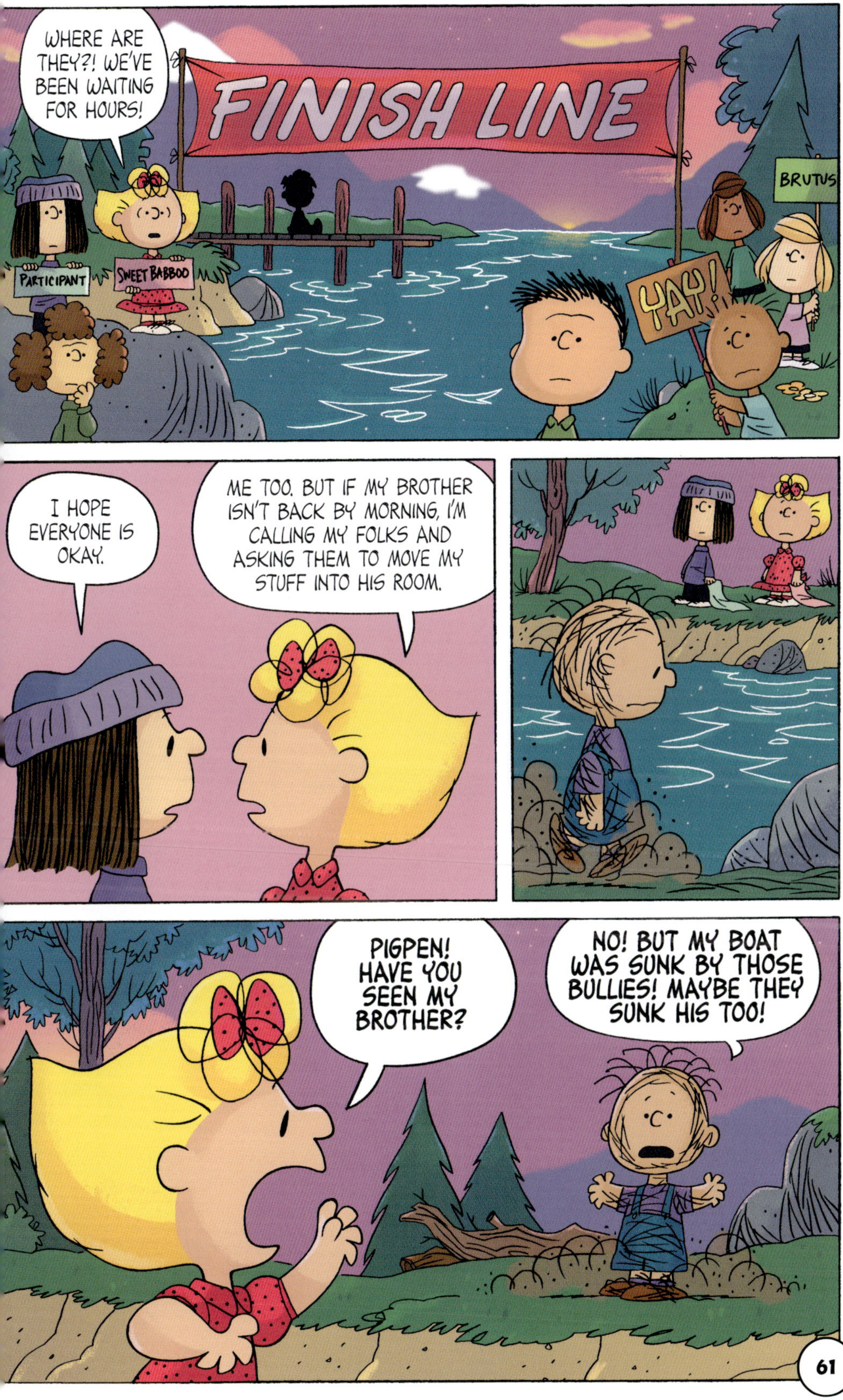
WHERE ARE THEY?! WE'VE BEEN WAITING FOR HOURS!
FINISH LINE
PARTICIPANT
SWEET BABBOO
YAY!
BRUTUS
I HOPE EVERYONE IS OKAY.
ME TOO. BUT IF MY BROTHER ISN'T BACK BY MORNING, I'M CALLING MY FOLKS AND ASKING THEM TO MOVE MY STUFF INTO HIS ROOM.
PIGPEN! HAVE YOU SEEN MY BROTHER?
NO! BUT MY BOAT WAS SUNK BY THOSE BULLIES! MAYBE THEY SUNK HIS TOO!

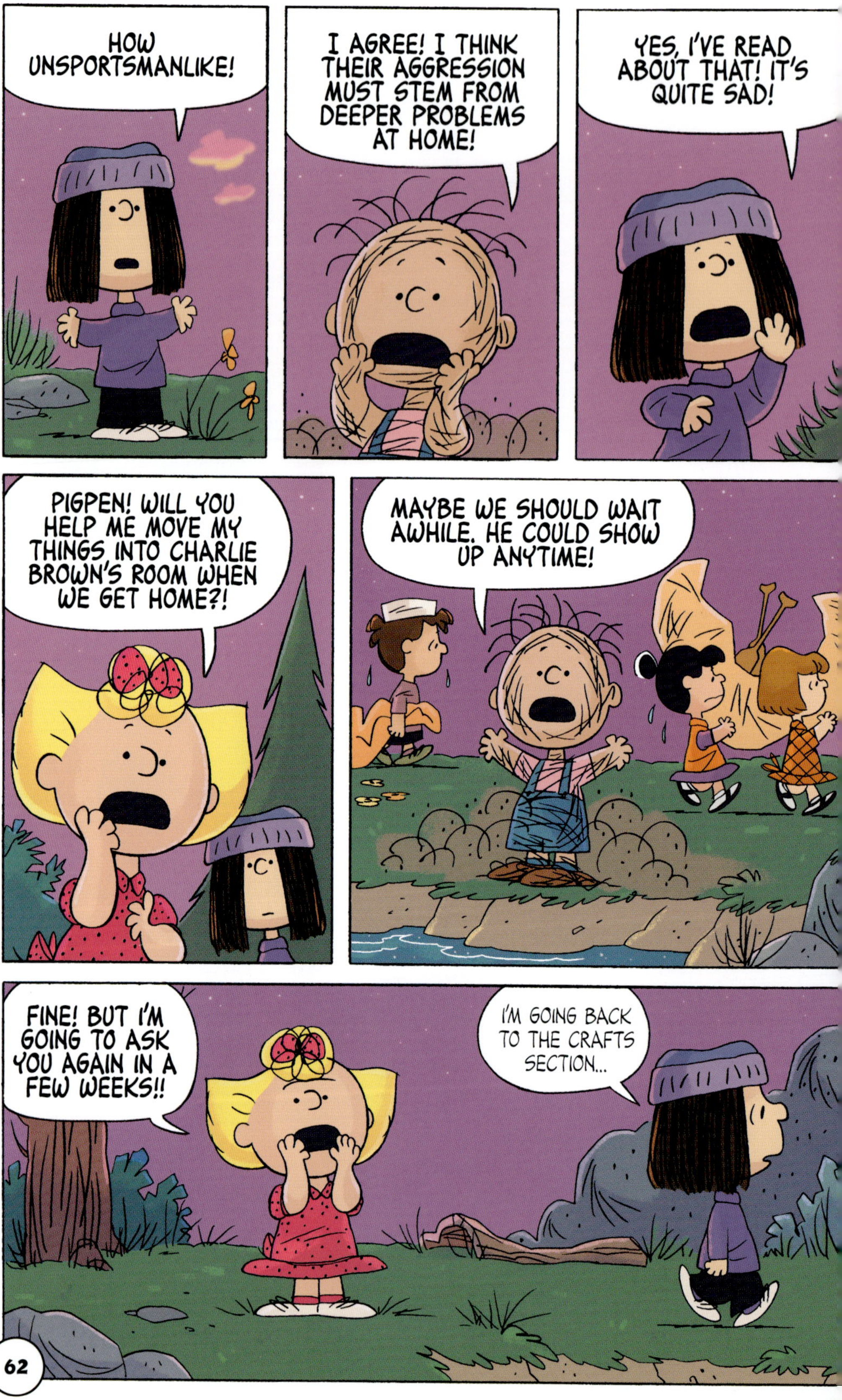
HOW UNSPORTSMANLIKE!
I AGREE! I THINK THEIR AGGRESSION MUST STEM FROM DEEPER PROBLEMS AT HOME!
YES, I'VE READ ABOUT THAT! IT'S QUITE SAD!
PIGPEN! WILL YOU HELP ME MOVE MY THINGS INTO CHARLIE BROWN'S ROOM WHEN WE GET HOME?!
MAYBE WE SHOULD WAIT AWHILE. HE COULD SHOW UP ANYTIME!
FINE! BUT I'M GOING TO ASK YOU AGAIN IN A FEW WEEKS!!
I'M GOING BACK TO THE CRAFTS SECTION...

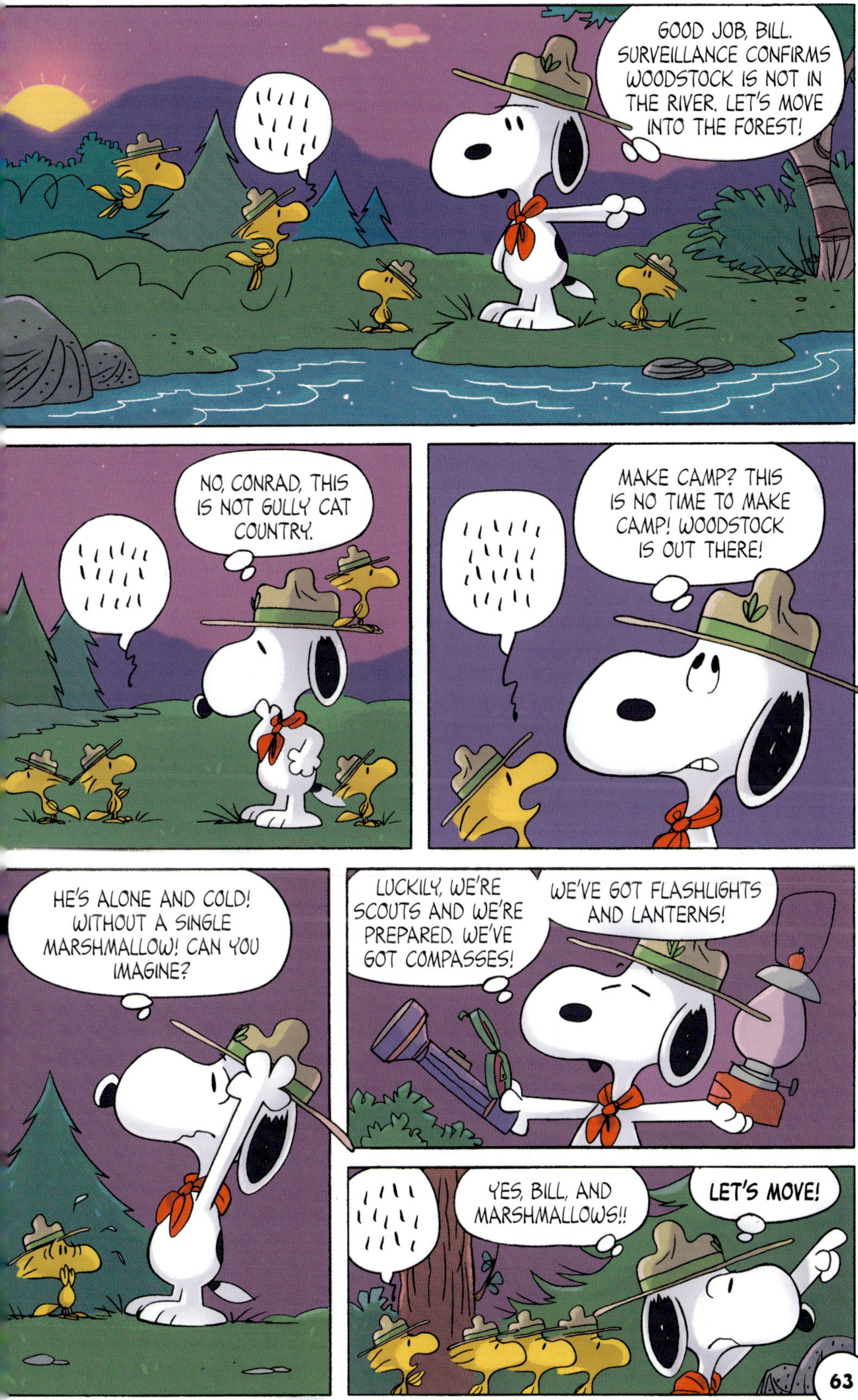
GOOD JOB, BILL. SURVEILLANCE CONFIRMS WOODSTOCK IS NOT IN THE RIVER. LET'S MOVE INTO THE FOREST!
NO, CONRAD, THIS IS NOT GULLY CAT COUNTRY.
MAKE CAMP? THIS IS NO TIME TO MAKE CAMP! WOODSTOCK IS OUT THERE!
HE'S ALONE AND COLD! WITHOUT A SINGLE MARSHMALLOW! CAN YOU IMAGINE?
LUCKILY, WE'RE SCOUTS AND WE'RE PREPARED. WE'VE GOT COMPASSES!
WE'VE GOT FLASHLIGHTS AND LANTERNS!
YES, BILL, AND MARSHMALLOWS!!
LET'S MOVE!

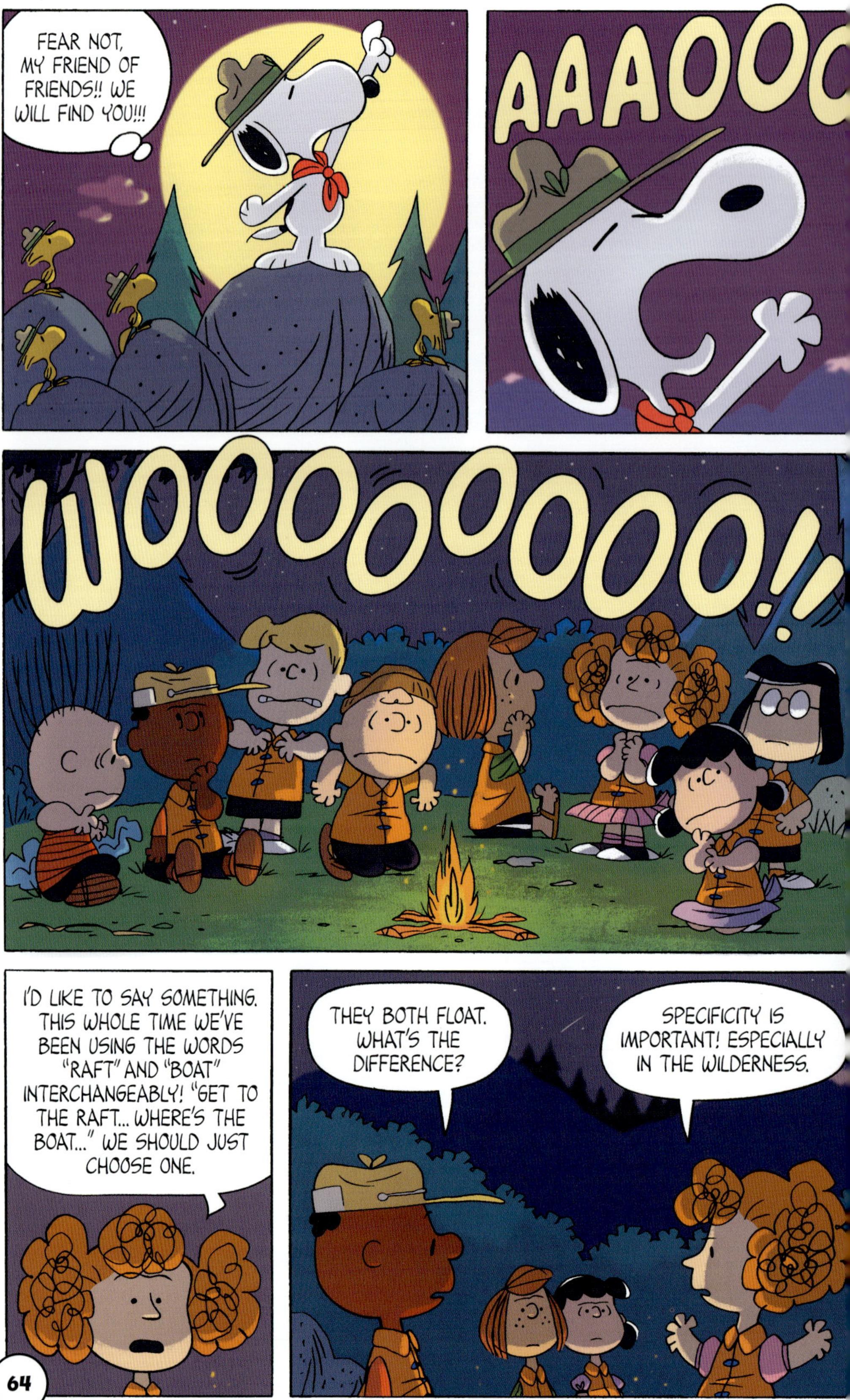
FEAR NOT, MY FRIEND OF FRIENDS!! WE WILL FIND YOU!!!
AAAOOO
WOOOOOOOO!!
I'D LIKE TO SAY SOMETHING. THIS WHOLE TIME WE'VE BEEN USING THE WORDS "RAFT" AND "BOAT" INTERCHANGEABLY! "GET TO THE RAFT... WHERE'S THE BOAT..." WE SHOULD JUST CHOOSE ONE.
THEY BOTH FLOAT. WHAT'S THE DIFFERENCE?
SPECIFICITY IS IMPORTANT! ESPECIALLY IN THE WILDERNESS.

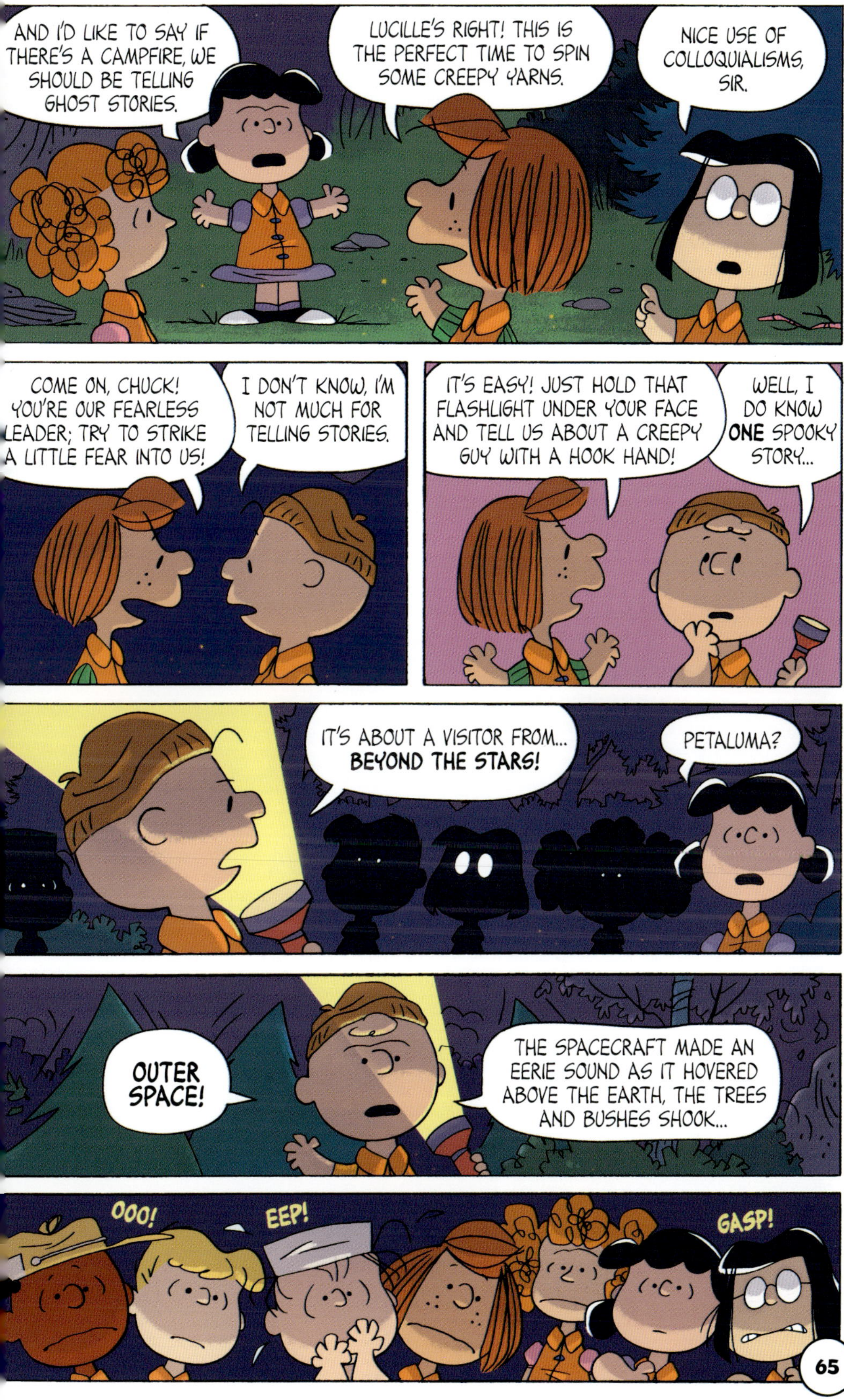
AND I'D LIKE TO SAY IF THERE'S A CAMPFIRE, WE SHOULD BE TELLING GHOST STORIES.
LUCILLE'S RIGHT! THIS IS THE PERFECT TIME TO SPIN SOME CREEPY YARNS.
NICE USE OF COLLOQUIALISMS, SIR.
COME ON, CHUCK! YOU'RE OUR FEARLESS LEADER; TRY TO STRIKE A LITTLE FEAR INTO US!
I DON'T KNOW, I'M NOT MUCH FOR TELLING STORIES.
IT'S EASY! JUST HOLD THAT FLASHLIGHT UNDER YOUR FACE AND TELL US ABOUT A CREEPY GUY WITH A HOOK HAND!
WELL, I DO KNOW **ONE** SPOOKY STORY...
IT'S ABOUT A VISITOR FROM... **BEYOND THE STARS!**
PETALUMA?
OUTER SPACE!
THE SPACECRAFT MADE AN EERIE SOUND AS IT HOVERED ABOVE THE EARTH, THE TREES AND BUSHES SHOOK...
OOO!
EEP!
GASP!

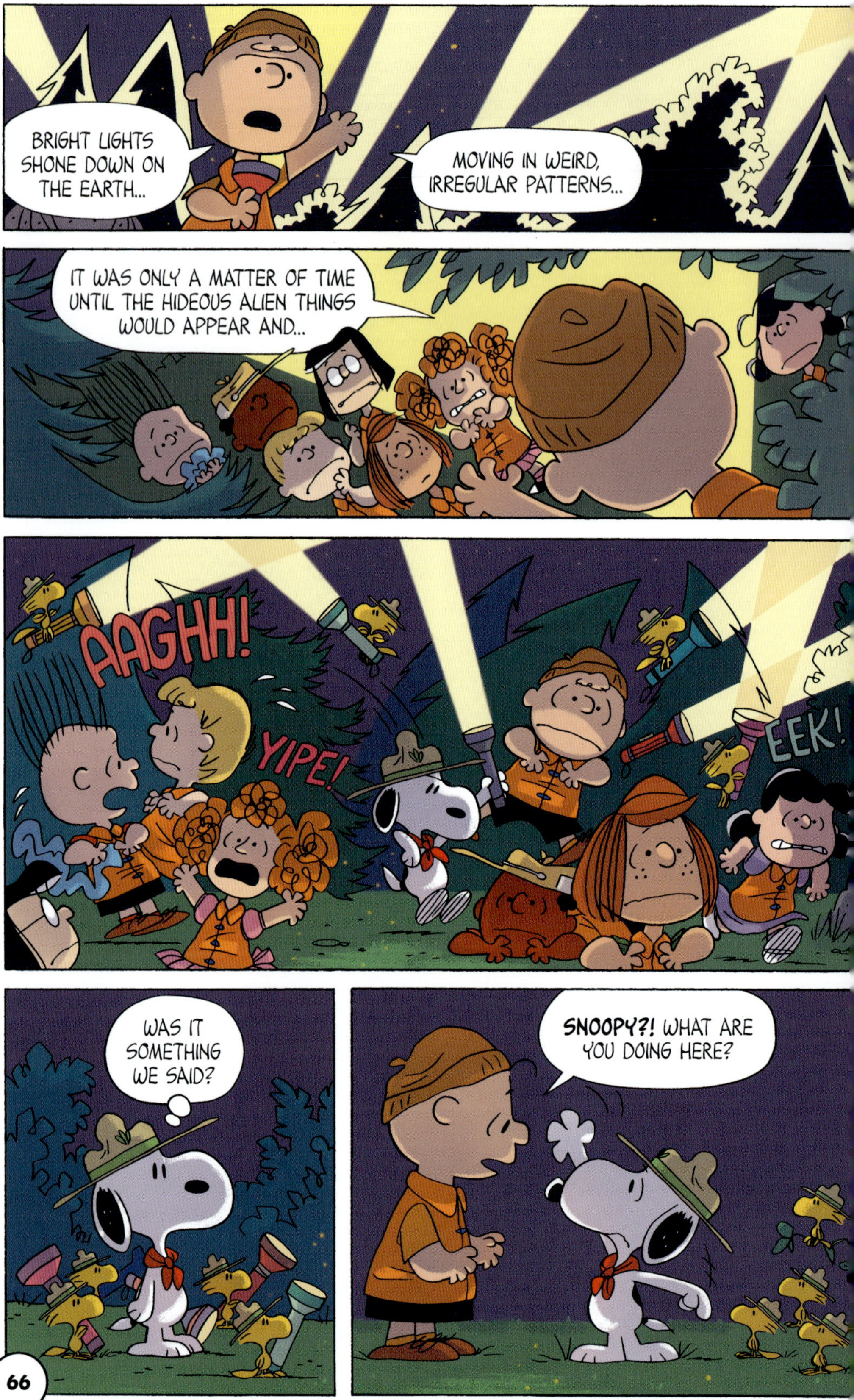

BRIGHT LIGHTS SHONE DOWN ON THE EARTH...
MOVING IN WEIRD, IRREGULAR PATTERNS...
IT WAS ONLY A MATTER OF TIME UNTIL THE HIDEOUS ALIEN THINGS WOULD APPEAR AND...
AAGHH!
YIPE!
EEK!
WAS IT SOMETHING WE SAID?
SNOOPY?! WHAT ARE YOU DOING HERE?

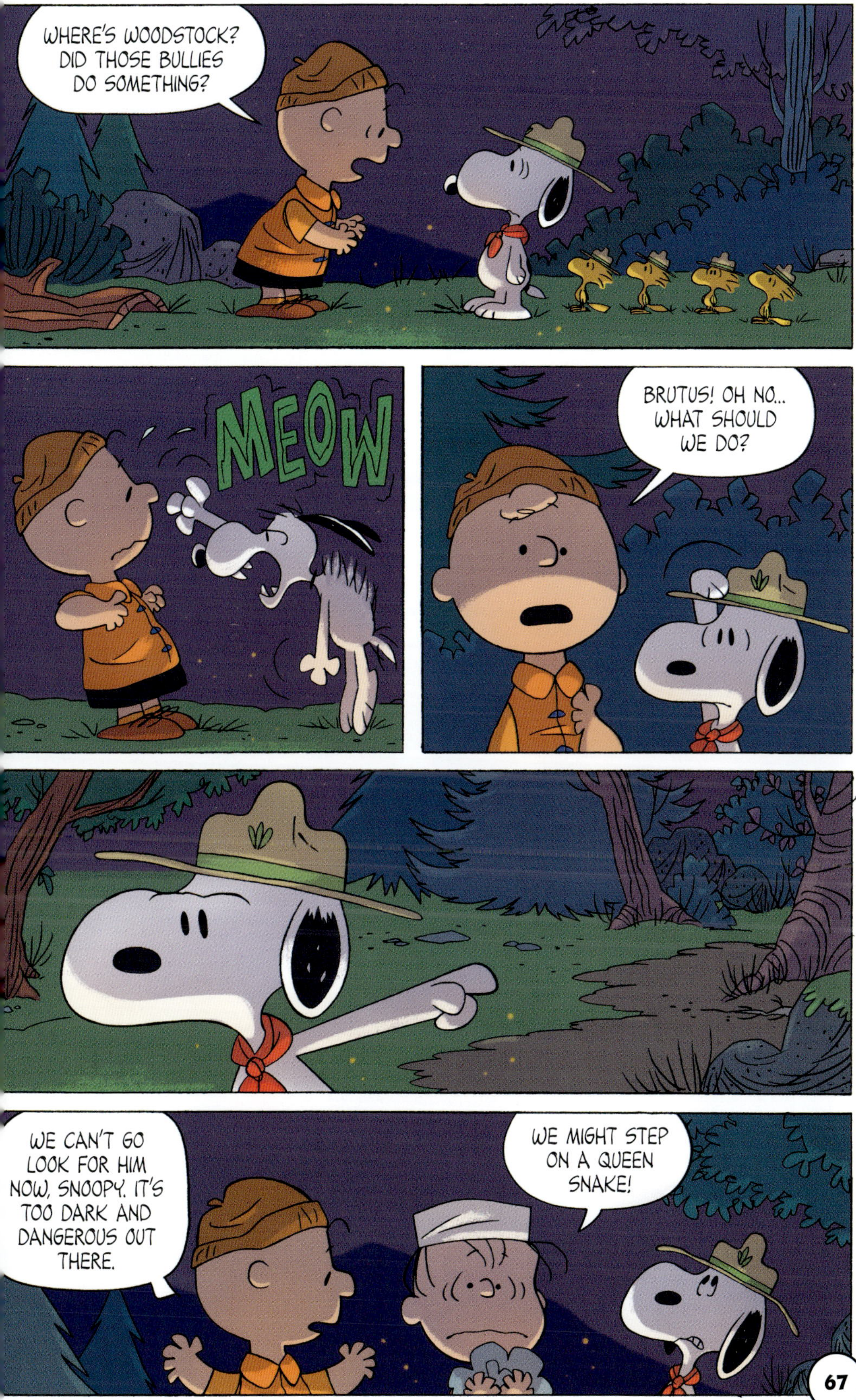
WHERE'S WOODSTOCK? DID THOSE BULLIES DO SOMETHING?
MEOW
BRUTUS! OH NO... WHAT SHOULD WE DO?
WE CAN'T GO LOOK FOR HIM NOW, SNOOPY. IT'S TOO DARK AND DANGEROUS OUT THERE.
WE MIGHT STEP ON A QUEEN SNAKE!

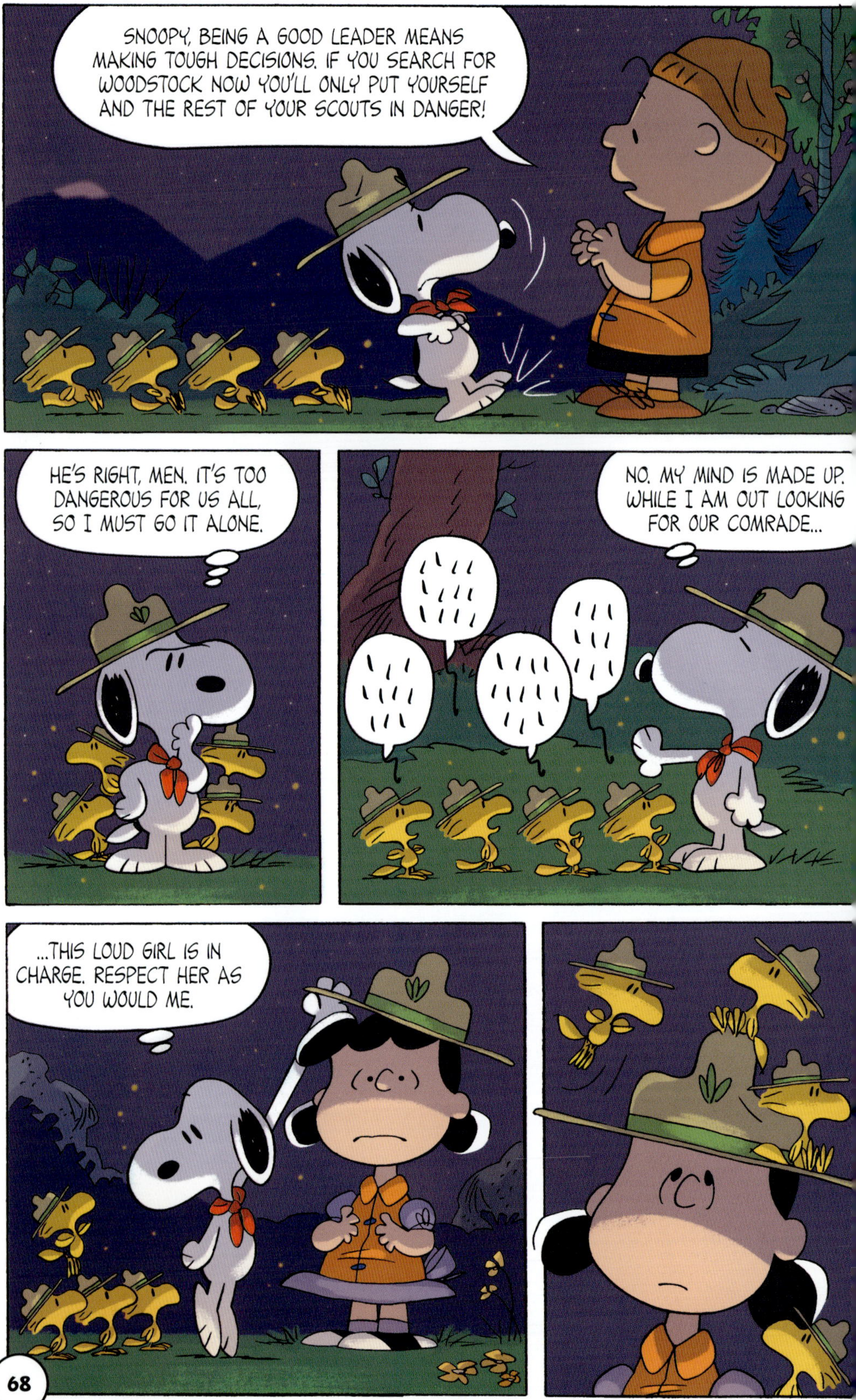
SNOOPY, BEING A GOOD LEADER MEANS MAKING TOUGH DECISIONS. IF YOU SEARCH FOR WOODSTOCK NOW YOU'LL ONLY PUT YOURSELF AND THE REST OF YOUR SCOUTS IN DANGER!
HE'S RIGHT, MEN. IT'S TOO DANGEROUS FOR US ALL, SO I MUST GO IT ALONE.
NO. MY MIND IS MADE UP. WHILE I AM OUT LOOKING FOR OUR COMRADE...
...THIS LOUD GIRL IS IN CHARGE. RESPECT HER AS YOU WOULD ME.

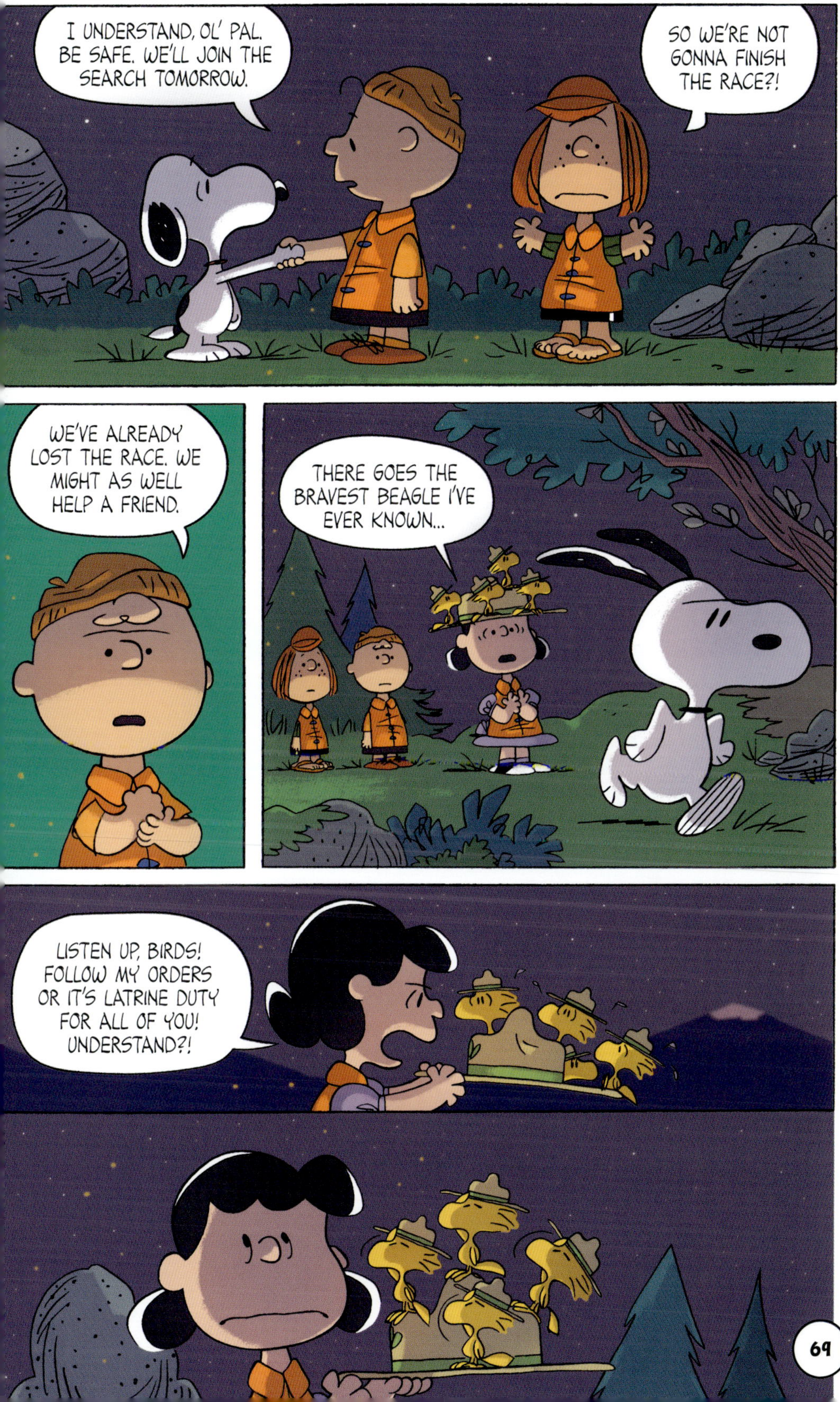
I UNDERSTAND, OL' PAL. BE SAFE. WE'LL JOIN THE SEARCH TOMORROW.
SO WE'RE NOT GONNA FINISH THE RACE?!
WE'VE ALREADY LOST THE RACE. WE MIGHT AS WELL HELP A FRIEND.
THERE GOES THE BRAVEST BEAGLE I'VE EVER KNOWN...
LISTEN UP, BIRDS! FOLLOW MY ORDERS OR IT'S LATRINE DUTY FOR ALL OF YOU! UNDERSTAND?!

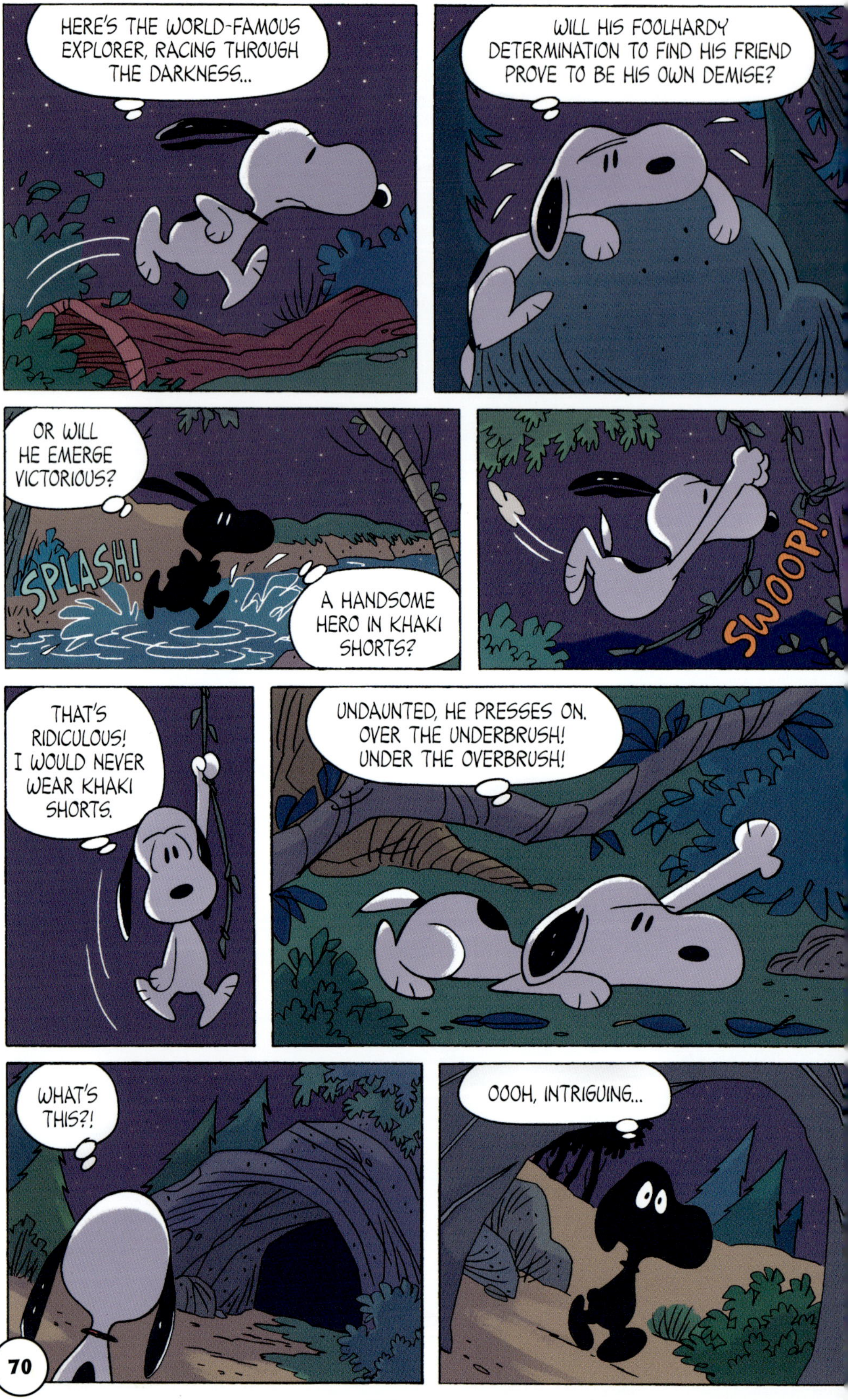
HERE'S THE WORLD-FAMOUS EXPLORER, RACING THROUGH THE DARKNESS...
WILL HIS FOOLHARDY DETERMINATION TO FIND HIS FRIEND PROVE TO BE HIS OWN DEMISE?
OR WILL HE EMERGE VICTORIOUS?
SPLASH!
A HANDSOME HERO IN KHAKI SHORTS?
SWOOP!
THAT'S RIDICULOUS! I WOULD NEVER WEAR KHAKI SHORTS.
UNDAUNTED, HE PRESSES ON. OVER THE UNDERBRUSH! UNDER THE OVERBRUSH!
WHAT'S THIS?!
OOOH, INTRIGUING...

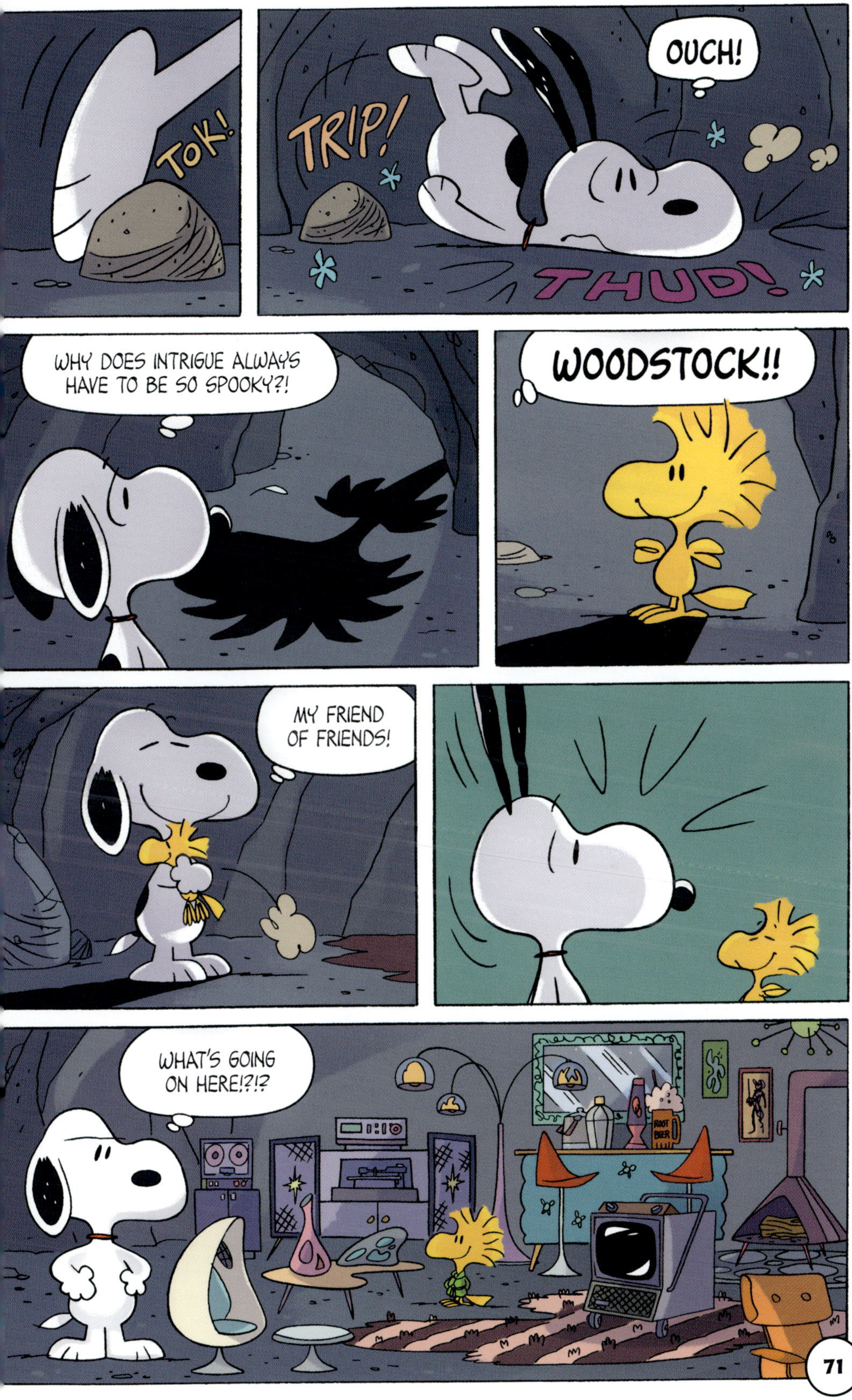
TOK!
TRIP!
OUCH!
THUD!
WHY DOES INTRIGUE ALWAYS HAVE TO BE SO SPOOKY?!
WOODSTOCK!!
MY FRIEND OF FRIENDS!
WHAT'S GOING ON HERE!?!?
ROOT BEER

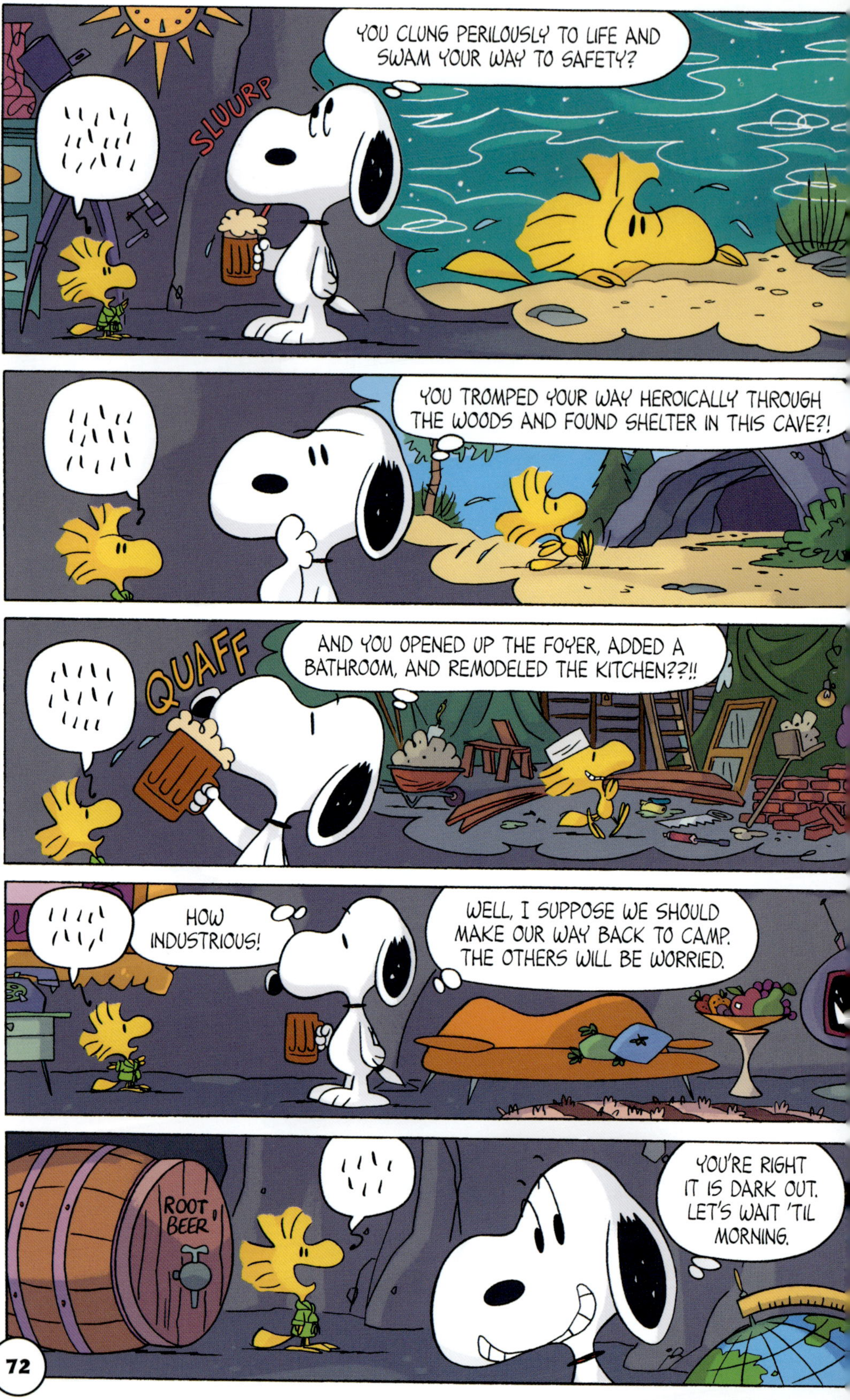
YOU CLUNG PERILOUSLY TO LIFE AND SWAM YOUR WAY TO SAFETY?
SLUURP
YOU TROMPED YOUR WAY HEROICALLY THROUGH THE WOODS AND FOUND SHELTER IN THIS CAVE?!
QUAFF
AND YOU OPENED UP THE FOYER, ADDED A BATHROOM, AND REMODELED THE KITCHEN??!!
HOW INDUSTRIOUS!
WELL, I SUPPOSE WE SHOULD MAKE OUR WAY BACK TO CAMP. THE OTHERS WILL BE WORRIED.
ROOT BEER
YOU'RE RIGHT IT IS DARK OUT. LET'S WAIT 'TIL MORNING.

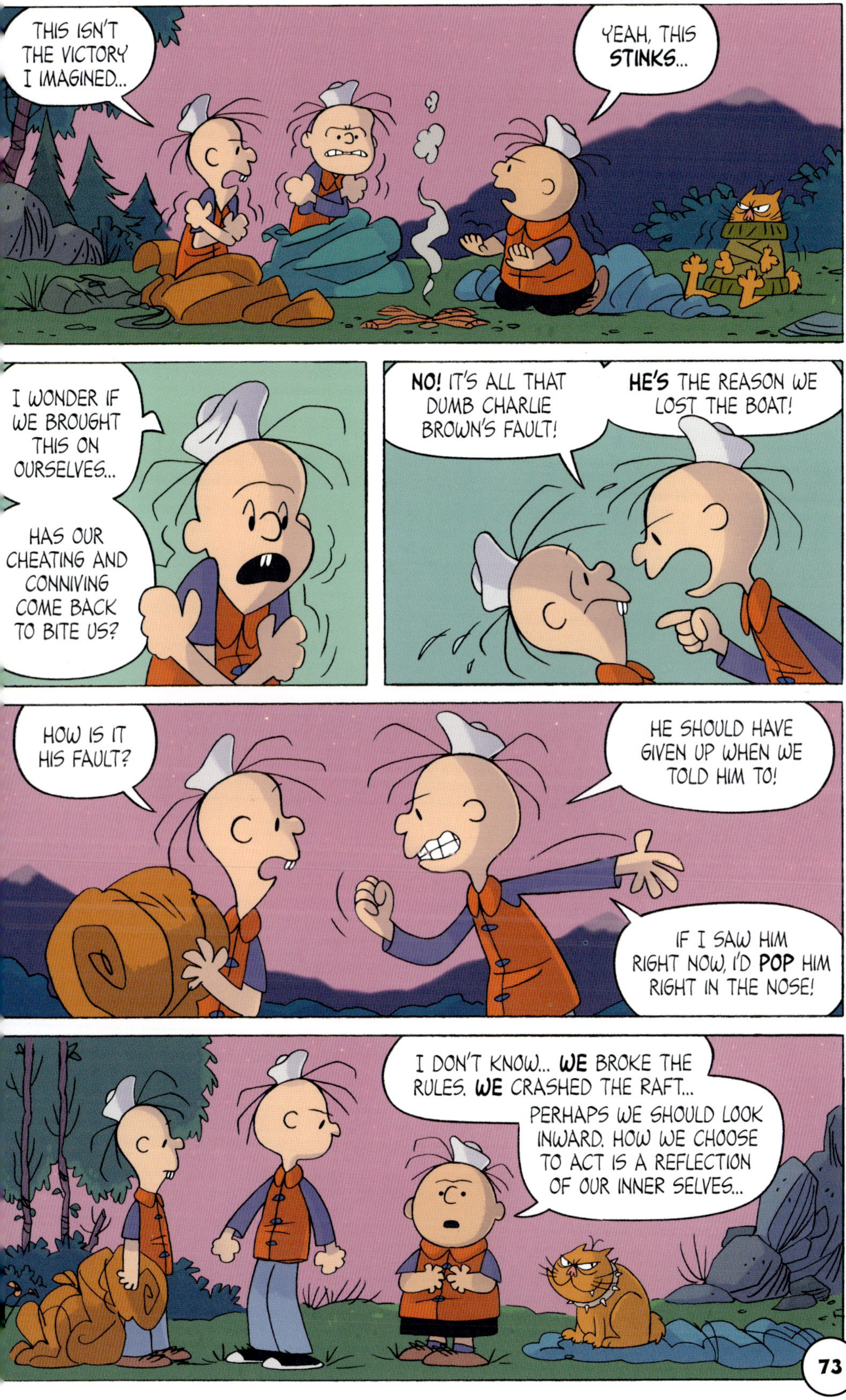
THIS ISN'T THE VICTORY I IMAGINED...
YEAH, THIS **STINKS**...
I WONDER IF WE BROUGHT THIS ON OURSELVES...
HAS OUR CHEATING AND CONNIVING COME BACK TO BITE US?
NO! IT'S ALL THAT DUMB CHARLIE BROWN'S FAULT!
HE'S THE REASON WE LOST THE BOAT!
HOW IS IT HIS FAULT?
HE SHOULD HAVE GIVEN UP WHEN WE TOLD HIM TO!
IF I SAW HIM RIGHT NOW, I'D **POP** HIM RIGHT IN THE NOSE!
I DON'T KNOW... **WE** BROKE THE RULES. **WE** CRASHED THE RAFT...
PERHAPS WE SHOULD LOOK INWARD. HOW WE CHOOSE TO ACT IS A REFLECTION OF OUR INNER SELVES...

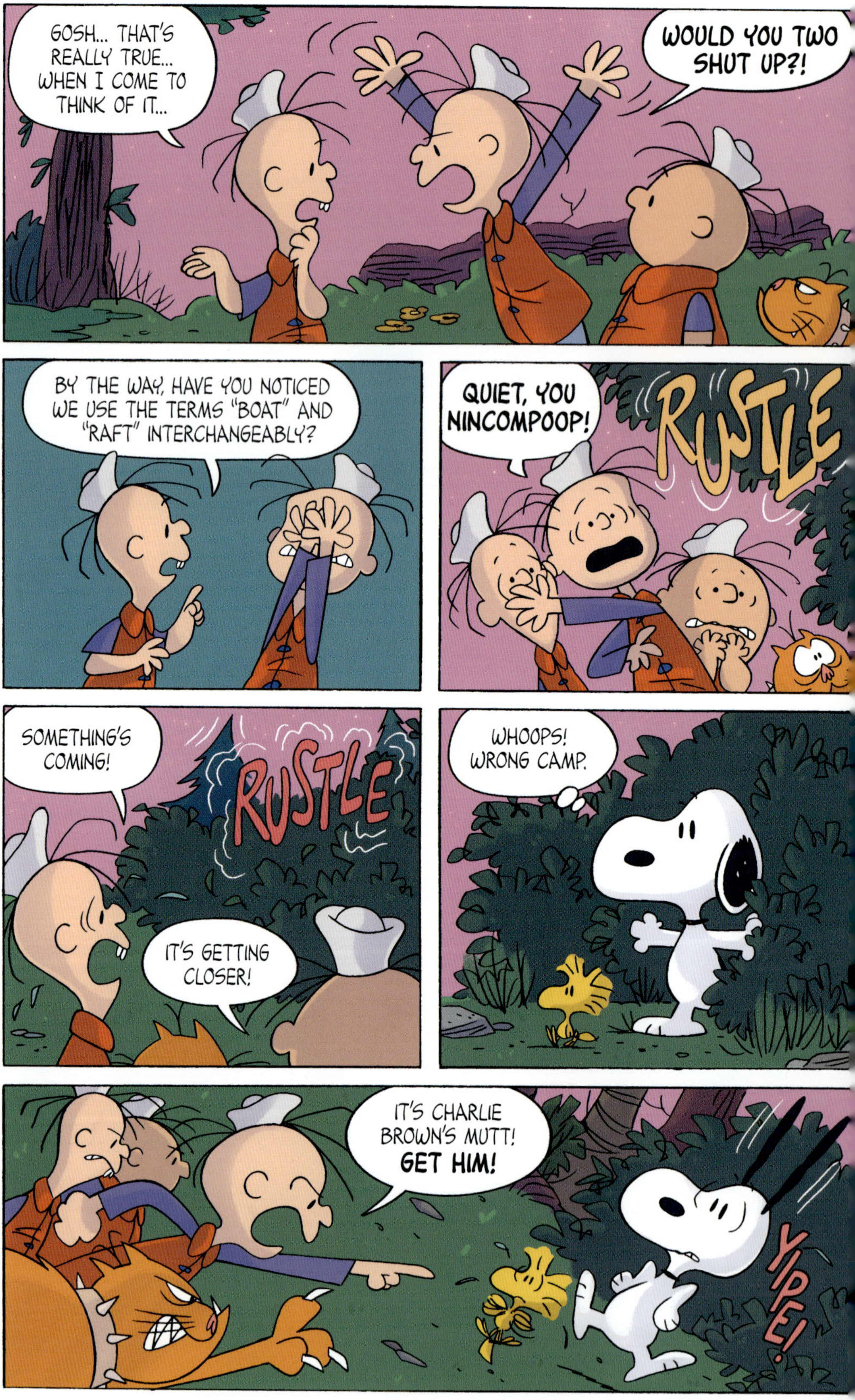
GOSH... THAT'S REALLY TRUE... WHEN I COME TO THINK OF IT...
WOULD YOU TWO SHUT UP?!
BY THE WAY, HAVE YOU NOTICED WE USE THE TERMS "BOAT" AND "RAFT" INTERCHANGEABLY?
QUIET, YOU NINCOMPOOP!
RUSTLE
SOMETHING'S COMING!
RUSTLE
IT'S GETTING CLOSER!
WHOOPS! WRONG CAMP.
IT'S CHARLIE BROWN'S MUTT! GET HIM!
YIPE!

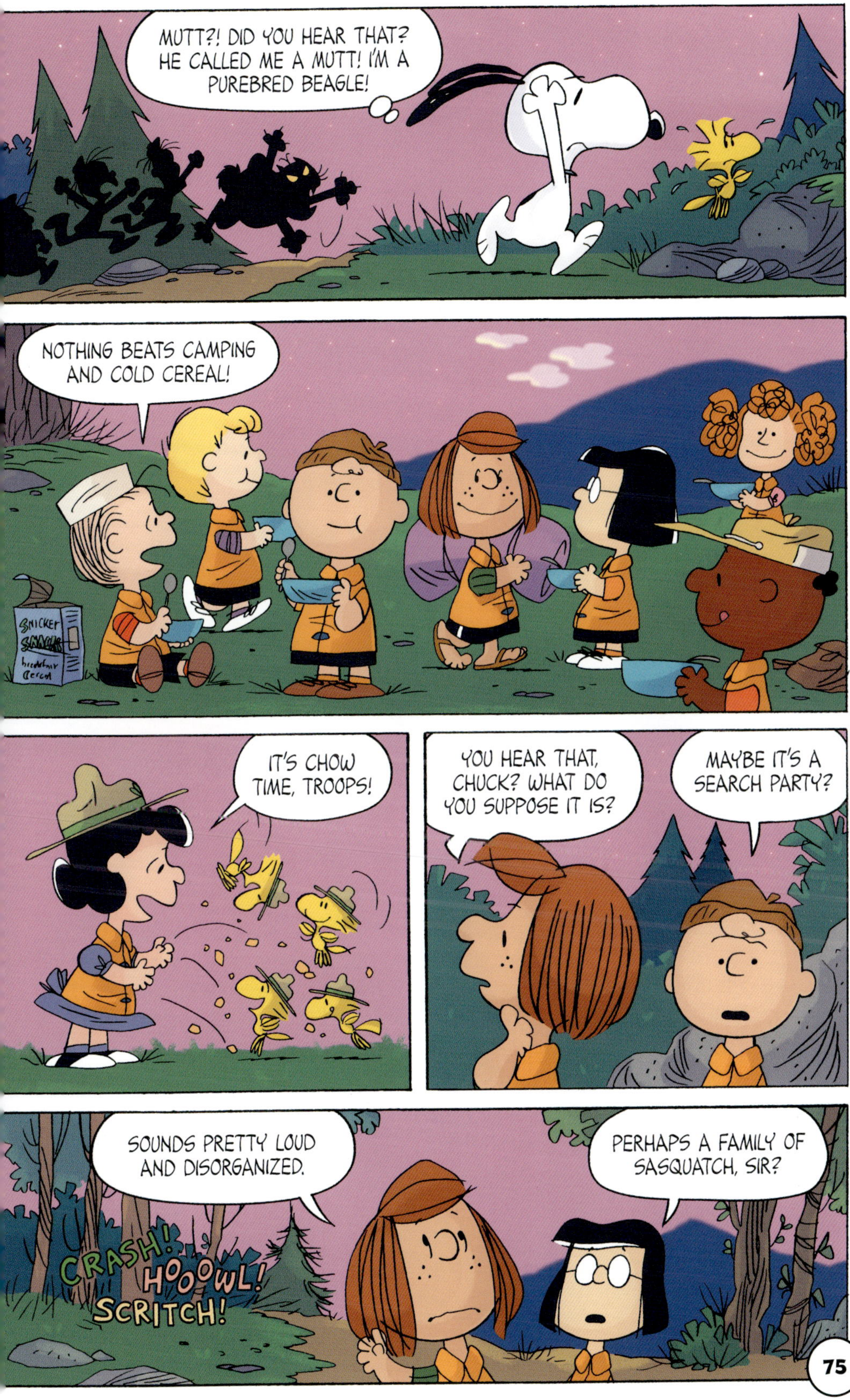
MUTT?! DID YOU HEAR THAT? HE CALLED ME A MUTT! I'M A PUREBRED BEAGLE!
NOTHING BEATS CAMPING AND COLD CEREAL!
IT'S CHOW TIME, TROOPS!
YOU HEAR THAT, CHUCK? WHAT DO YOU SUPPOSE IT IS?
MAYBE IT'S A SEARCH PARTY?
SOUNDS PRETTY LOUD AND DISORGANIZED.
PERHAPS A FAMILY OF SASQUATCH, SIR?
CRASH!
HOOOWL!
SCRITCH!

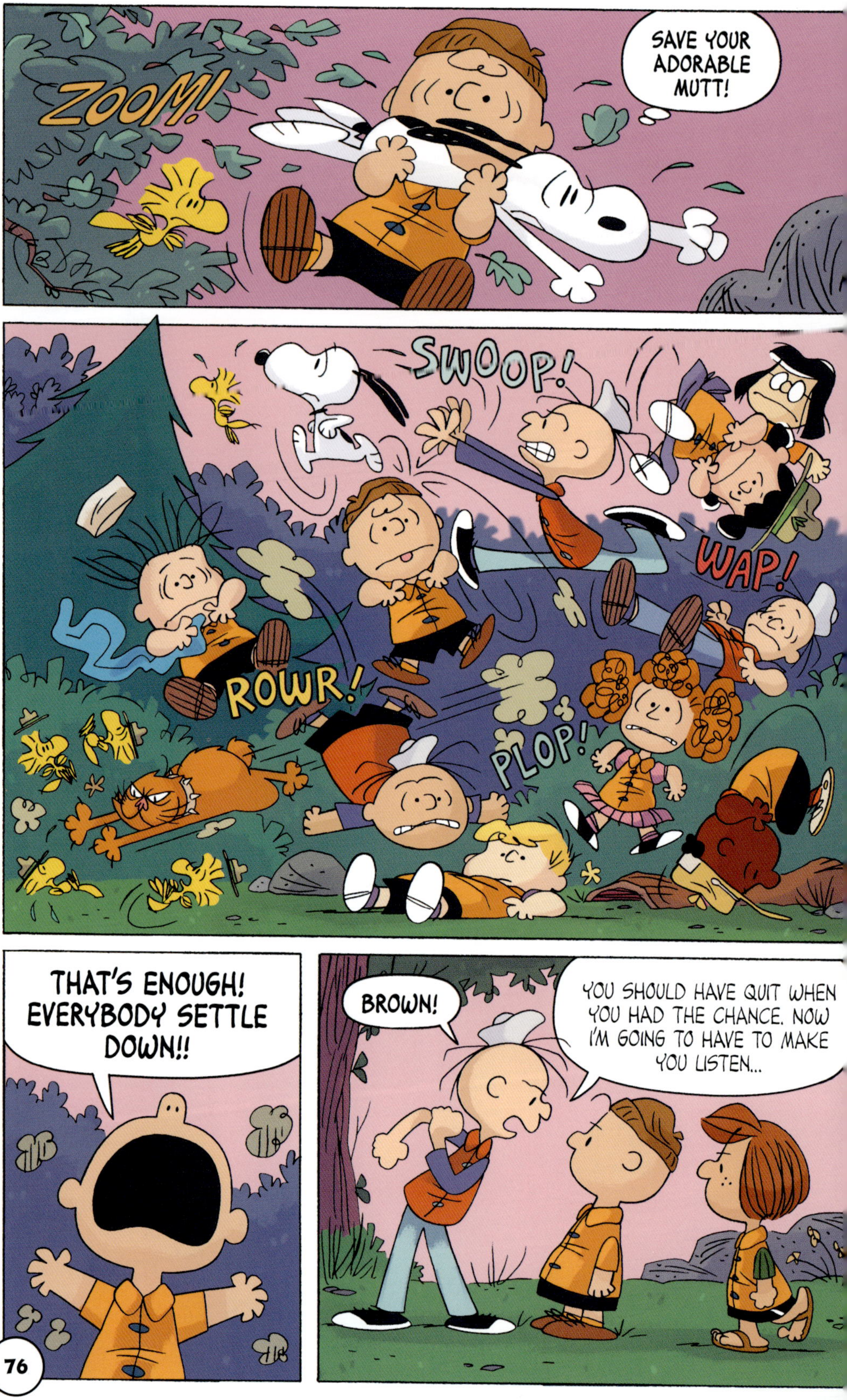
ZOOM!
SAVE YOUR ADORABLE MUTT!
SWOOP!
WAP!
ROWR!
PLOP!
THAT'S ENOUGH! EVERYBODY SETTLE DOWN!!
BROWN!
YOU SHOULD HAVE QUIT WHEN YOU HAD THE CHANCE. NOW I'M GOING TO HAVE TO MAKE YOU LISTEN...

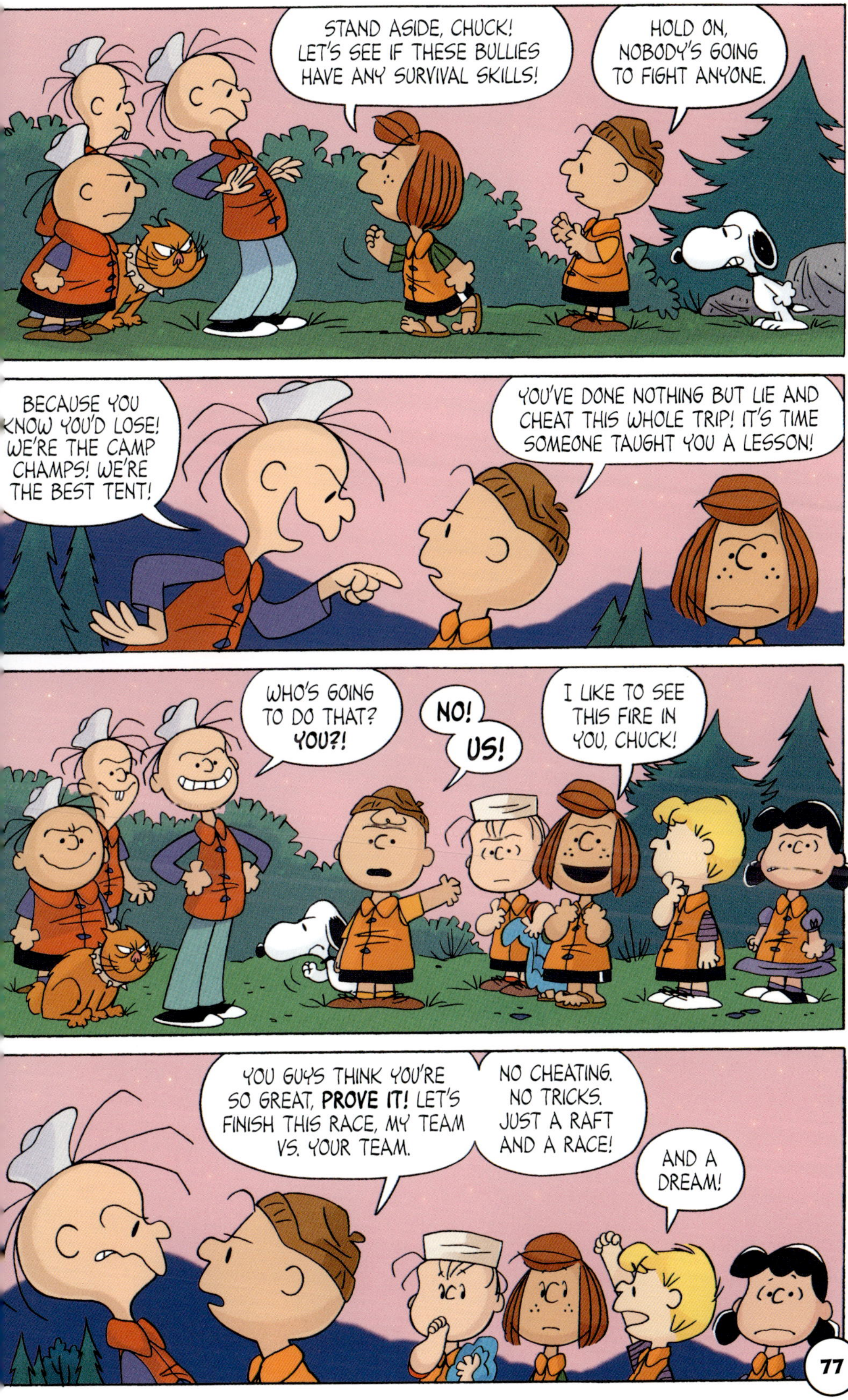
STAND ASIDE, CHUCK! LET'S SEE IF THESE BULLIES HAVE ANY SURVIVAL SKILLS!
HOLD ON, NOBODY'S GOING TO FIGHT ANYONE.
BECAUSE YOU KNOW YOU'D LOSE! WE'RE THE CAMP CHAMPS! WE'RE THE BEST TENT!
YOU'VE DONE NOTHING BUT LIE AND CHEAT THIS WHOLE TRIP! IT'S TIME SOMEONE TAUGHT YOU A LESSON!
WHO'S GOING TO DO THAT? **YOU?!**
NO!
US!
I LIKE TO SEE THIS FIRE IN YOU, CHUCK!
YOU GUYS THINK YOU'RE SO GREAT, **PROVE IT!** LET'S FINISH THIS RACE, MY TEAM VS. YOUR TEAM.
NO CHEATING. NO TRICKS. JUST A RAFT AND A RACE!
AND A DREAM!

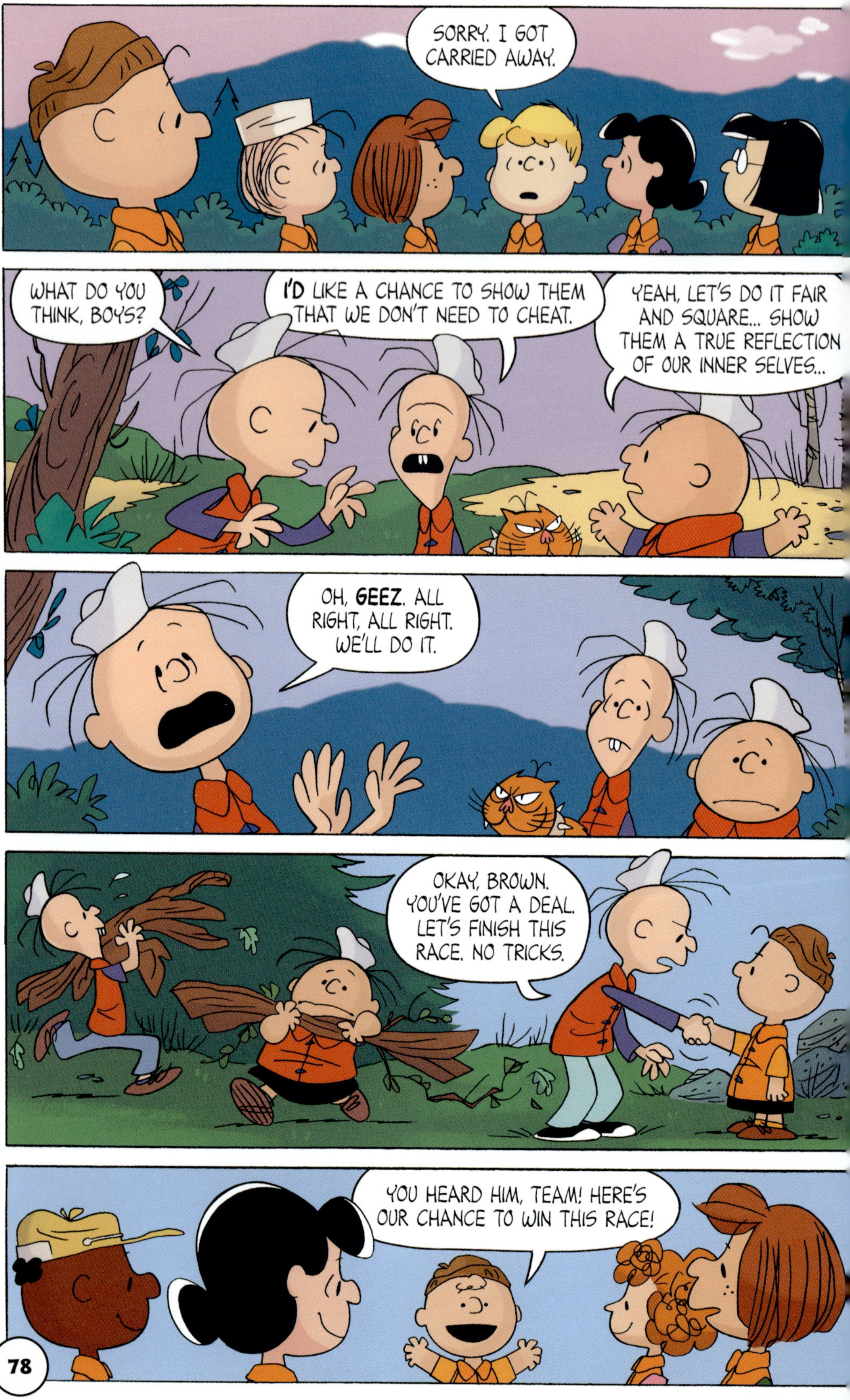
SORRY. I GOT CARRIED AWAY.
WHAT DO YOU THINK, BOYS?
I'D LIKE A CHANCE TO SHOW THEM THAT WE DON'T NEED TO CHEAT.
YEAH, LET'S DO IT FAIR AND SQUARE... SHOW THEM A TRUE REFLECTION OF OUR INNER SELVES...
OH, GEEZ. ALL RIGHT, ALL RIGHT. WE'LL DO IT.
OKAY, BROWN. YOU'VE GOT A DEAL. LET'S FINISH THIS RACE. NO TRICKS.
YOU HEARD HIM, TEAM! HERE'S OUR CHANCE TO WIN THIS RACE!

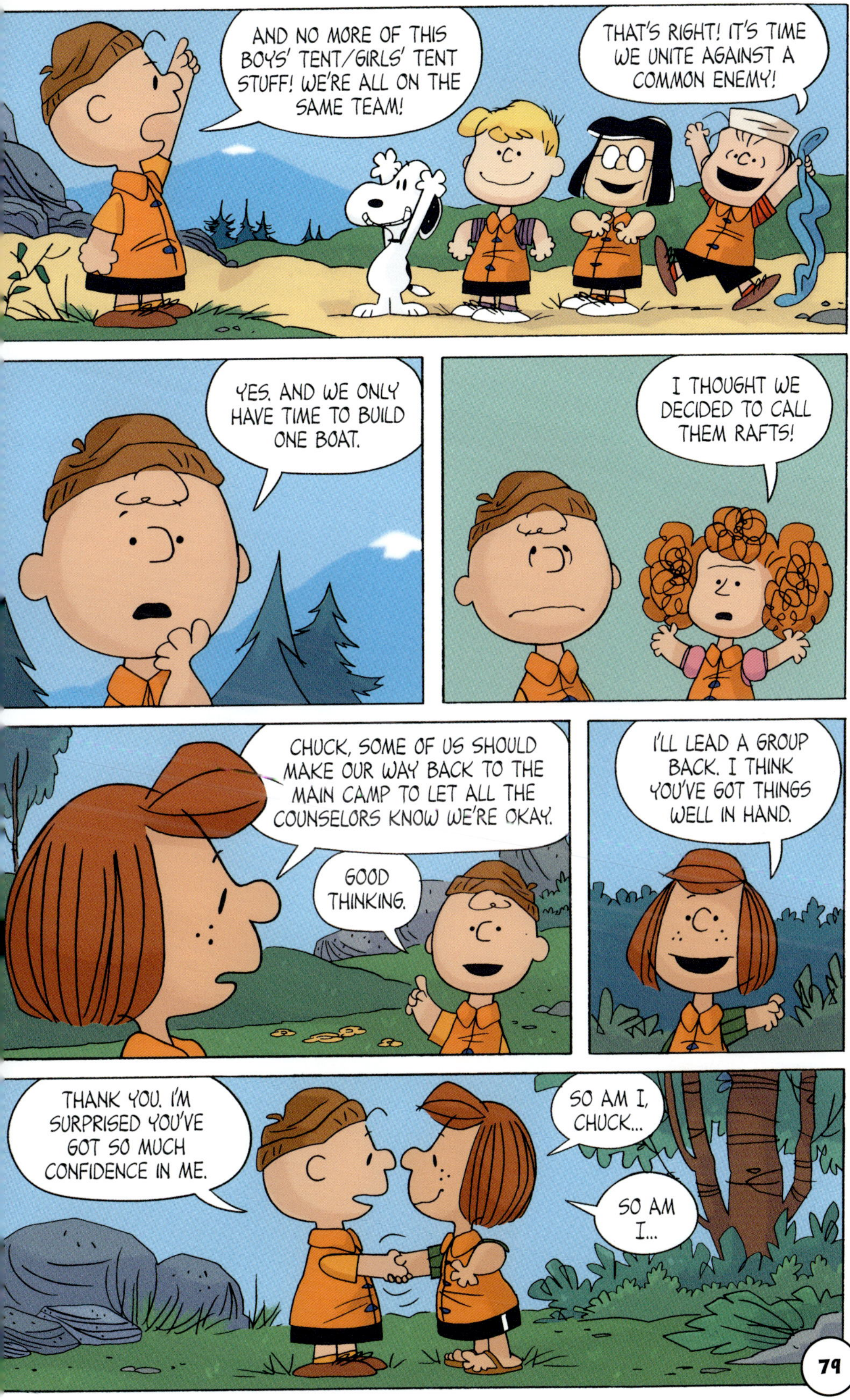
AND NO MORE OF THIS BOYS' TENT/GIRLS' TENT STUFF! WE'RE ALL ON THE SAME TEAM!
THAT'S RIGHT! IT'S TIME WE UNITE AGAINST A COMMON ENEMY!
YES. AND WE ONLY HAVE TIME TO BUILD ONE BOAT.
I THOUGHT WE DECIDED TO CALL THEM RAFTS!
CHUCK, SOME OF US SHOULD MAKE OUR WAY BACK TO THE MAIN CAMP TO LET ALL THE COUNSELORS KNOW WE'RE OKAY.
GOOD THINKING.
I'LL LEAD A GROUP BACK. I THINK YOU'VE GOT THINGS WELL IN HAND.
THANK YOU. I'M SURPRISED YOU'VE GOT SO MUCH CONFIDENCE IN ME.
SO AM I, CHUCK...
SO AM I...

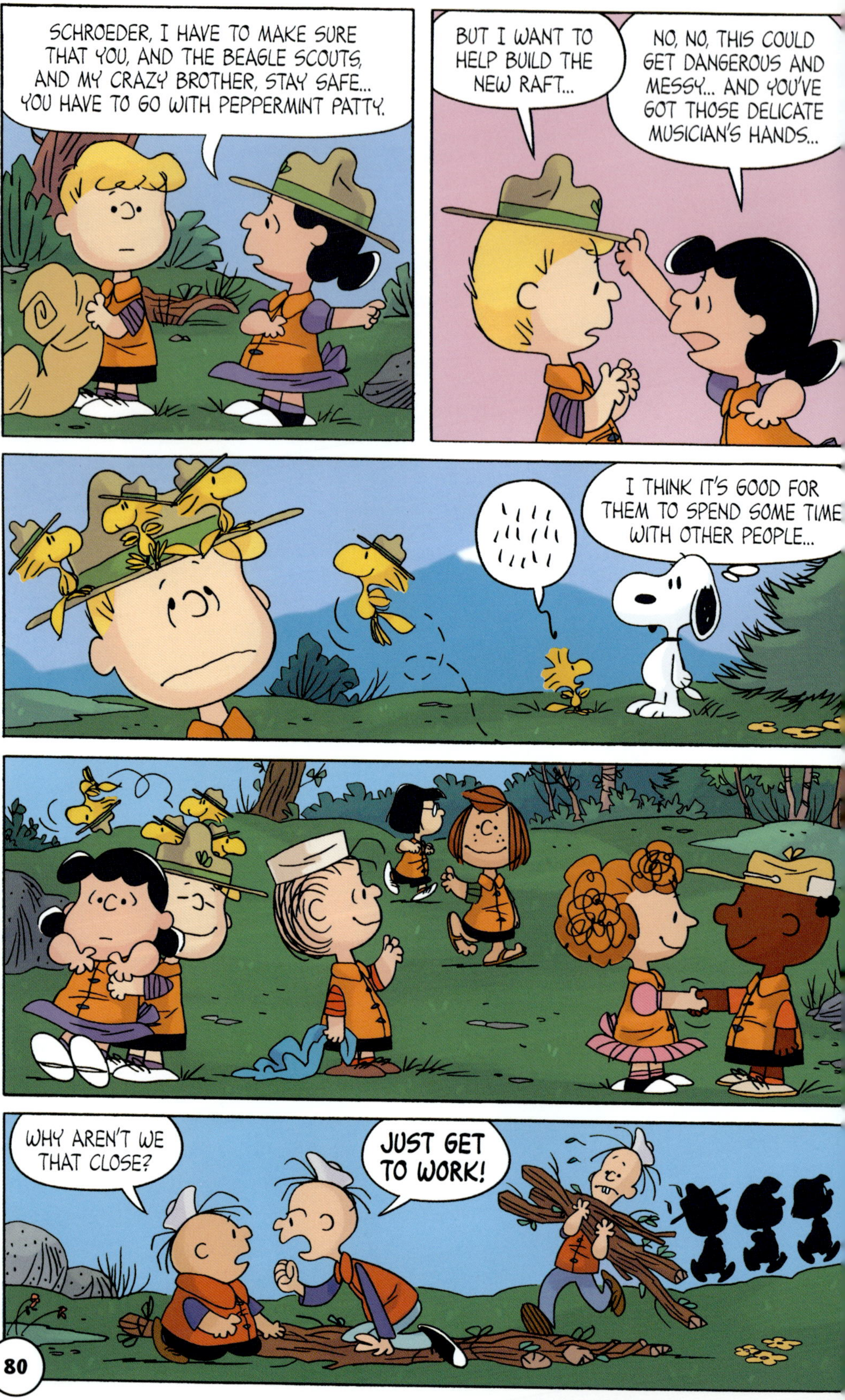
SCHROEDER, I HAVE TO MAKE SURE THAT YOU, AND THE BEAGLE SCOUTS, AND MY CRAZY BROTHER, STAY SAFE... YOU HAVE TO GO WITH PEPPERMINT PATTY.
BUT I WANT TO HELP BUILD THE NEW RAFT...
NO, NO, THIS COULD GET DANGEROUS AND MESSY... AND YOU'VE GOT THOSE DELICATE MUSICIAN'S HANDS...
I THINK IT'S GOOD FOR THEM TO SPEND SOME TIME WITH OTHER PEOPLE...
WHY AREN'T WE THAT CLOSE?
JUST GET TO WORK!

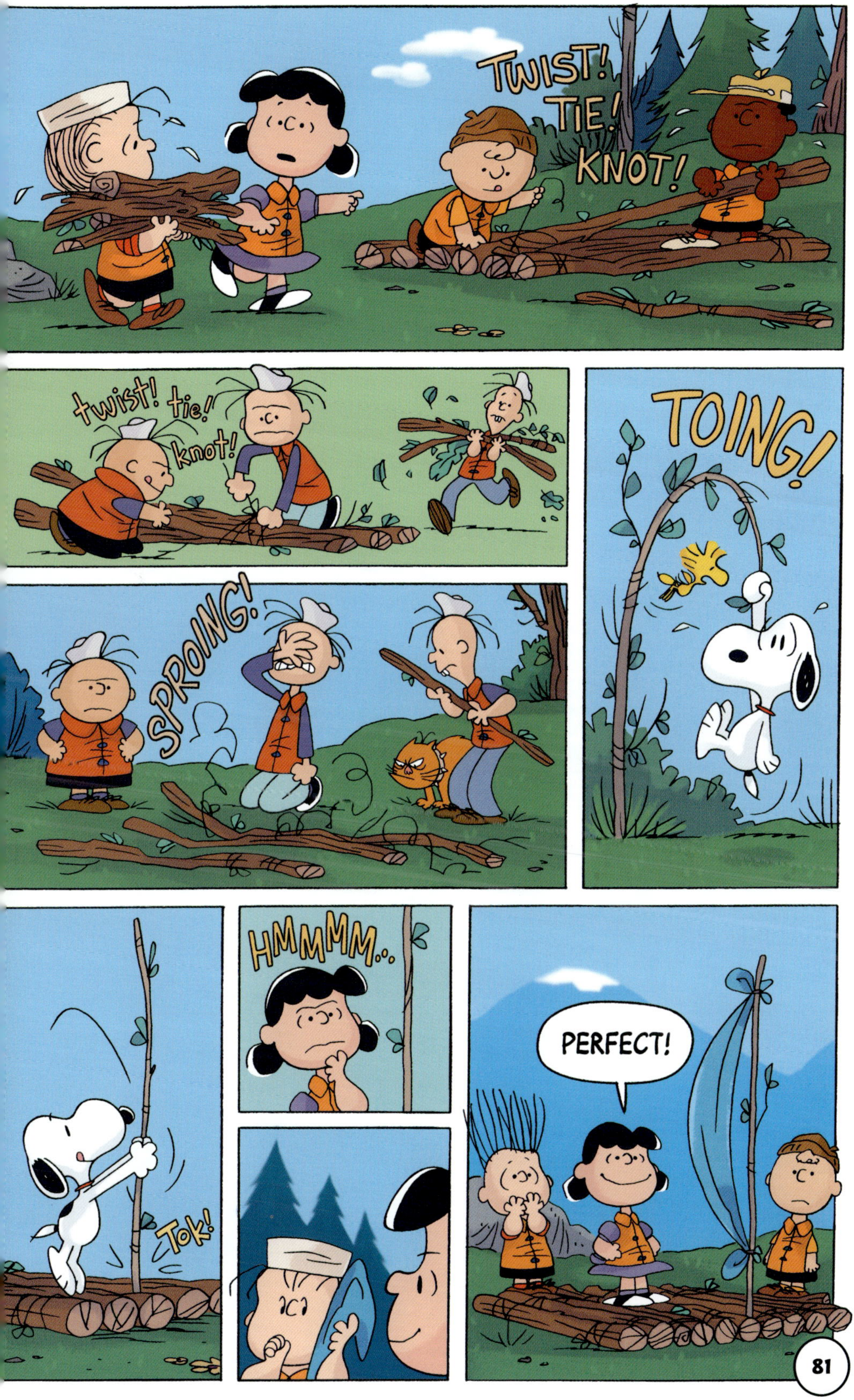

TWIST! TIE! KNOT!
twist! tie! knot!
TOING!
SPROING!
Tok!
HMMMM...
PERFECT!

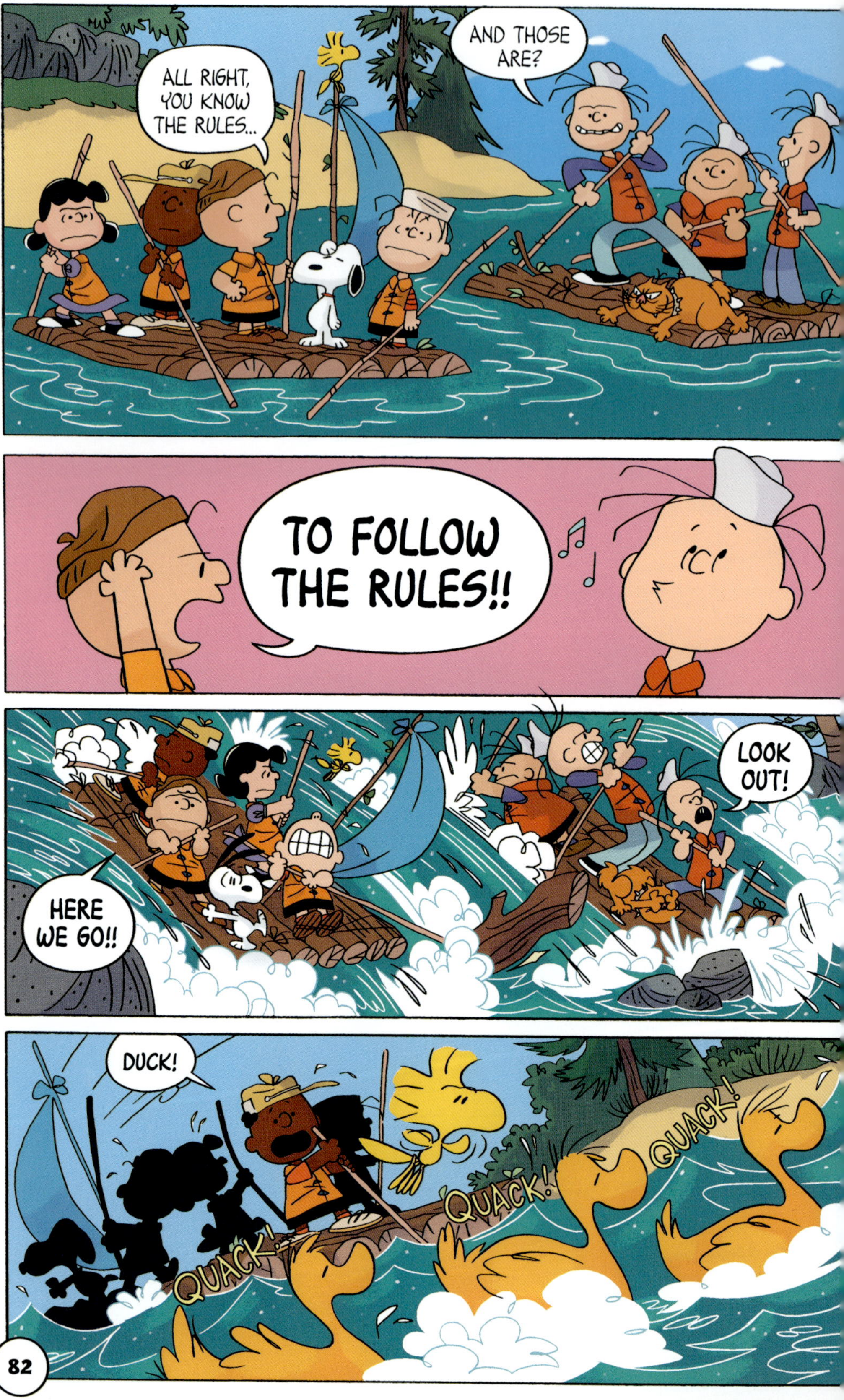
ALL RIGHT, YOU KNOW THE RULES...
AND THOSE ARE?
TO FOLLOW THE RULES!!
LOOK OUT!
HERE WE GO!!
DUCK!
QUACK!
QUACK!
QUACK!

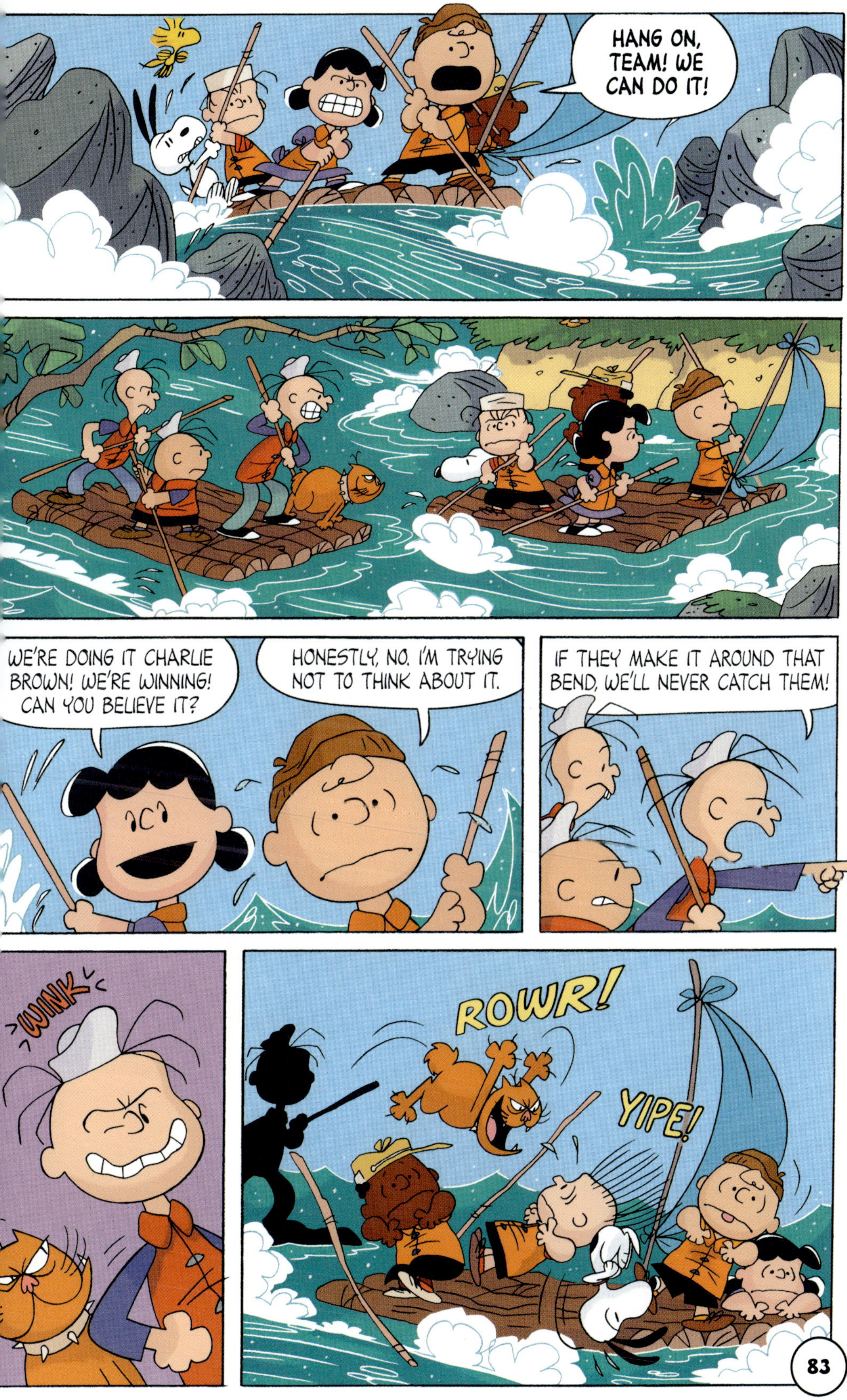
HANG ON, TEAM! WE CAN DO IT!
WE'RE DOING IT CHARLIE BROWN! WE'RE WINNING! CAN YOU BELIEVE IT?
HONESTLY, NO. I'M TRYING NOT TO THINK ABOUT IT.
IF THEY MAKE IT AROUND THAT BEND, WE'LL NEVER CATCH THEM!
WINK
ROWR!
YIPE!

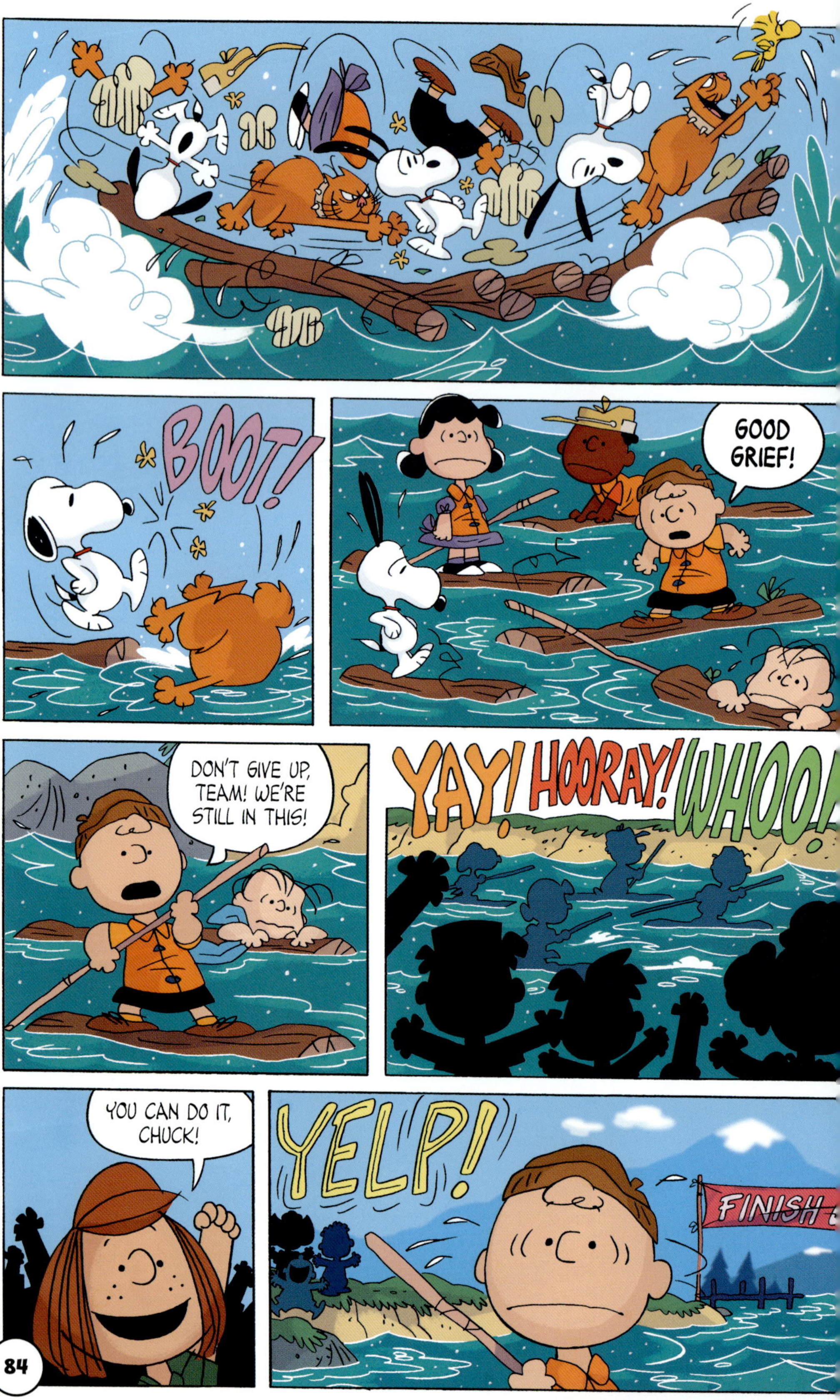
BOOT!
GOOD GRIEF!
DON'T GIVE UP, TEAM! WE'RE STILL IN THIS!
YAY! HOORAY! WHOO!
YOU CAN DO IT, CHUCK!
YELP!
FINISH

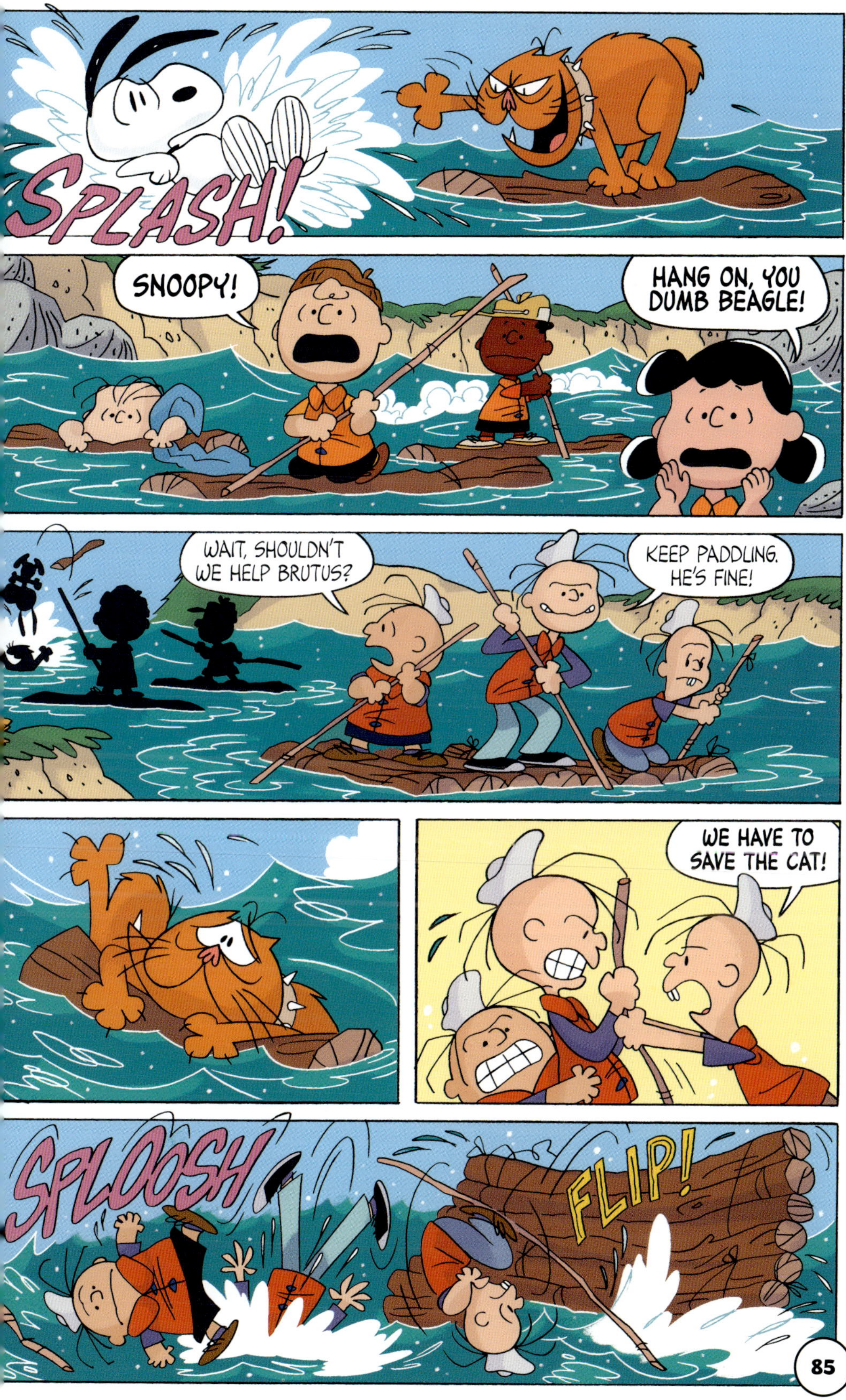
SPLASH!
SNOOPY!
HANG ON, YOU DUMB BEAGLE!
WAIT, SHOULDN'T WE HELP BRUTUS?
KEEP PADDLING. HE'S FINE!
WE HAVE TO SAVE THE CAT!
SPLOOSH
FLIP!

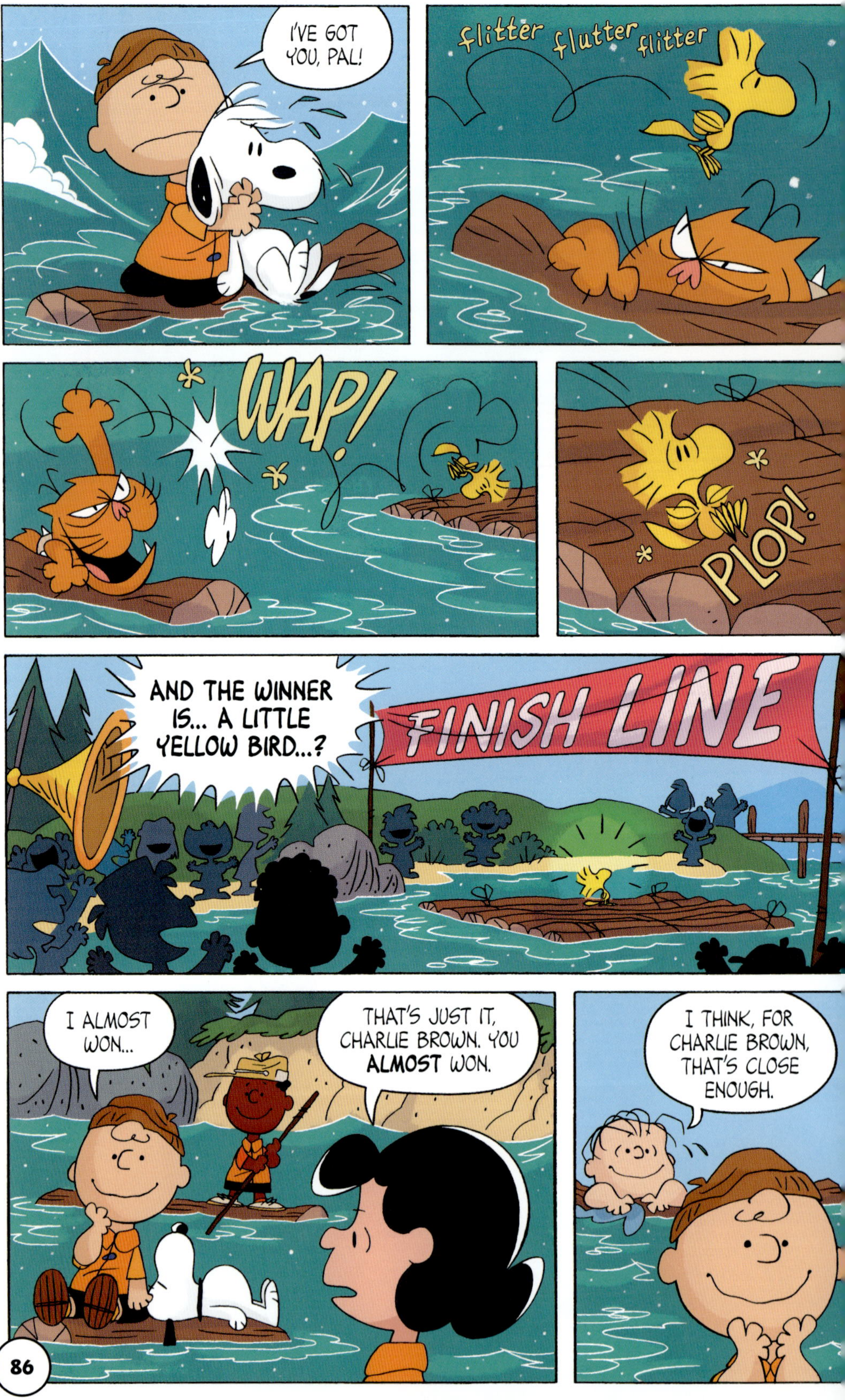
I'VE GOT YOU, PAL!
flitter flutter flitter
WAP!
PLOP!
AND THE WINNER IS... A LITTLE YELLOW BIRD...?
FINISH LINE
I ALMOST WON...
THAT'S JUST IT, CHARLIE BROWN. YOU **ALMOST** WON.
I THINK, FOR CHARLIE BROWN, THAT'S CLOSE ENOUGH.

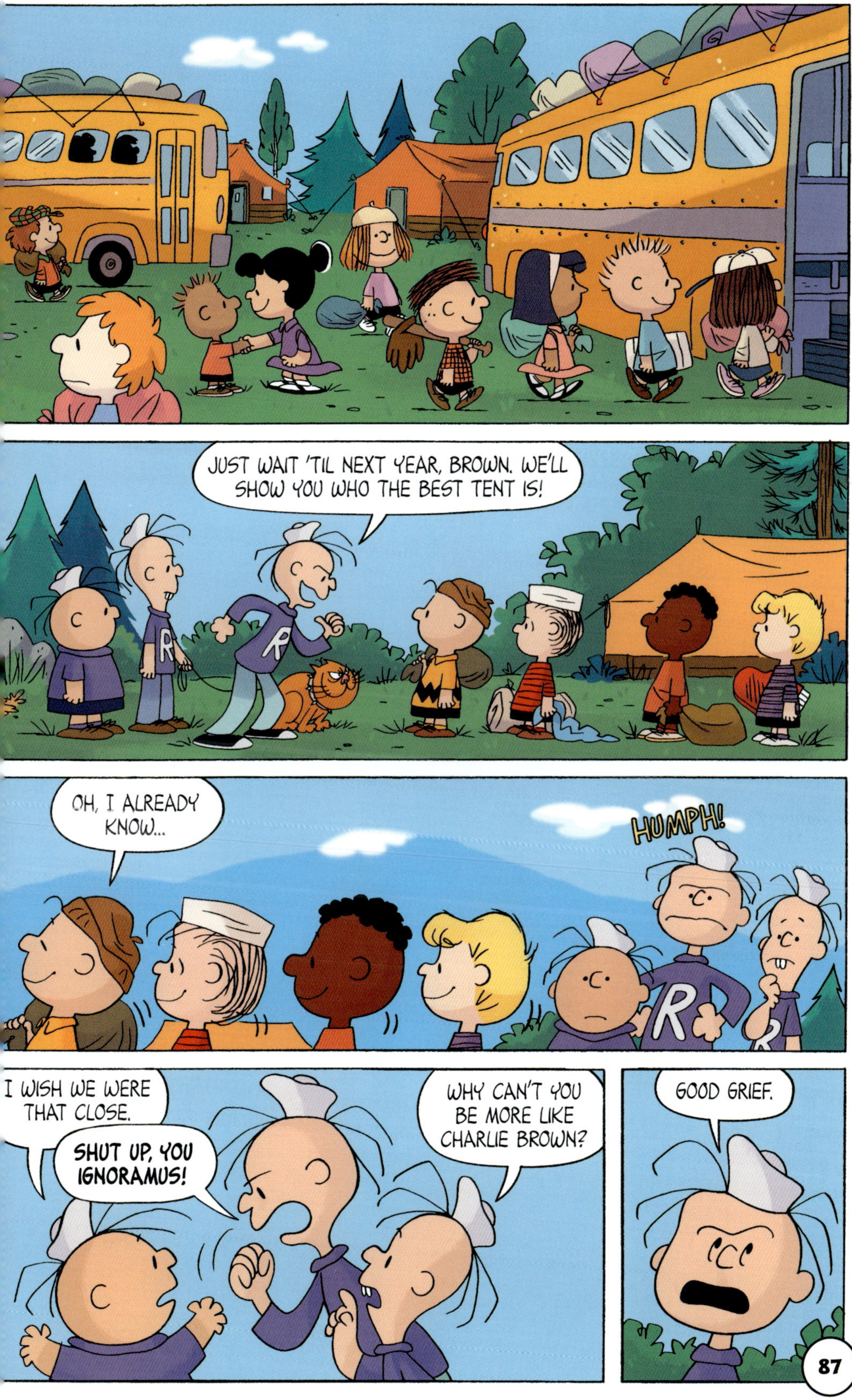

JUST WAIT 'TIL NEXT YEAR, BROWN. WE'LL SHOW YOU WHO THE BEST TENT IS!
OH, I ALREADY KNOW...
HUMPH!
I WISH WE WERE THAT CLOSE.
SHUT UP, YOU IGNORAMUS!
WHY CAN'T YOU BE MORE LIKE CHARLIE BROWN?
GOOD GRIEF.

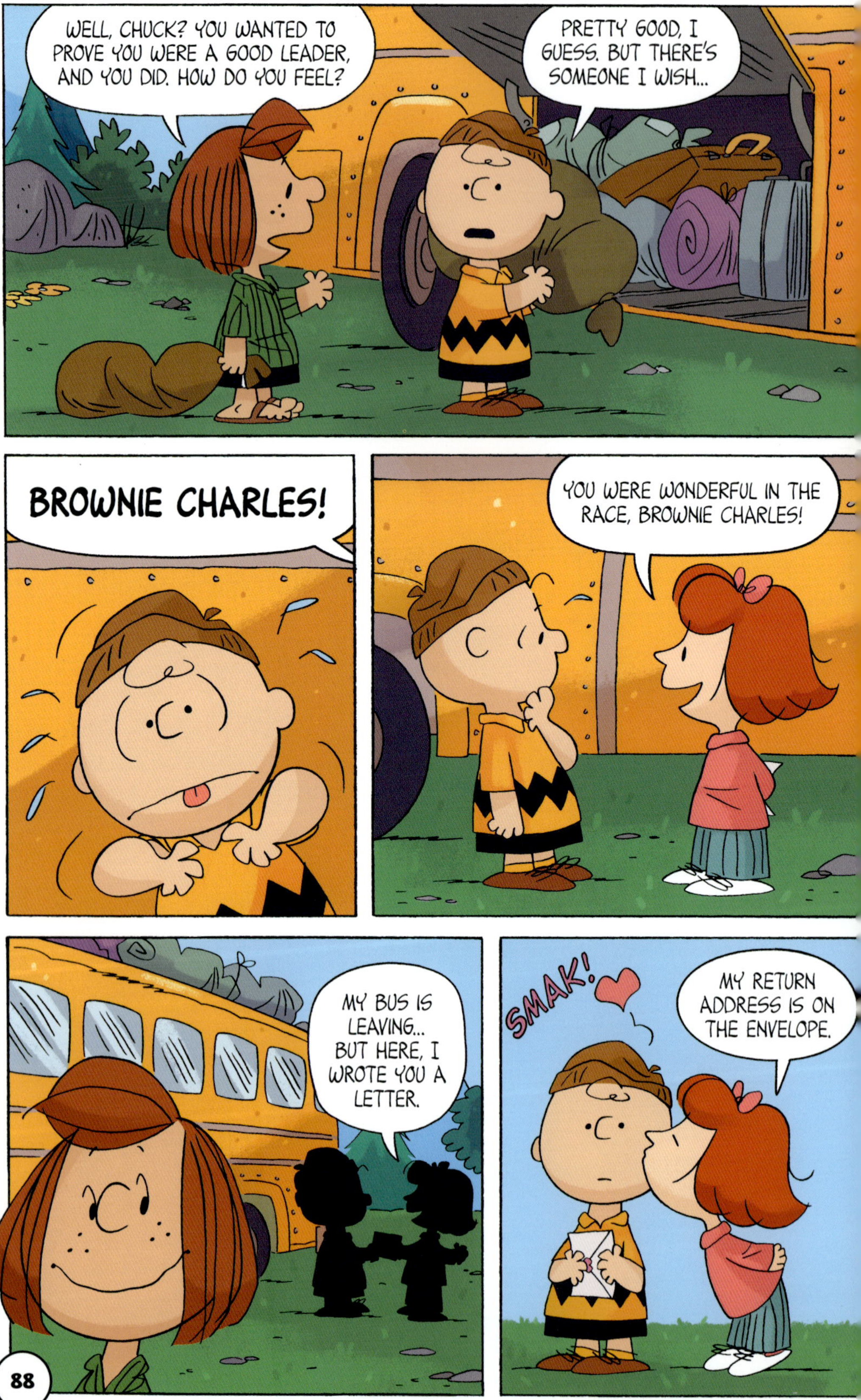
WELL, CHUCK? YOU WANTED TO PROVE YOU WERE A GOOD LEADER, AND YOU DID. HOW DO YOU FEEL?
PRETTY GOOD, I GUESS. BUT THERE'S SOMEONE I WISH...
BROWNIE CHARLES!
YOU WERE WONDERFUL IN THE RACE, BROWNIE CHARLES!
MY BUS IS LEAVING... BUT HERE, I WROTE YOU A LETTER.
SMAK!
MY RETURN ADDRESS IS ON THE ENVELOPE.

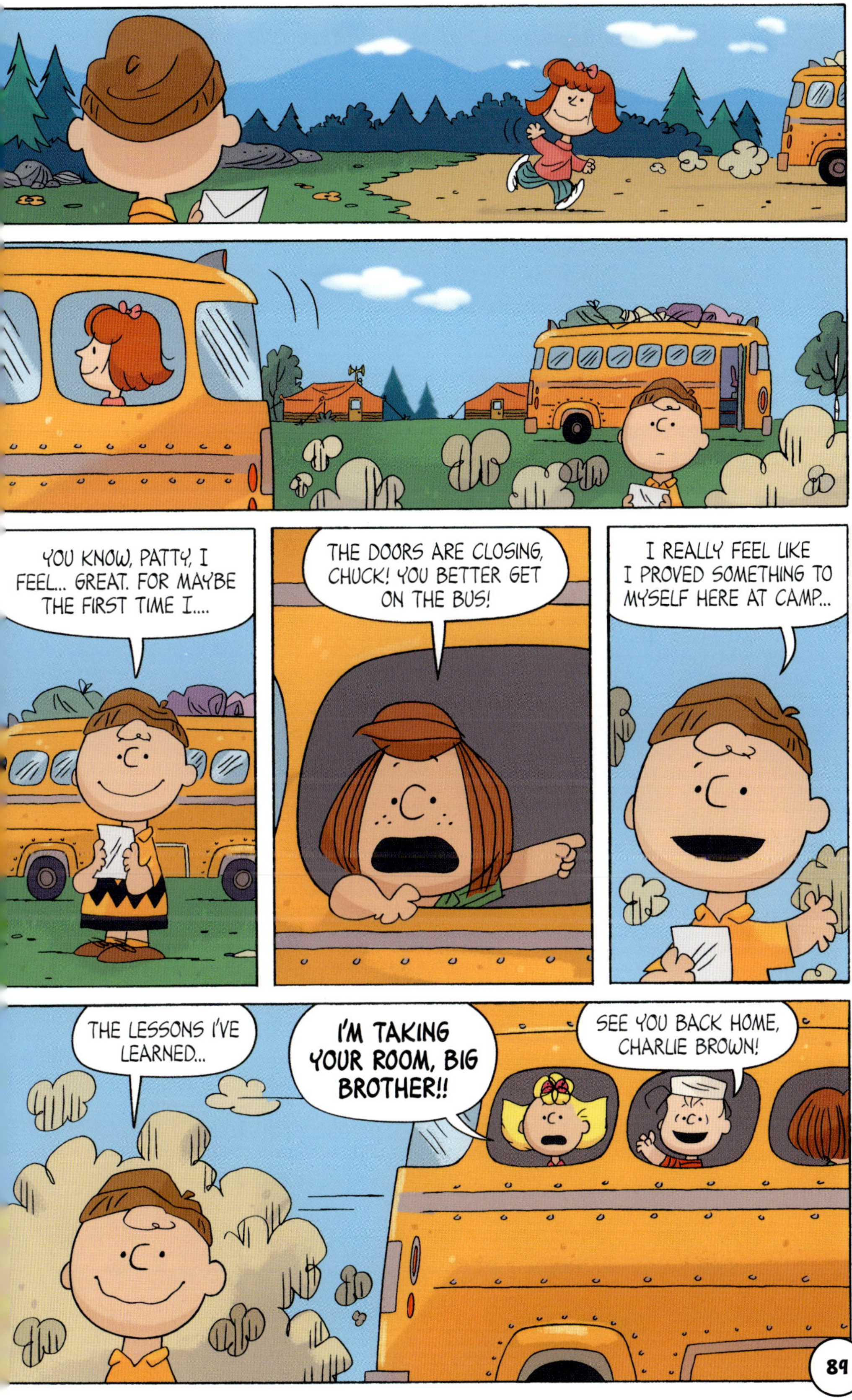
YOU KNOW, PATTY, I FEEL... GREAT. FOR MAYBE THE FIRST TIME I....
THE DOORS ARE CLOSING, CHUCK! YOU BETTER GET ON THE BUS!
I REALLY FEEL LIKE I PROVED SOMETHING TO MYSELF HERE AT CAMP...
THE LESSONS I'VE LEARNED...
I'M TAKING YOUR ROOM, BIG BROTHER!!
SEE YOU BACK HOME, CHARLIE BROWN!

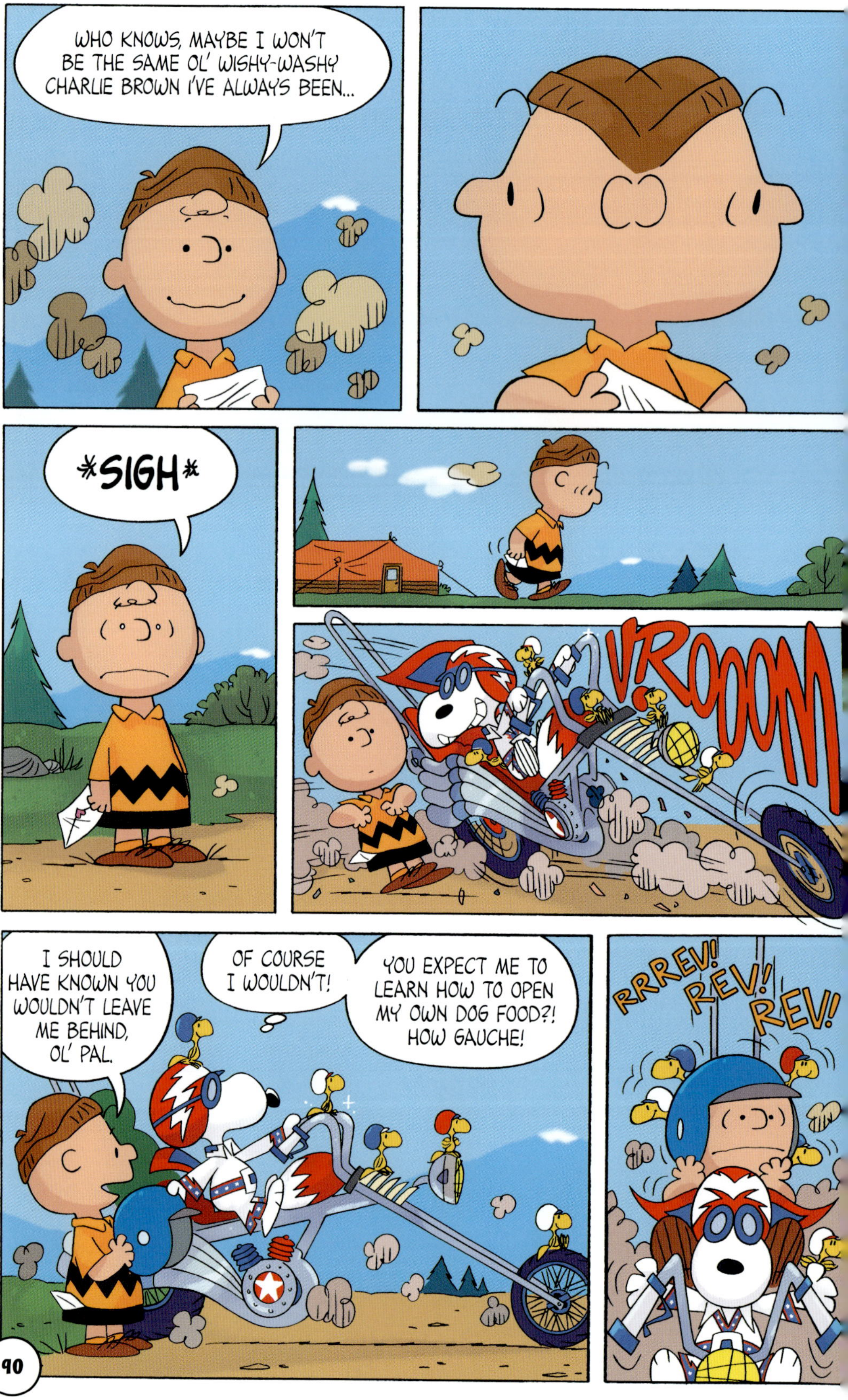
WHO KNOWS, MAYBE I WON'T BE THE SAME OL' WISHY-WASHY CHARLIE BROWN I'VE ALWAYS BEEN...
SIGH
VROOOM
I SHOULD HAVE KNOWN YOU WOULDN'T LEAVE ME BEHIND, OL' PAL.
OF COURSE I WOULDN'T!
YOU EXPECT ME TO LEARN HOW TO OPEN MY OWN DOG FOOD?! HOW GAUCHE!
RRREV! REV! REV!

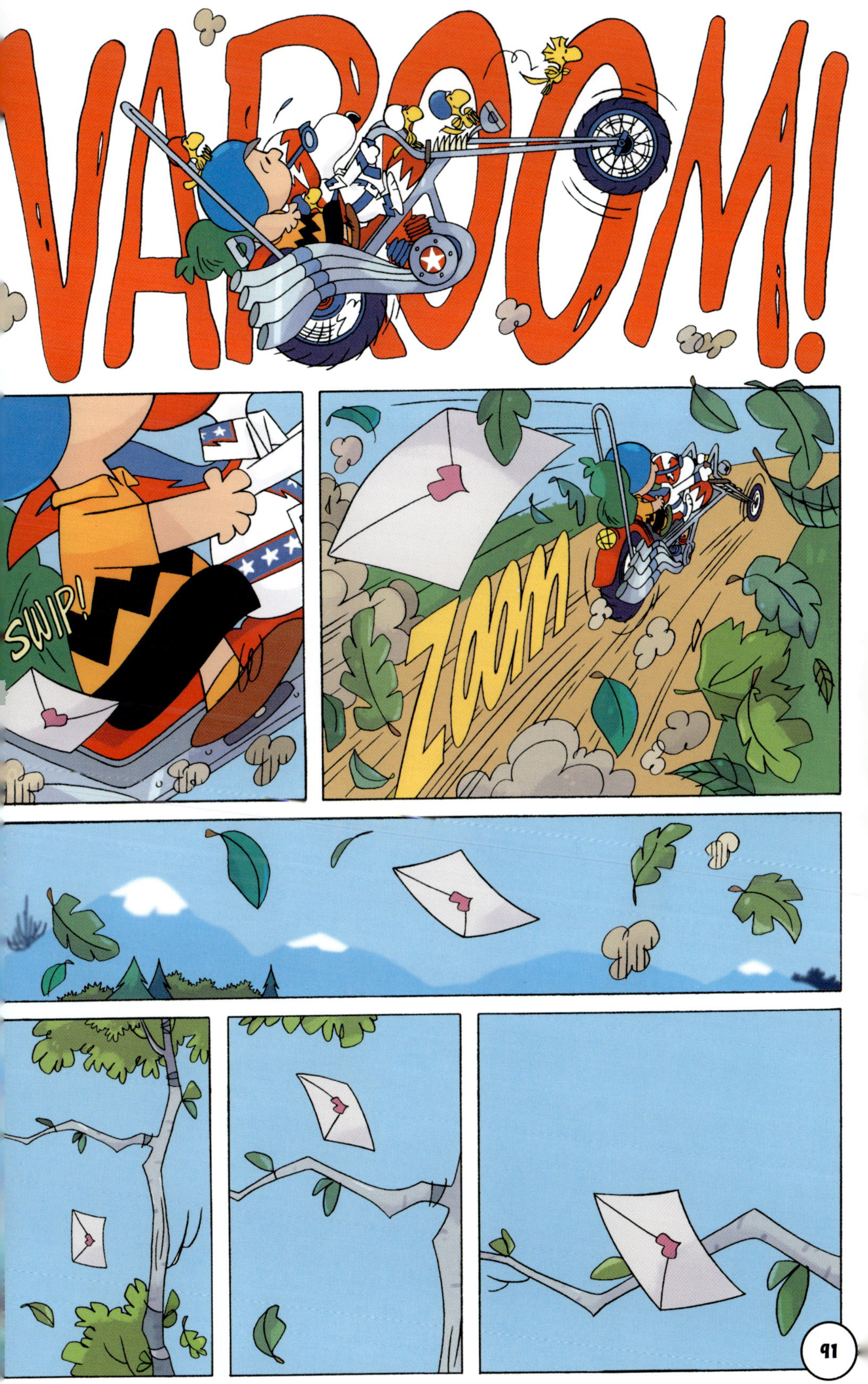
VAROOM!
SWIP!
ZOOM

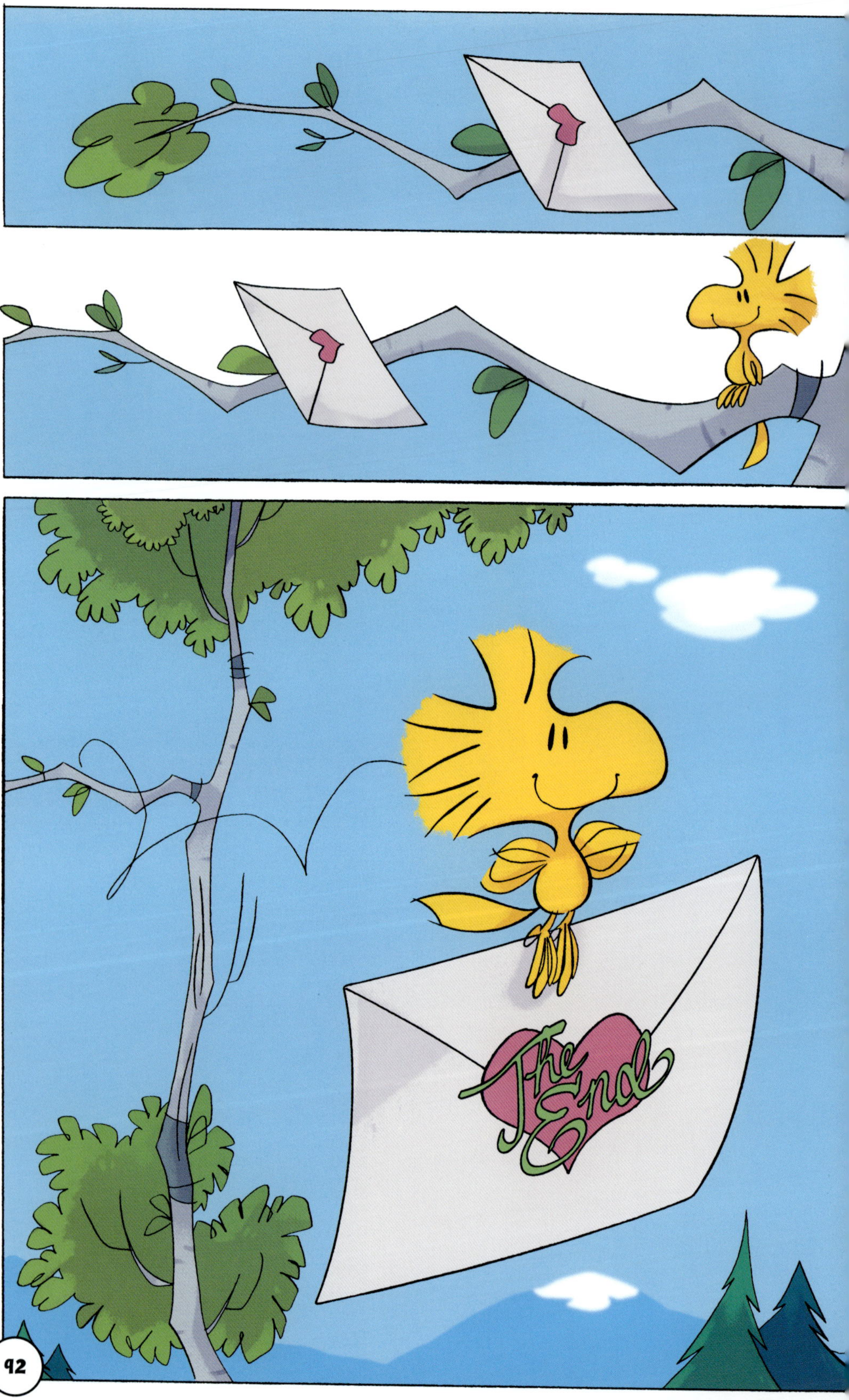
The End

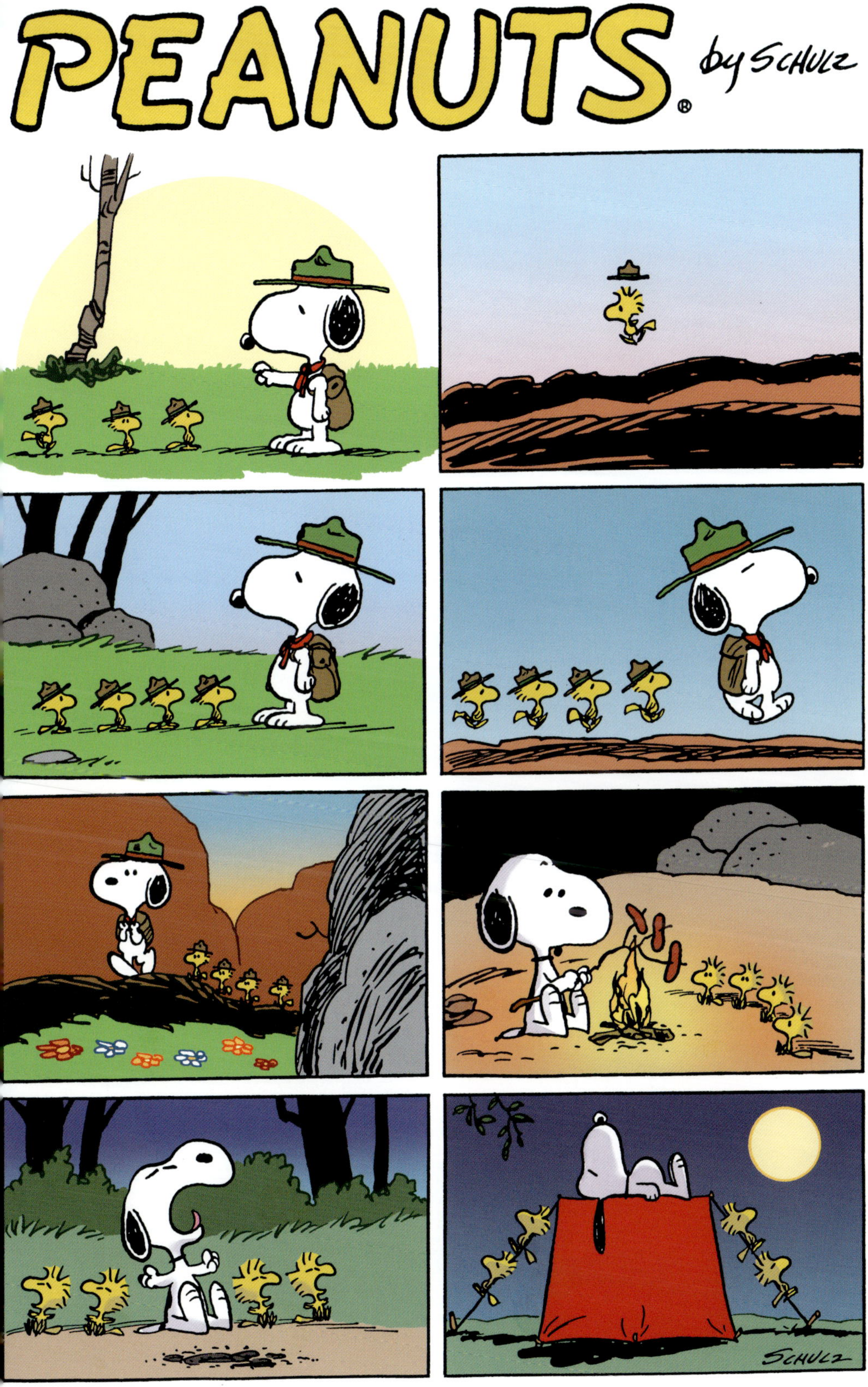
PEANUTS
by SCHULZ
SCHULZ

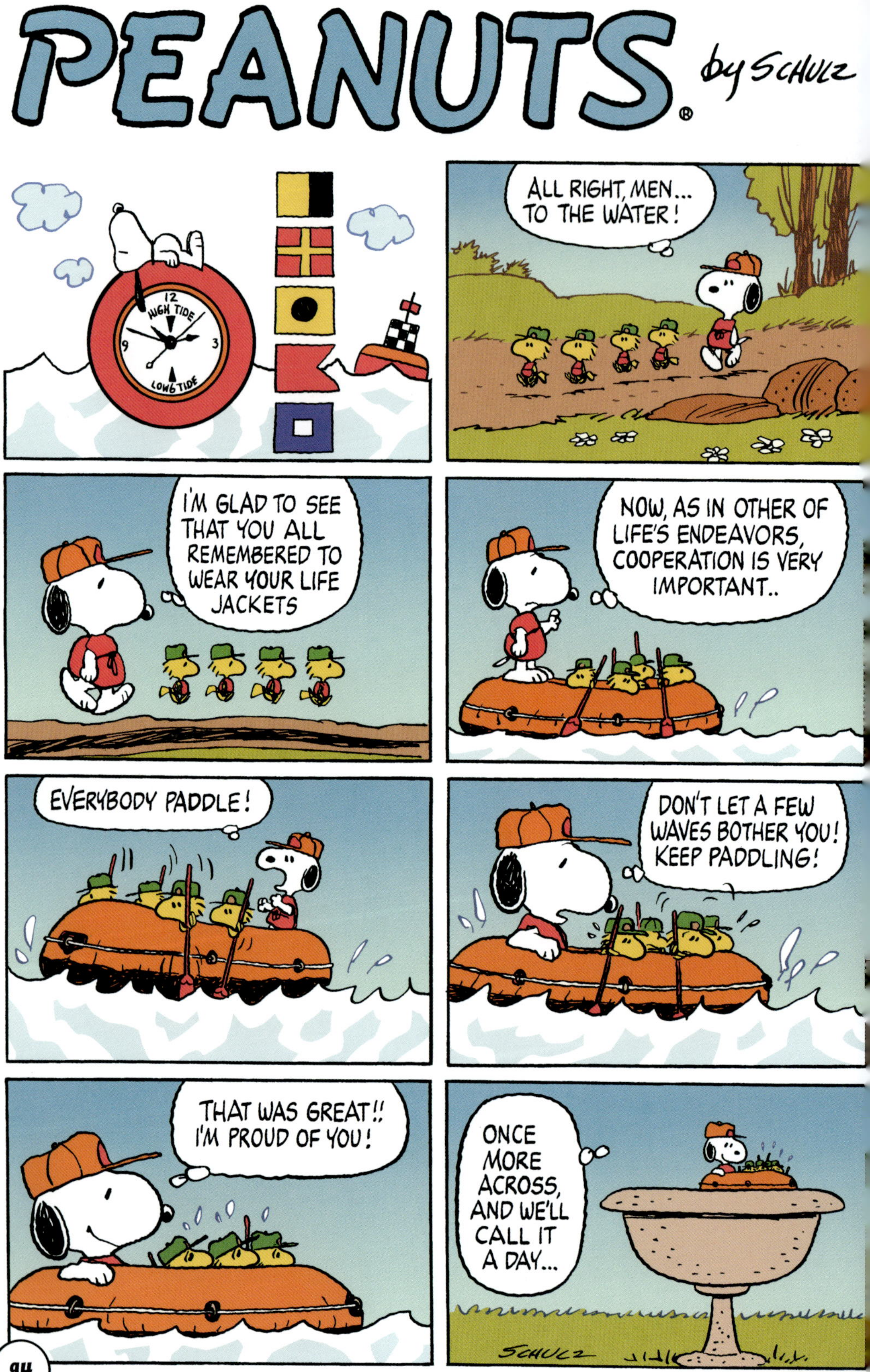
PEANUTS
by SCHULZ
12
HIGH TIDE
9
3
LOW TIDE
ALL RIGHT, MEN... TO THE WATER!
I'M GLAD TO SEE THAT YOU ALL REMEMBERED TO WEAR YOUR LIFE JACKETS
NOW, AS IN OTHER OF LIFE'S ENDEAVORS, COOPERATION IS VERY IMPORTANT..
EVERYBODY PADDLE!
DON'T LET A FEW WAVES BOTHER YOU! KEEP PADDLING!
THAT WAS GREAT!! I'M PROUD OF YOU!
ONCE MORE ACROSS, AND WE'LL CALL IT A DAY...
SCHULZ

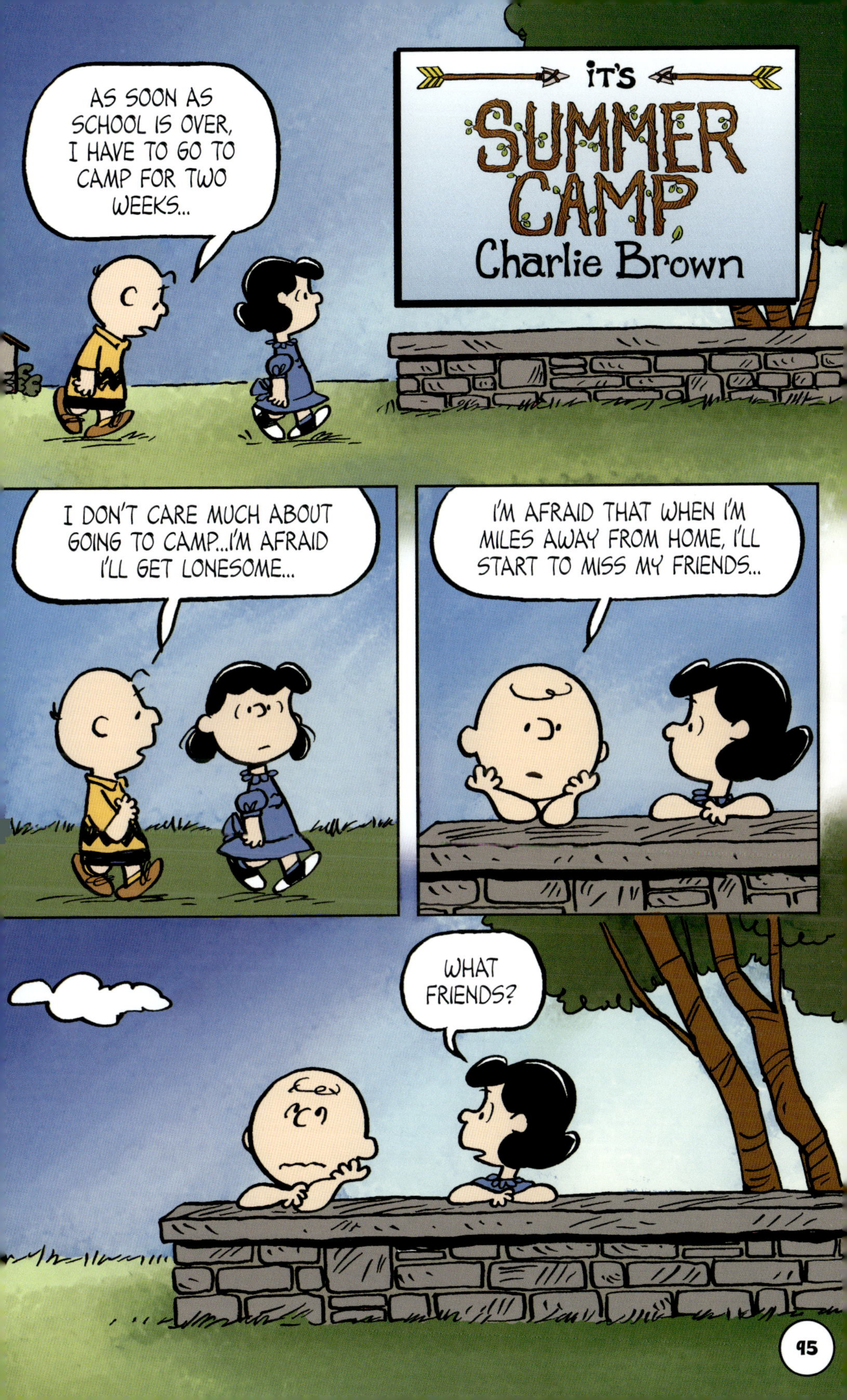
AS SOON AS SCHOOL IS OVER, I HAVE TO GO TO CAMP FOR TWO WEEKS...
IT'S
SUMMER CAMP
Charlie Brown
I DON'T CARE MUCH ABOUT GOING TO CAMP...I'M AFRAID I'LL GET LONESOME...
I'M AFRAID THAT WHEN I'M MILES AWAY FROM HOME, I'LL START TO MISS MY FRIENDS...
WHAT FRIENDS?

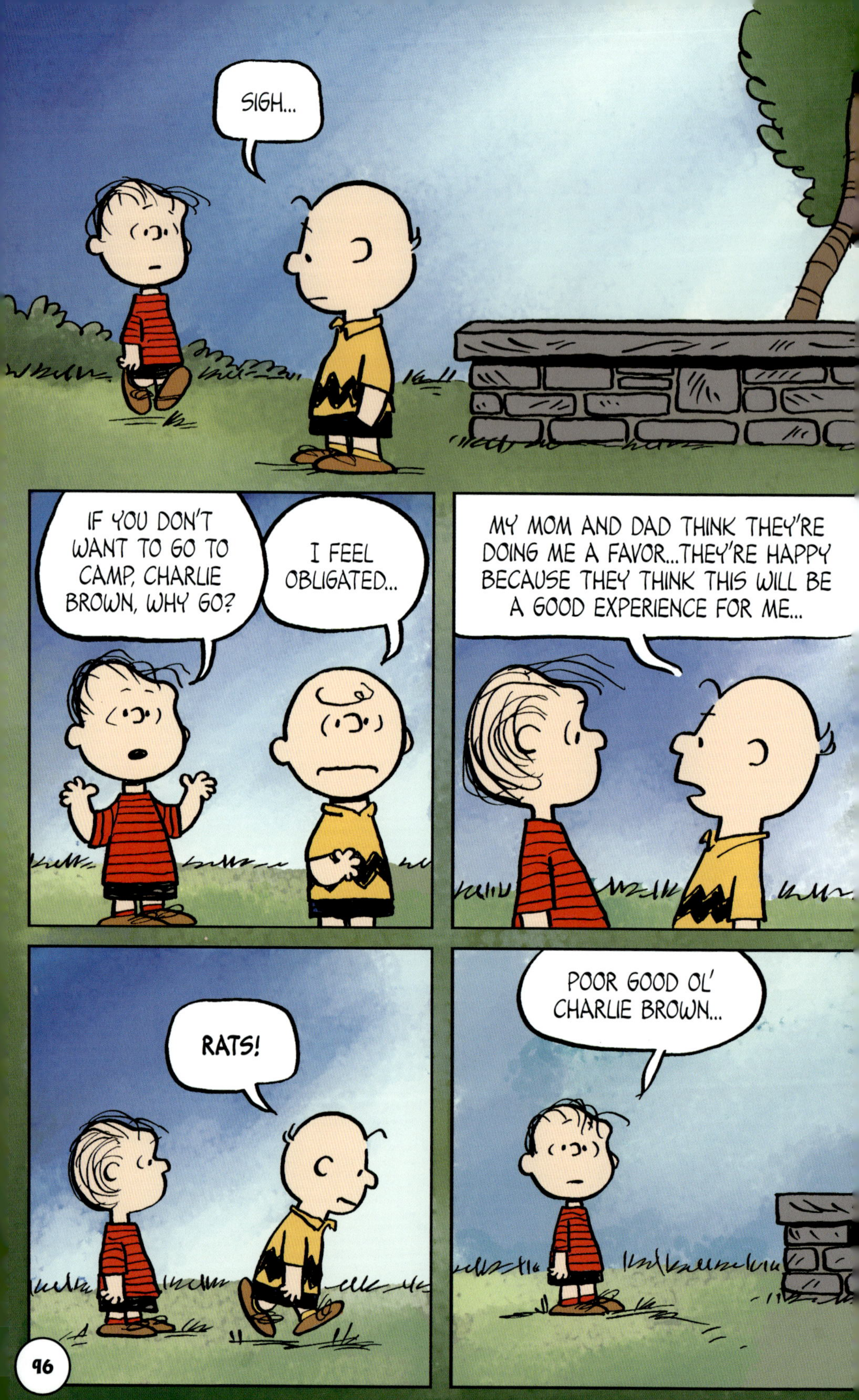
SIGH...
IF YOU DON'T WANT TO GO TO CAMP, CHARLIE BROWN, WHY GO?
I FEEL OBLIGATED...
MY MOM AND DAD THINK THEY'RE DOING ME A FAVOR...THEY'RE HAPPY BECAUSE THEY THINK THIS WILL BE A GOOD EXPERIENCE FOR ME...
RATS!
POOR GOOD OL' CHARLIE BROWN...

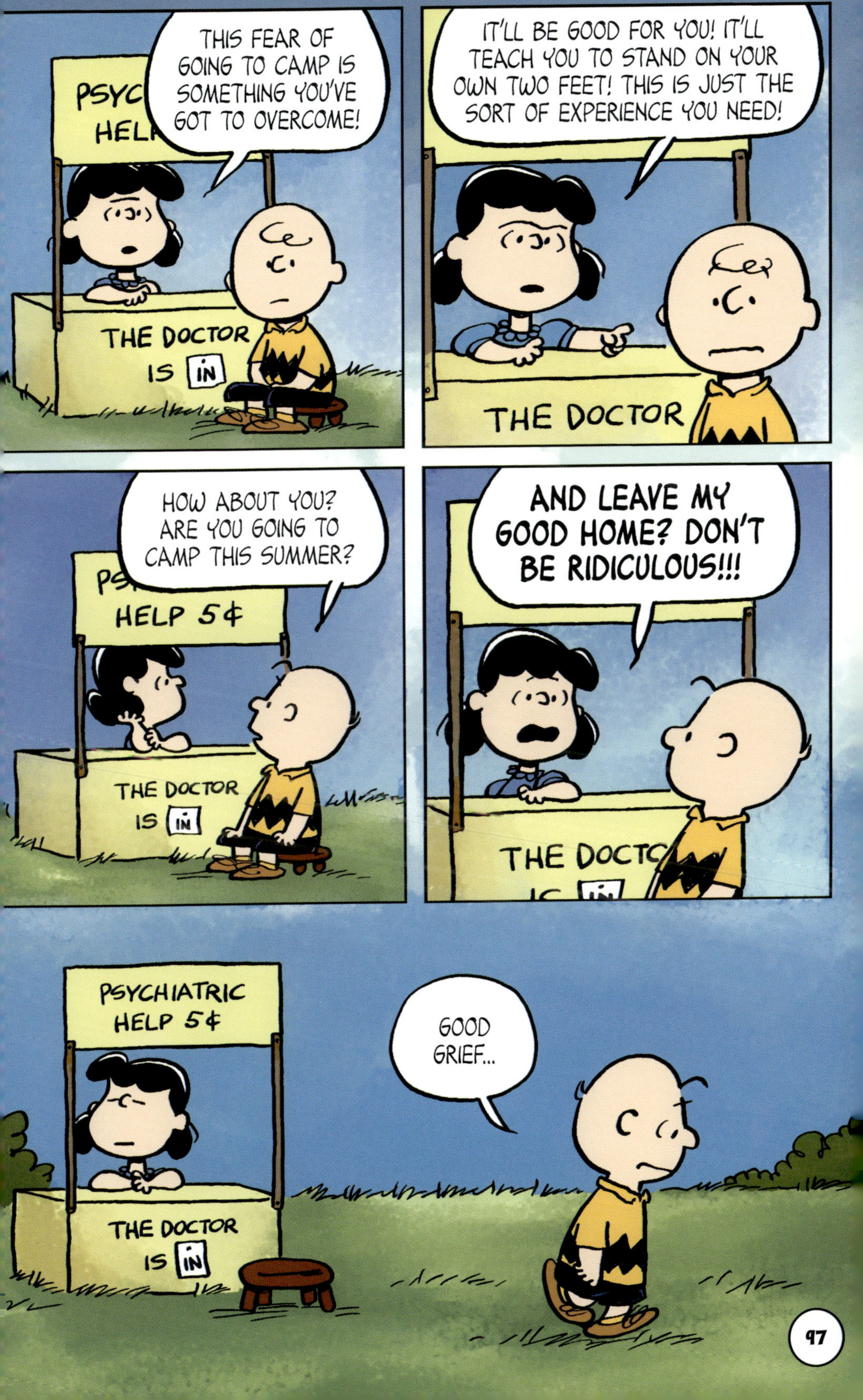
THIS FEAR OF GOING TO CAMP IS SOMETHING YOU'VE GOT TO OVERCOME!
THE DOCTOR IS IN
IT'LL BE GOOD FOR YOU! IT'LL TEACH YOU TO STAND ON YOUR OWN TWO FEET! THIS IS JUST THE SORT OF EXPERIENCE YOU NEED!
THE DOCTOR
HOW ABOUT YOU? ARE YOU GOING TO CAMP THIS SUMMER?
HELP 5¢
THE DOCTOR IS IN
AND LEAVE MY GOOD HOME? DON'T BE RIDICULOUS!!!
PSYCHIATRIC HELP 5¢
THE DOCTOR IS IN
GOOD GRIEF...

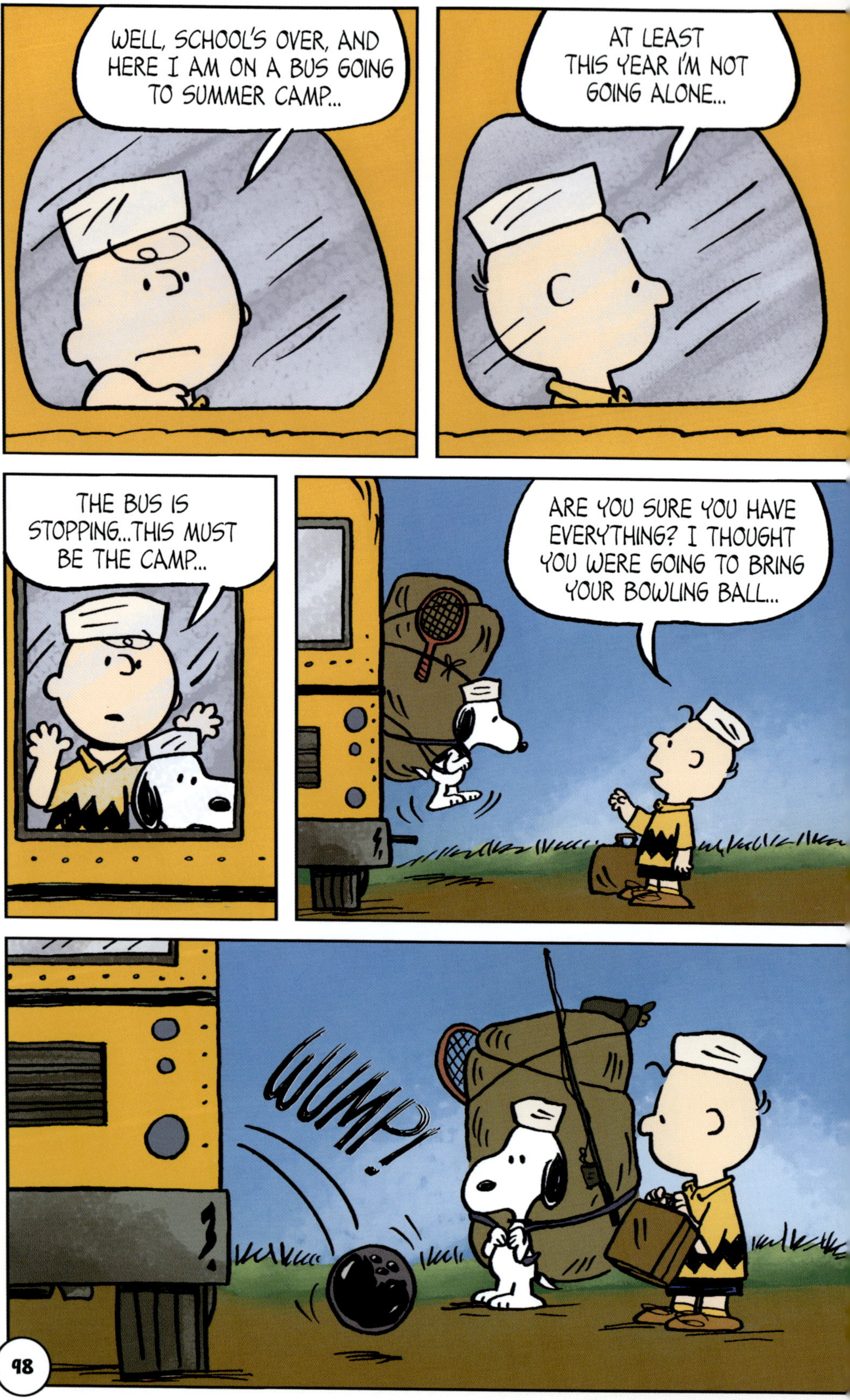
WELL, SCHOOL'S OVER, AND HERE I AM ON A BUS GOING TO SUMMER CAMP...
AT LEAST THIS YEAR I'M NOT GOING ALONE...
THE BUS IS STOPPING...THIS MUST BE THE CAMP...
ARE YOU SURE YOU HAVE EVERYTHING? I THOUGHT YOU WERE GOING TO BRING YOUR BOWLING BALL...
WUMP!

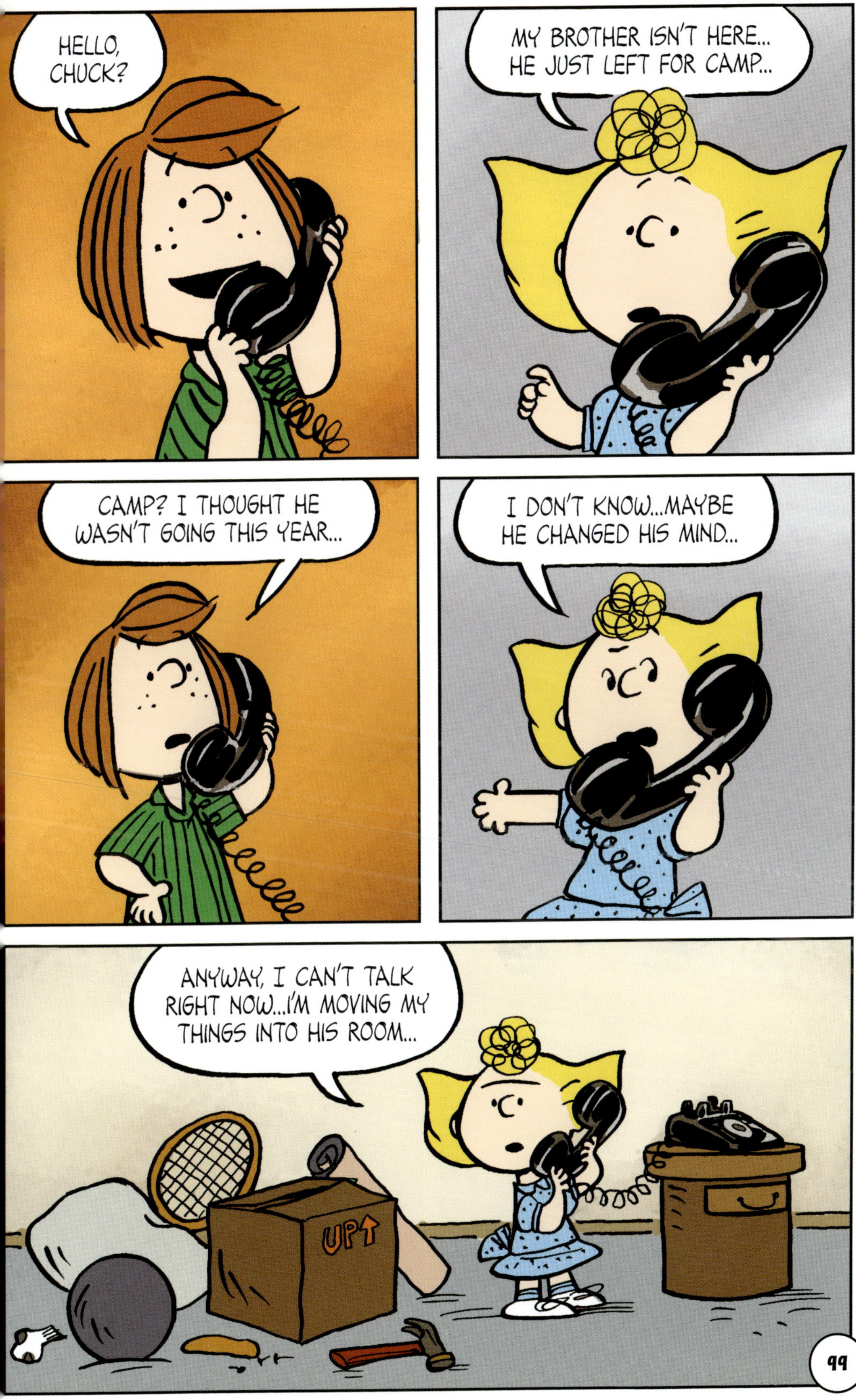
HELLO, CHUCK?
MY BROTHER ISN'T HERE... HE JUST LEFT FOR CAMP...
CAMP? I THOUGHT HE WASN'T GOING THIS YEAR...
I DON'T KNOW...MAYBE HE CHANGED HIS MIND...
ANYWAY, I CAN'T TALK RIGHT NOW...I'M MOVING MY THINGS INTO HIS ROOM...
UP

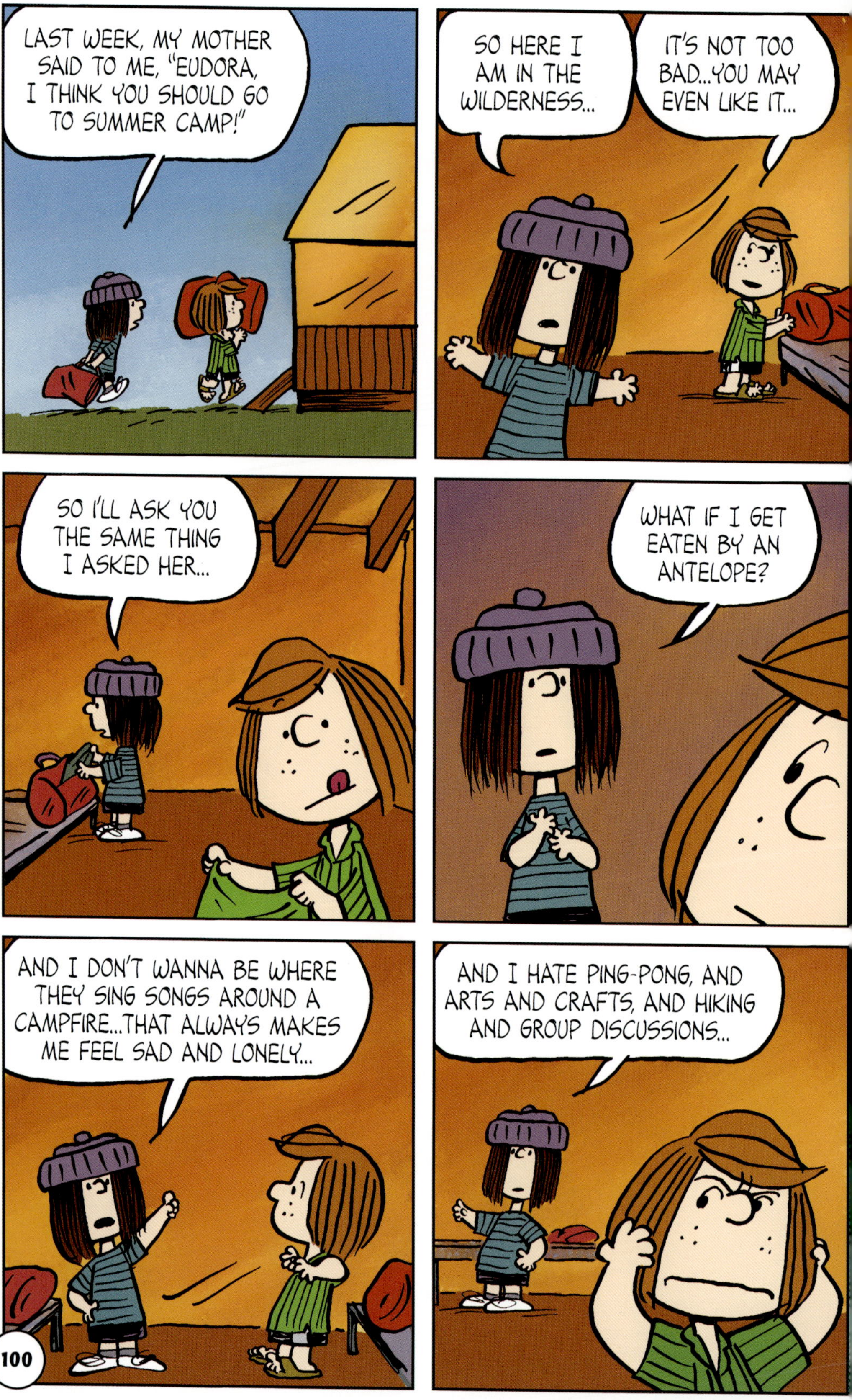
LAST WEEK, MY MOTHER SAID TO ME, "EUDORA, I THINK YOU SHOULD GO TO SUMMER CAMP!"
SO HERE I AM IN THE WILDERNESS...
IT'S NOT TOO BAD...YOU MAY EVEN LIKE IT...
SO I'LL ASK YOU THE SAME THING I ASKED HER...
WHAT IF I GET EATEN BY AN ANTELOPE?
AND I DON'T WANNA BE WHERE THEY SING SONGS AROUND A CAMPFIRE...THAT ALWAYS MAKES ME FEEL SAD AND LONELY...
AND I HATE PING-PONG, AND ARTS AND CRAFTS, AND HIKING AND GROUP DISCUSSIONS...

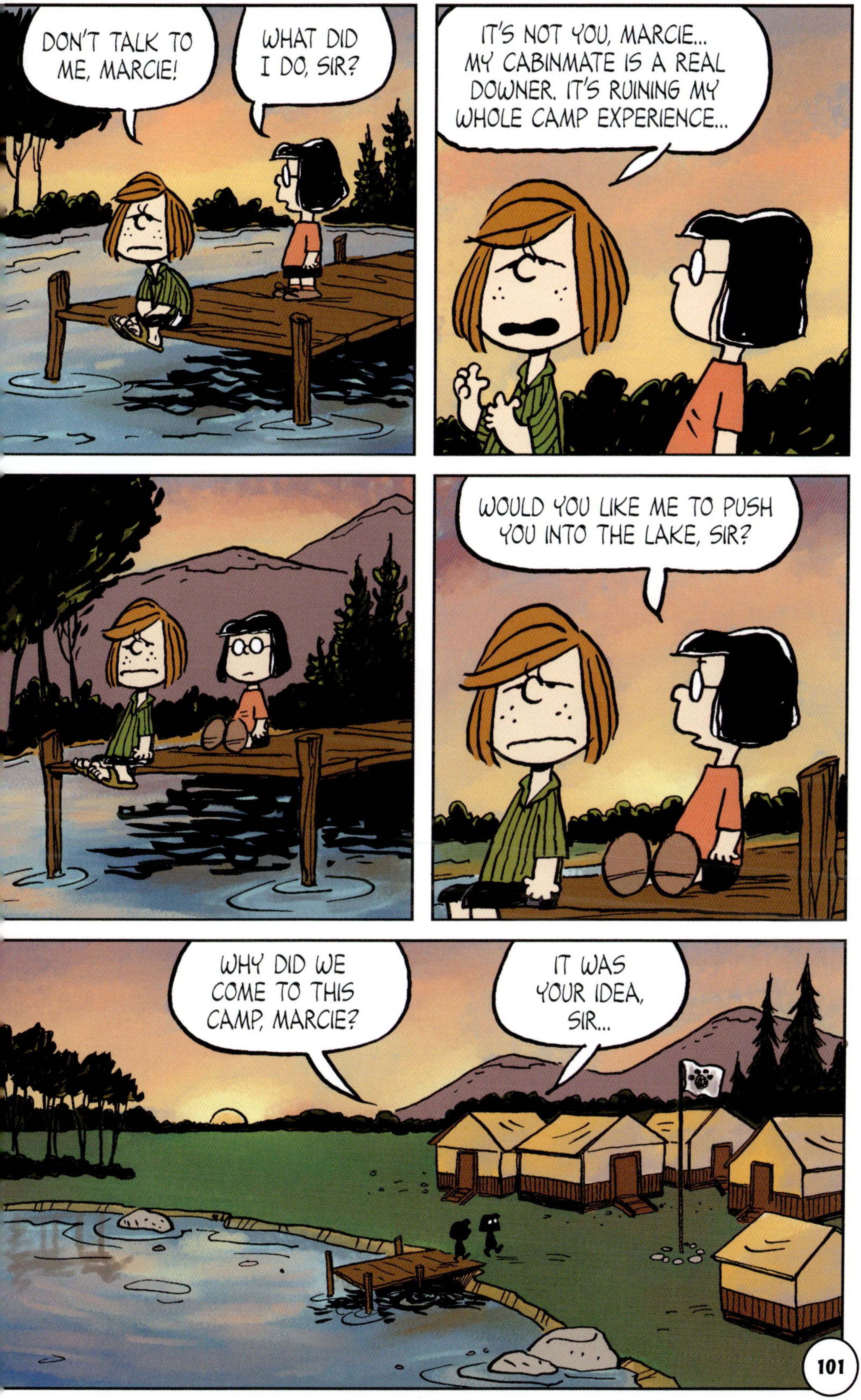
DON'T TALK TO ME, MARCIE!
WHAT DID I DO, SIR?
IT'S NOT YOU, MARCIE... MY CABINMATE IS A REAL DOWNER. IT'S RUINING MY WHOLE CAMP EXPERIENCE...
WOULD YOU LIKE ME TO PUSH YOU INTO THE LAKE, SIR?
WHY DID WE COME TO THIS CAMP, MARCIE?
IT WAS YOUR IDEA, SIR...

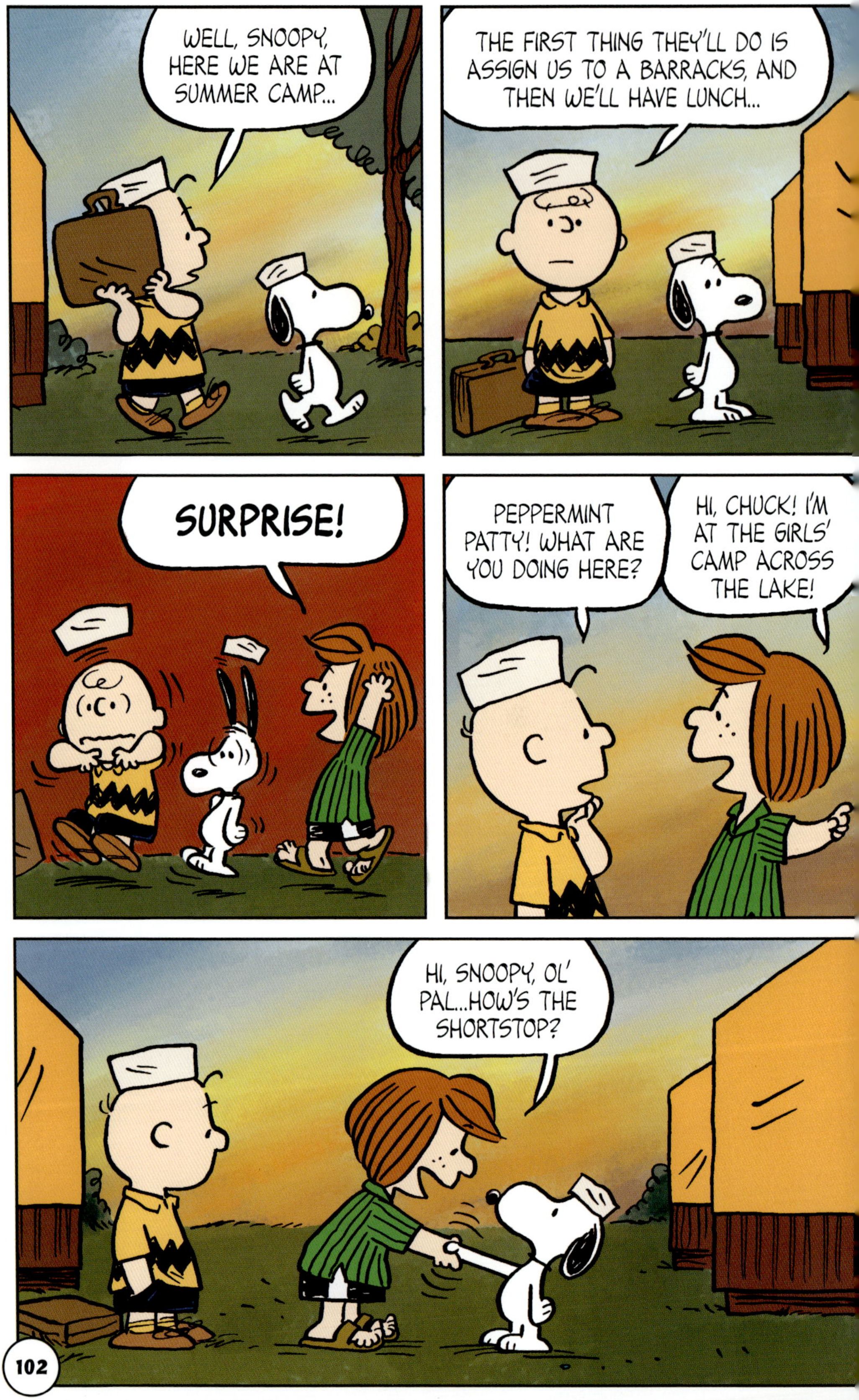
WELL, SNOOPY, HERE WE ARE AT SUMMER CAMP...
THE FIRST THING THEY'LL DO IS ASSIGN US TO A BARRACKS, AND THEN WE'LL HAVE LUNCH...
SURPRISE!
PEPPERMINT PATTY! WHAT ARE YOU DOING HERE?
HI, CHUCK! I'M AT THE GIRLS' CAMP ACROSS THE LAKE!
HI, SNOOPY, OL' PAL...HOW'S THE SHORTSTOP?

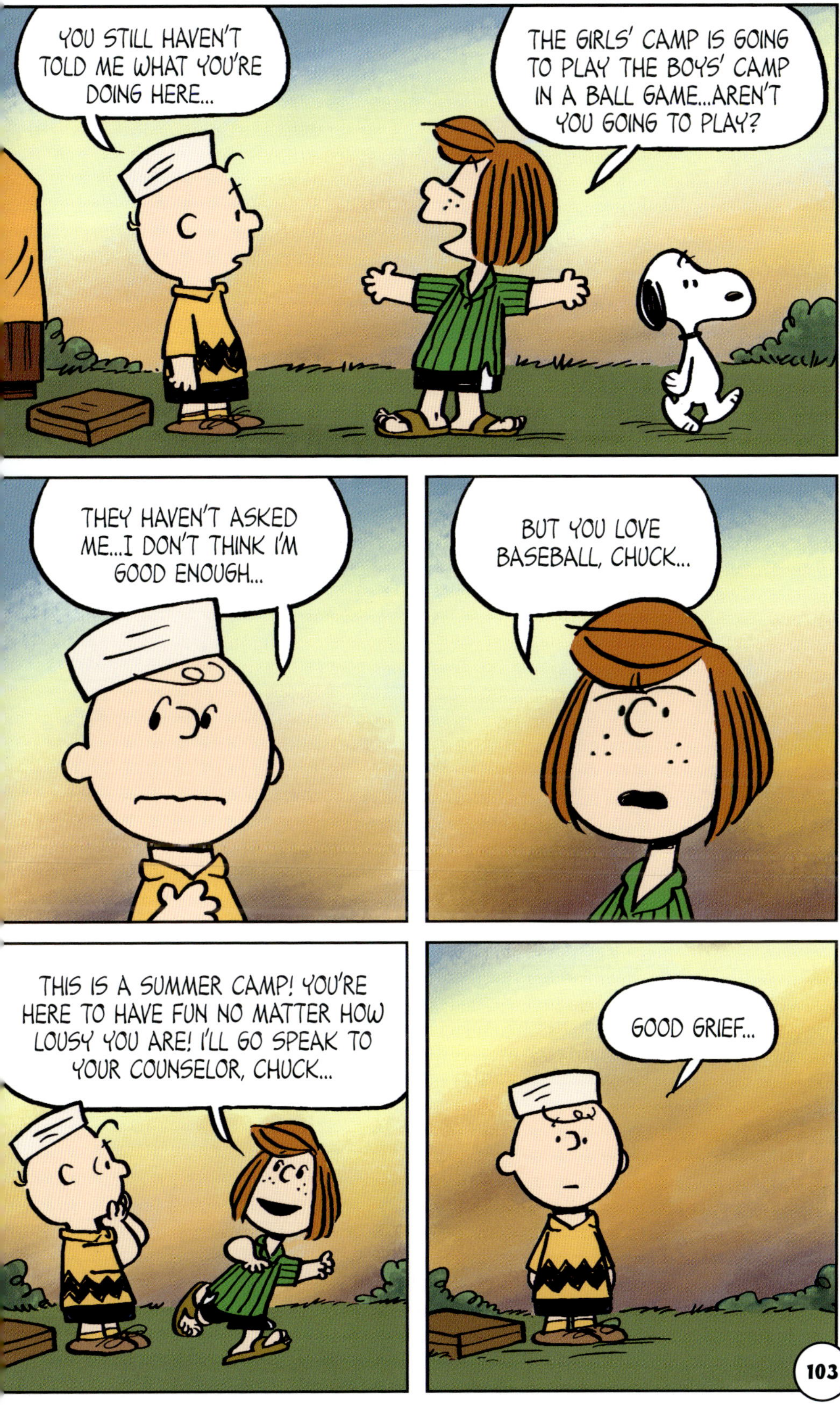
YOU STILL HAVEN'T TOLD ME WHAT YOU'RE DOING HERE...
THE GIRLS' CAMP IS GOING TO PLAY THE BOYS' CAMP IN A BALL GAME...AREN'T YOU GOING TO PLAY?
THEY HAVEN'T ASKED ME...I DON'T THINK I'M GOOD ENOUGH...
BUT YOU LOVE BASEBALL, CHUCK...
THIS IS A SUMMER CAMP! YOU'RE HERE TO HAVE FUN NO MATTER HOW LOUSY YOU ARE! I'LL GO SPEAK TO YOUR COUNSELOR, CHUCK...
GOOD GRIEF...

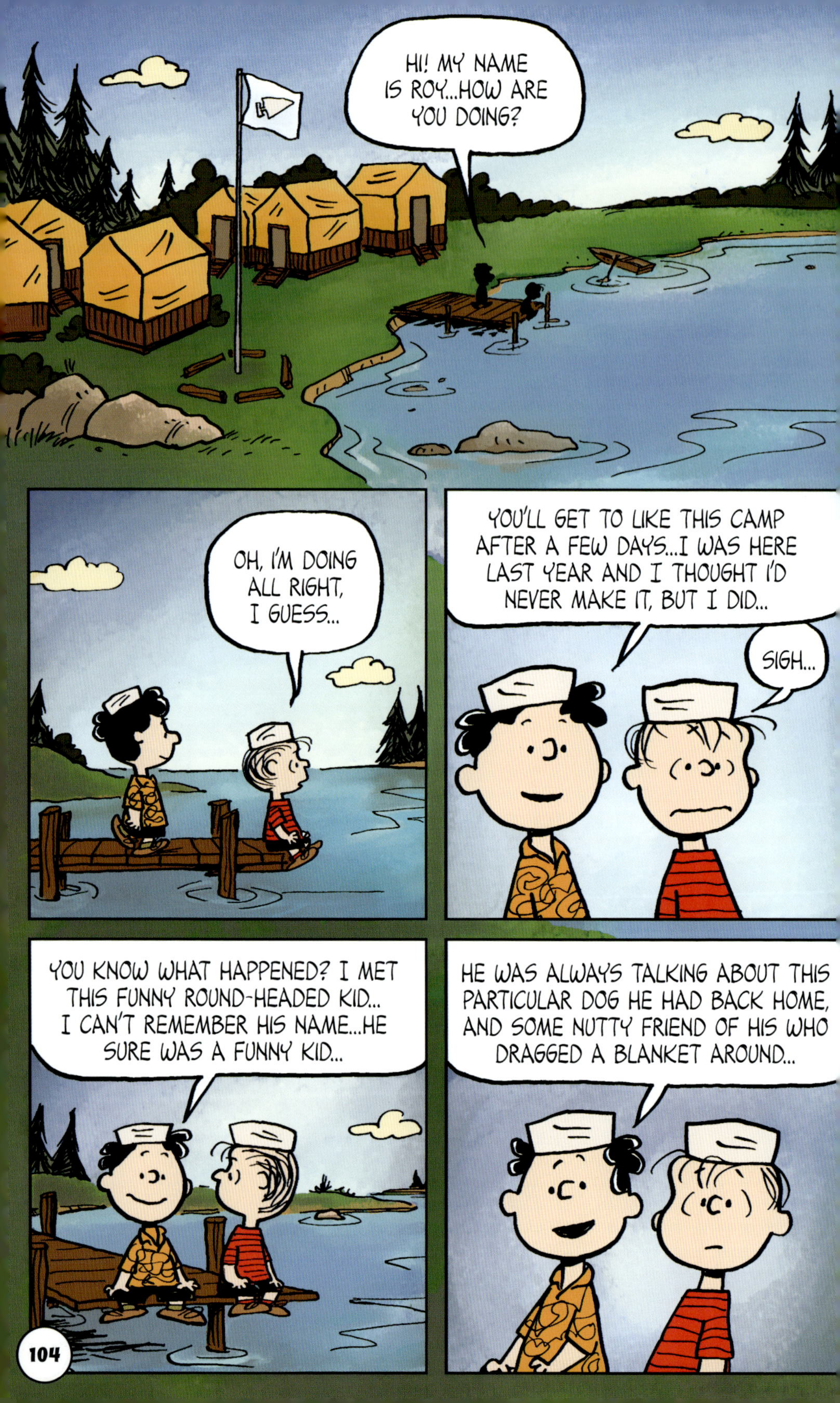
HI! MY NAME IS ROY...HOW ARE YOU DOING?
OH, I'M DOING ALL RIGHT, I GUESS...
YOU'LL GET TO LIKE THIS CAMP AFTER A FEW DAYS...I WAS HERE LAST YEAR AND I THOUGHT I'D NEVER MAKE IT, BUT I DID...
SIGH...
YOU KNOW WHAT HAPPENED? I MET THIS FUNNY ROUND-HEADED KID... I CAN'T REMEMBER HIS NAME...HE SURE WAS A FUNNY KID...
HE WAS ALWAYS TALKING ABOUT THIS PARTICULAR DOG HE HAD BACK HOME, AND SOME NUTTY FRIEND OF HIS WHO DRAGGED A BLANKET AROUND...

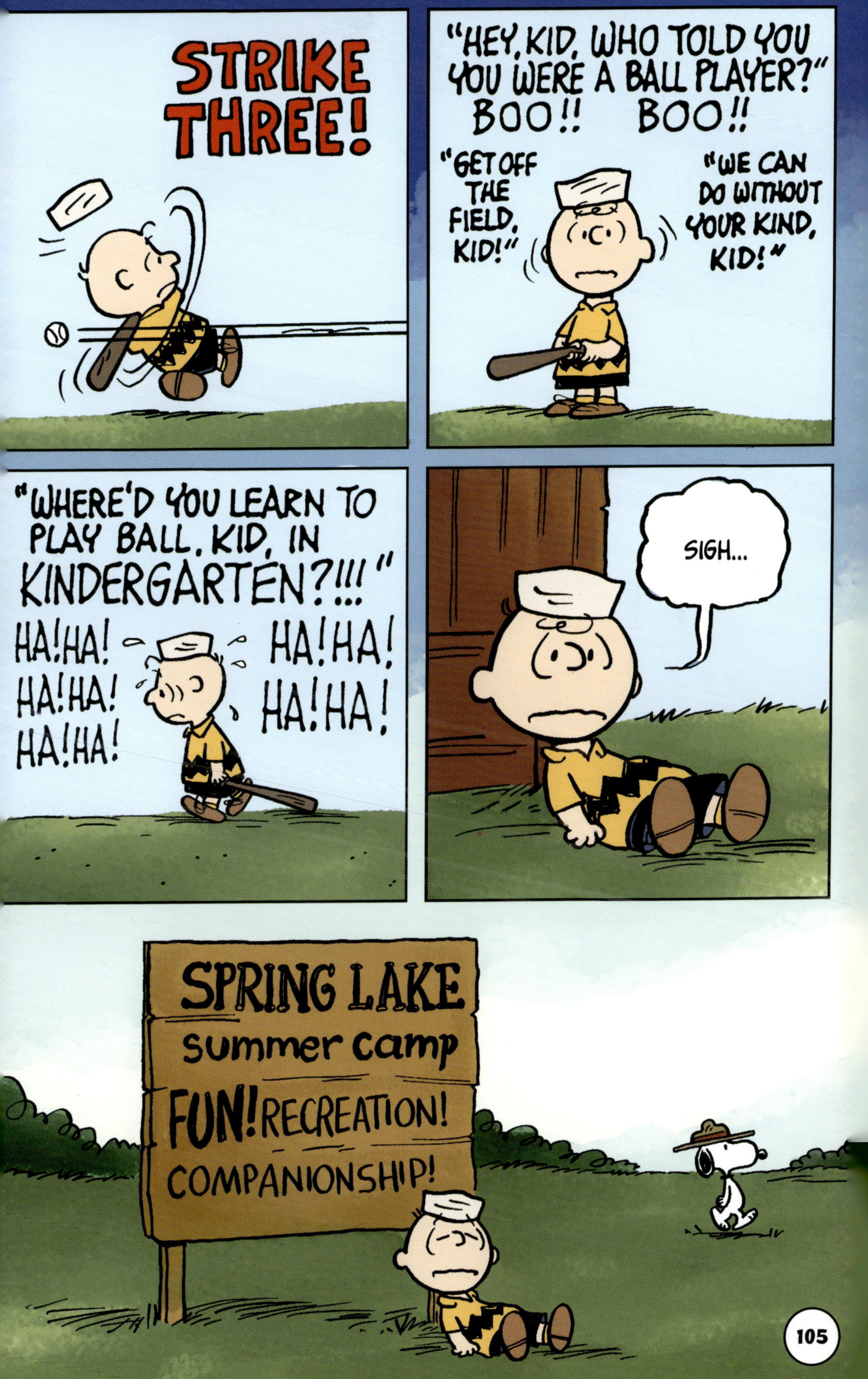
STRIKE THREE!
"HEY, KID, WHO TOLD YOU YOU WERE A BALL PLAYER?"
BOO!! BOO!!
"GET OFF THE FIELD, KID!"
"WE CAN DO WITHOUT YOUR KIND, KID!"
"WHERE'D YOU LEARN TO PLAY BALL, KID, IN KINDERGARTEN?!!!"
HA!HA! HA!HA! HA!HA!
HA!HA! HA!HA!
SIGH...
SPRING LAKE
summer camp
FUN! RECREATION!
COMPANIONSHIP!

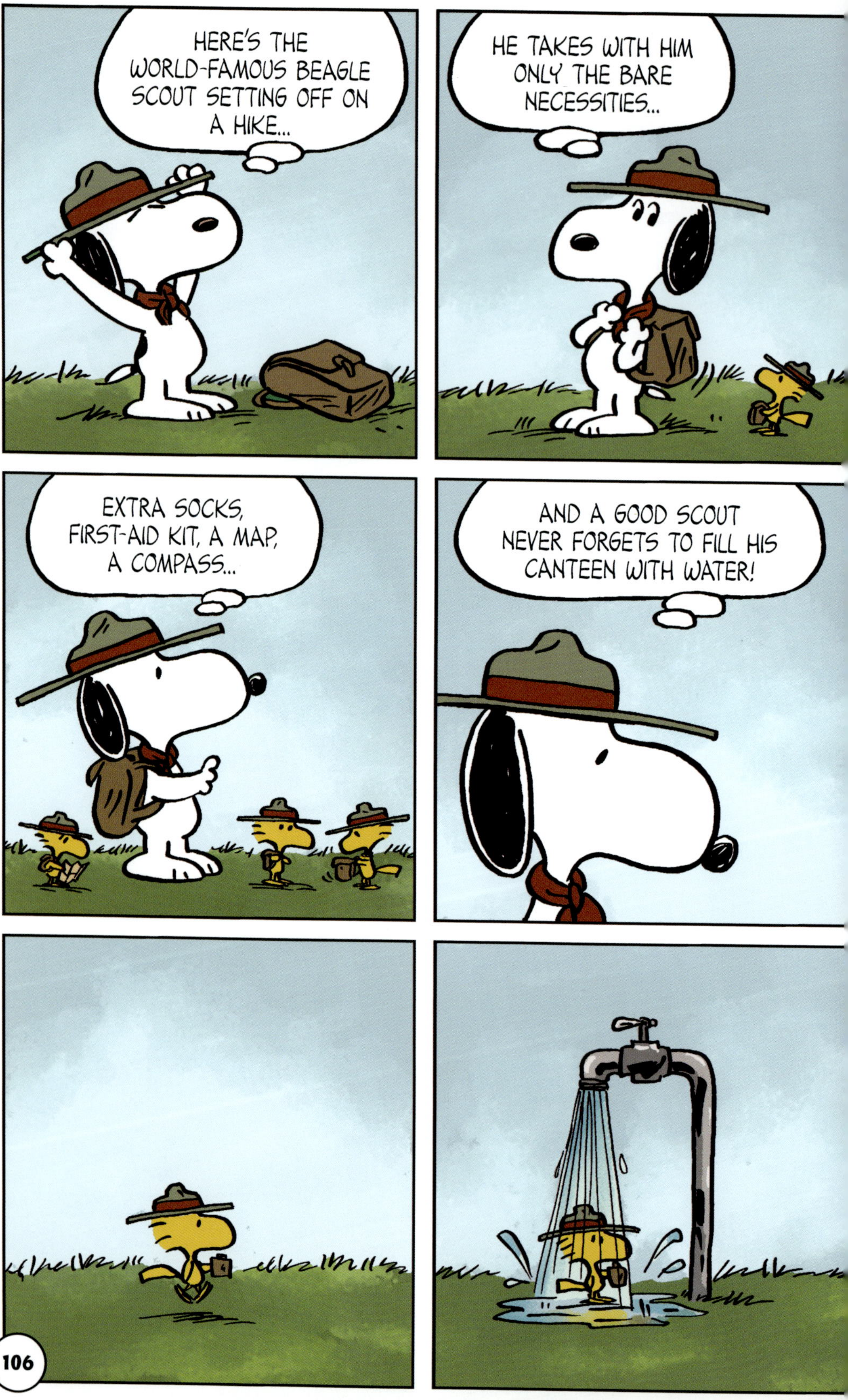
HERE'S THE WORLD-FAMOUS BEAGLE SCOUT SETTING OFF ON A HIKE...
HE TAKES WITH HIM ONLY THE BARE NECESSITIES...
EXTRA SOCKS, FIRST-AID KIT, A MAP, A COMPASS...
AND A GOOD SCOUT NEVER FORGETS TO FILL HIS CANTEEN WITH WATER!

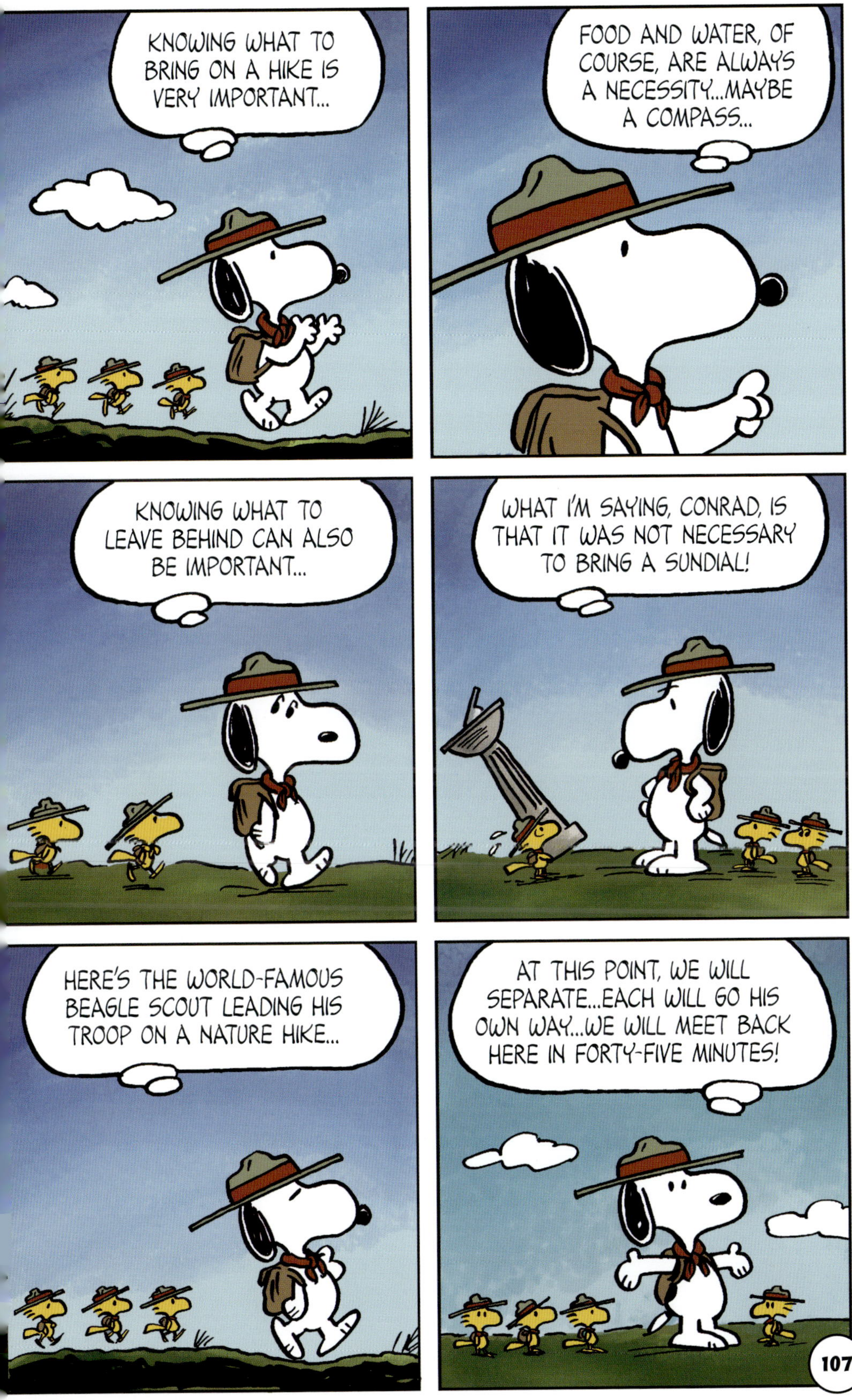
KNOWING WHAT TO BRING ON A HIKE IS VERY IMPORTANT...
FOOD AND WATER, OF COURSE, ARE ALWAYS A NECESSITY...MAYBE A COMPASS...
KNOWING WHAT TO LEAVE BEHIND CAN ALSO BE IMPORTANT...
WHAT I'M SAYING, CONRAD, IS THAT IT WAS NOT NECESSARY TO BRING A SUNDIAL!
HERE'S THE WORLD-FAMOUS BEAGLE SCOUT LEADING HIS TROOP ON A NATURE HIKE...
AT THIS POINT, WE WILL SEPARATE...EACH WILL GO HIS OWN WAY...WE WILL MEET BACK HERE IN FORTY-FIVE MINUTES!

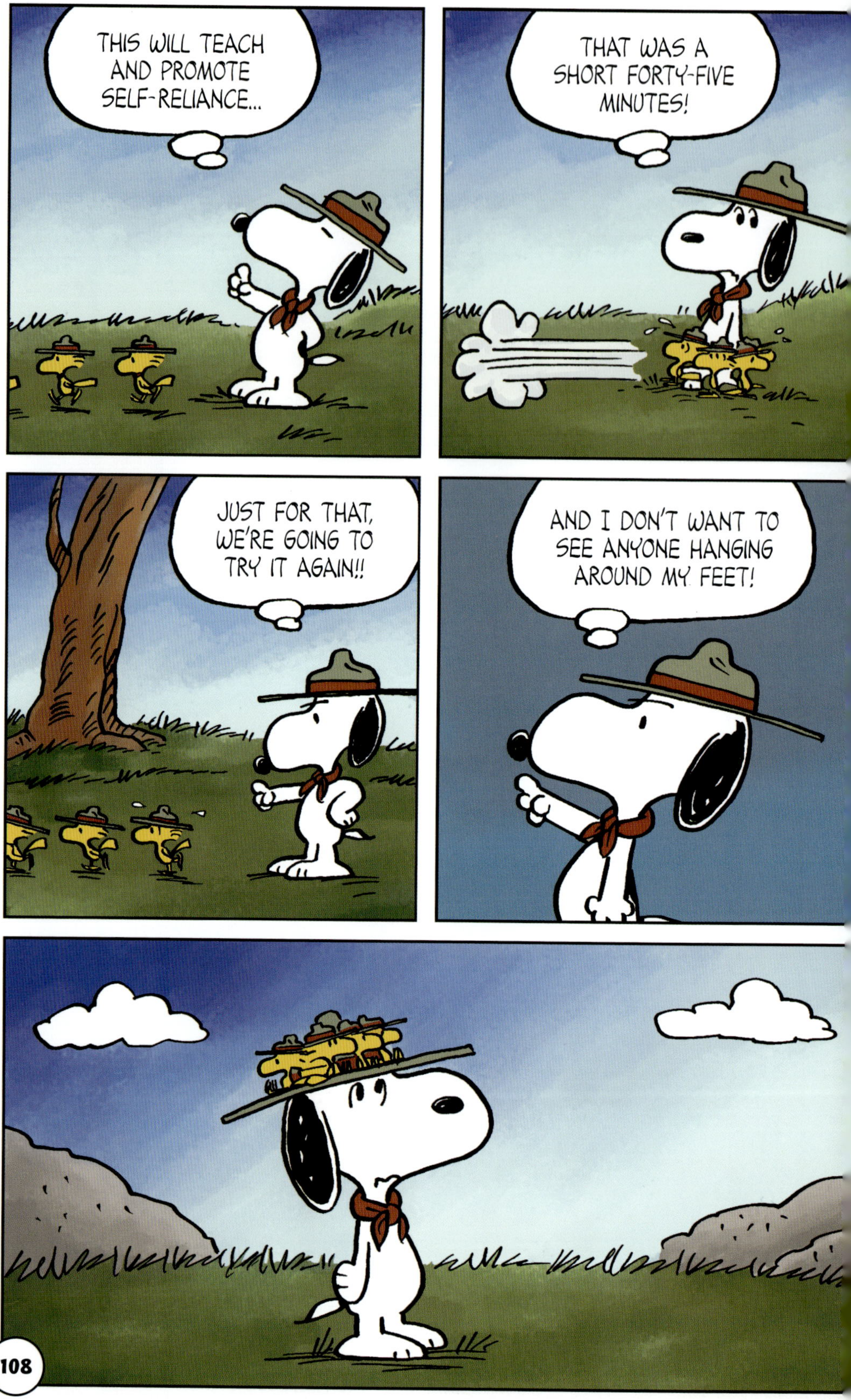
THIS WILL TEACH AND PROMOTE SELF-RELIANCE...
THAT WAS A SHORT FORTY-FIVE MINUTES!
JUST FOR THAT, WE'RE GOING TO TRY IT AGAIN!!
AND I DON'T WANT TO SEE ANYONE HANGING AROUND MY FEET!

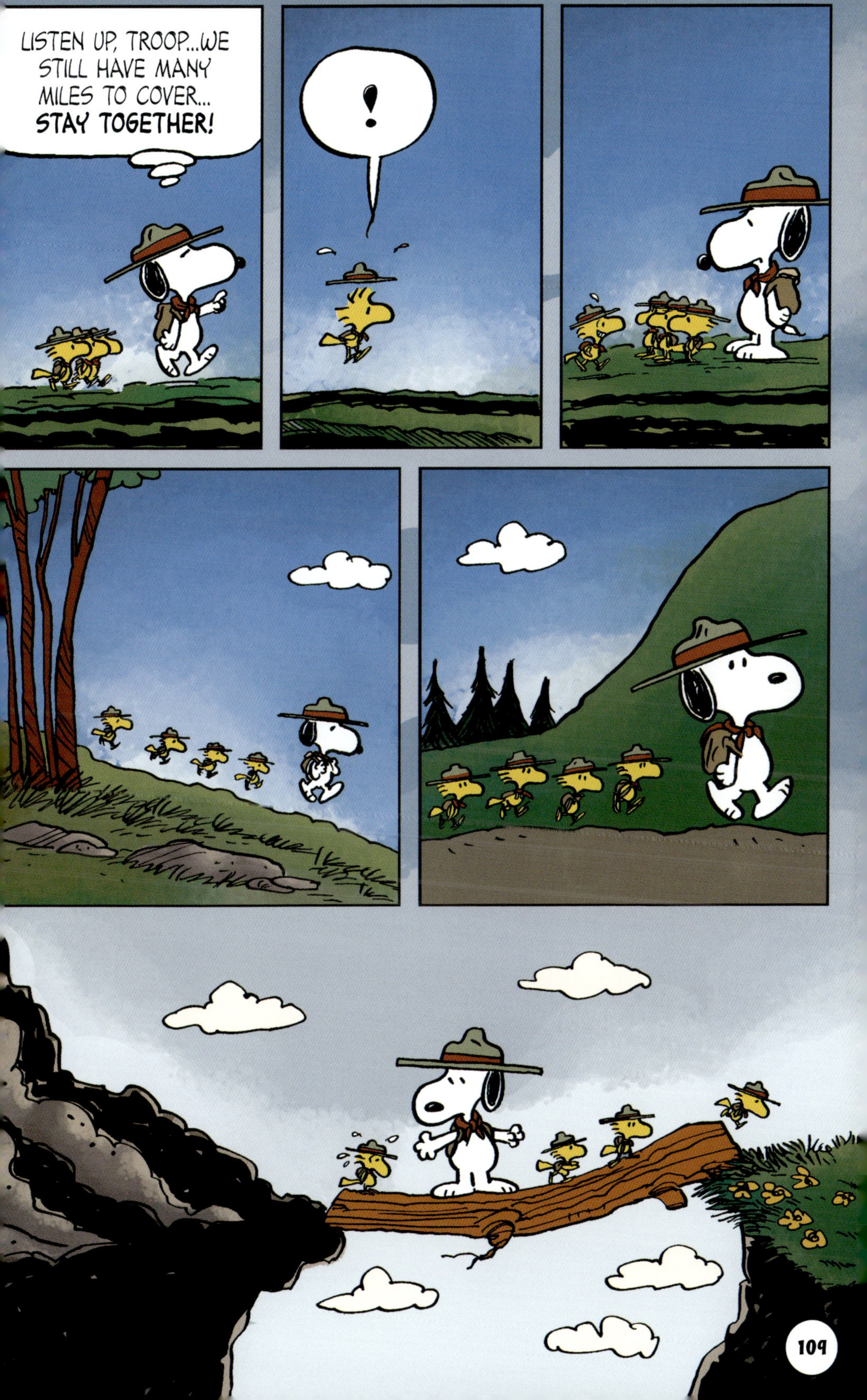
LISTEN UP, TROOP...WE STILL HAVE MANY MILES TO COVER... STAY TOGETHER!
!

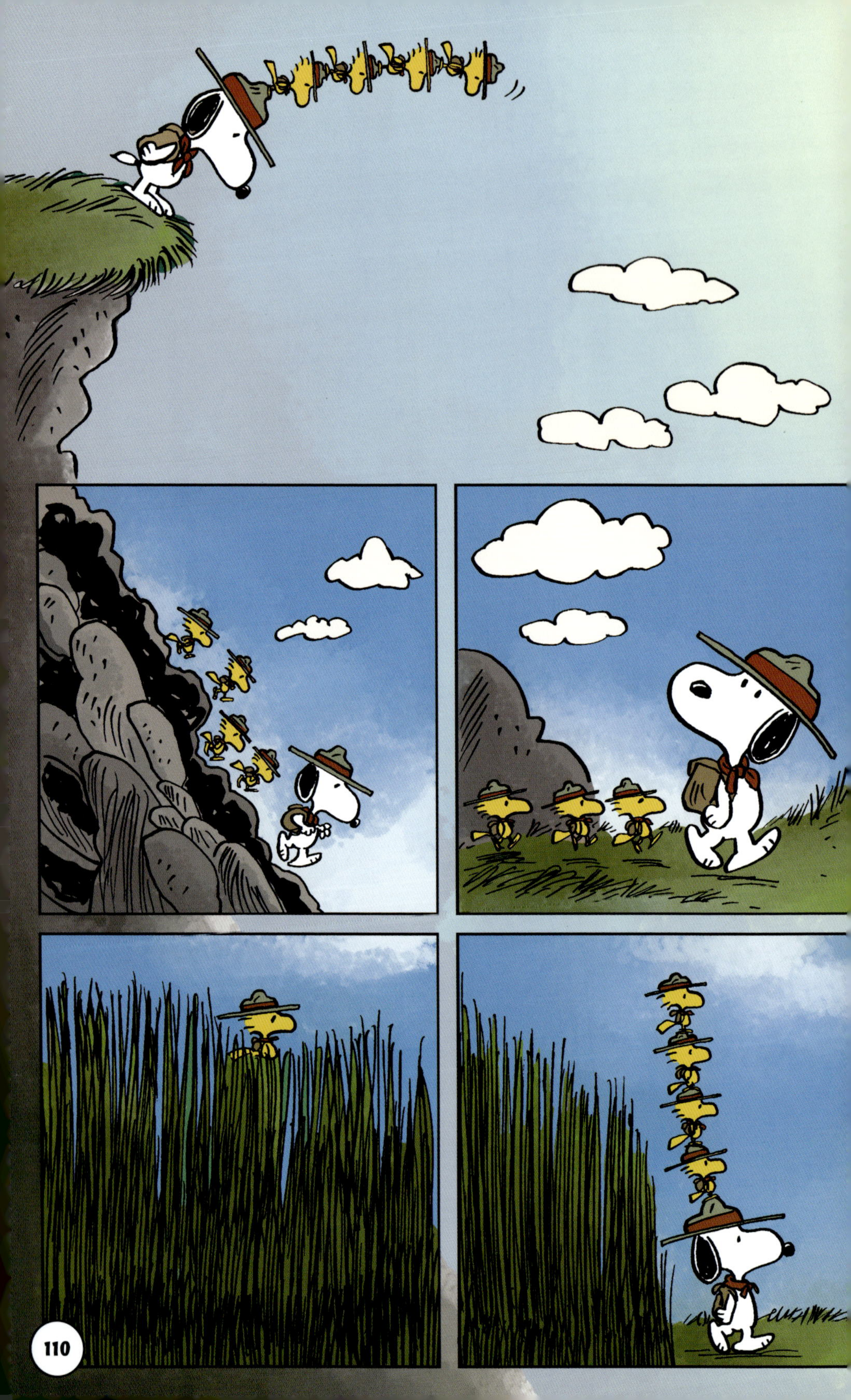

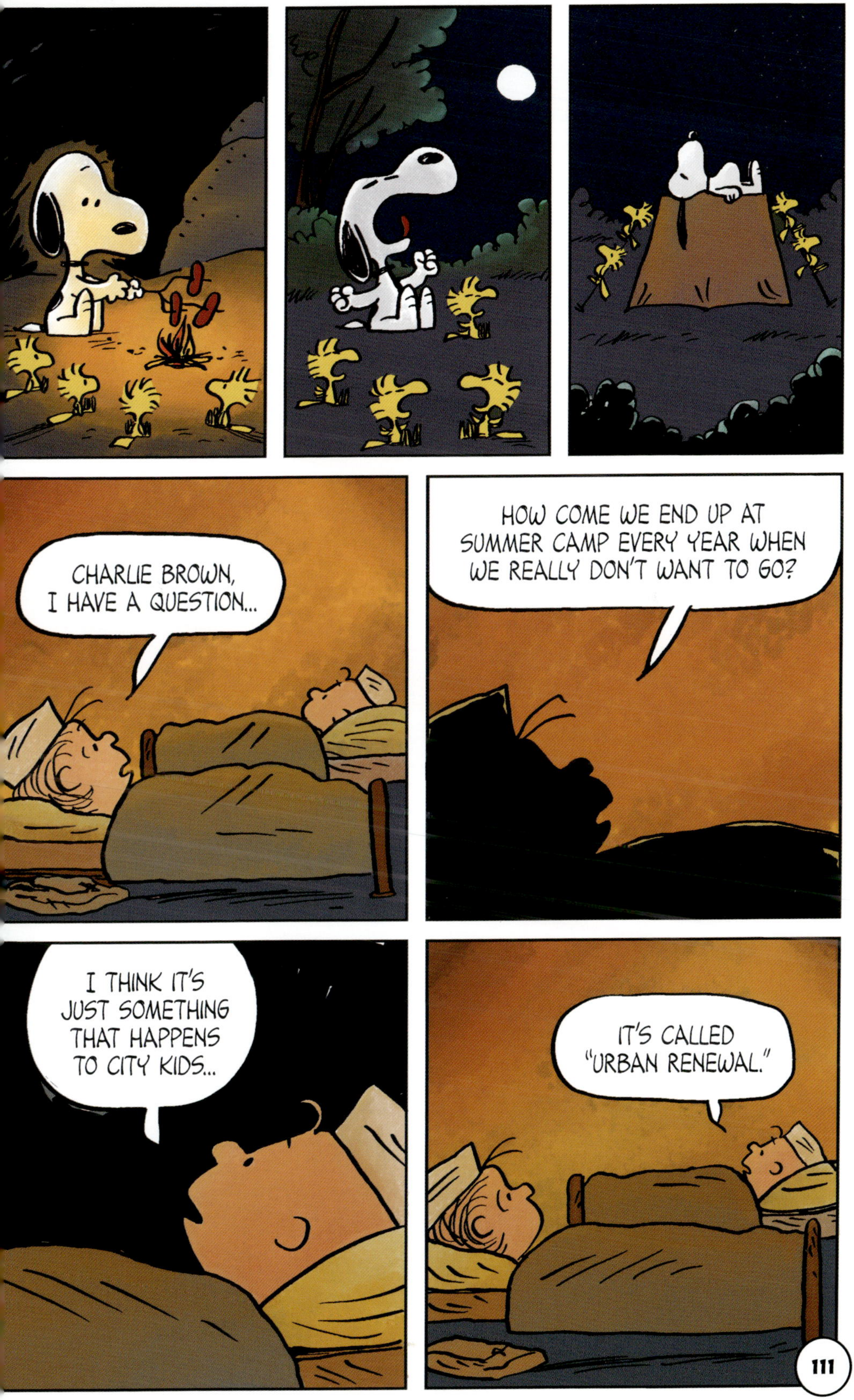
CHARLIE BROWN, I HAVE A QUESTION...
HOW COME WE END UP AT SUMMER CAMP EVERY YEAR WHEN WE REALLY DON'T WANT TO GO?
I THINK IT'S JUST SOMETHING THAT HAPPENS TO CITY KIDS...
IT'S CALLED "URBAN RENEWAL."

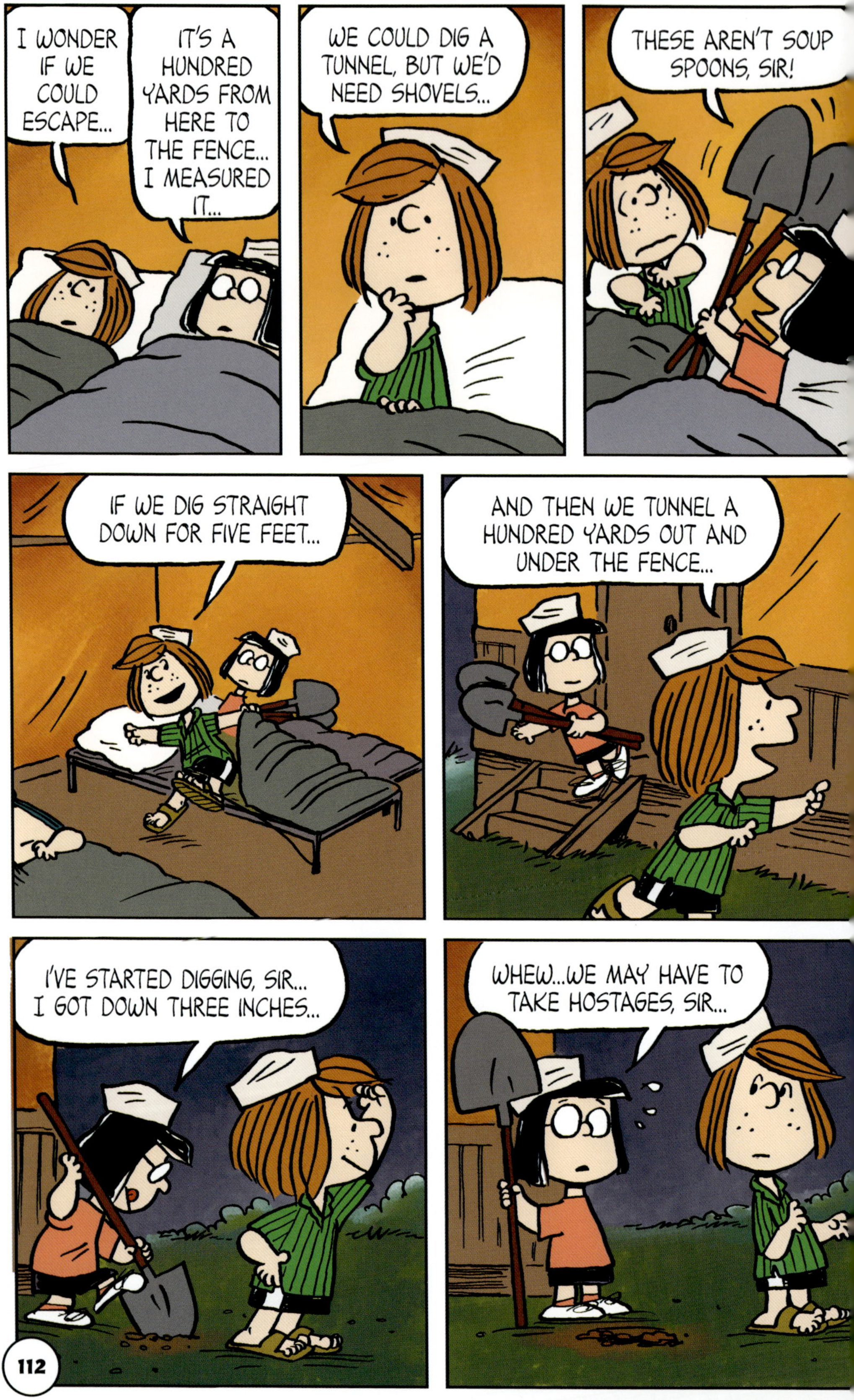
I WONDER IF WE COULD ESCAPE...
IT'S A HUNDRED YARDS FROM HERE TO THE FENCE... I MEASURED IT...
WE COULD DIG A TUNNEL, BUT WE'D NEED SHOVELS...
THESE AREN'T SOUP SPOONS, SIR!
IF WE DIG STRAIGHT DOWN FOR FIVE FEET...
AND THEN WE TUNNEL A HUNDRED YARDS OUT AND UNDER THE FENCE...
I'VE STARTED DIGGING, SIR... I GOT DOWN THREE INCHES...
WHEW...WE MAY HAVE TO TAKE HOSTAGES, SIR...

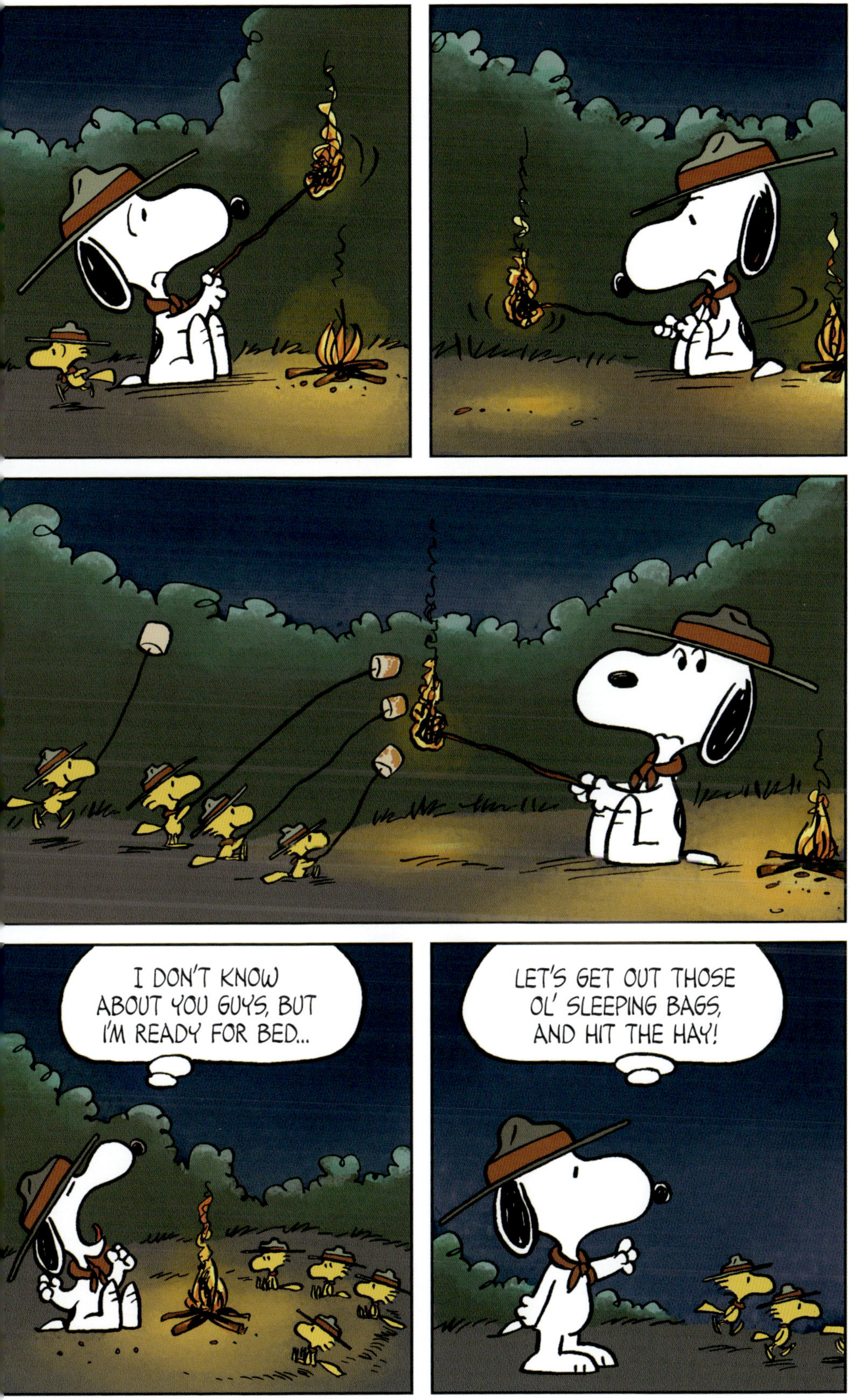
I DON'T KNOW ABOUT YOU GUYS, BUT I'M READY FOR BED...
LET'S GET OUT THOSE OL' SLEEPING BAGS, AND HIT THE HAY!

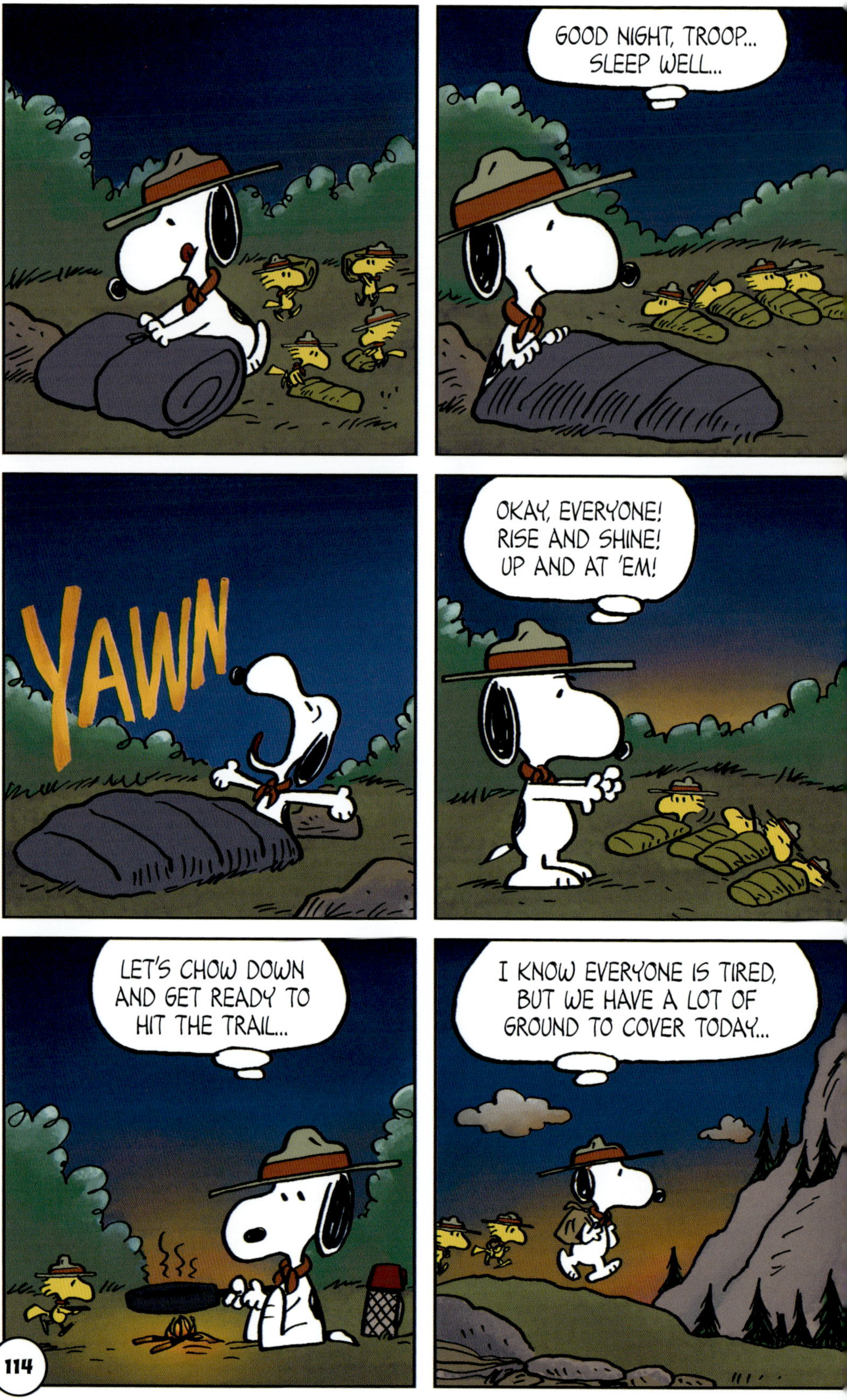
GOOD NIGHT, TROOP... SLEEP WELL...
YAWN
OKAY, EVERYONE! RISE AND SHINE! UP AND AT 'EM!
LET'S CHOW DOWN AND GET READY TO HIT THE TRAIL...
I KNOW EVERYONE IS TIRED, BUT WE HAVE A LOT OF GROUND TO COVER TODAY...

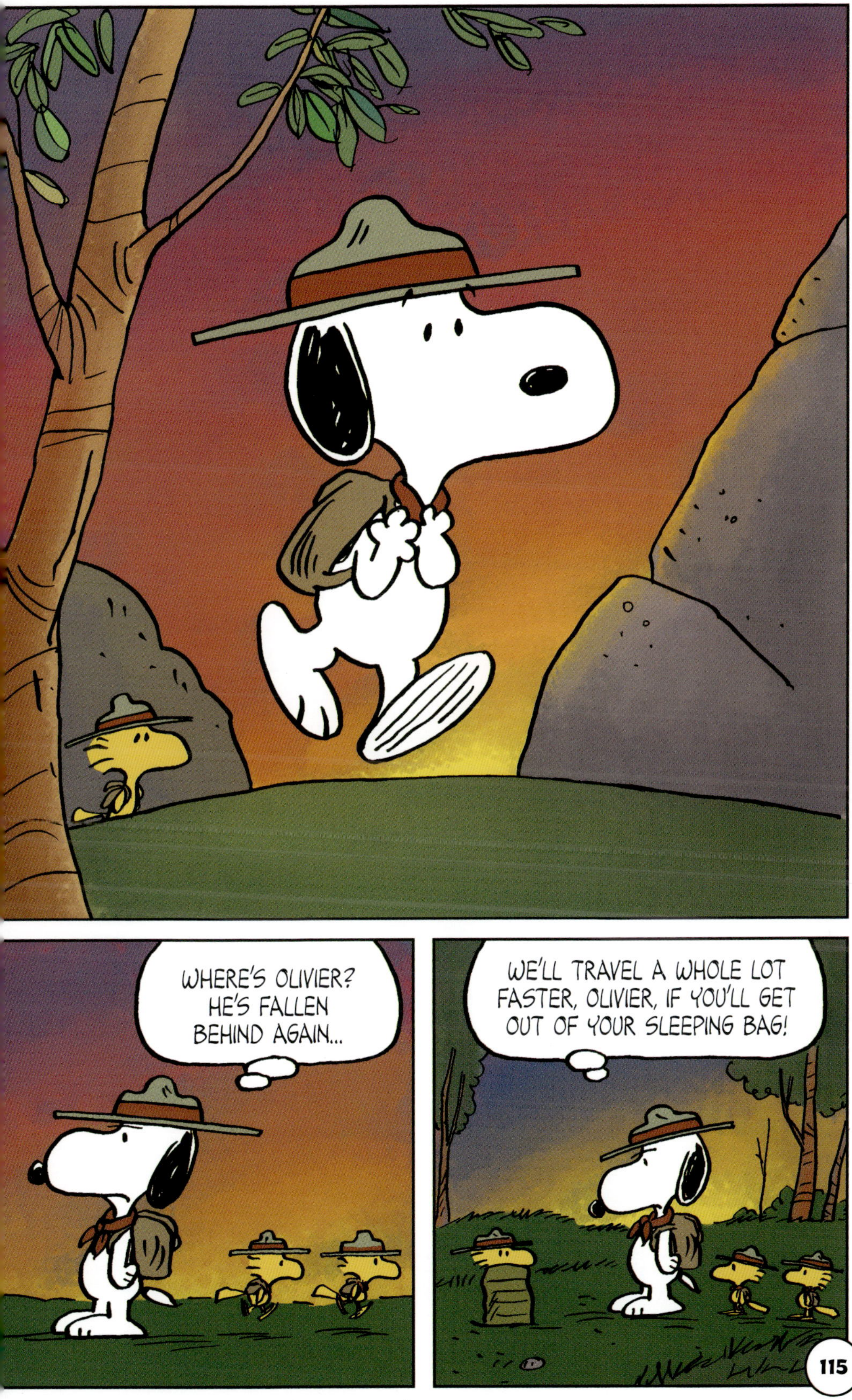
WHERE'S OLIVIER? HE'S FALLEN BEHIND AGAIN...
WE'LL TRAVEL A WHOLE LOT FASTER, OLIVIER, IF YOU'LL GET OUT OF YOUR SLEEPING BAG!

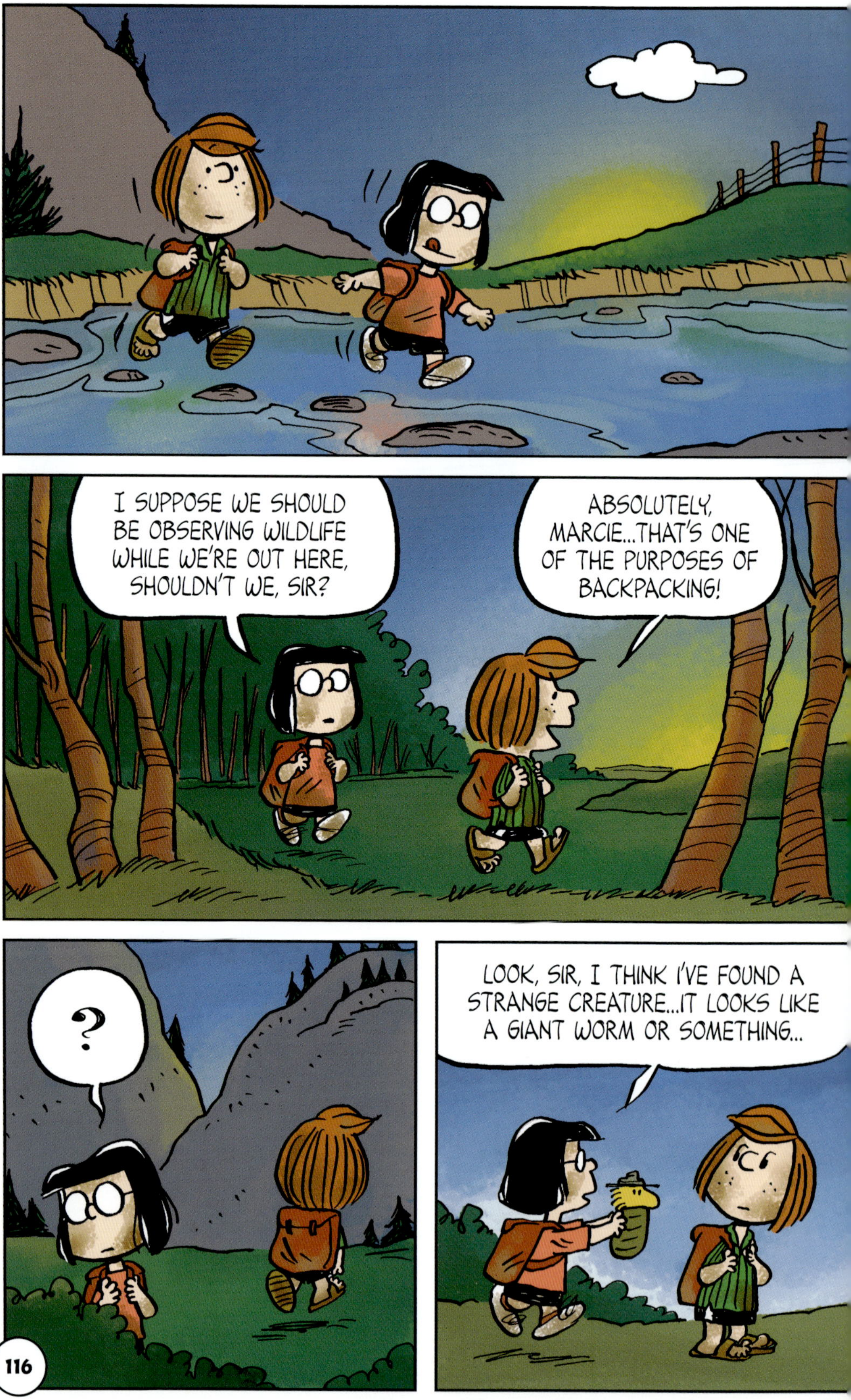
I SUPPOSE WE SHOULD BE OBSERVING WILDLIFE WHILE WE'RE OUT HERE, SHOULDN'T WE, SIR?
ABSOLUTELY, MARCIE...THAT'S ONE OF THE PURPOSES OF BACKPACKING!
?
LOOK, SIR, I THINK I'VE FOUND A STRANGE CREATURE...IT LOOKS LIKE A GIANT WORM OR SOMETHING...

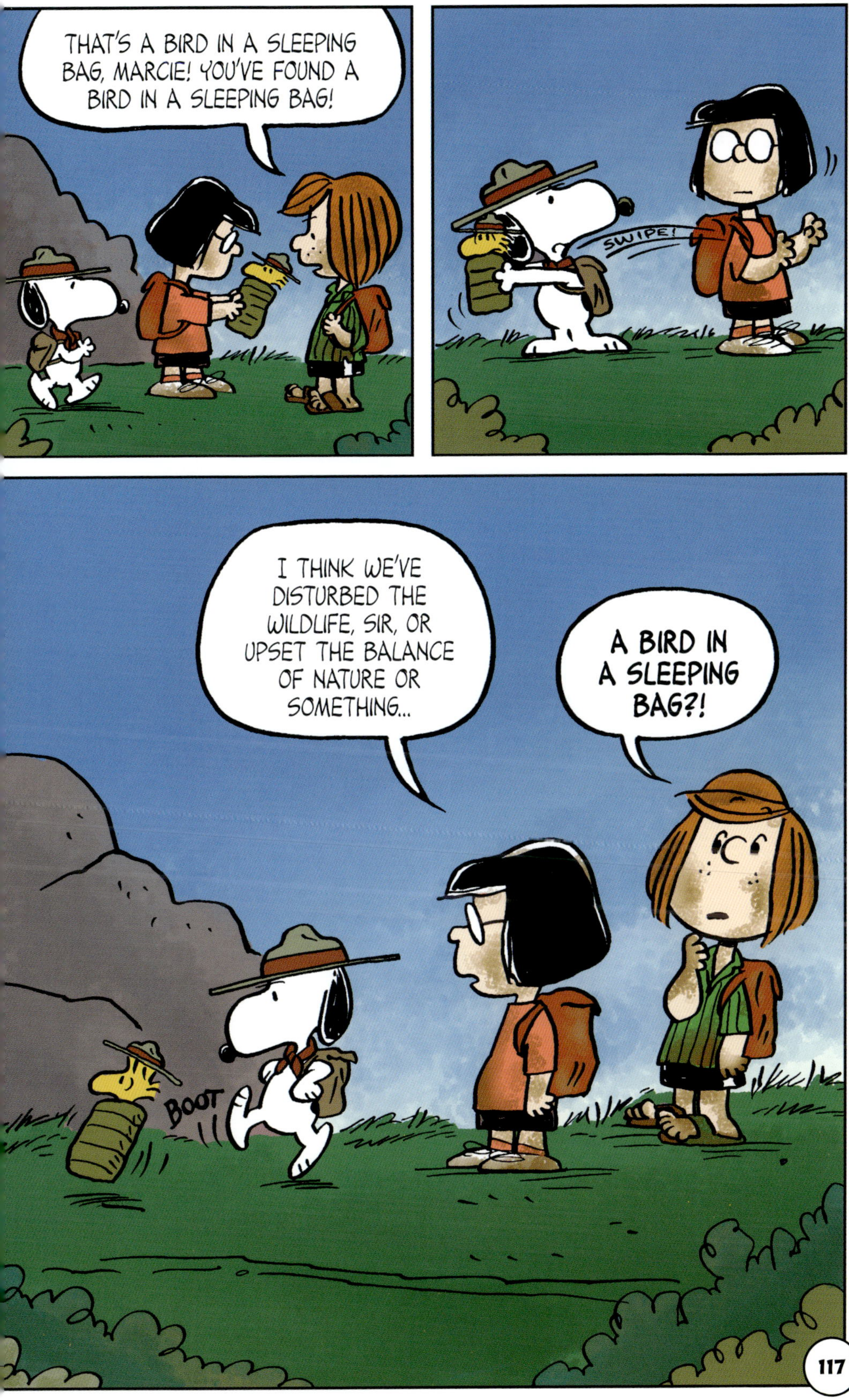
THAT'S A BIRD IN A SLEEPING BAG, MARCIE! YOU'VE FOUND A BIRD IN A SLEEPING BAG!
SWIPE!
I THINK WE'VE DISTURBED THE WILDLIFE, SIR, OR UPSET THE BALANCE OF NATURE OR SOMETHING...
A BIRD IN A SLEEPING BAG?!
BOOT

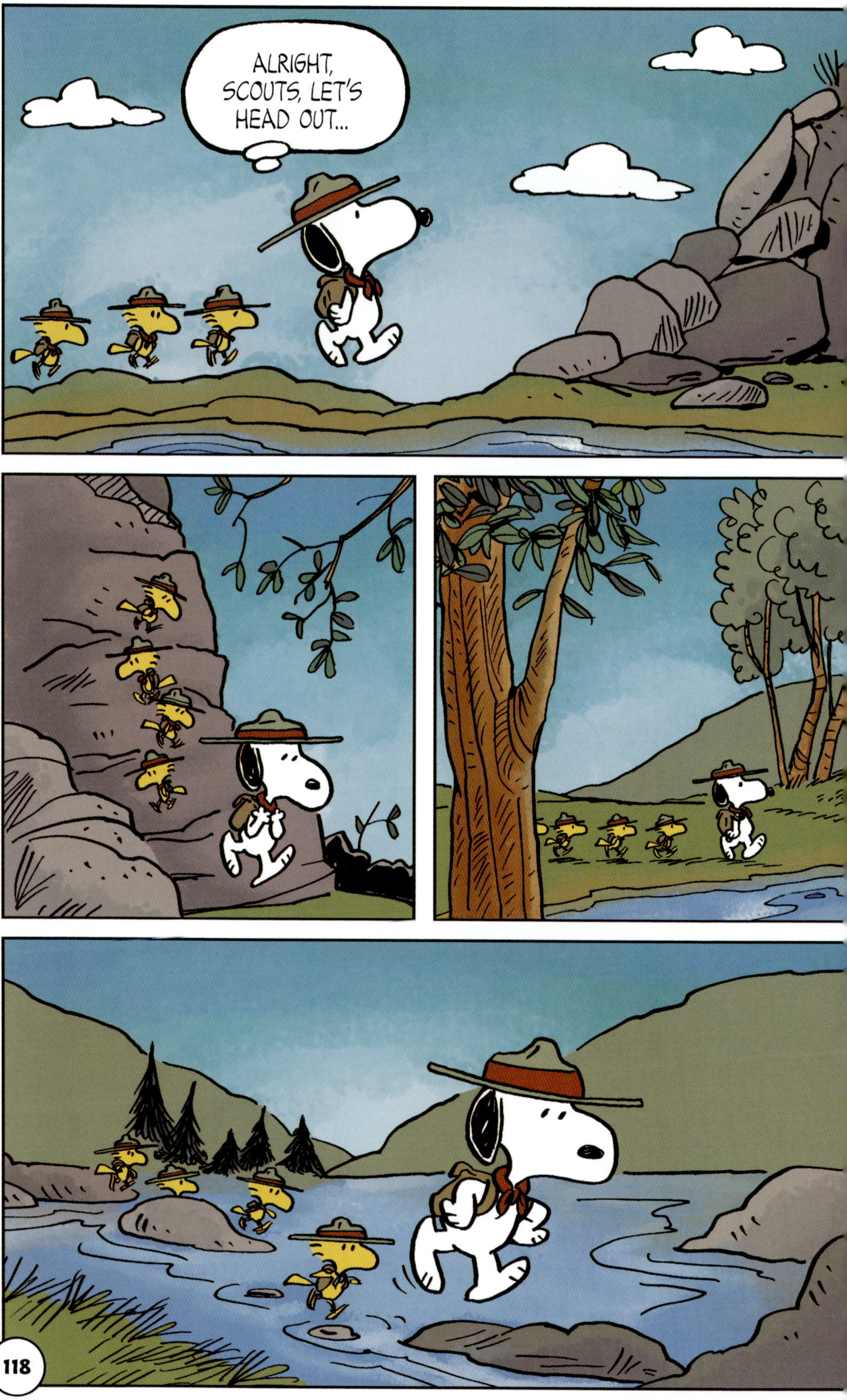
ALRIGHT, SCOUTS, LET'S HEAD OUT...

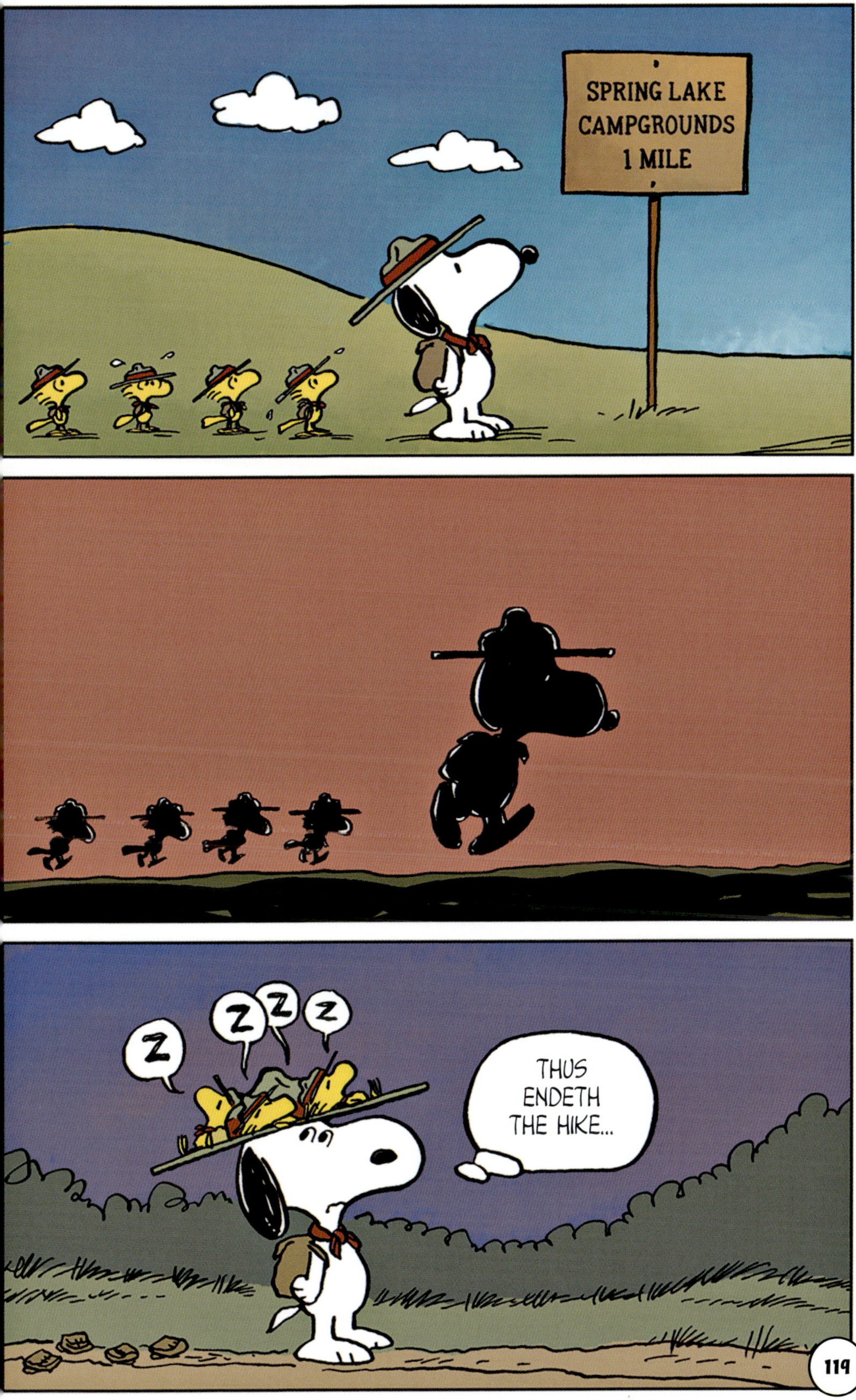
SPRING LAKE
CAMPGROUNDS
1 MILE
Z
Z
Z
Z
THUS
ENDETH
THE HIKE...

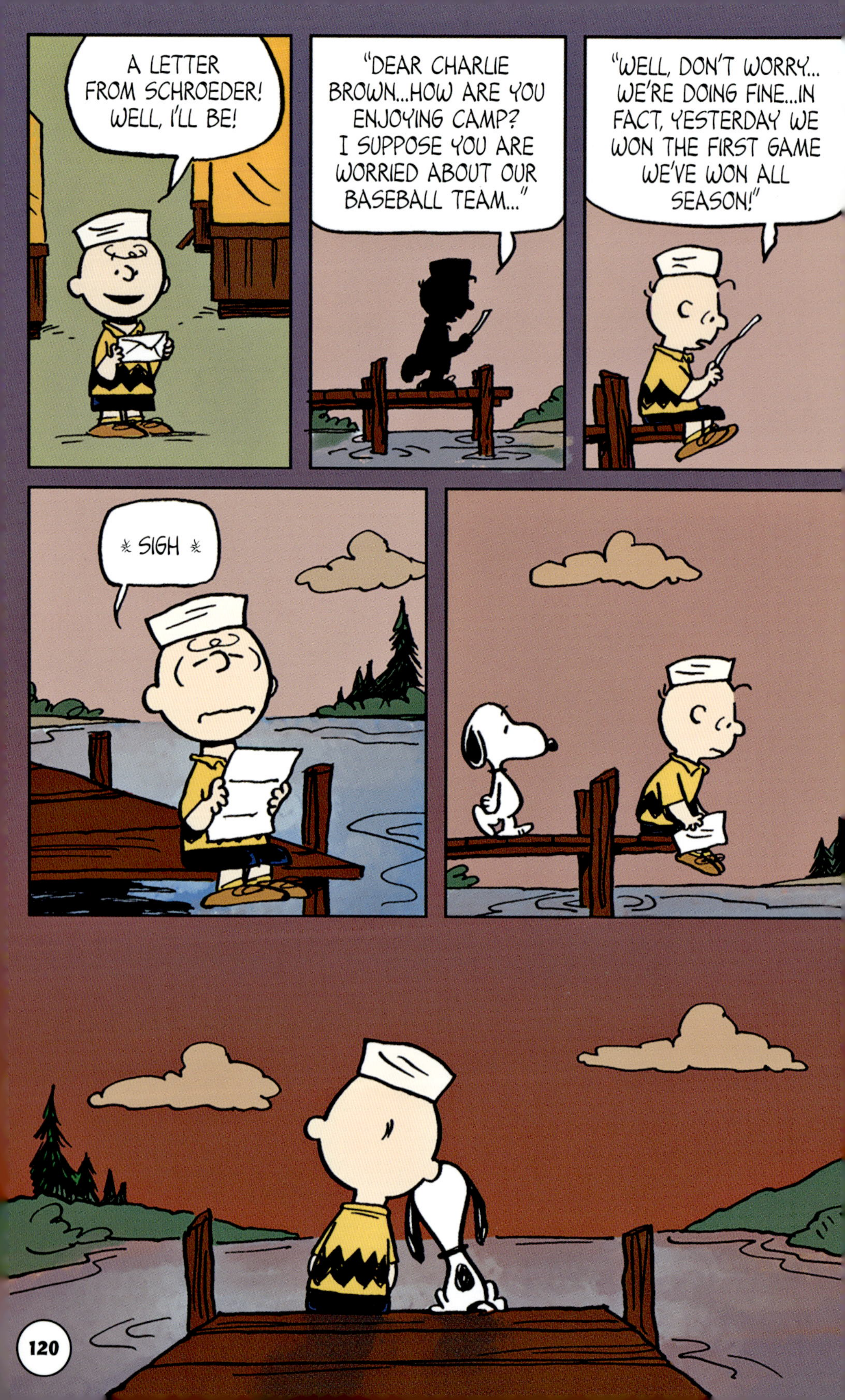
A LETTER FROM SCHROEDER! WELL, I'LL BE!
"DEAR CHARLIE BROWN...HOW ARE YOU ENJOYING CAMP? I SUPPOSE YOU ARE WORRIED ABOUT OUR BASEBALL TEAM..."
"WELL, DON'T WORRY... WE'RE DOING FINE...IN FACT, YESTERDAY WE WON THE FIRST GAME WE'VE WON ALL SEASON!"
SIGH

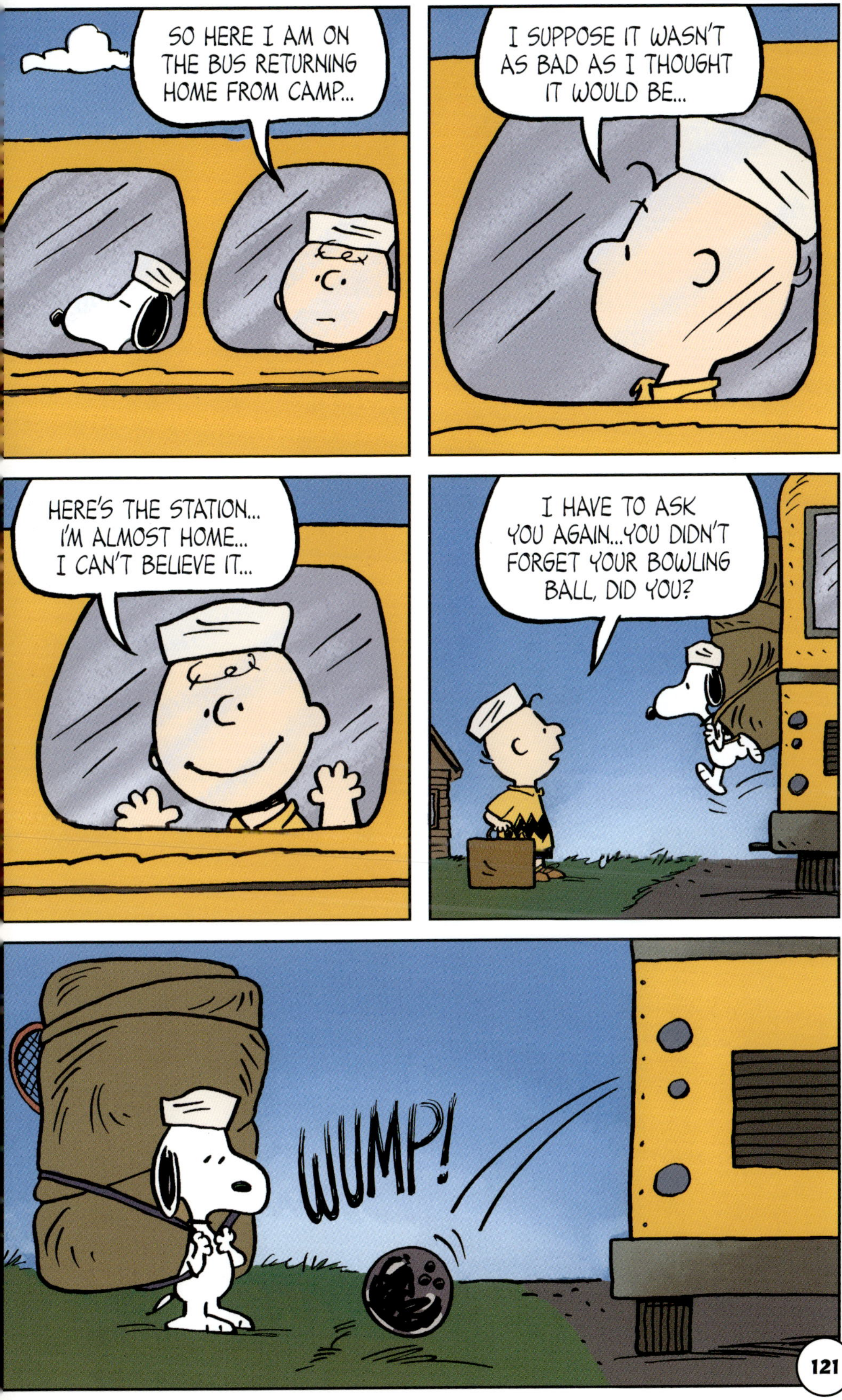
SO HERE I AM ON THE BUS RETURNING HOME FROM CAMP...
I SUPPOSE IT WASN'T AS BAD AS I THOUGHT IT WOULD BE...
HERE'S THE STATION... I'M ALMOST HOME... I CAN'T BELIEVE IT...
I HAVE TO ASK YOU AGAIN...YOU DIDN'T FORGET YOUR BOWLING BALL, DID YOU?
WUMP!

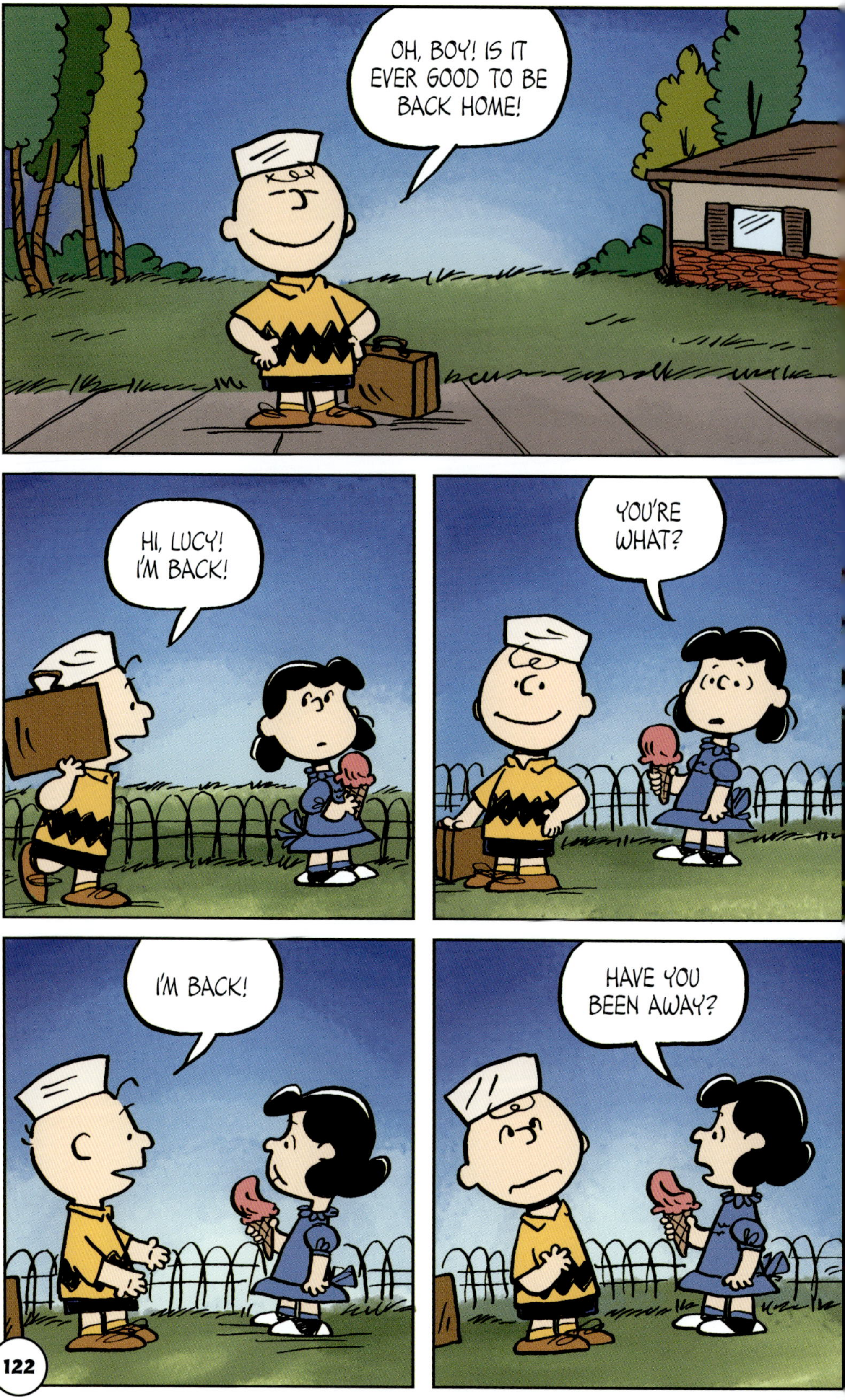
OH, BOY! IS IT EVER GOOD TO BE BACK HOME!
HI, LUCY! I'M BACK!
YOU'RE WHAT?
I'M BACK!
HAVE YOU BEEN AWAY?

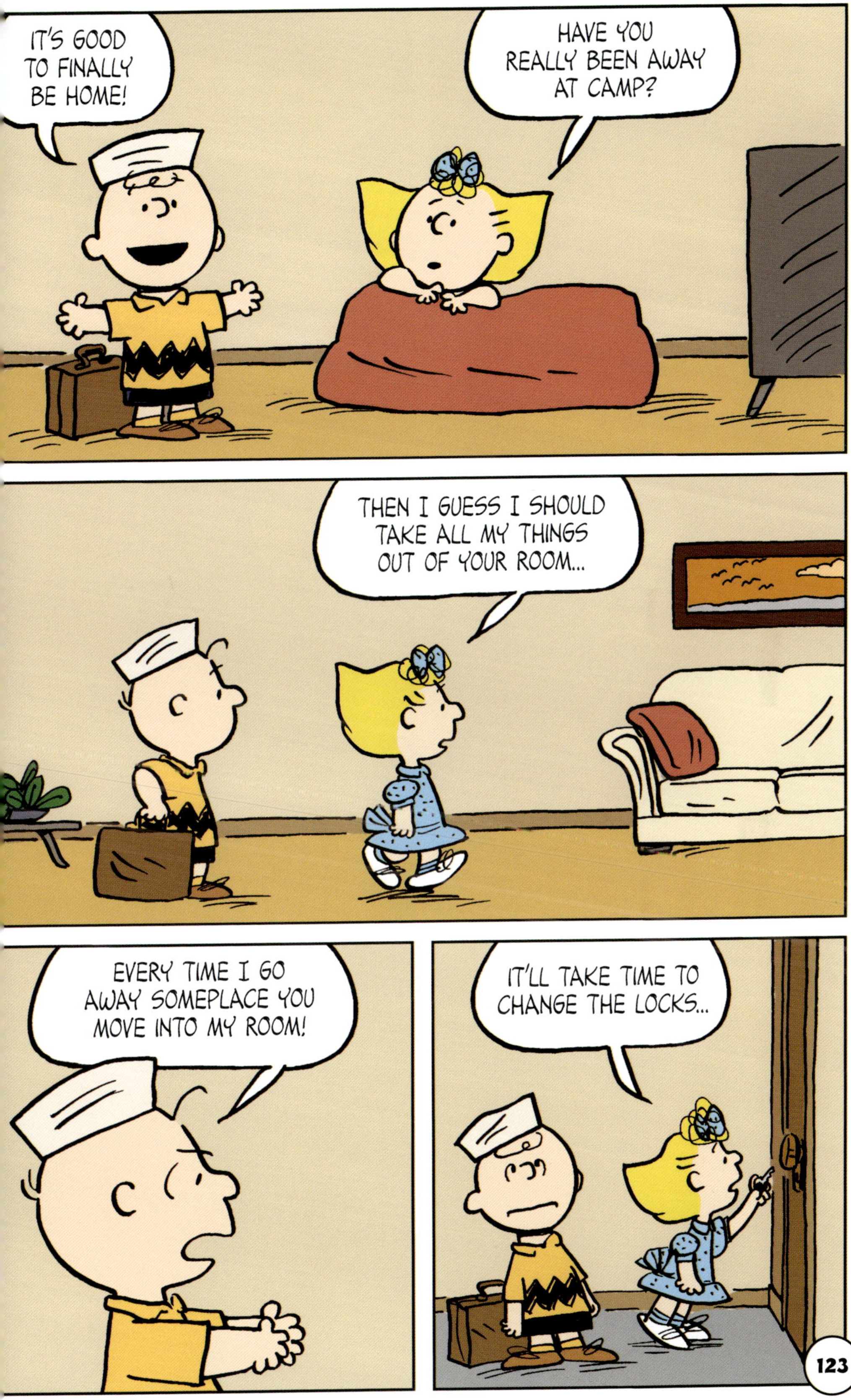
IT'S GOOD TO FINALLY BE HOME!
HAVE YOU REALLY BEEN AWAY AT CAMP?
THEN I GUESS I SHOULD TAKE ALL MY THINGS OUT OF YOUR ROOM...
EVERY TIME I GO AWAY SOMEPLACE YOU MOVE INTO MY ROOM!
IT'LL TAKE TIME TO CHANGE THE LOCKS...

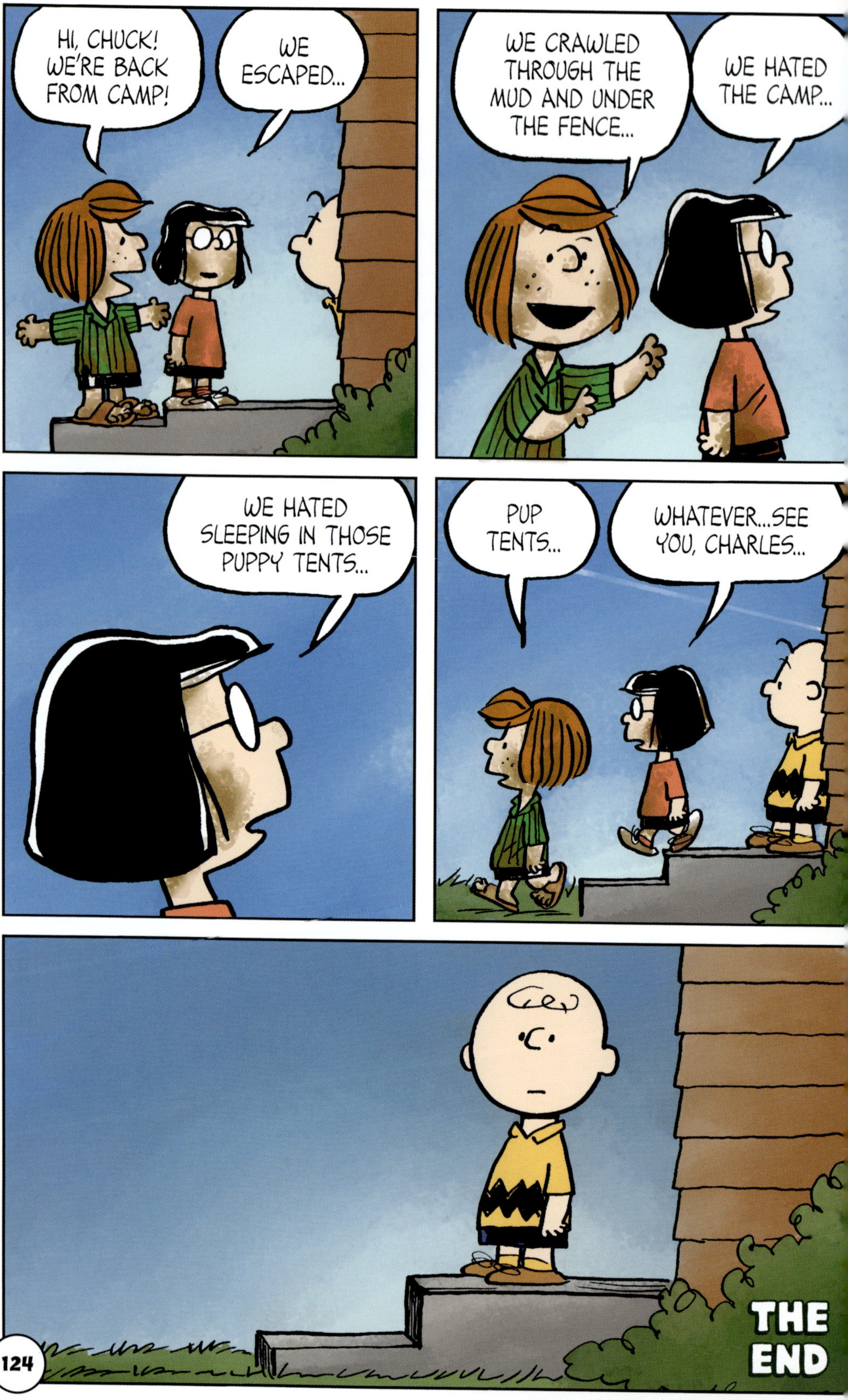
HI, CHUCK! WE'RE BACK FROM CAMP!
WE ESCAPED...
WE CRAWLED THROUGH THE MUD AND UNDER THE FENCE...
WE HATED THE CAMP...
WE HATED SLEEPING IN THOSE PUPPY TENTS...
PUP TENTS...
WHATEVER...SEE YOU, CHARLES...
THE END

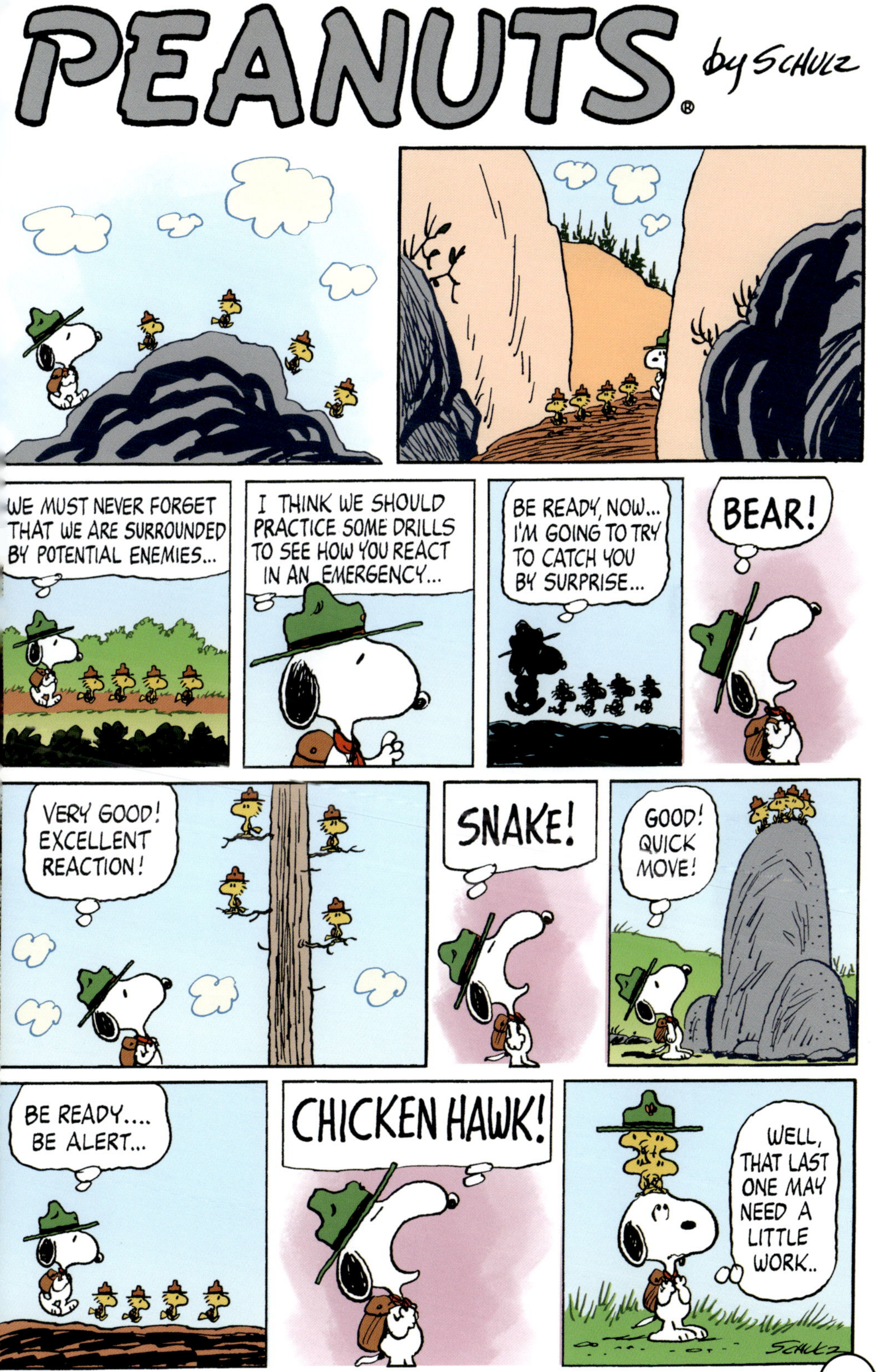
PEANUTS®
by SCHULZ
WE MUST NEVER FORGET THAT WE ARE SURROUNDED BY POTENTIAL ENEMIES...
I THINK WE SHOULD PRACTICE SOME DRILLS TO SEE HOW YOU REACT IN AN EMERGENCY...
BE READY, NOW... I'M GOING TO TRY TO CATCH YOU BY SURPRISE...
BEAR!
VERY GOOD! EXCELLENT REACTION!
SNAKE!
GOOD! QUICK MOVE!
BE READY.... BE ALERT...
CHICKEN HAWK!
WELL, THAT LAST ONE MAY NEED A LITTLE WORK..
SCHULZ

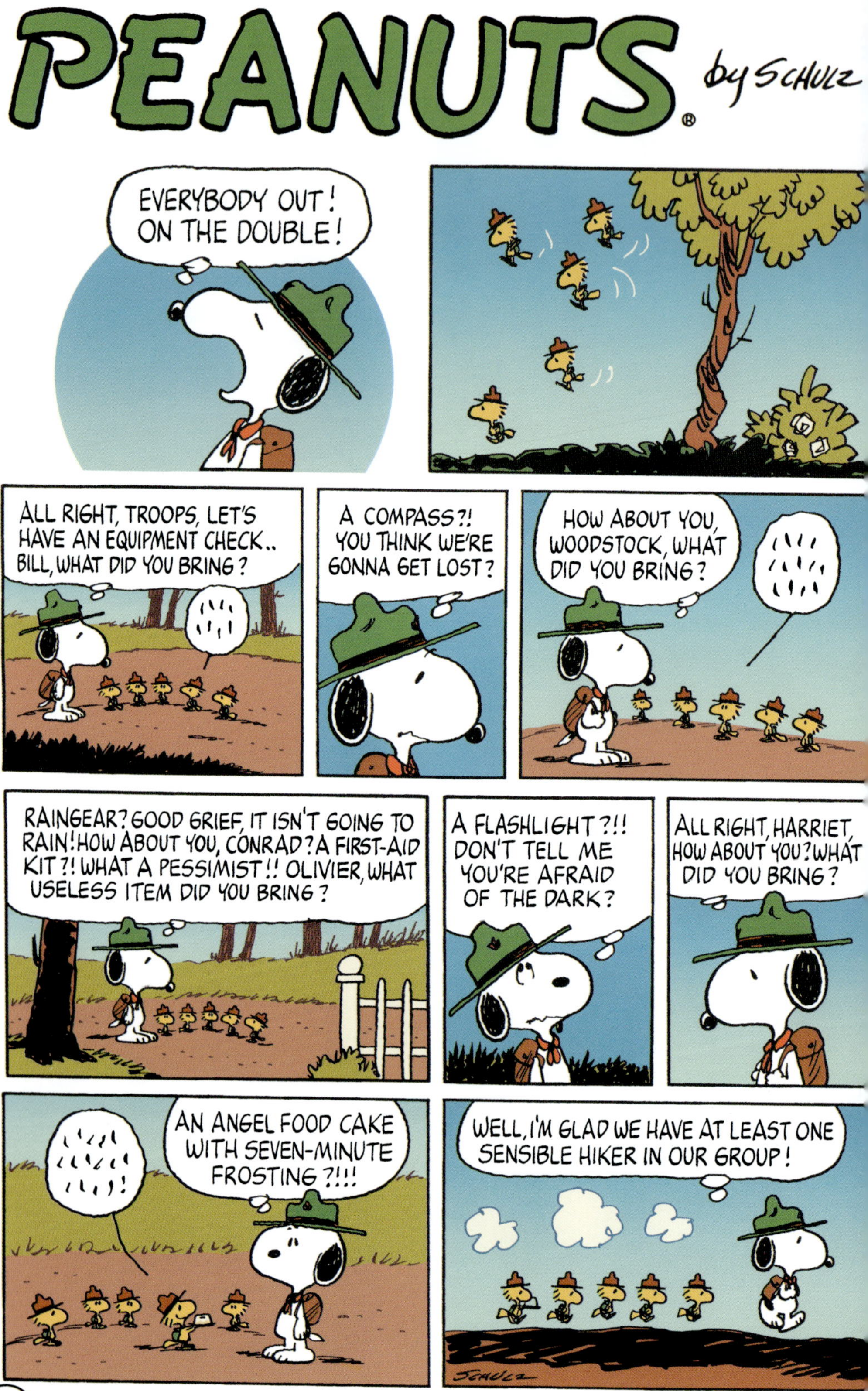
PEANUTS by SCHULZ
EVERYBODY OUT! ON THE DOUBLE!
ALL RIGHT, TROOPS, LET'S HAVE AN EQUIPMENT CHECK.. BILL, WHAT DID YOU BRING?
A COMPASS?! YOU THINK WE'RE GONNA GET LOST?
HOW ABOUT YOU, WOODSTOCK, WHAT DID YOU BRING?
RAINGEAR? GOOD GRIEF, IT ISN'T GOING TO RAIN! HOW ABOUT YOU, CONRAD? A FIRST-AID KIT?! WHAT A PESSIMIST!! OLIVIER, WHAT USELESS ITEM DID YOU BRING?
A FLASHLIGHT?!! DON'T TELL ME YOU'RE AFRAID OF THE DARK?
ALL RIGHT, HARRIET, HOW ABOUT YOU? WHAT DID YOU BRING?
AN ANGEL FOOD CAKE WITH SEVEN-MINUTE FROSTING?!!!
WELL, I'M GLAD WE HAVE AT LEAST ONE SENSIBLE HIKER IN OUR GROUP!
SCHULZ

SNOOPY in MOVIE TIME

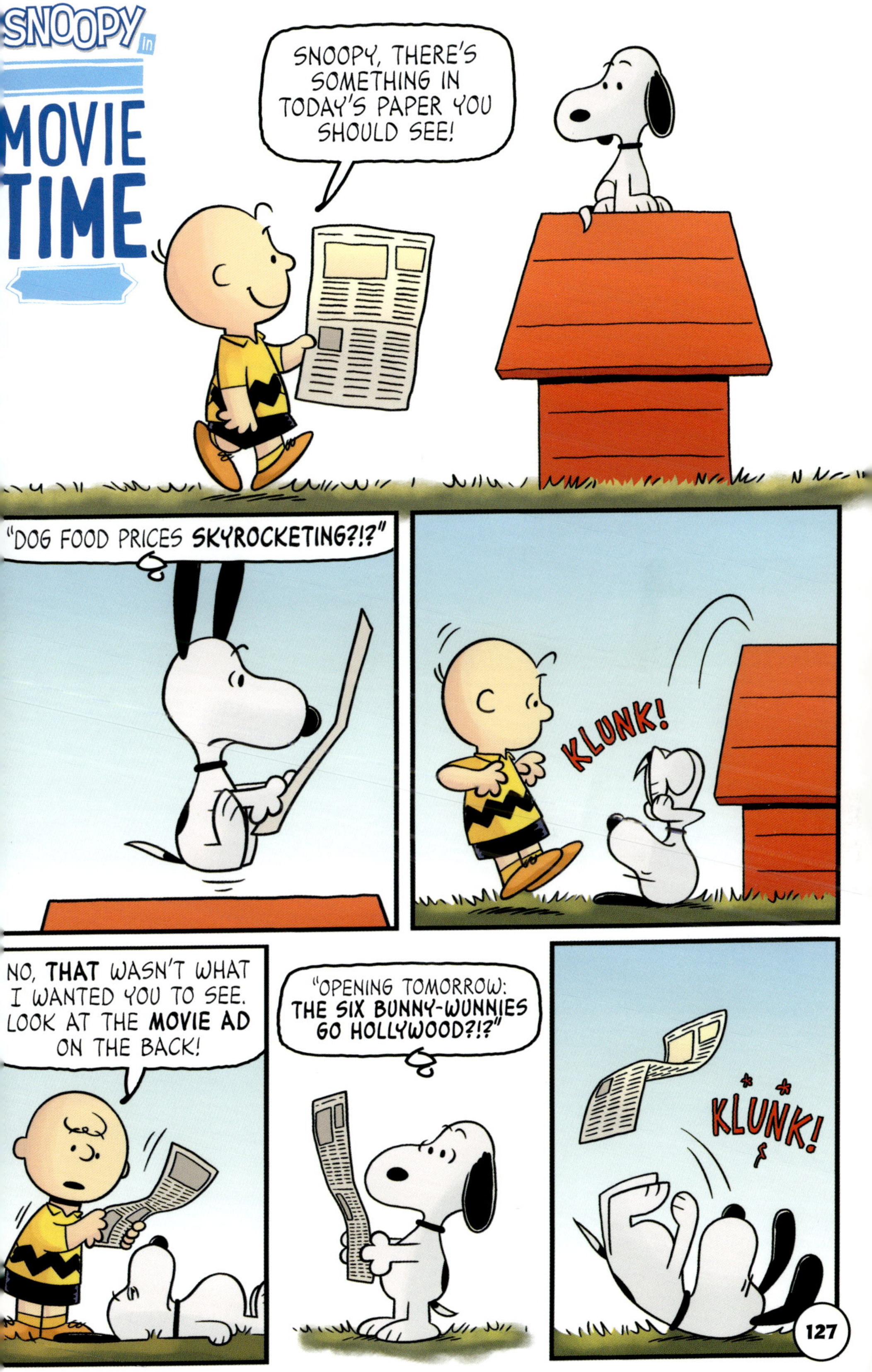

SNOOPY, THERE'S SOMETHING IN TODAY'S PAPER YOU SHOULD SEE!
"DOG FOOD PRICES SKYROCKETING?!?"
KLUNK!
NO, THAT WASN'T WHAT I WANTED YOU TO SEE. LOOK AT THE MOVIE AD ON THE BACK!
"OPENING TOMORROW: THE SIX BUNNY-WUNNIES GO HOLLYWOOD?!?"
KLUNK!

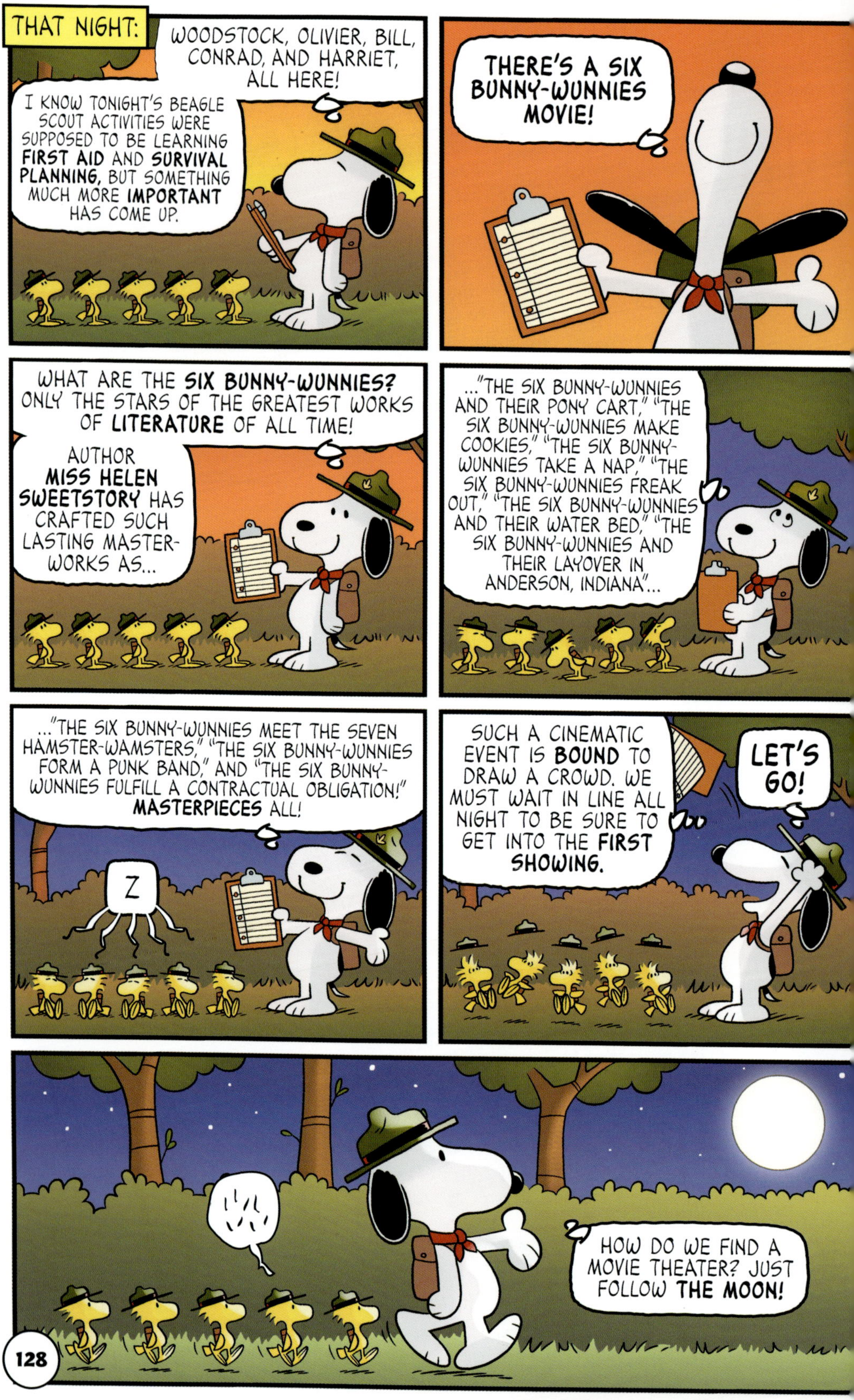
THAT NIGHT:
WOODSTOCK, OLIVIER, BILL, CONRAD, AND HARRIET, ALL HERE!
I KNOW TONIGHT'S BEAGLE SCOUT ACTIVITIES WERE SUPPOSED TO BE LEARNING FIRST AID AND SURVIVAL PLANNING, BUT SOMETHING MUCH MORE IMPORTANT HAS COME UP.
THERE'S A SIX BUNNY-WUNNIES MOVIE!
WHAT ARE THE SIX BUNNY-WUNNIES? ONLY THE STARS OF THE GREATEST WORKS OF LITERATURE OF ALL TIME!
AUTHOR MISS HELEN SWEETSTORY HAS CRAFTED SUCH LASTING MASTER-WORKS AS...
..."THE SIX BUNNY-WUNNIES AND THEIR PONY CART," "THE SIX BUNNY-WUNNIES MAKE COOKIES," "THE SIX BUNNY-WUNNIES TAKE A NAP," "THE SIX BUNNY-WUNNIES FREAK OUT," "THE SIX BUNNY-WUNNIES AND THEIR WATER BED," "THE SIX BUNNY-WUNNIES AND THEIR LAYOVER IN ANDERSON, INDIANA"...
..."THE SIX BUNNY-WUNNIES MEET THE SEVEN HAMSTER-WAMSTERS," "THE SIX BUNNY-WUNNIES FORM A PUNK BAND," AND "THE SIX BUNNY-WUNNIES FULFILL A CONTRACTUAL OBLIGATION!" MASTERPIECES ALL!
Z
SUCH A CINEMATIC EVENT IS BOUND TO DRAW A CROWD. WE MUST WAIT IN LINE ALL NIGHT TO BE SURE TO GET INTO THE FIRST SHOWING.
LET'S GO!
HOW DO WE FIND A MOVIE THEATER? JUST FOLLOW THE MOON!

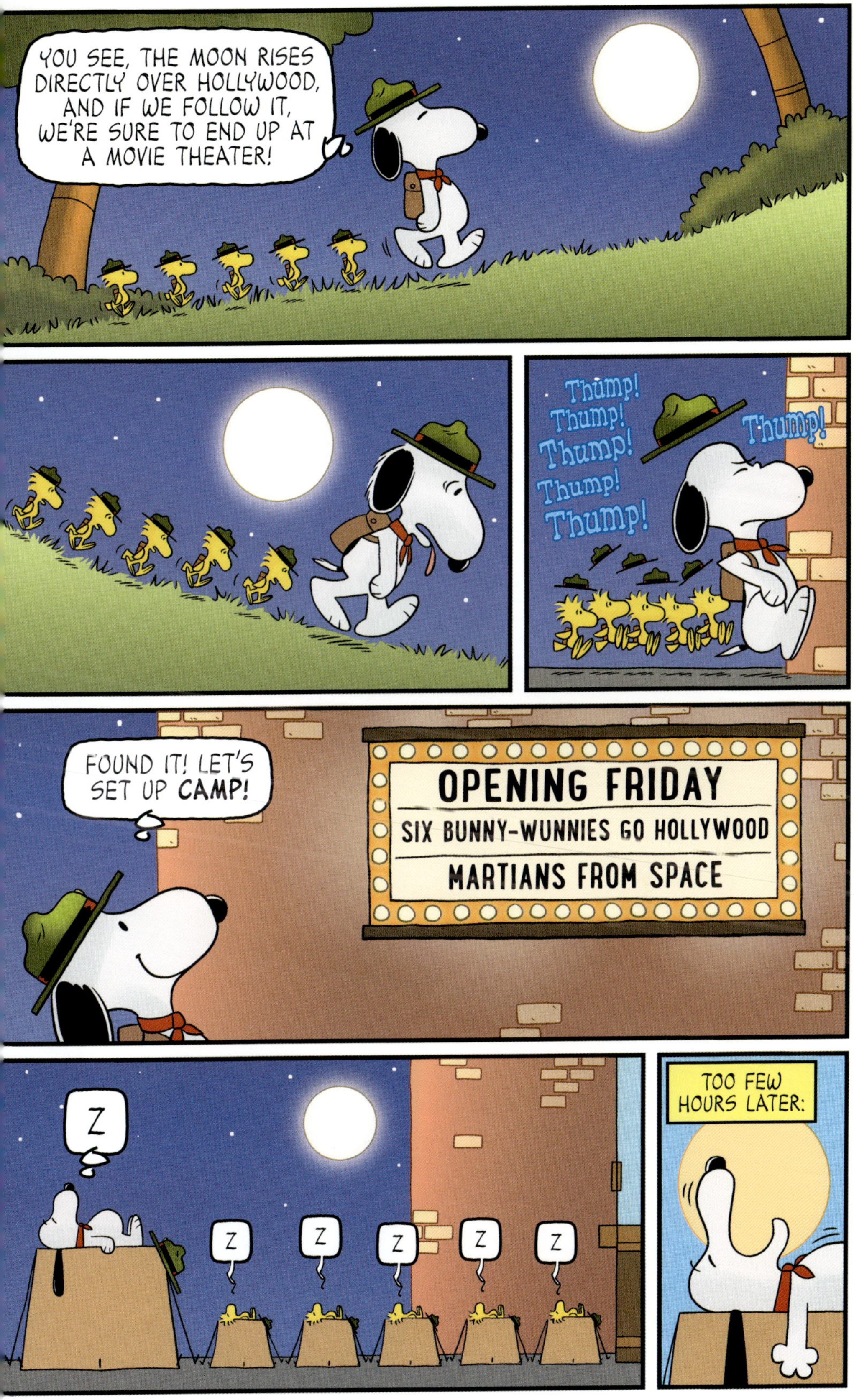
YOU SEE, THE MOON RISES DIRECTLY OVER HOLLYWOOD, AND IF WE FOLLOW IT, WE'RE SURE TO END UP AT A MOVIE THEATER!
Thump! Thump! Thump! Thump! Thump!
Thump!
FOUND IT! LET'S SET UP CAMP!
OPENING FRIDAY
SIX BUNNY-WUNNIES GO HOLLYWOOD
MARTIANS FROM SPACE
Z
Z
Z
Z
Z
Z
TOO FEW HOURS LATER:

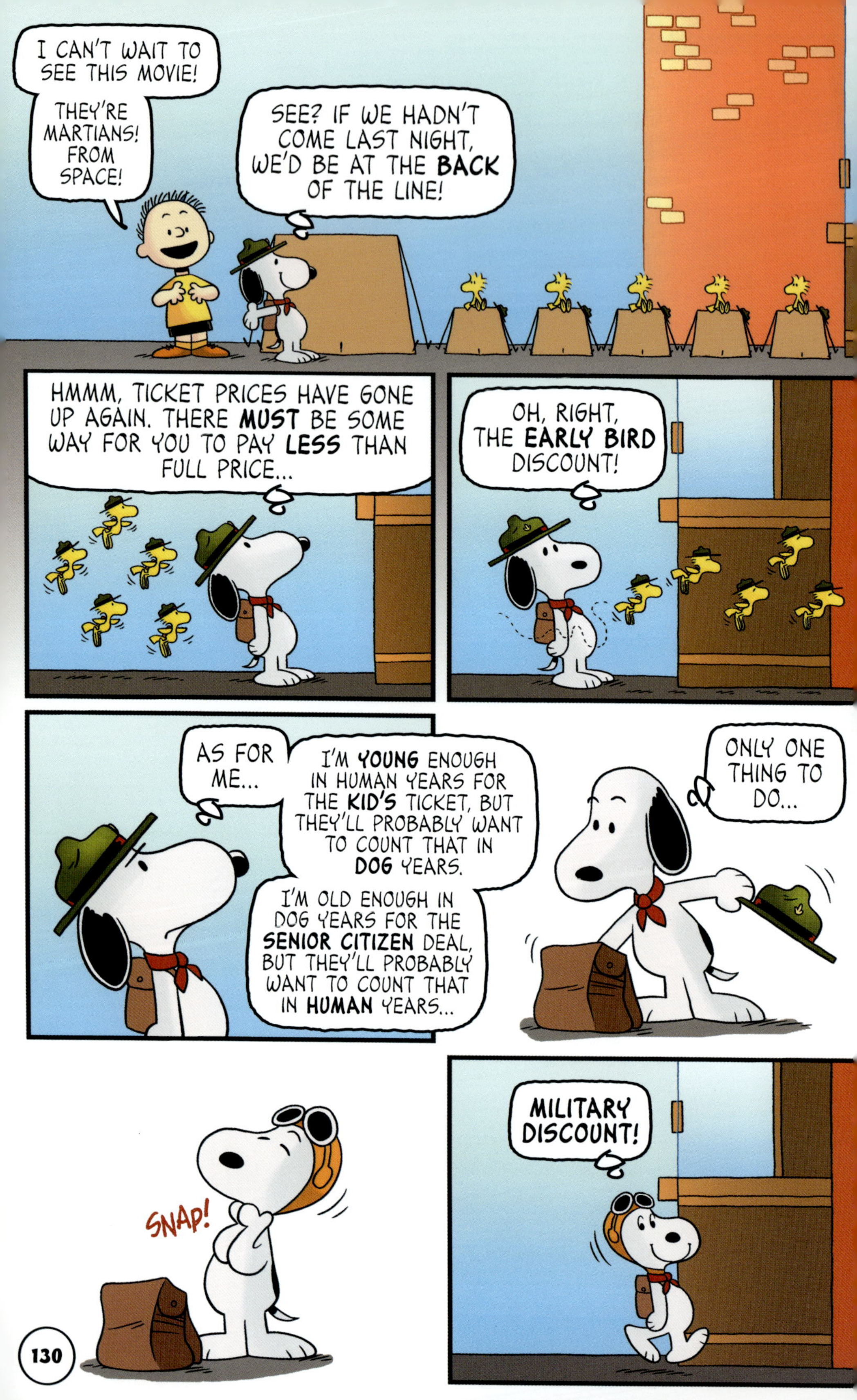
I CAN'T WAIT TO SEE THIS MOVIE!
THEY'RE MARTIANS! FROM SPACE!
SEE? IF WE HADN'T COME LAST NIGHT, WE'D BE AT THE **BACK** OF THE LINE!
HMMM, TICKET PRICES HAVE GONE UP AGAIN. THERE **MUST** BE SOME WAY FOR YOU TO PAY **LESS** THAN FULL PRICE...
OH, RIGHT, THE **EARLY BIRD** DISCOUNT!
AS FOR ME...
I'M **YOUNG** ENOUGH IN HUMAN YEARS FOR THE **KID'S** TICKET, BUT THEY'LL PROBABLY WANT TO COUNT THAT IN **DOG** YEARS.
I'M OLD ENOUGH IN DOG YEARS FOR THE **SENIOR CITIZEN** DEAL, BUT THEY'LL PROBABLY WANT TO COUNT THAT IN **HUMAN** YEARS...
ONLY ONE THING TO DO...
SNAP!
MILITARY DISCOUNT!

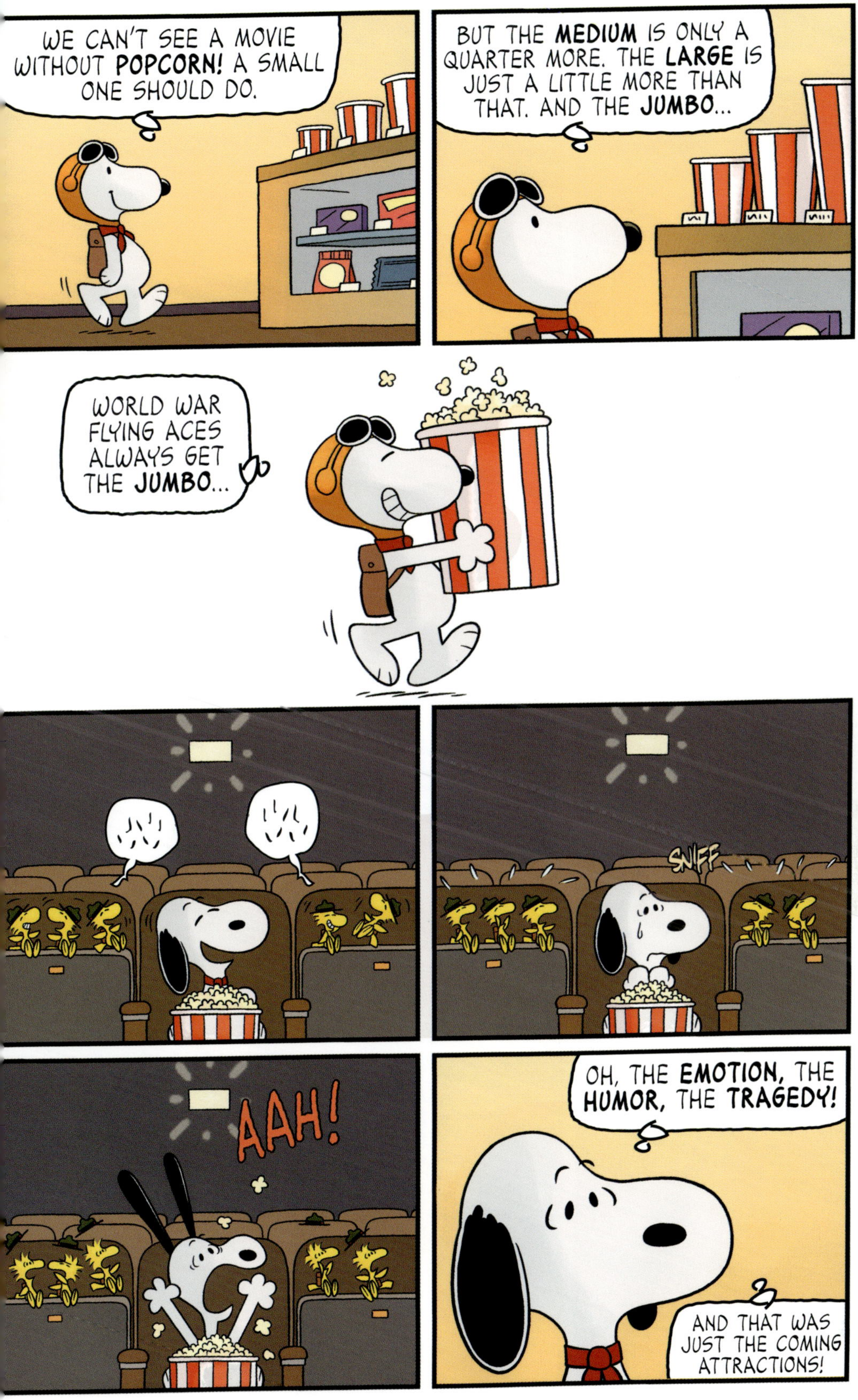
WE CAN'T SEE A MOVIE WITHOUT POPCORN! A SMALL ONE SHOULD DO.
BUT THE MEDIUM IS ONLY A QUARTER MORE. THE LARGE IS JUST A LITTLE MORE THAN THAT. AND THE JUMBO...
WORLD WAR FLYING ACES ALWAYS GET THE JUMBO...
SNIFF
AAH!
OH, THE EMOTION, THE HUMOR, THE TRAGEDY!
AND THAT WAS JUST THE COMING ATTRACTIONS!

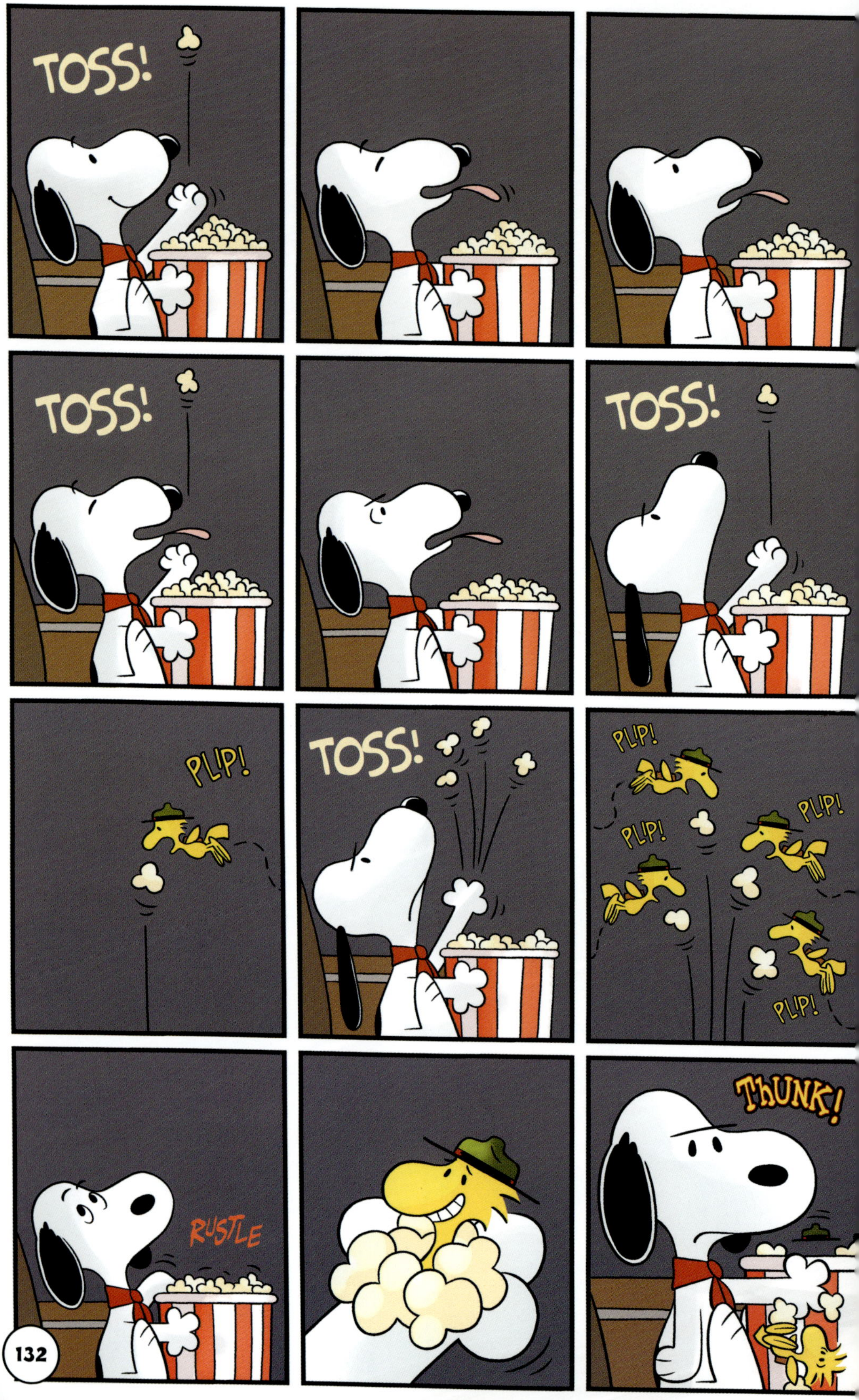
TOSS!
TOSS!
TOSS!
PLIP!
TOSS!
PLIP!
PLIP!
PLIP!
PLIP!
RUSTLE
THUNK!

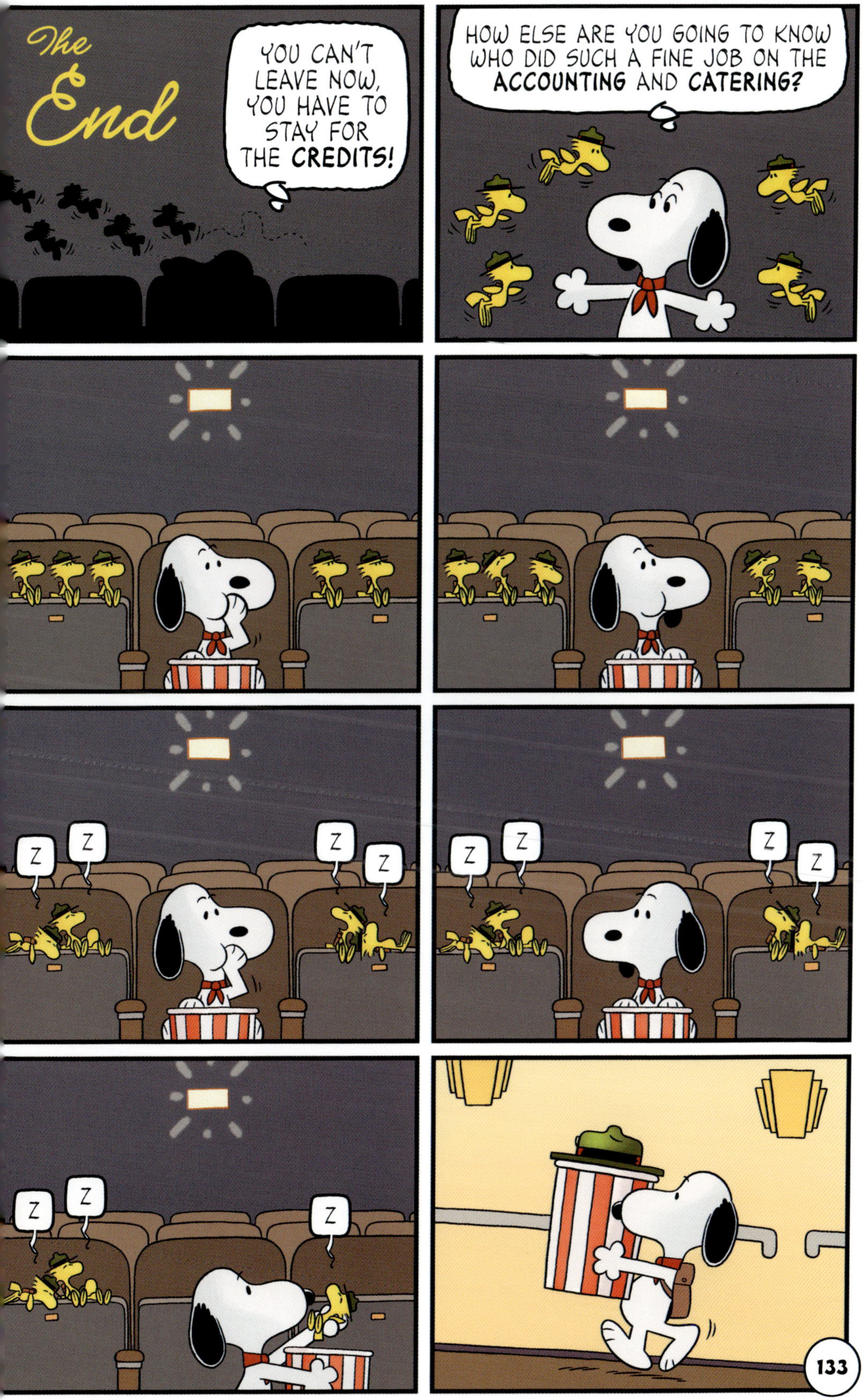
The End
YOU CAN'T LEAVE NOW, YOU HAVE TO STAY FOR THE CREDITS!
HOW ELSE ARE YOU GOING TO KNOW WHO DID SUCH A FINE JOB ON THE ACCOUNTING AND CATERING?
Z Z Z Z
Z Z Z Z
Z Z Z

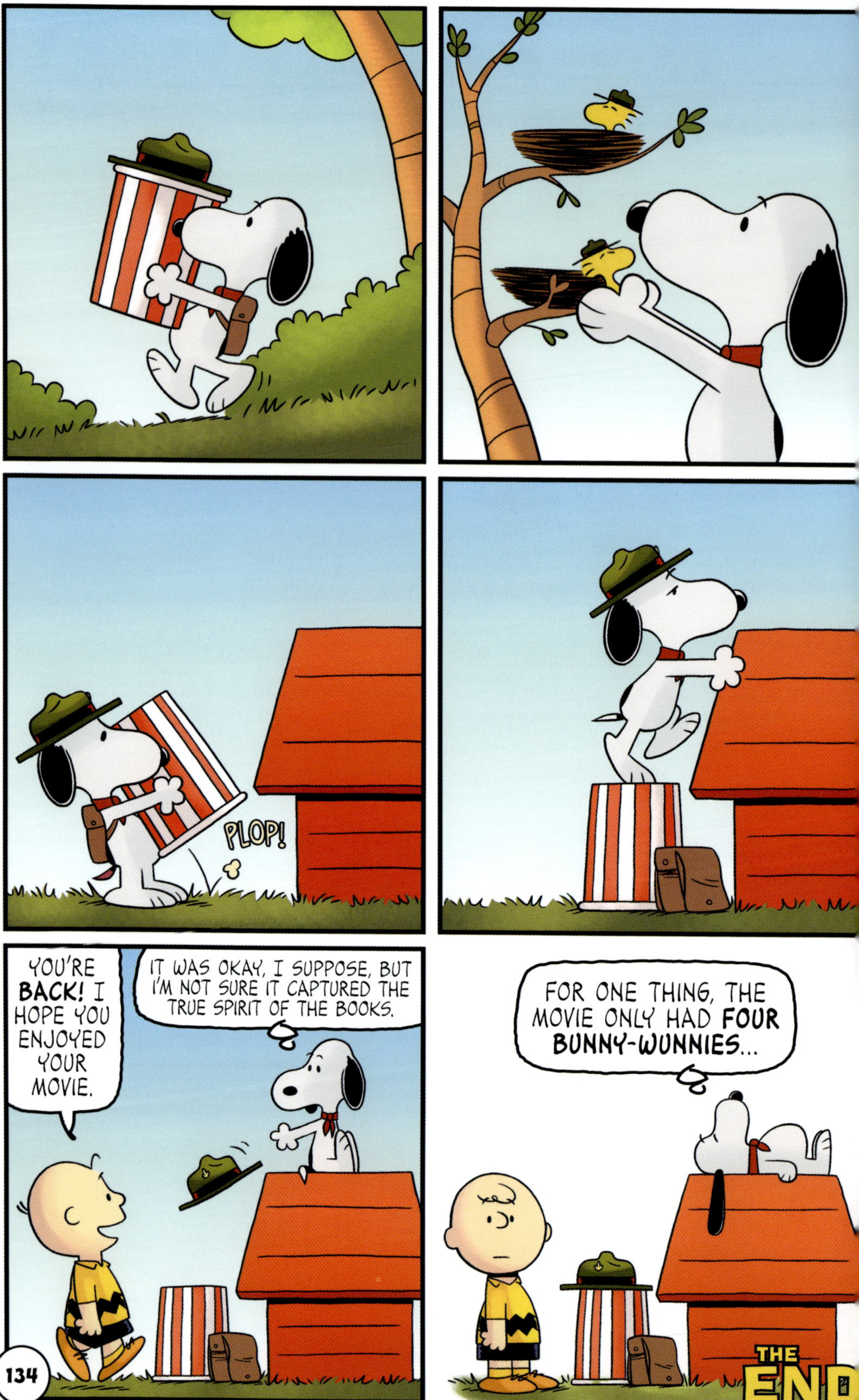
PLOP!
YOU'RE BACK! I HOPE YOU ENJOYED YOUR MOVIE.
IT WAS OKAY, I SUPPOSE, BUT I'M NOT SURE IT CAPTURED THE TRUE SPIRIT OF THE BOOKS.
FOR ONE THING, THE MOVIE ONLY HAD FOUR BUNNY-WUNNIES...
THE END

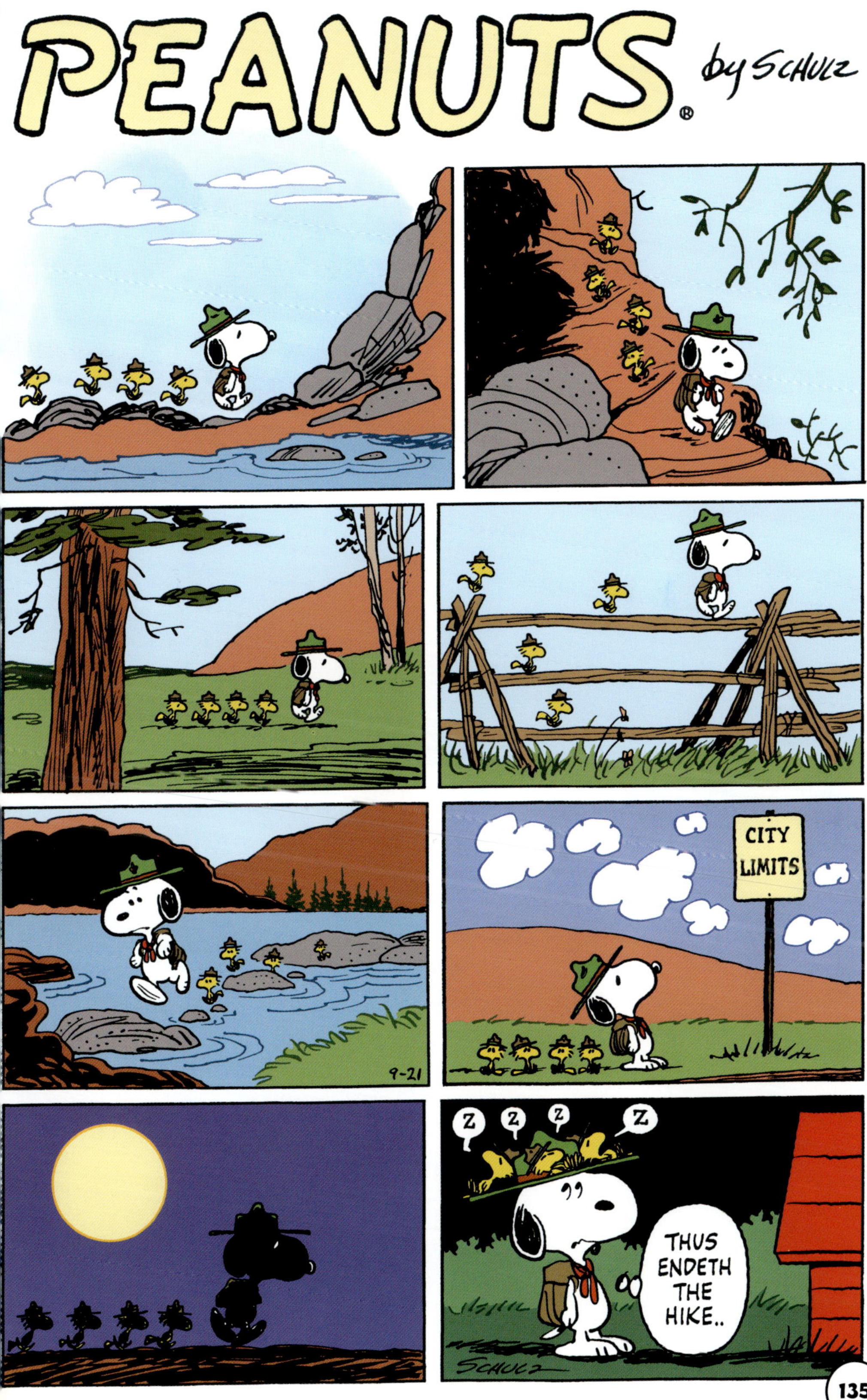
PEANUTS
by SCHULZ
9-21
CITY LIMITS
Z
Z
Z
Z
THUS ENDETH THE HIKE..
SCHULZ

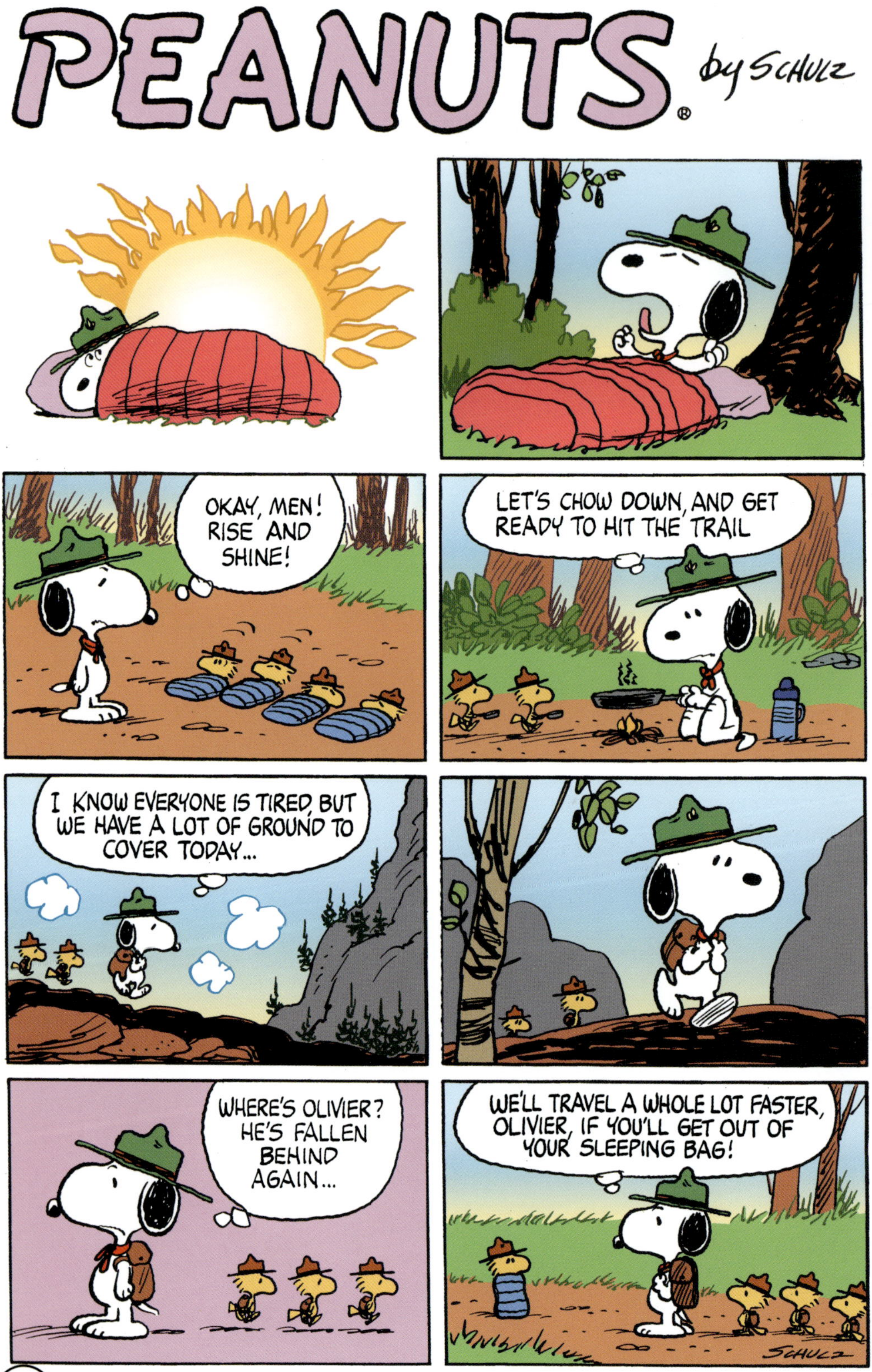
PEANUTS
by SCHULZ
OKAY, MEN! RISE AND SHINE!
LET'S CHOW DOWN, AND GET READY TO HIT THE TRAIL
I KNOW EVERYONE IS TIRED, BUT WE HAVE A LOT OF GROUND TO COVER TODAY...
WHERE'S OLIVIER? HE'S FALLEN BEHIND AGAIN...
WE'LL TRAVEL A WHOLE LOT FASTER, OLIVIER, IF YOU'LL GET OUT OF YOUR SLEEPING BAG!
SCHULZ

Toodle-oo, Caribou!

A Tale of the Frozen North

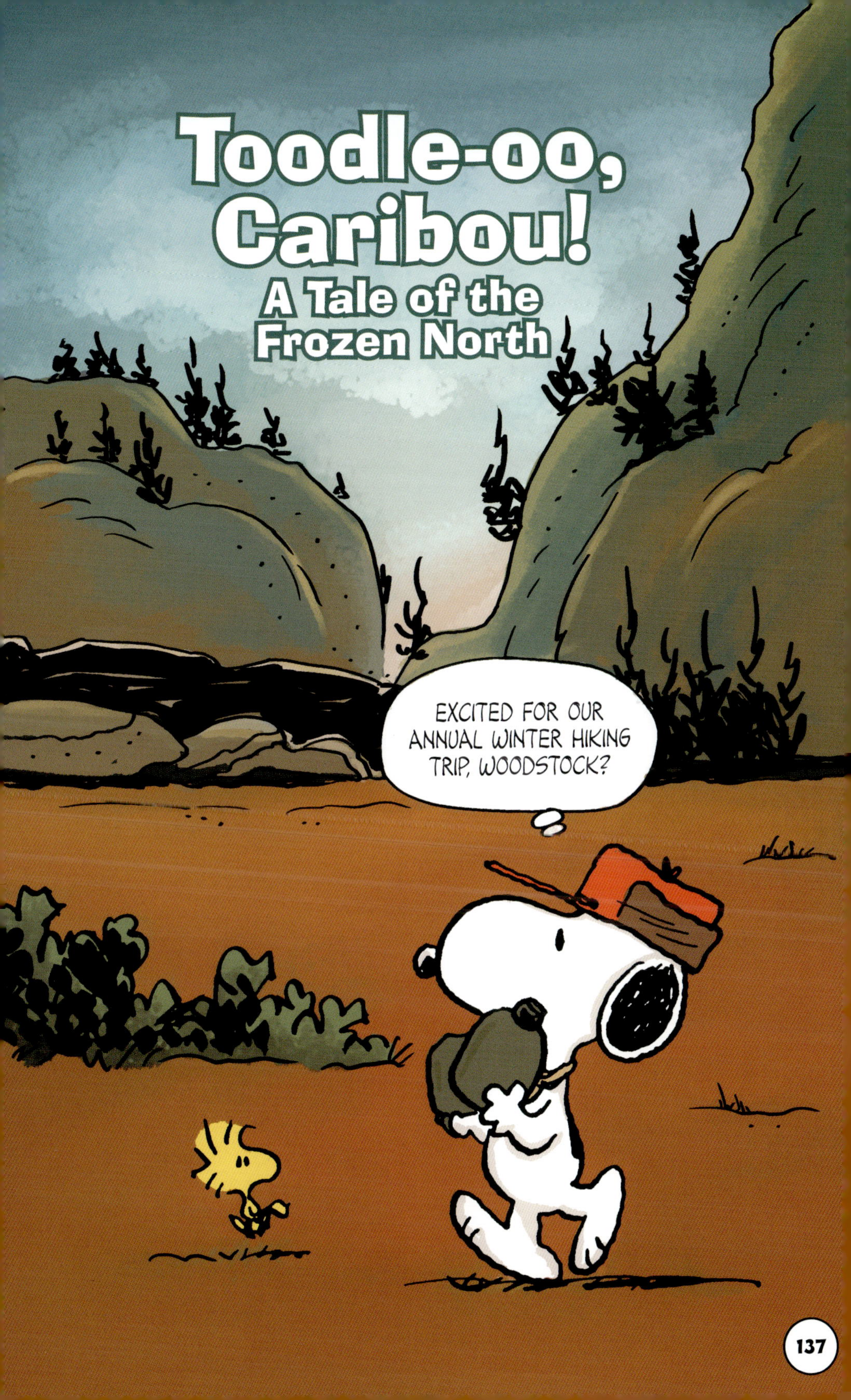
EXCITED FOR OUR ANNUAL WINTER HIKING TRIP, WOODSTOCK?

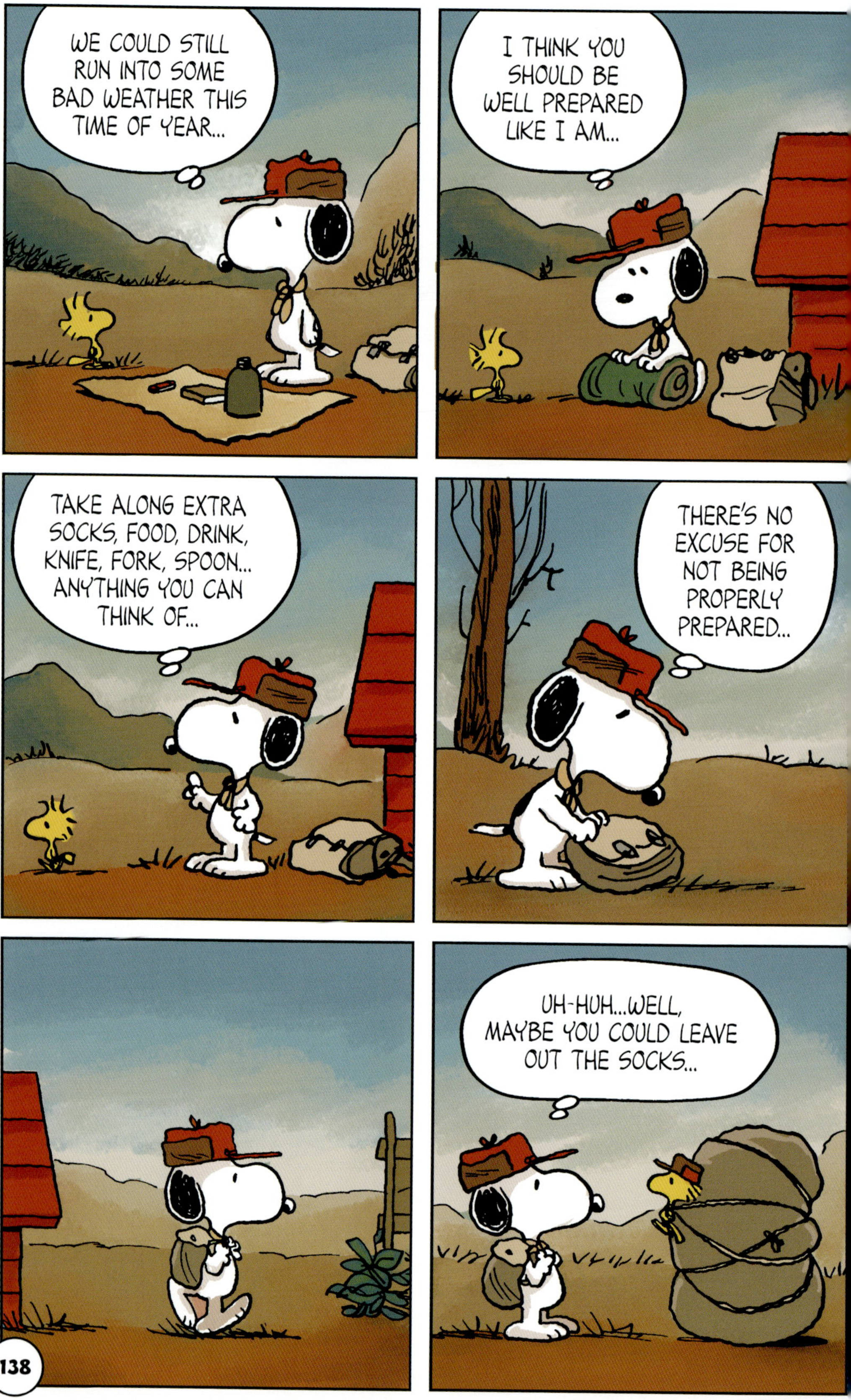
WE COULD STILL RUN INTO SOME BAD WEATHER THIS TIME OF YEAR...
I THINK YOU SHOULD BE WELL PREPARED LIKE I AM...
TAKE ALONG EXTRA SOCKS, FOOD, DRINK, KNIFE, FORK, SPOON... ANYTHING YOU CAN THINK OF...
THERE'S NO EXCUSE FOR NOT BEING PROPERLY PREPARED...
UH-HUH...WELL, MAYBE YOU COULD LEAVE OUT THE SOCKS...

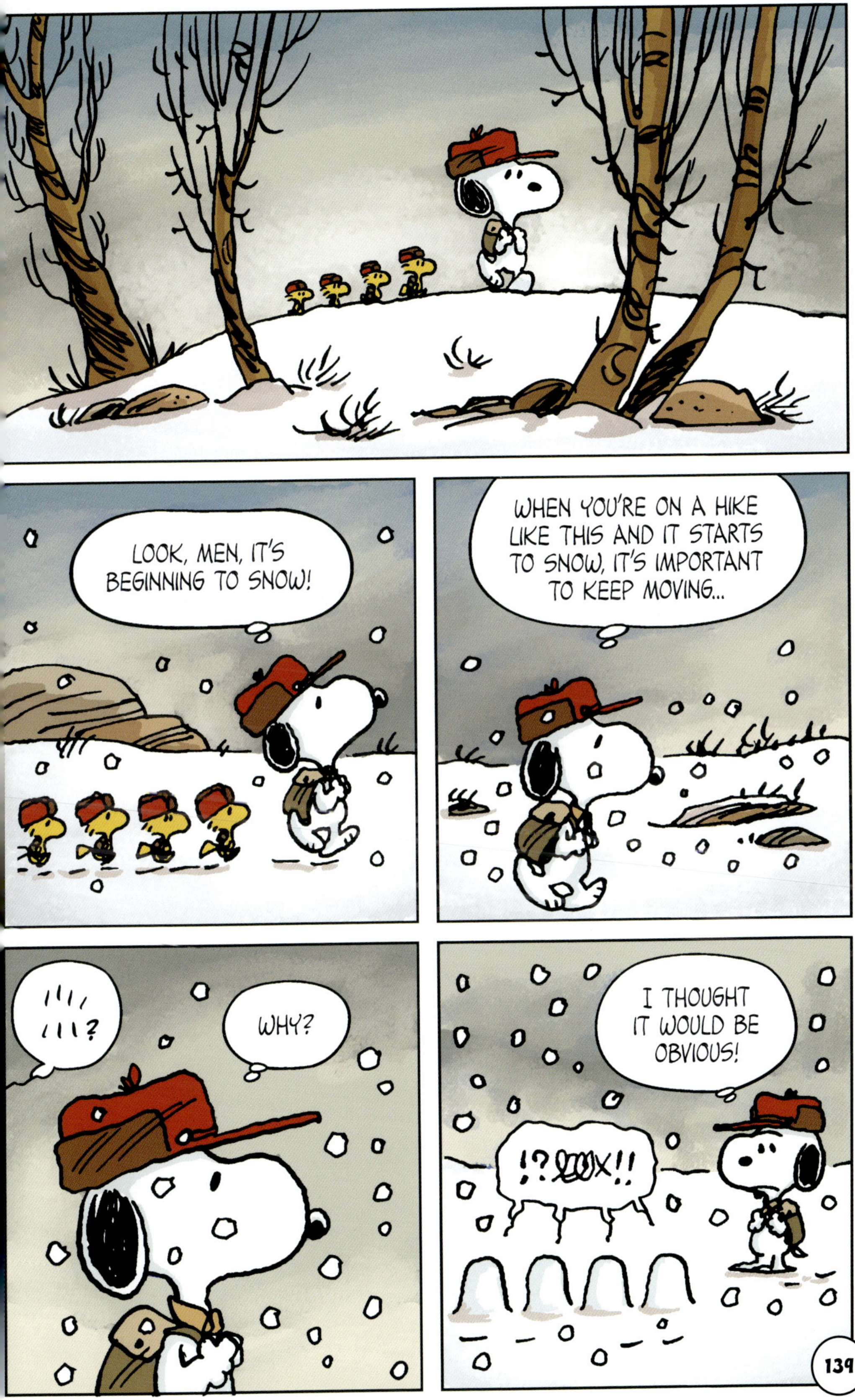
LOOK, MEN, IT'S BEGINNING TO SNOW!
WHEN YOU'RE ON A HIKE LIKE THIS AND IT STARTS TO SNOW, IT'S IMPORTANT TO KEEP MOVING...
WHY?
I THOUGHT IT WOULD BE OBVIOUS!

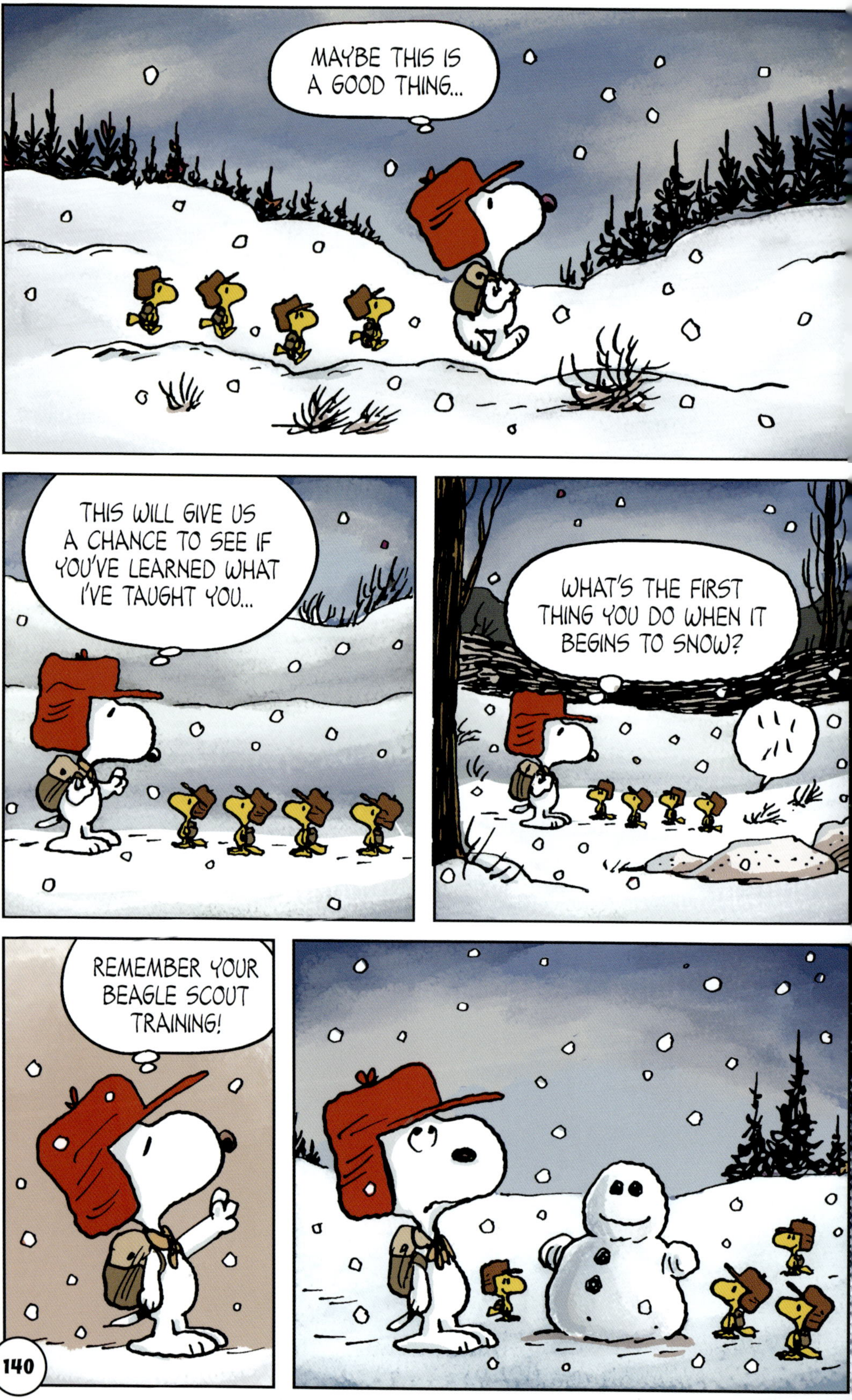
MAYBE THIS IS A GOOD THING...
THIS WILL GIVE US A CHANCE TO SEE IF YOU'VE LEARNED WHAT I'VE TAUGHT YOU...
WHAT'S THE FIRST THING YOU DO WHEN IT BEGINS TO SNOW?
REMEMBER YOUR BEAGLE SCOUT TRAINING!

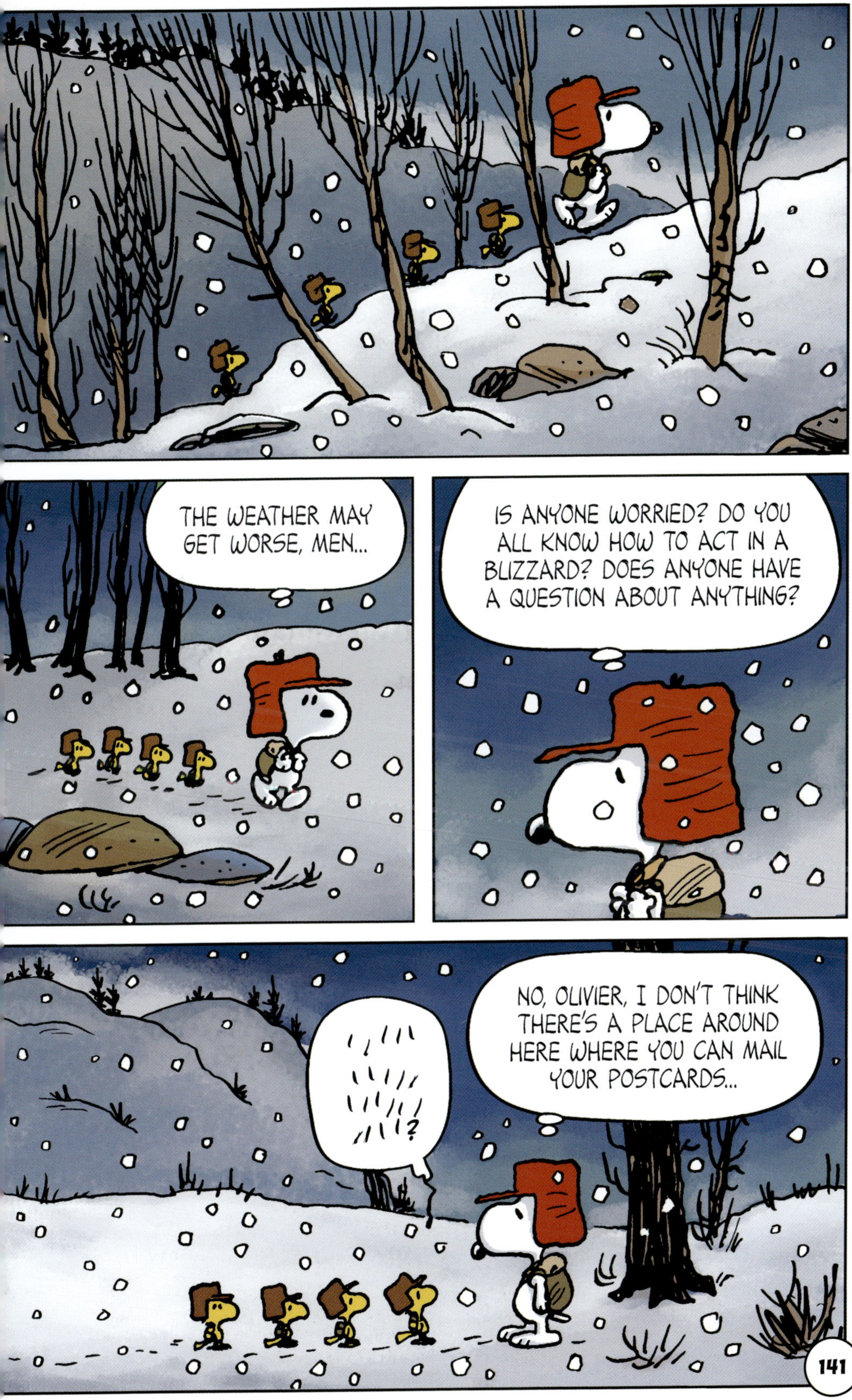
THE WEATHER MAY GET WORSE, MEN...
IS ANYONE WORRIED? DO YOU ALL KNOW HOW TO ACT IN A BLIZZARD? DOES ANYONE HAVE A QUESTION ABOUT ANYTHING?
NO, OLIVIER, I DON'T THINK THERE'S A PLACE AROUND HERE WHERE YOU CAN MAIL YOUR POSTCARDS...

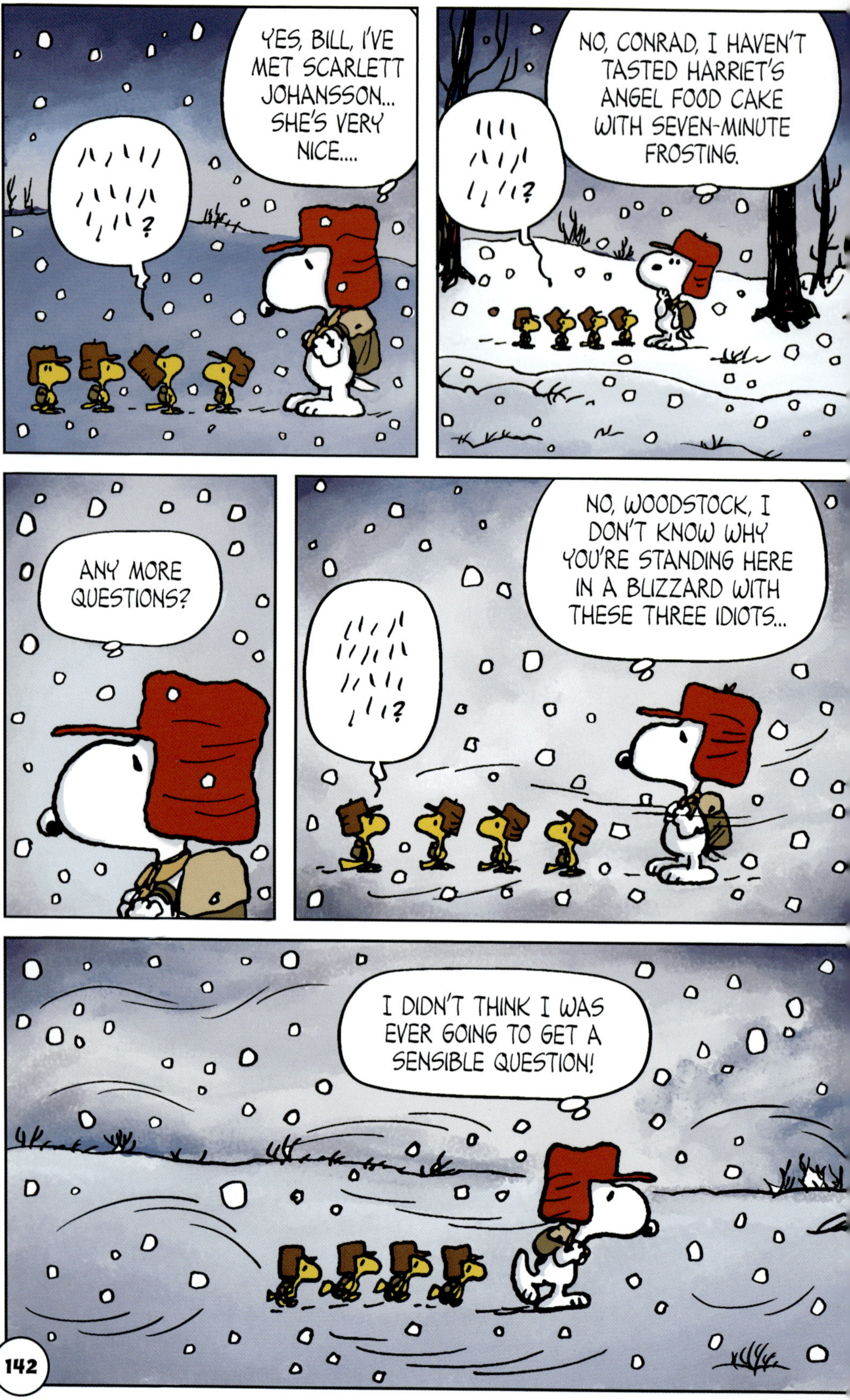
YES, BILL, I'VE MET SCARLETT JOHANSSON... SHE'S VERY NICE....
NO, CONRAD, I HAVEN'T TASTED HARRIET'S ANGEL FOOD CAKE WITH SEVEN-MINUTE FROSTING.
ANY MORE QUESTIONS?
NO, WOODSTOCK, I DON'T KNOW WHY YOU'RE STANDING HERE IN A BLIZZARD WITH THESE THREE IDIOTS...
I DIDN'T THINK I WAS EVER GOING TO GET A SENSIBLE QUESTION!

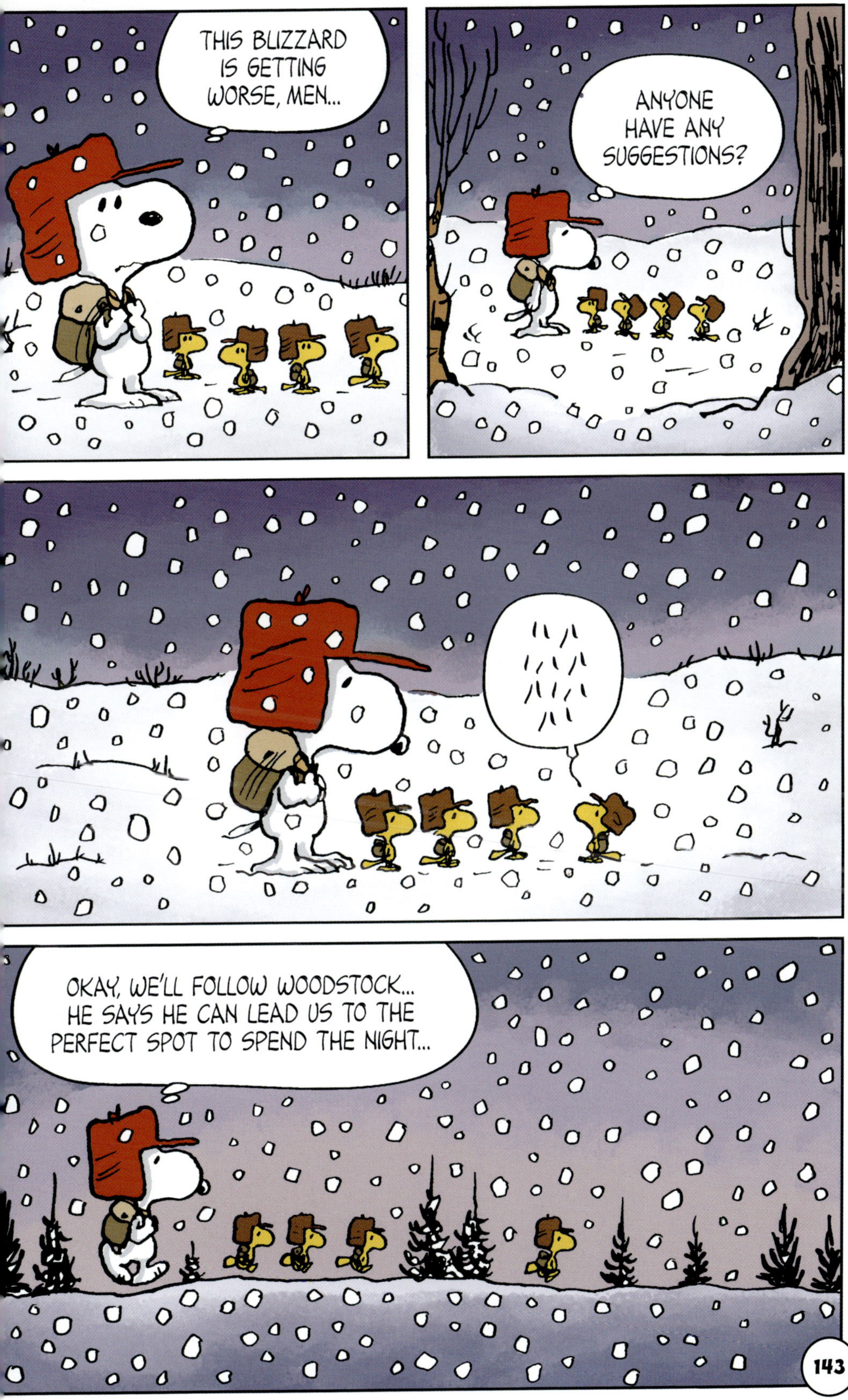
THIS BLIZZARD IS GETTING WORSE, MEN...
ANYONE HAVE ANY SUGGESTIONS?
OKAY, WE'LL FOLLOW WOODSTOCK... HE SAYS HE CAN LEAD US TO THE PERFECT SPOT TO SPEND THE NIGHT...

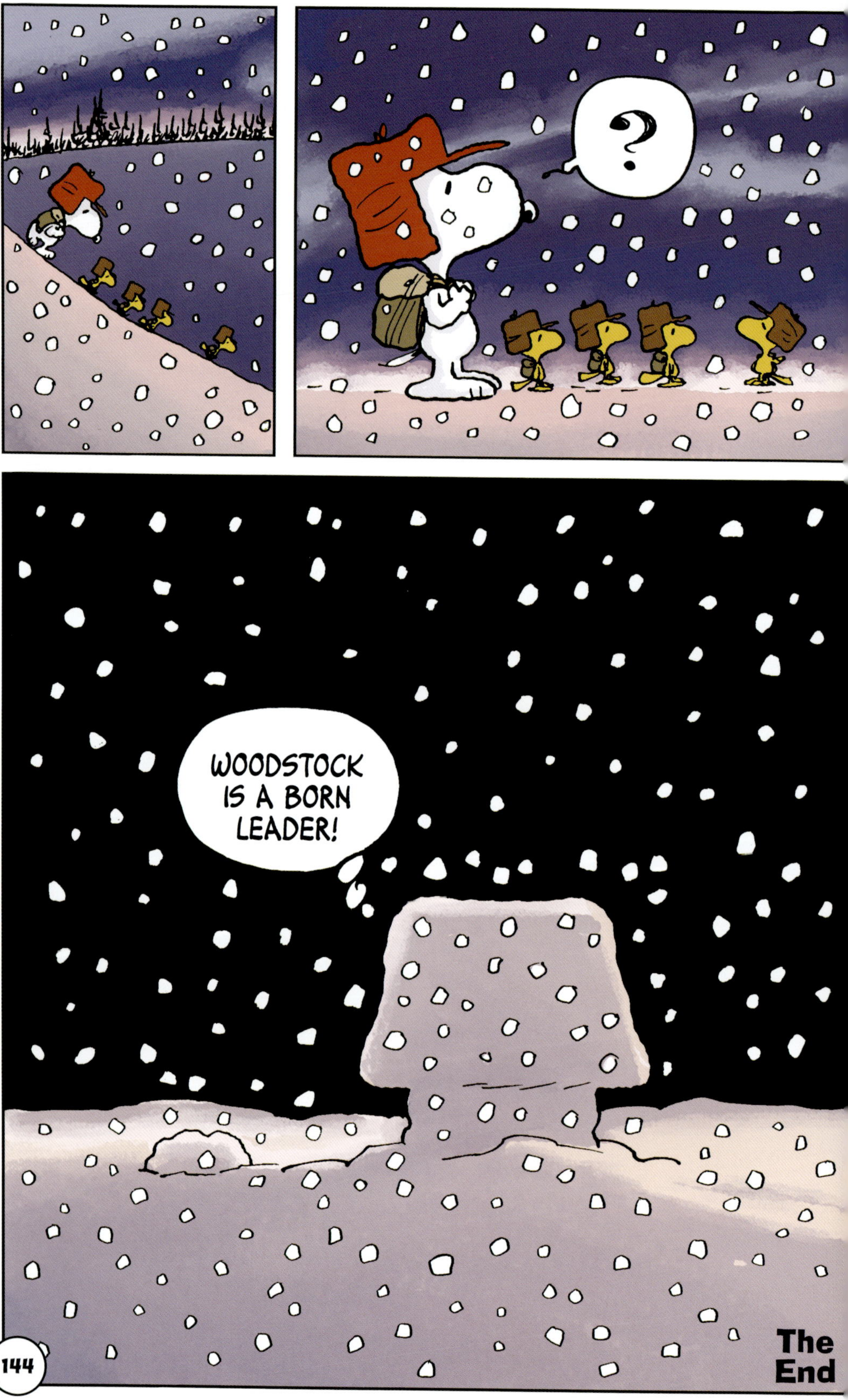
?
WOODSTOCK IS A BORN LEADER!
The End

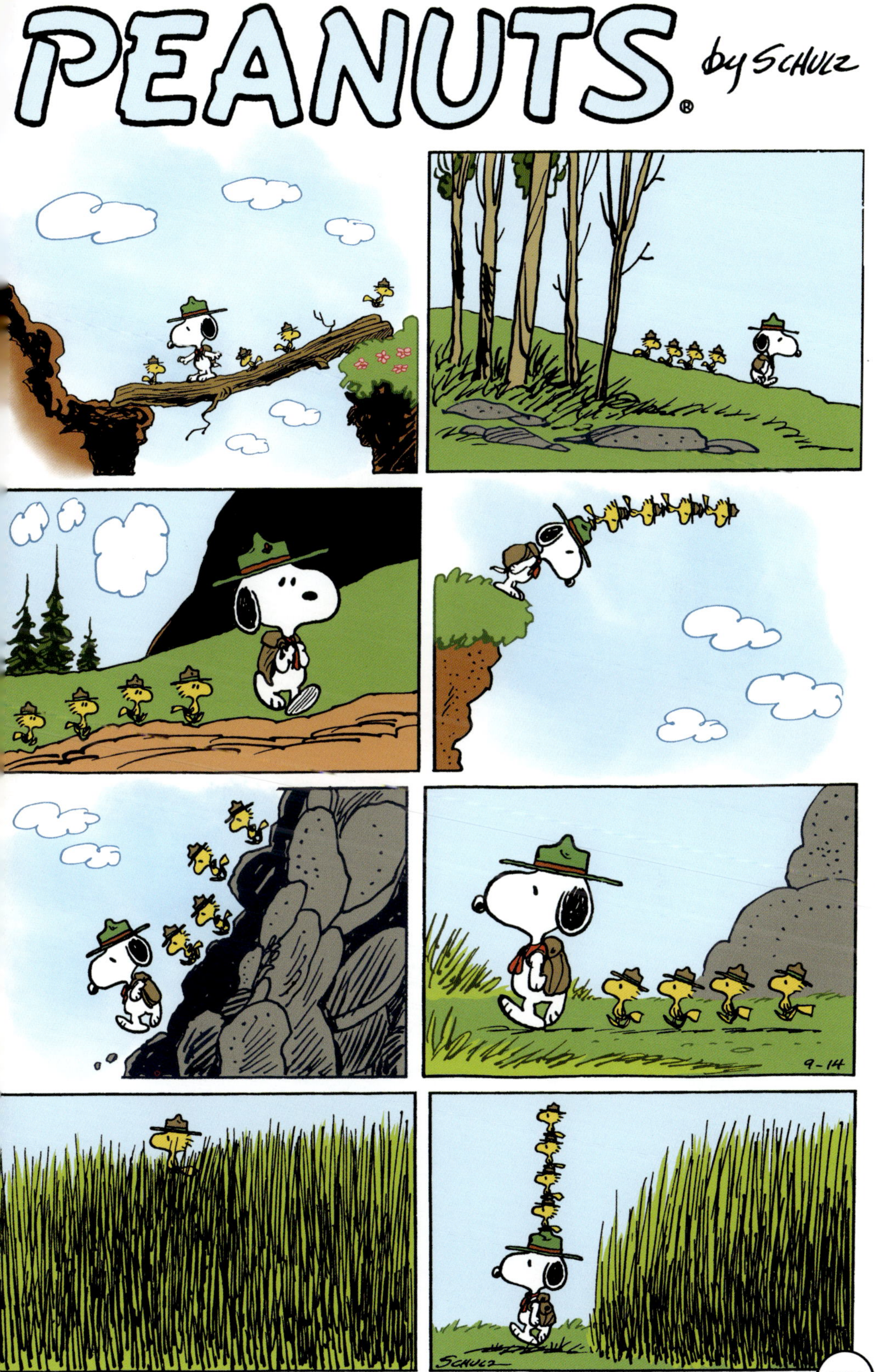
PEANUTS® by SCHULZ
9-14
SCHULZ

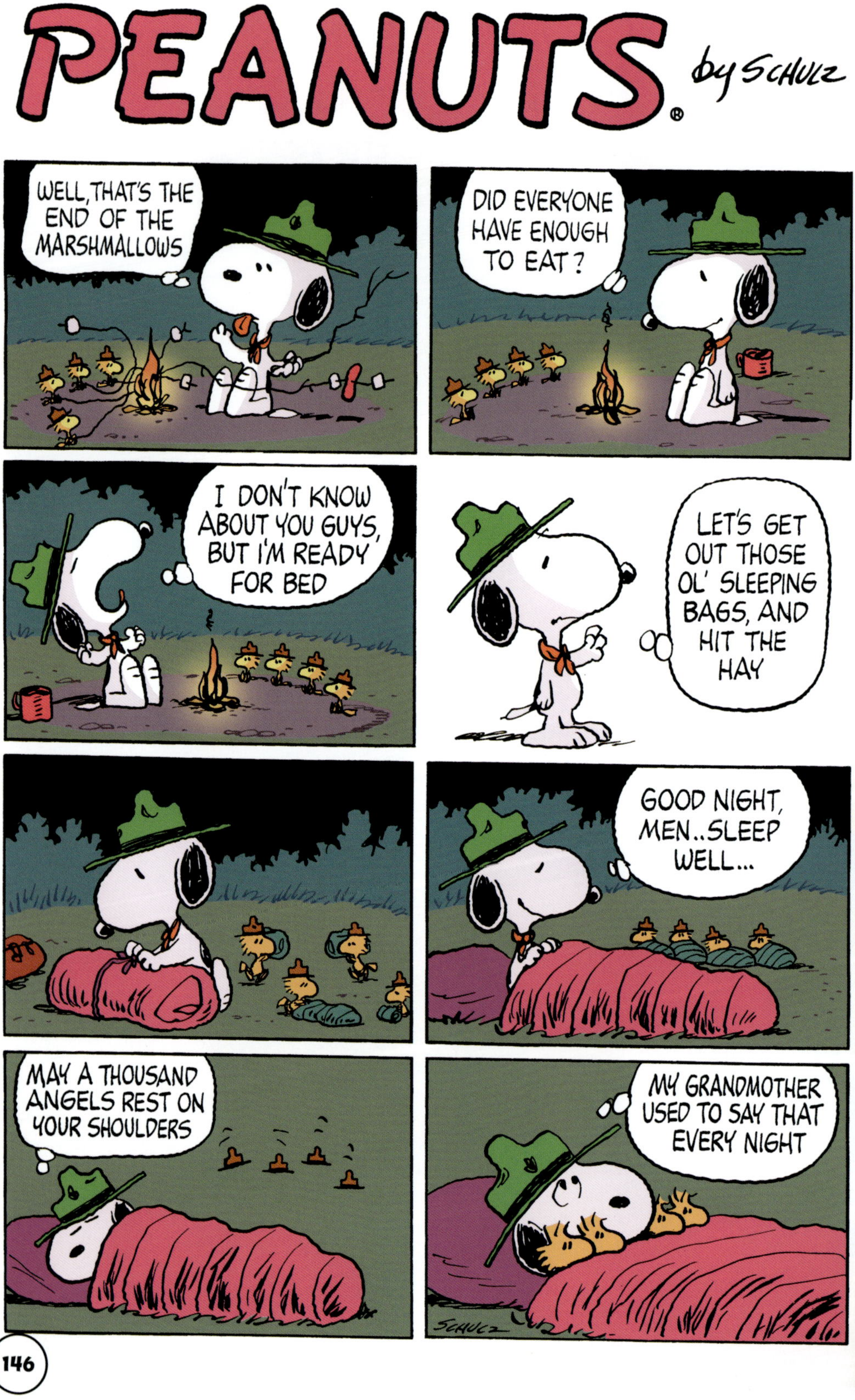
PEANUTS
by SCHULZ
WELL, THAT'S THE END OF THE MARSHMALLOWS
DID EVERYONE HAVE ENOUGH TO EAT?
I DON'T KNOW ABOUT YOU GUYS, BUT I'M READY FOR BED
LET'S GET OUT THOSE OL' SLEEPING BAGS, AND HIT THE HAY
GOOD NIGHT, MEN..SLEEP WELL...
MAY A THOUSAND ANGELS REST ON YOUR SHOULDERS
MY GRANDMOTHER USED TO SAY THAT EVERY NIGHT
SCHULZ

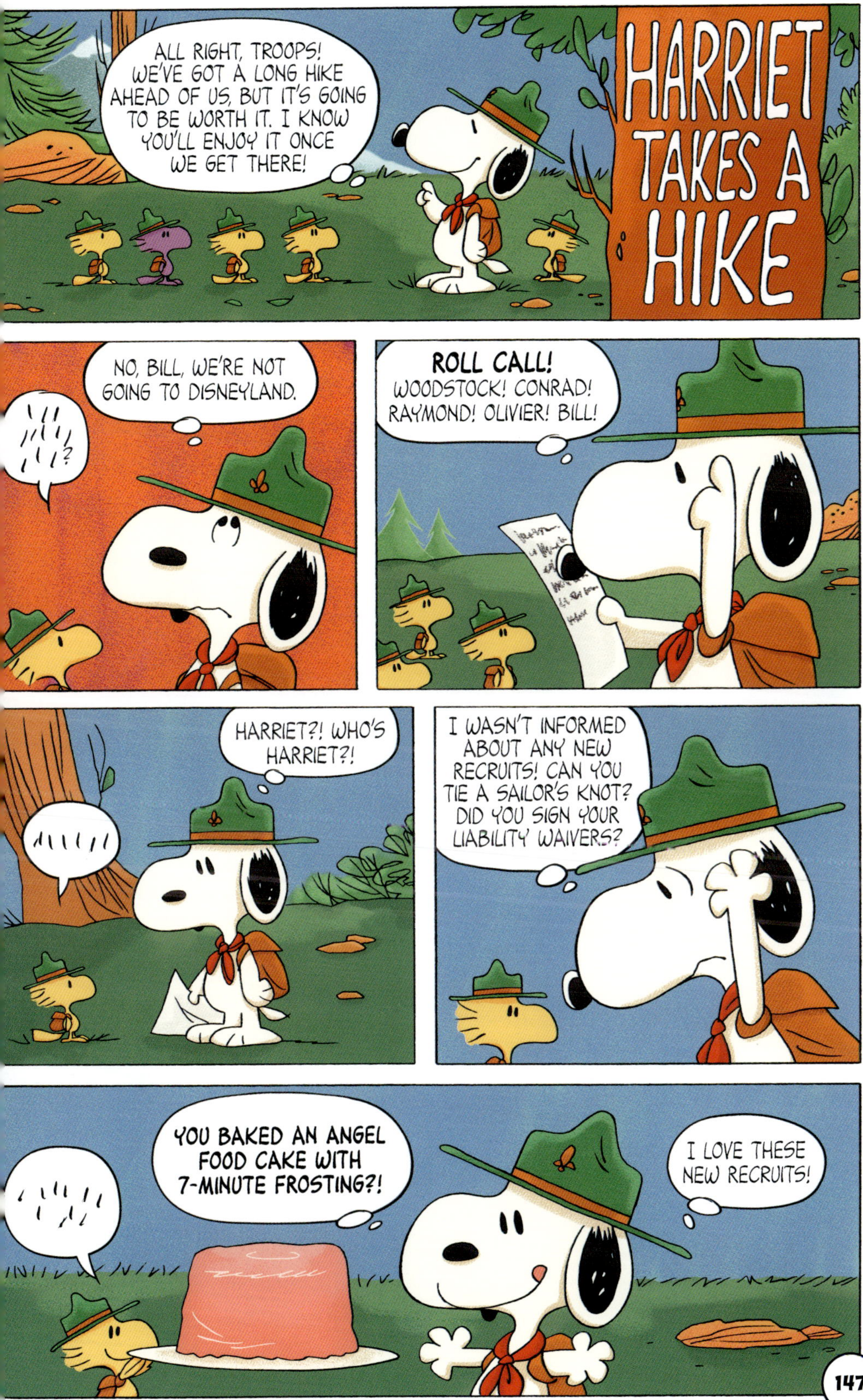

ALL RIGHT, TROOPS! WE'VE GOT A LONG HIKE AHEAD OF US, BUT IT'S GOING TO BE WORTH IT. I KNOW YOU'LL ENJOY IT ONCE WE GET THERE!
HARRIET TAKES A HIKE
NO, BILL, WE'RE NOT GOING TO DISNEYLAND.
ROLL CALL! WOODSTOCK! CONRAD! RAYMOND! OLIVIER! BILL!
HARRIET?! WHO'S HARRIET?!
I WASN'T INFORMED ABOUT ANY NEW RECRUITS! CAN YOU TIE A SAILOR'S KNOT? DID YOU SIGN YOUR LIABILITY WAIVERS?
YOU BAKED AN ANGEL FOOD CAKE WITH 7-MINUTE FROSTING?!
I LOVE THESE NEW RECRUITS!

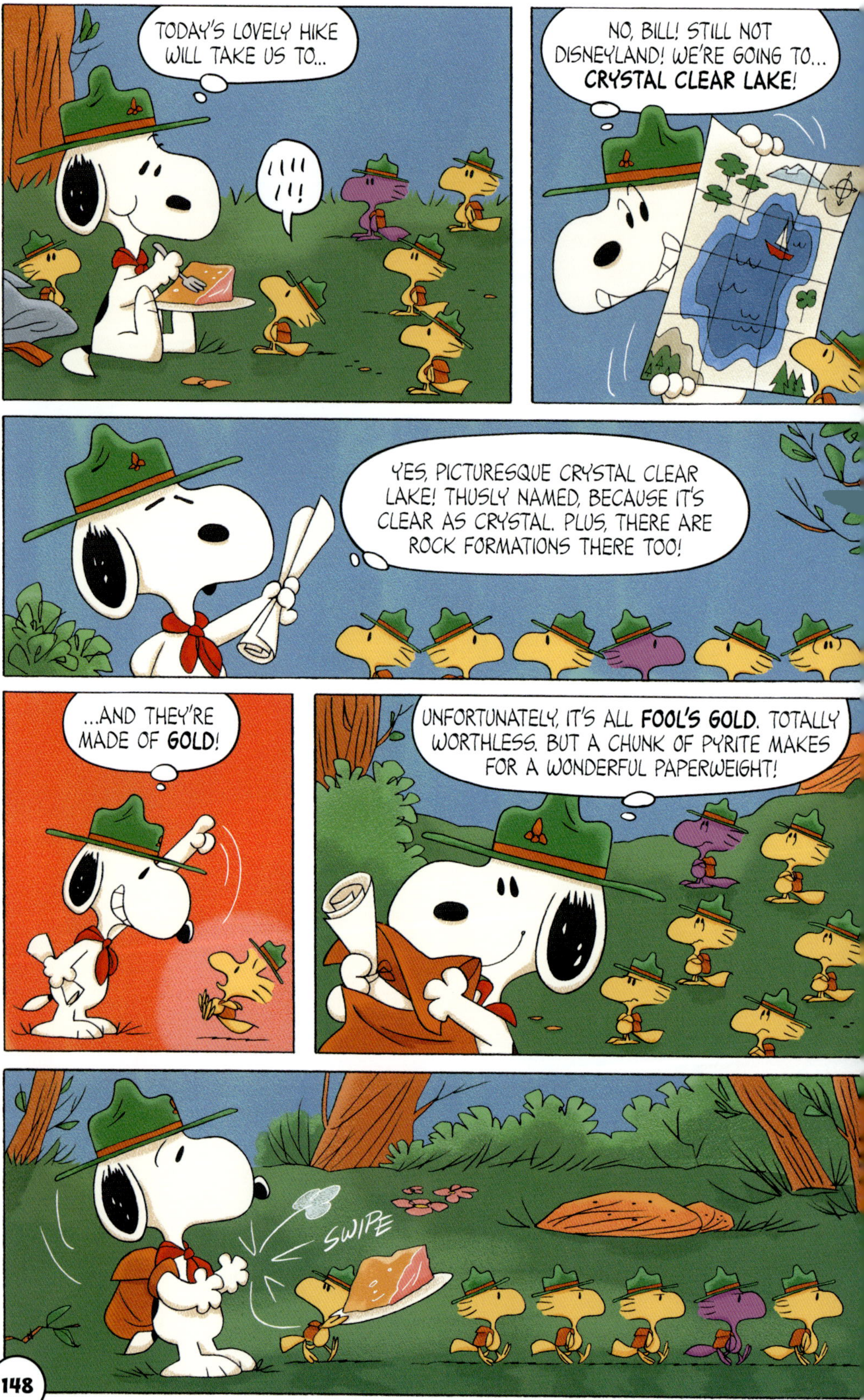
TODAY'S LOVELY HIKE WILL TAKE US TO...
NO, BILL! STILL NOT DISNEYLAND! WE'RE GOING TO... CRYSTAL CLEAR LAKE!
YES, PICTURESQUE CRYSTAL CLEAR LAKE! THUSLY NAMED, BECAUSE IT'S CLEAR AS CRYSTAL. PLUS, THERE ARE ROCK FORMATIONS THERE TOO!
...AND THEY'RE MADE OF GOLD!
UNFORTUNATELY, IT'S ALL FOOL'S GOLD. TOTALLY WORTHLESS. BUT A CHUNK OF PYRITE MAKES FOR A WONDERFUL PAPERWEIGHT!
SWIPE

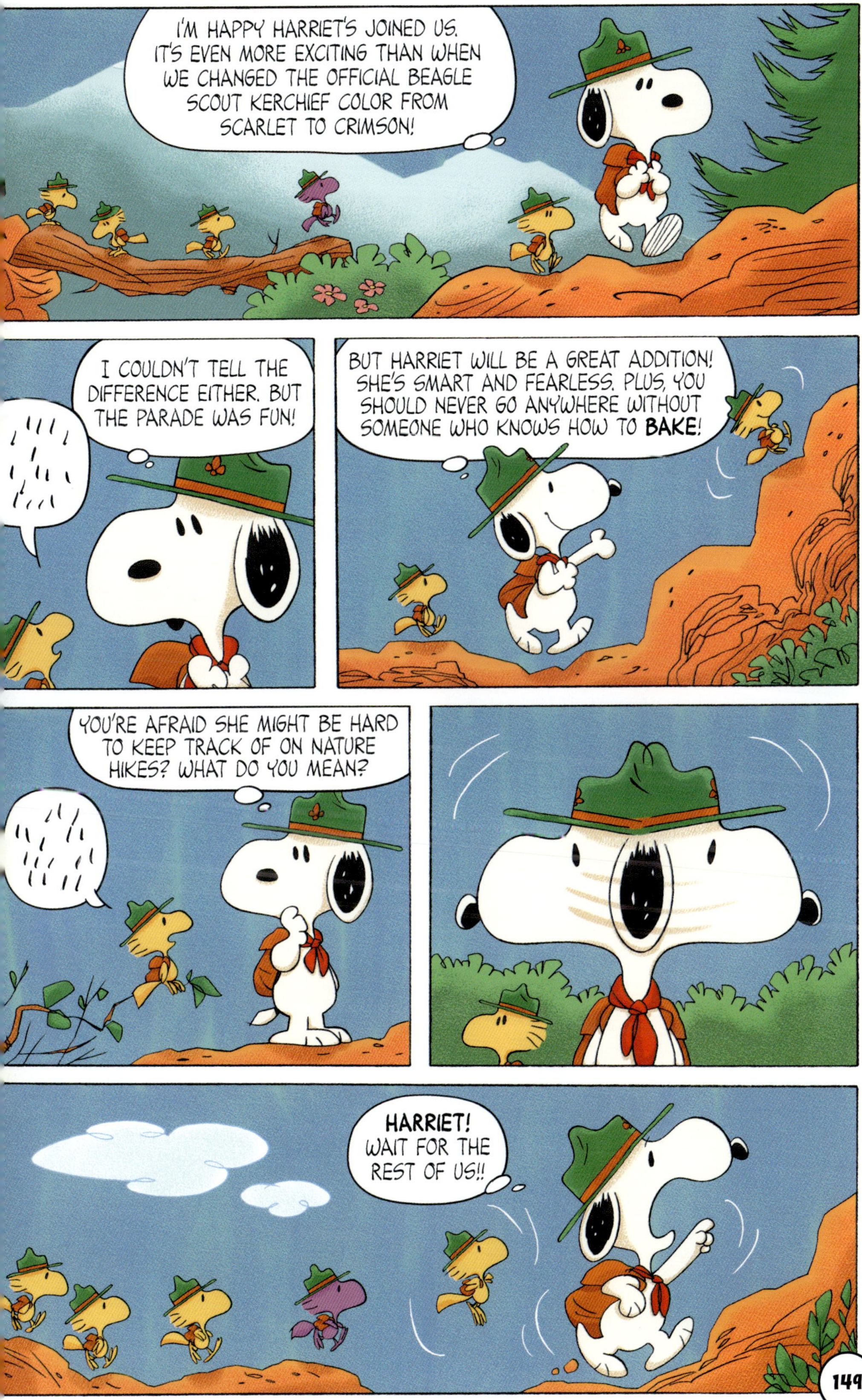
I'M HAPPY HARRIET'S JOINED US. IT'S EVEN MORE EXCITING THAN WHEN WE CHANGED THE OFFICIAL BEAGLE SCOUT KERCHIEF COLOR FROM SCARLET TO CRIMSON!
I COULDN'T TELL THE DIFFERENCE EITHER. BUT THE PARADE WAS FUN!
BUT HARRIET WILL BE A GREAT ADDITION! SHE'S SMART AND FEARLESS. PLUS, YOU SHOULD NEVER GO ANYWHERE WITHOUT SOMEONE WHO KNOWS HOW TO **BAKE**!
YOU'RE AFRAID SHE MIGHT BE HARD TO KEEP TRACK OF ON NATURE HIKES? WHAT DO YOU MEAN?
HARRIET! WAIT FOR THE REST OF US!!

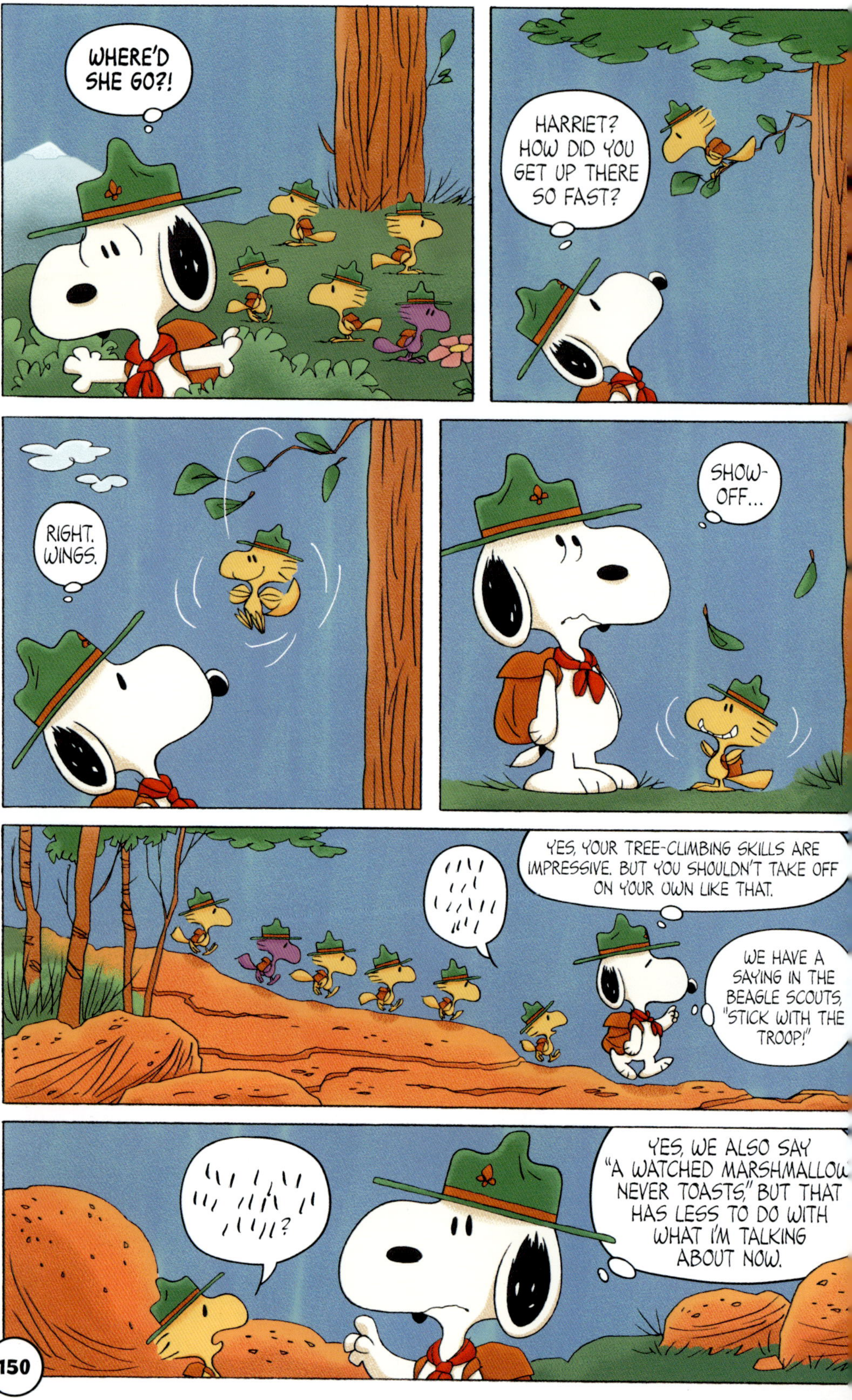
WHERE'D SHE GO?!
HARRIET? HOW DID YOU GET UP THERE SO FAST?
RIGHT. WINGS.
SHOW-OFF...
YES, YOUR TREE-CLIMBING SKILLS ARE IMPRESSIVE. BUT YOU SHOULDN'T TAKE OFF ON YOUR OWN LIKE THAT.
WE HAVE A SAYING IN THE BEAGLE SCOUTS, "STICK WITH THE TROOP!"
YES, WE ALSO SAY "A WATCHED MARSHMALLOW NEVER TOASTS," BUT THAT HAS LESS TO DO WITH WHAT I'M TALKING ABOUT NOW.

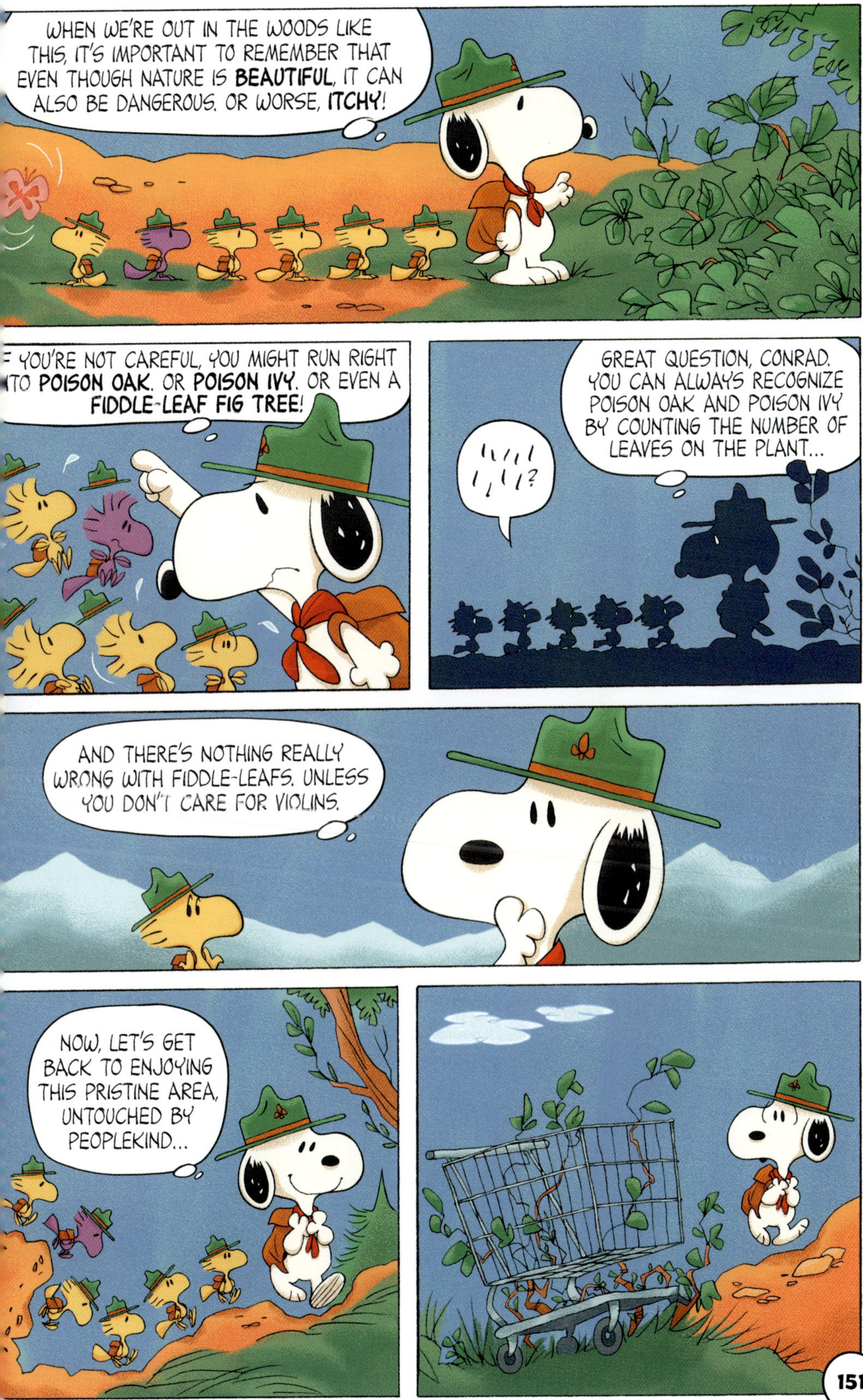
WHEN WE'RE OUT IN THE WOODS LIKE THIS, IT'S IMPORTANT TO REMEMBER THAT EVEN THOUGH NATURE IS **BEAUTIFUL**, IT CAN ALSO BE DANGEROUS. OR WORSE, **ITCHY**!
YOU'RE NOT CAREFUL, YOU MIGHT RUN RIGHT TO **POISON OAK**. OR **POISON IVY**. OR EVEN A **FIDDLE-LEAF FIG TREE**!
!!!!?
GREAT QUESTION, CONRAD. YOU CAN ALWAYS RECOGNIZE POISON OAK AND POISON IVY BY COUNTING THE NUMBER OF LEAVES ON THE PLANT...
AND THERE'S NOTHING REALLY WRONG WITH FIDDLE-LEAFS. UNLESS YOU DON'T CARE FOR VIOLINS.
NOW, LET'S GET BACK TO ENJOYING THIS PRISTINE AREA, UNTOUCHED BY PEOPLEKIND...

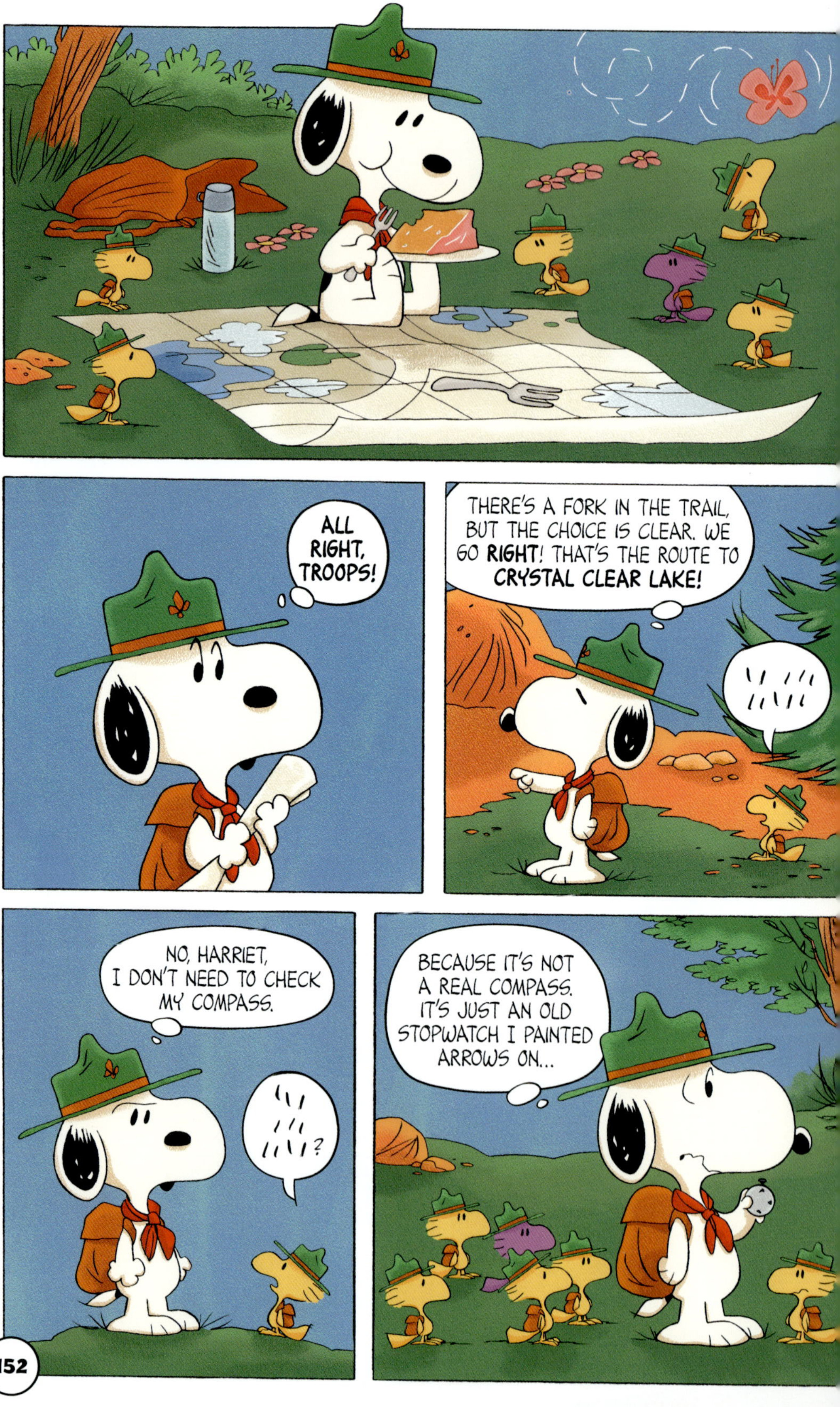
ALL RIGHT, TROOPS!
THERE'S A FORK IN THE TRAIL, BUT THE CHOICE IS CLEAR. WE GO **RIGHT**! THAT'S THE ROUTE TO **CRYSTAL CLEAR LAKE!**
NO, HARRIET, I DON'T NEED TO CHECK MY COMPASS.
BECAUSE IT'S NOT A REAL COMPASS. IT'S JUST AN OLD STOPWATCH I PAINTED ARROWS ON...

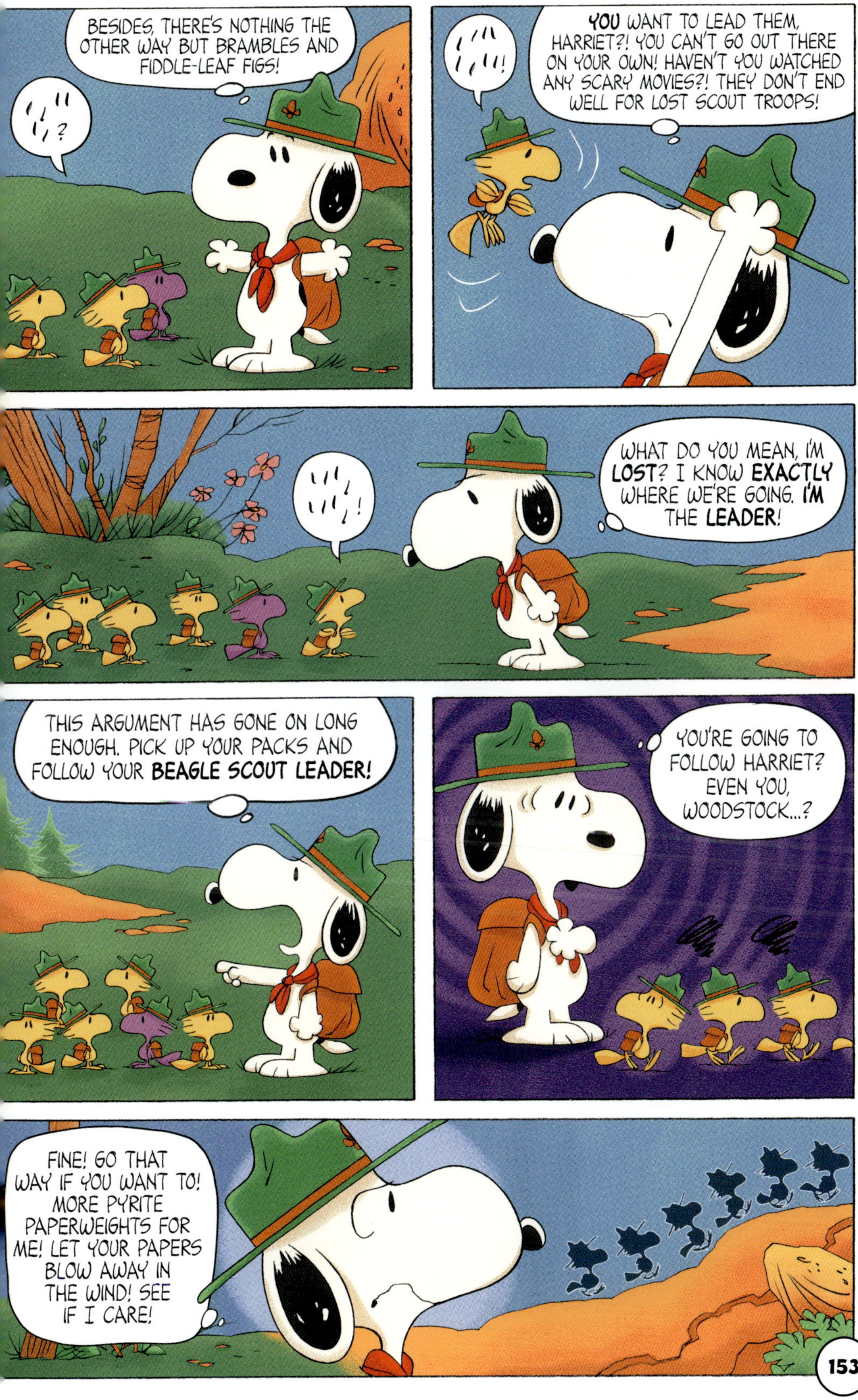
BESIDES, THERE'S NOTHING THE OTHER WAY BUT BRAMBLES AND FIDDLE-LEAF FIGS!
YOU WANT TO LEAD THEM, HARRIET?! YOU CAN'T GO OUT THERE ON YOUR OWN! HAVEN'T YOU WATCHED ANY SCARY MOVIES?! THEY DON'T END WELL FOR LOST SCOUT TROOPS!
WHAT DO YOU MEAN, I'M LOST? I KNOW EXACTLY WHERE WE'RE GOING. I'M THE LEADER!
THIS ARGUMENT HAS GONE ON LONG ENOUGH. PICK UP YOUR PACKS AND FOLLOW YOUR BEAGLE SCOUT LEADER!
YOU'RE GOING TO FOLLOW HARRIET? EVEN YOU, WOODSTOCK...?
FINE! GO THAT WAY IF YOU WANT TO! MORE PYRITE PAPERWEIGHTS FOR ME! LET YOUR PAPERS BLOW AWAY IN THE WIND! SEE IF I CARE!

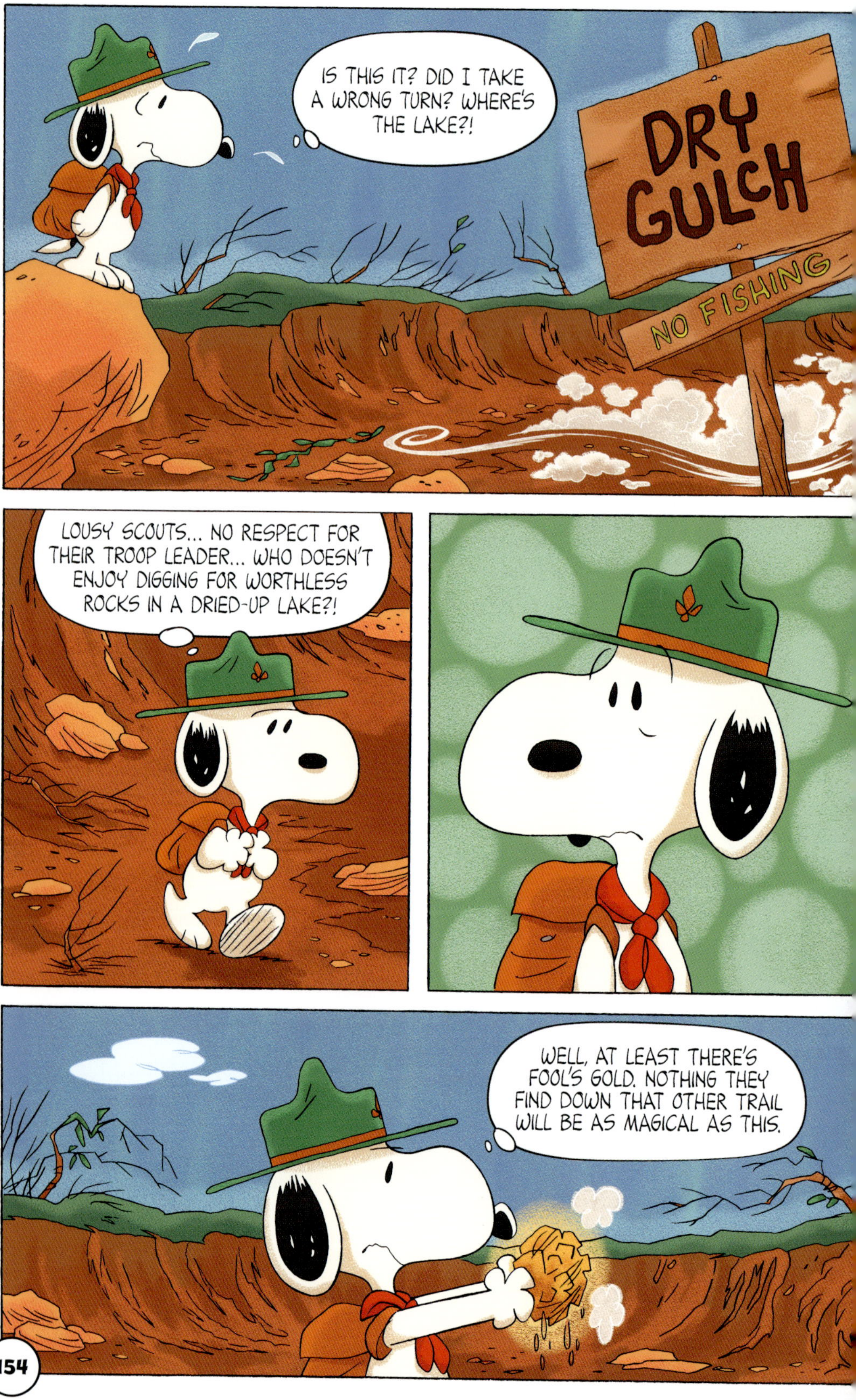
IS THIS IT? DID I TAKE A WRONG TURN? WHERE'S THE LAKE?!
DRY GULCH
NO FISHING
LOUSY SCOUTS... NO RESPECT FOR THEIR TROOP LEADER... WHO DOESN'T ENJOY DIGGING FOR WORTHLESS ROCKS IN A DRIED-UP LAKE?!
WELL, AT LEAST THERE'S FOOL'S GOLD. NOTHING THEY FIND DOWN THAT OTHER TRAIL WILL BE AS MAGICAL AS THIS.

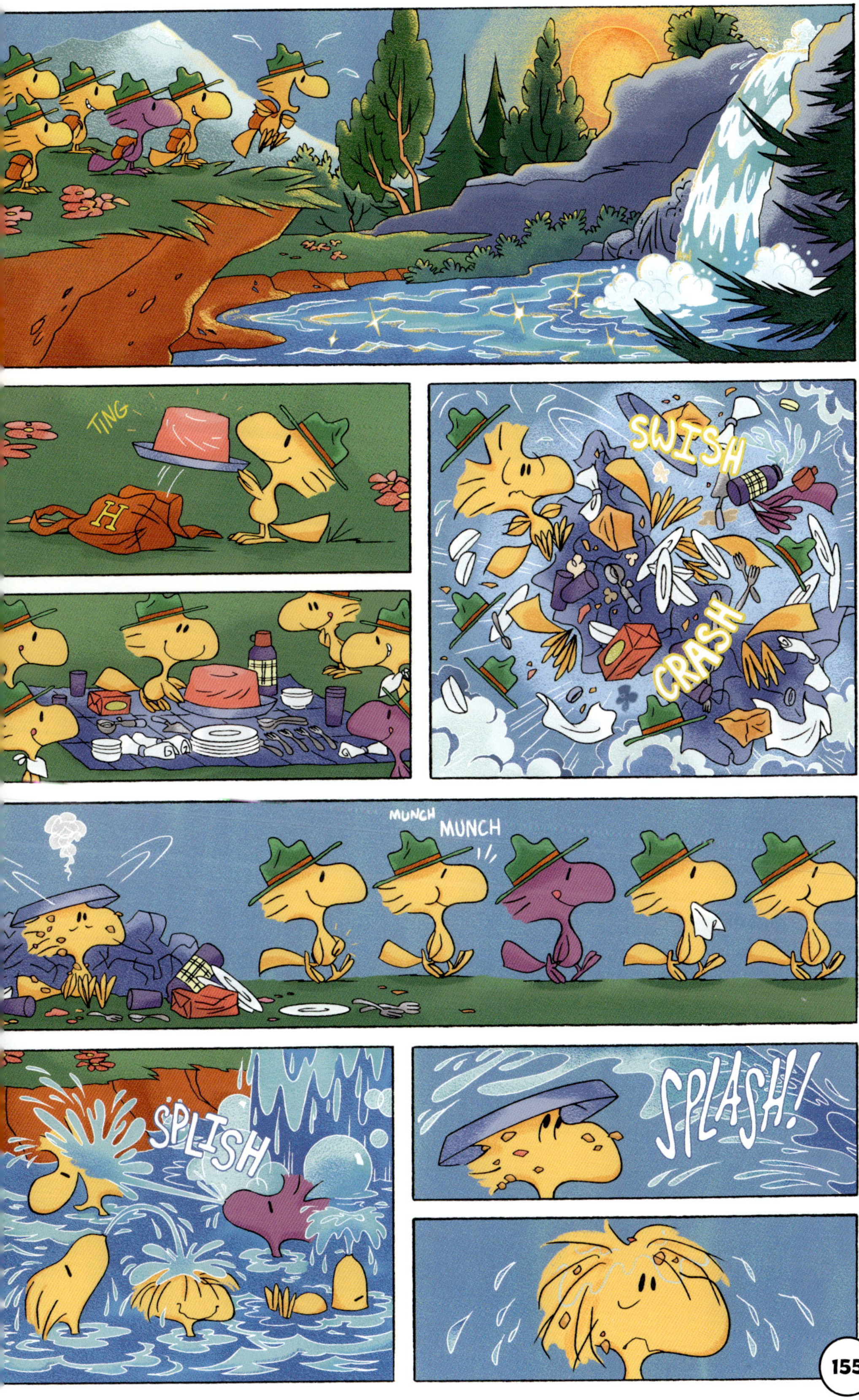

TING
SWISH
CRASH
MUNCH
MUNCH
SPLISH
SPLASH!

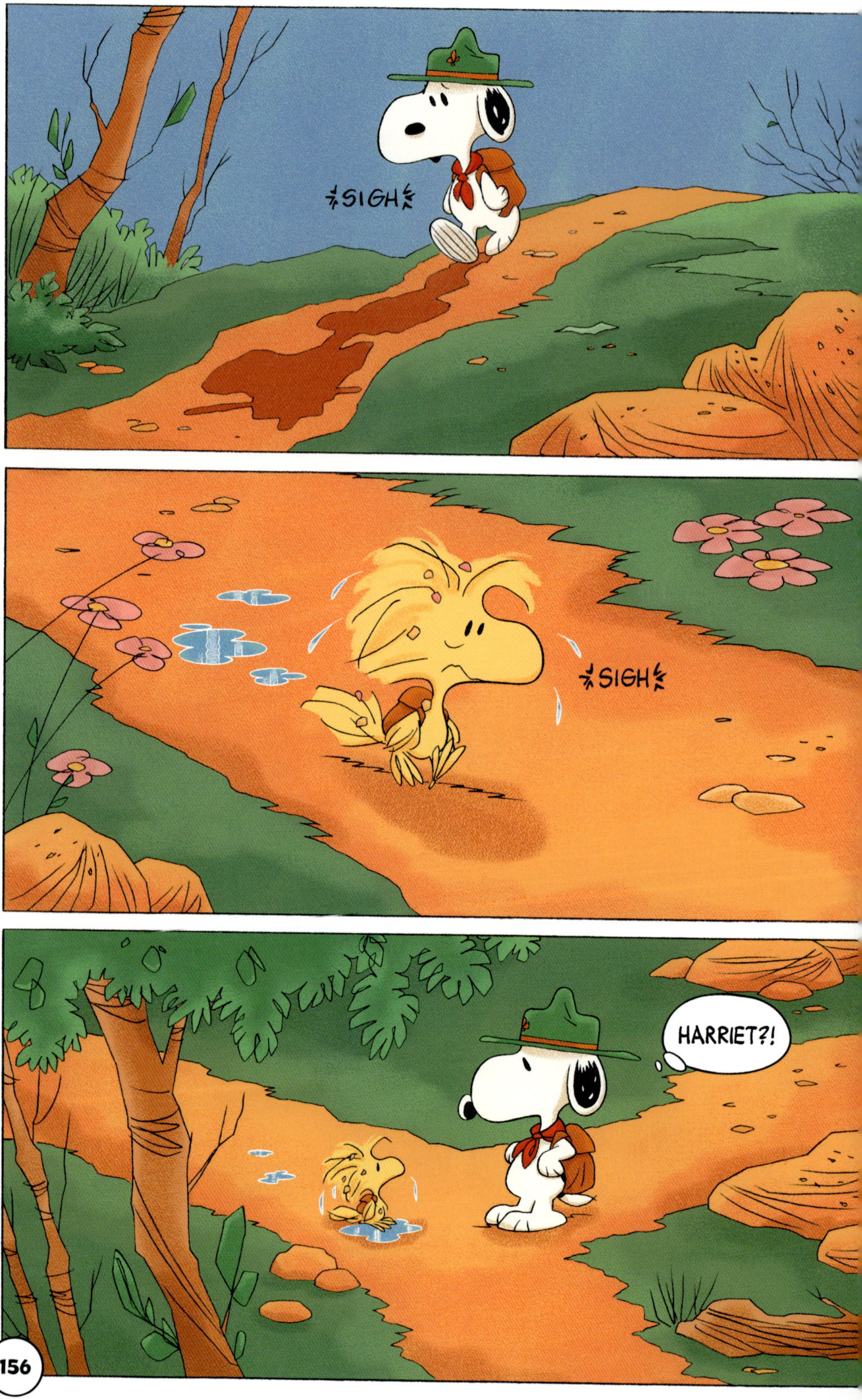
SIGH
SIGH
HARRIET?!

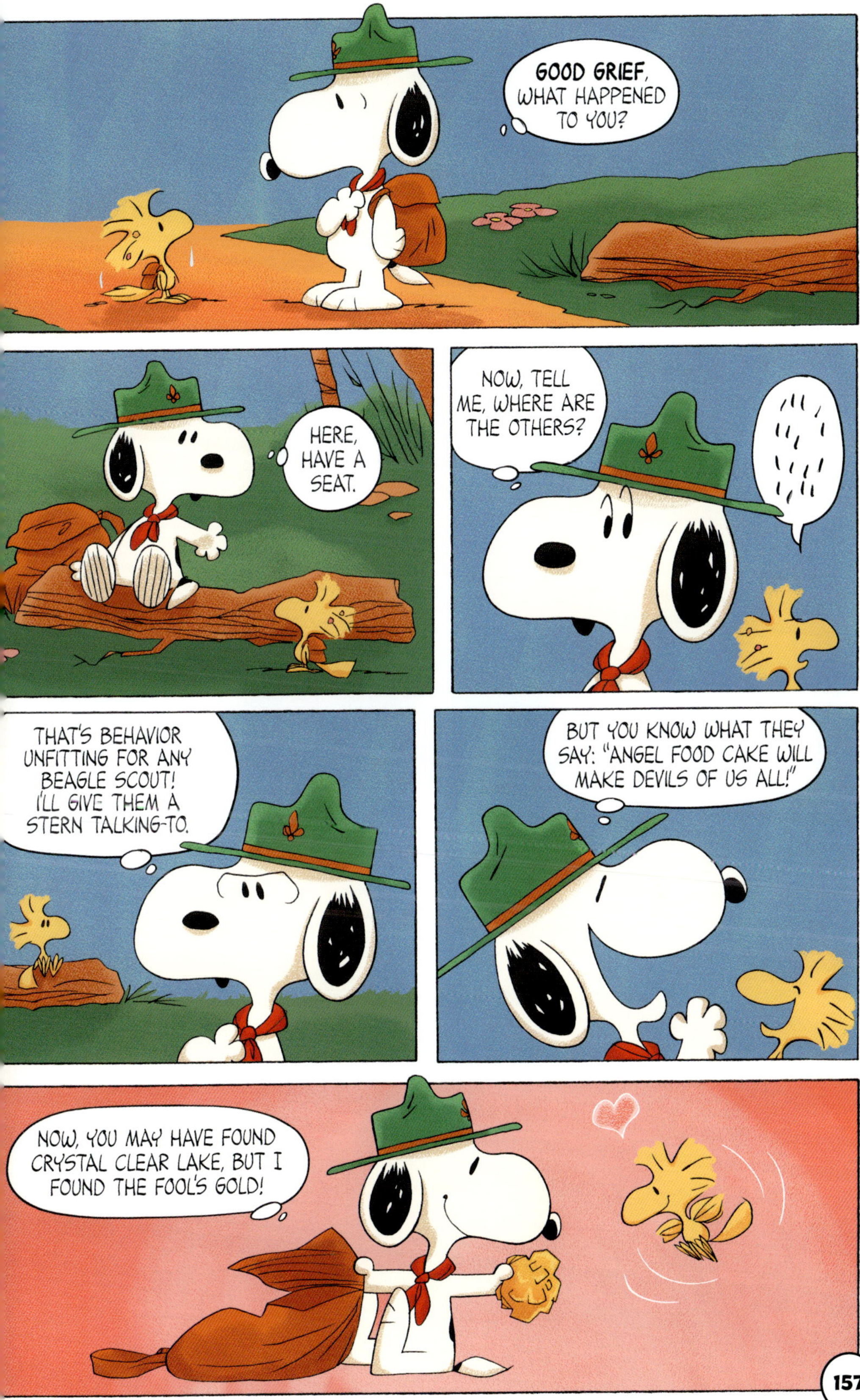
GOOD GRIEF, WHAT HAPPENED TO YOU?
HERE, HAVE A SEAT.
NOW, TELL ME, WHERE ARE THE OTHERS?
THAT'S BEHAVIOR UNFITTING FOR ANY BEAGLE SCOUT! I'LL GIVE THEM A STERN TALKING-TO.
BUT YOU KNOW WHAT THEY SAY: "ANGEL FOOD CAKE WILL MAKE DEVILS OF US ALL!"
NOW, YOU MAY HAVE FOUND CRYSTAL CLEAR LAKE, BUT I FOUND THE FOOL'S GOLD!

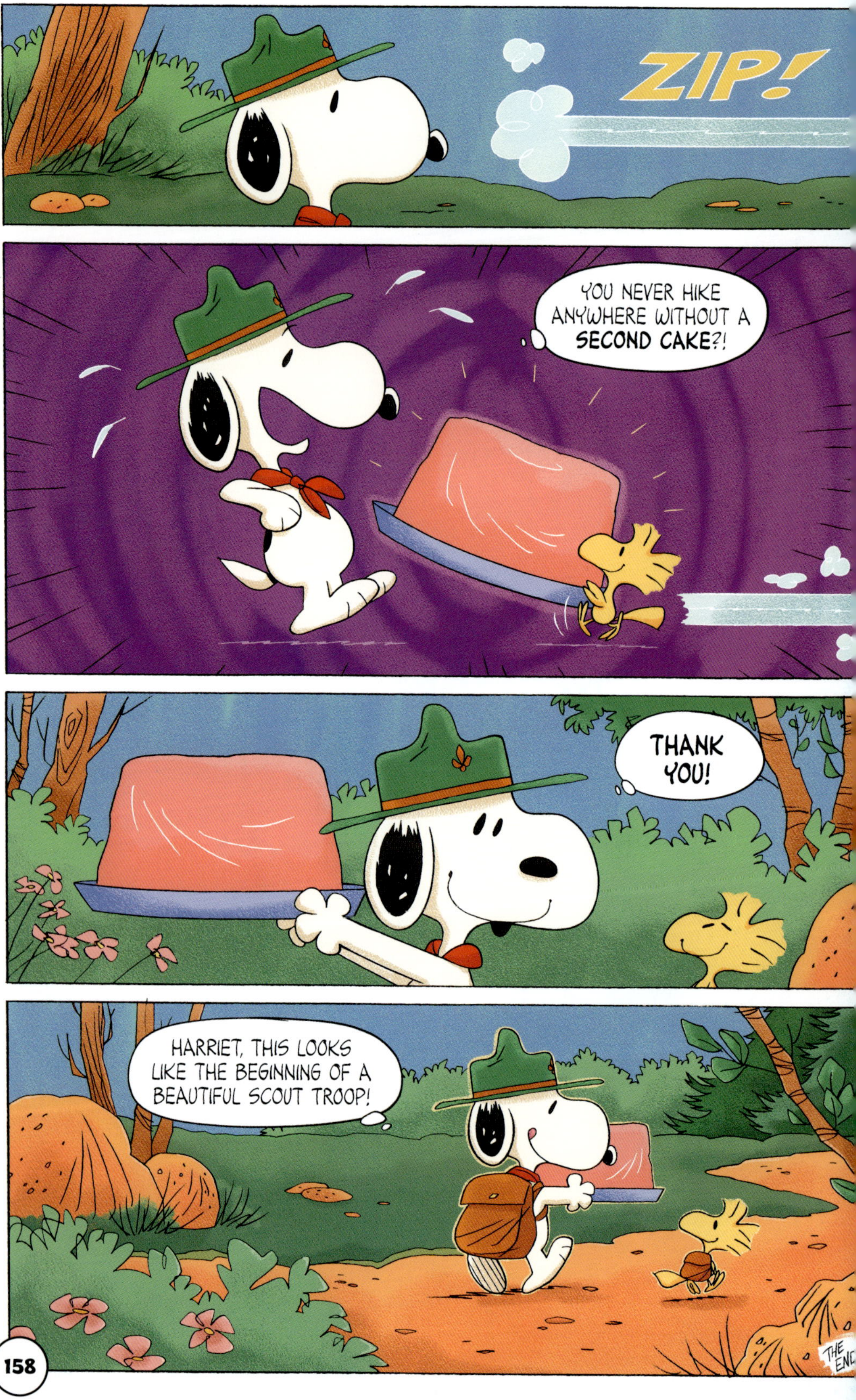
ZIP!
YOU NEVER HIKE ANYWHERE WITHOUT A SECOND CAKE?!
THANK YOU!
HARRIET, THIS LOOKS LIKE THE BEGINNING OF A BEAUTIFUL SCOUT TROOP!
THE END

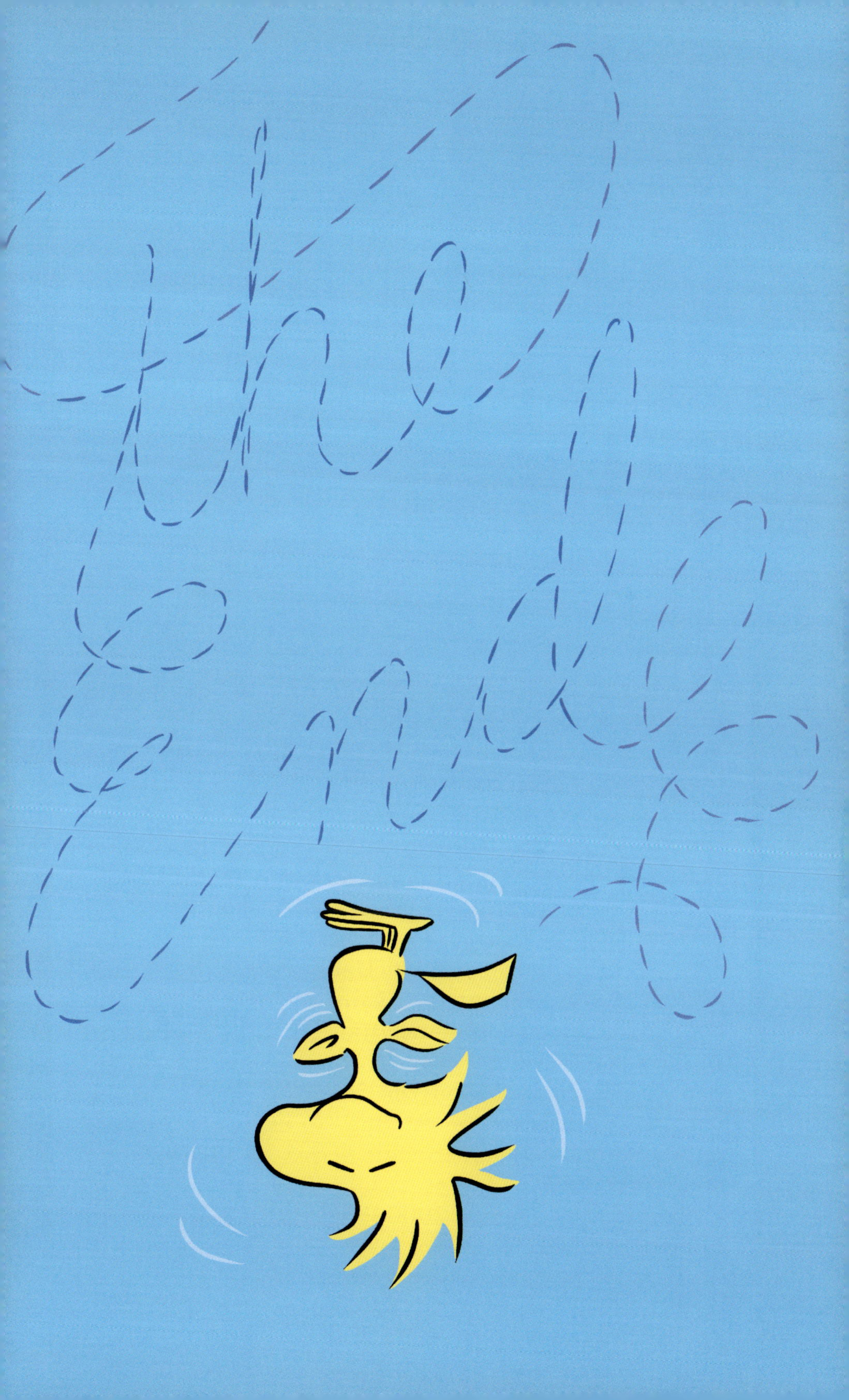
The End

Charles M. Schulz once described himself as "born to draw comic strips." He was born in Minneapolis, and at just two days old, an uncle nicknamed him "Sparky" after the cartoon horse Spark Plug from the *Barney Google* comic strip. Throughout his youth, Schulz and his father shared a Sunday morning ritual reading newspaper comics. After serving in the army during World War II, Schulz's first big break came in 1947 when he sold a cartoon feature called *Li'l Folks* to the St. Paul *Pioneer Press*. In 1950, Schulz met with United Feature Syndicate, and on October 2 of that year Schulz's comic strip *Peanuts* debuted in seven newspapers. Schulz would go on to write and draw *Peanuts* for the next fifty years, and create cultural icons in Snoopy, Charlie Brown, and the rest of the Peanuts gang. At its height, *Peanuts* appeared in 2,600 newspapers across 75 countries and in 21 languages. Charles Schulz died in Santa Rosa, California, in February 2000—just hours before his last original strip was to appear in the Sunday papers.